Devil's Paw

Debra Dunbar

Anessa Books, Bethesda, Maryland

ISBN:1491295783
ISBN-13:9781491295786

DEDICATION

To Dr. Hadley Tremaine (1939-2001), Chairman of the Department of English, Hood College, Frederick, Maryland, who taught me that there is great treasure to be found in what others consign to Hell.

~1~

It was rent day and I was loitering on a sidewalk, surrounded by plastic action figures, an obscene wad of cash in my pocket.

"Can I be Godzilla?" I asked the five-year-old boy before me. "Stomp them all and scatter them into the streets?"

"No," he protested, his dark eyes indignant at the suggestion. "You have to be the good guy."

Angelo Perez was one of many children belonging to a tenant: a tenant who was perpetually late on her rent; a tenant I gave unusual slack to, just so I had the opportunity to hang out with her youngest child.

"But I don't want to be the good guy," I protested. "I want to kick them and crush them under my foot."

Angelo shook a reproving Spiderman figure at me. "Nope. You're the good guy."

But I wasn't. I was the Iblis, the Ha-Satan, the titular leader of the demons. I was an imp, delighting in naughty pranks. And I was female, at least in this human form I'd worn for the last forty years.

"Mama says everyone has good in them, even Satan," he added, flying Spiderman down the sidewalk to scoop up Batman in a protective embrace.

I didn't use to have good in me, at least none that I remembered. But now . . . I wasn't sure if it was the forty years I'd spent here, outside of Hel among what had become my human friends, my relationship with my human boyfriend, Wyatt, or the red-purple chunk of angel I'd seized and squirreled away inside of me. Something had changed. Yes, I was still a bad girl, but sometimes, when the shit hit the fan, I was unaccountably good. I hadn't figured it out, but I'd decided to just go with it. Life was always better if one followed one's instincts. And my instincts right now were telling me to smash the green plastic dude in front of me.

"No, Ms. Martin!" Angelo squealed. My foot hovered. "The Hulk is a good guy too. Here, smash this stick instead."

It was a poor substitute, but I complied, crushing the evil stick into smaller, less evil sticks. Cars rushed past us on the street, people shuffled by, carefully stepping around the various toys, rocks, and sticks fueling the imaginations of an imp and a five-year-old boy. Everyone else was rushing on their way somewhere — even if it was to the corner liquor store, but I was in no hurry. Yes, there was a stack of angelic reports I had to peruse, and a few details left involving Wyatt's birthday gift, but for once I wasn't worrying over someone, demon or angel, trying to kill me. I was enjoying the sunny afternoon. It was just me, Angelo, Mrs. Hosprit rocking on her porch across the street, and that suspicious-looking guy that kept peeking around the corner of the alley.

I paused in my destruction to look his way. He leaned against a building, trying a little too hard to look casual as he glanced up and down the road. I couldn't quite make out his appearance beyond the baggy jeans and gray hoodie. Who the heck wears a hoodie in mid-June and doesn't expect to draw attention? His uneasy stance and hunched shoulders added to the stereotypical image. No doubt he was a drug dealer waiting to meet a customer. Still . . . .. I glanced down at Angelo and admired his wild black curls that desperately needed a trim.

The loiterer dug a hand in his pocket, causing his gray hoodie to bunch up. I saw a brief flash of dull metal, a solid item at the back of his waistband.

"Angelo, go in the house," I commanded in a low, hushed voice.

His protest died as he saw the stern expression on my face. It was that kind of neighborhood. The boy scooped up his superhero figures with practiced speed and darted toward the front of his house. No sooner had the door closed behind him then a second man stopped at the corner. He, too, glanced down the street my way, his eyes skimming past me to generally assess the area as he spoke to the dealer. Satisfied, the two vanished into the alley and out of sight.

I waited a few seconds then began walking down the block toward my car. Neither party looked particularly contentious. Odds were good that this would just be a routine transaction and everyone would go on their merry way. Still, it was best to be cautious, especially with a young child around. There had been too many human bystanders caught in crossfire this year, and I was particularly fond of Angelo Perez. Woe would befall anyone who hit him with a bullet, stray or otherwise.

"Thanks, Dante," I told the teen boy guarding my Corvette. He grinned, accepting the twenty that I palmed him as we shook hands. Somehow all these humans, tenants or not, had become "my people". Mine.

"Was worried that delivery guy was gonna knock your mirror off," he told me, nodding at the large truck halfway up the block. "He came awful close."

The truck was double parked, taking up one whole lane. Cars were backed up behind him, cautiously alternating turns in the other lane of the two-way street. Oblivious, the driver stood on the sidewalk outside his truck, slowly filling out paperwork. An elderly lady scolded him, waving her arms between the driver and the truck to emphasize her point.

"Ms. Moyer can't get her car out, and the guy won't move," Dante explained, his voice excited. "She's probably going to start smacking him with her purse."

Now that was something I wanted to see. I walked toward the elderly woman, who was indeed beginning to punctuate her words with an angry swish of the huge purple handbag.

"Lady, I got a delivery to make," the man said, not even bothering to look at her.

"There's a spot not three spaces behind you. Just move back there. I got a doctor's appointment I need to get to."

The man ignored her and continued to scribble at the papers on his clipboard. The purple bag rose through the air in a wide arc. Just before it impacted, the delivery guy grabbed the purse, wrenched it in a quick movement from Ms. Moyer, and threw it into the street. She let out a cry and shuffled toward it, her gait stiff and awkward.

"Here, let me," I told her, swooping in and grabbing the bag from the gutter. She held it close and met my eyes, her lower lip trembling. Something thick and hot surged up inside me — anger and a fierce need to protect. Mine.

Ms. Moyer wasn't my tenant. I didn't own any of the houses on this particular block of All Saints Street. I barely knew this woman, had never spoken more than monosyllabic pleasantries to her in over a decade, but I couldn't help the snarl that curled my lip, or the strong desire to beat this delivery man into a pulpy mess on the sidewalk. Ms. Moyer's eyes widened as she saw my expression, and she took a step backward. Careful not to alarm her further, I pushed down my instincts and decided to try and handle this like a human instead of a demon.

Walking slowly to the man, I tried to keep a tight leash on my temper.

"Move your truck, or I'll do it for you," I said, my voice cold. He looked up in brief surprise from his clipboard and eyed me from head to toe before shaking his head and looking back down at his paperwork.

"Door's locked. Not sure how you think you're going to move it."

I used to be much better at this whole intimidation thing, but I must have lost my touch. The guy was clearly unimpressed, his tone as dismissive as his actions. Once again, I stuffed my murderous urges deep down and took what I hoped to be a cleansing breath. I could take care of this in a non-violent fashion. Yes, I could.

"Fine. I'll move it myself."

He gave me a little sideways look, curious, but still wanting to appear nonchalant. I turned my back on him and faced the vehicle a GMC C-7500 heavy-duty delivery truck. The thing had to weigh thirty-thousand pounds, even without whatever it was in the back. Still, this trick should work, regardless of size or weight.

I surrounded the truck with a narrow field of energy, like a bubble, and created a buffer that negated the gravitational field inside. I'd done this with water globes, with lawn chairs, even with a rather notable statue downtown. I'd never practiced on anything quite this size before. Concentrating, I lifted. There was a lot of creaking and squawking of springs and metal as the massive vehicle rose slightly.

I heard the clipboard hit the ground. Purple flashed by my side as Ms. Moyer retreated with a gasp to the safety of a neighbor's driveway. The truck continued to rise, rocking a bit as it hovered six inches off the pavement. This really wasn't any harder than the globes of water I'd formed and suspended, but the truck was an irregular shape, and it wiggled a bit inside the non-gravitational field.

"Fuck," I muttered under my breath as the vehicle lurched to the side. The cars that had been waiting behind it raced past, eager to put as much space between themselves and the levitating truck as possible.

I raised the truck an additional six inches and attempted to move it backwards down the road, into an open parking space. The thing was like a damned slinky, twisting and shifting with every inch. I struggled to keep the field surrounding it intact and concentrated on holding the truck upright.

By this point, I'd drawn a bit of a crowd. Ms. Moyer had reappeared from the driveway and was standing next to me, Dante beside her. Out of the corner of my eye, I could see a woman in a sundress lurking in a doorway, clutching a child to her legs. Down near the open space, where the truck's destination was to be, stood the drug dealer from before, his eyes big, his mouth an "O" of shock. I frowned, feeling a nagging sense of concern over his presence.

The swaying became more exaggerated as the truck floated down the street. Excited, the crowd began to voice encouragement, shouting "whoa, whoa" as the bed tilted dangerously close to the parked cars. A bead of sweat tickled my forehead. Just a few feet more, and then sideways into the parking space.

With a groan of metal, the truck shifted, and I overcompensated the energy field, pushing the truck toward the middle of the road. The crowd leaned their bodies in unison with the truck, and as one said, "Oooooo".

I pulled, frantically trying to wrap the energy field back around the truck, but I was too late. With a crash that set off car alarms all the way down the street, the vehicle landed on its side, completely blocking the road. The crowd erupted with cheers and clapping.

"Oops." I turned to face the delivery man. His crimson cheeks were puffing in and out as he spluttered. "I think you may need a tow truck. Or a crane. Yes, probably a crane."

The man snapped his jaw shut and glared at me a moment as he dug his cell phone from his pocket.

"I'm calling the police. You can't smash my truck and get away with it."

I laughed. What an asshole. He could care less about inconveniencing others, didn't give one flying fuck about anyone else's feelings or needs. Jerk

"What are you going to tell them? That I turned your truck on its side with my amazing Jedi mind powers?"

He looked around at the crowd. "There are witnesses. They'll back me up."

"I ain't seen nothing," Ms. Moyer said as she unlocked her car door.

The others agreed, meandering back to their homes with comments about how the load must have been unbalanced, or the driver particularly unskilled.

"Start thinking of a better story." I walked back to my car, only to realize that the entire road was blocked. I couldn't even drive the opposite way down the street since traffic was beginning to back up in both lanes behind the overturned delivery truck. Shit, I'd blocked myself in.

Resigned to the fact that it would be several hours before I could use my car, I began to walk the ten blocks to Michelle's office to drop off her cut of the cash rental payments. I never got there.

~2~

The number of pedestrians and homeowners relaxing on their stoops thinned out as I made my way past the second-hand store and a closed-up beauty shop. Several of the buildings in this section of town were boarded up and vacant, lending an air of desperation to the place. I'd tried to buy them a few years back, but the foreign investment firm that owned them didn't seem interested in selling. I couldn't see the benefit in having a bunch of rotted buildings on their balance sheet, but it wasn't my business.

The drug dealer followed me for a bit before vanishing down a side street, presumably to meet a client in one of the ramshackle brick structures. I was a bit disappointed that he didn't try to rob me — a good fight would have been the icing on top of what was shaping up to be a really great day.

The alley I took to cut through to Patrick Street was gloomy in the shadows of the buildings, its narrow path strewn with garbage and reeking of urine. A homeless person on the corner huddled like a lump under a dirty, green blanket, shivering in spite of the warm day. A strange unease came over me, just like I'd felt while watching the drug dealer, but I was a demon and this was my town, so I shrugged it off and kept moving. Ahead, golden rays of sunshine poked into the alley from the intersection with Patrick Street, like the light at the end of a tunnel. Motes of dust sparkled in the sunbeams, and I ran a hand along the brick wall beside me, musing over the contrast between the warm sun and the building's dank coolness.

Something soft brushed against my fingers, and I paused to watch a feather drift to the dirty pavement. An angel feather. Instinctively, I ducked and spun around, partially avoiding the blow that caught the edge of my head and numbed my shoulder. I pushed away from the wall, weighing the wisdom of having a solid structure at my back versus the increased maneuverability in the middle of the alley. Whoever had assaulted had missed his opportunity. There had been once chance to take me by surprise, and he'd failed. I'd fight him as a human, because I enjoyed that sort of thing, but regardless of how good he was, few humans could prevail against a demon.

Shaking my head to clear it, I looked around. Three men surrounded me. The drug dealer from before hefted a bat, presumably the one that had nearly splattered my brains on the blacktop. To my left was another human, built like a club bouncer with a shaved head, a blingy ring glowing oddly on his right hand. Behind me stood another, thin and wiry with a scar under one eye. I pivoted, trying to keep them all within sight as my adrenaline spiked. I'd wanted a fight, but three would be tough without using any demonic powers.

The dealer swung the bat in an arc toward my midsection, and I jumped, crashing an elbow backwards and up into flesh. Cartilage crunched, but the wiry guy behind me paid no heed to his injury, grabbing me and slamming a fist into my lower back and kidneys. I gasped and bent in half, giving the drug dealer a perfect opportunity to knee me in the face.

Blood spurted from my nose, and the ground before me swam as I tried to jerk free and avoid the fists raining down on my head from the drug dealer. Shit. I wasn't doing a great job defending myself against these two; who knows how bad things would get when Mr. Clean decided to join in. I'd better get with the program fast or I was going to be unconscious and relieved of my cash, which would be a rather embarrassing situation for a demon, even a lowly imp.

I jumped and lifted my legs, maximizing my downward momentum with the dead weight of my body. The wiry guy grunted and his hands slipped, unable to hold a hundred and twenty pound woman under the influence of gravity. I crashed to the pavement and rolled, avoiding the kicks that came my way. Where the fuck was Mr. Clean? And what the hell was an angel feather doing here?

"*Nyl gebian eawfaest drohtrun.*"

I felt the net constrict me as I froze. *Elven* magic. Here, in a back alley in Frederick Maryland? Mr. Clean was a *sorcerer*? Actually, he had to be a mage, and a rather low-level one at that, I thought as I probed the rough edges of the net that blinded me and kept me from using any of my demon energy.

"I think she broke one of my teeth," one lisped. The wiry guy, probably. I'd hit him with my elbow rather forcefully.

I kept probing the net. This guy was a hack. There had to be a hole somewhere. I could have just transformed my barrette into its more lethal form and blown the net apart with my Shotgun of the Iblis, but I was wary about discharging a firearm downtown, especially since I wasn't really sure what sort of magical bullets it was shooting or the effect they could have on neighboring buildings or passersby. Plus, I had enough reports to complete without adding to them by accidently killing random pedestrians.

"It took you long enough," another complained.

"You were supposed to be able to accomplish this yourself," a heavily accented voice replied.

The mage. Why in the world was a mage teaming up with two petty criminals? Why was he in a back alley, robbing a demon and risking the chance he'd get his ass cooked? Humans wouldn't recognize the danger, but he should have. But none of those questions mattered right now because I'd found what I was looking for— a hole in the net. Without a moment's thought, I grabbed the edges of the flaw and pulled, widening the hole and providing a window through which I could see and fight. The mage gasped, realizing what was happening just as I shot a burst of energy through the hole and into the legs within my sight.

The drug dealer screamed and collapsed as the lower part of his right leg exploded in a flash of red. The wiry guy ducked behind a garbage bin, and the mage raised his hands and began to chant. He was too late. I'd freed myself from his net and was on him, breaking his concentration and smashing his back against the doorway of a brick building flanking one side of the alley.

"You fucker. You're gonna wish you'd stayed in Hel," I snarled as I began to snake my energy into his body in preparation to Own him. "Eternity is a long time to be a demon's plaything."

I knew the drug dealer was bleeding-out in the alley behind me. I knew the wiry guy wouldn't risk his own neck to interfere, having watched his buddy's leg burst into chunks. It was just me and this mage, alone, in a shadowed alley. *And an angel feather*, something in the back of my mind prompted.

"No, no, no." I felt a hand on my shoulder and slippery, silicone whiteness began to cover my store of energy. "Bad little imp. We need this mage alive and in one piece."

An angel. And not my angel either. I'd become very familiar with how angels restrained us from using our energy, and I managed to hit his hand with a substantial amount before the rest snapped back into the slippery shell.

He yanked his hand away, momentarily breaking contact. He'd been unprepared for my attack, and I'd injured him beyond the flesh, down to his spirit self. I took advantage of the slip and made to bolt, but he reacted quickly, slapping another hand against my neck and restraining me completely this time.

"Feisty, huh? Well, you won't be able to do that again." Eyes narrowed in pain as he glared down at me. Yeah, I'd hurt him pretty good. Fucker.

"You'll come quietly with us, now," the angel said, the firm press of compulsion in his voice. I'd been shrugging off a far greater power for almost a year now. His command had no impact on me, but I turned in a show of docile obedience, waiting for a moment of inattention to give me an opening to break free. If he wasn't touching me, the restraint on my energy would break and I'd once again be able to attack and defend.

I didn't recognize this angel. He was one of the blond androgynous types that always seemed to look the same to me. Behind and to his left, wiry guy emerged from the protection of his doorway, casting a quick glance at drug dealer, who surely had to have been dead by this point. Damn it all, one more fucking report I'd need to fill out. How the hell was I going to explain this one to those assholes on the Ruling Council?

"She killed Duke! Killed him." Wiry guy walked toward the angel as he said this, gesturing at the body on the ground.

The angel shot him an irritated glance. "I had assumed the *three* of you could handle *one* demon. Especially this one—a paltry imp."

I wondered for a moment if he recognized me, knew that I wasn't just a paltry imp but the Iblis, and a demon bound by a powerful angel. How could one of Gregory's enforcers not have gotten the memo that I was off limits? Either he didn't know who I was, or he was some kind of vigilante, taking the law into his own hands. I wasn't exactly popular among the angelic host, even with my supposed title and status.

"But she was using demon stuff," the human argued. "You told us they wouldn't do that, that they're afraid of getting caught."

The mage had slipped out from behind me and was looking down at the dead human, his face pale. Wiry guy and the angel argued, their attention turning from me, supposedly restrained and compliant. I ran a hand down the door behind me, where the mage had been pressed. It was a fire door with no knob to grant access to the building from the outside. A human couldn't get in, but I wasn't a human.

The angel's hand on my arm moved a fraction of an inch, and I was able to grab a small amount of my energy to channel into the door. While their voices grew heated, I dissolved the lock and snapped the hinges that would have prevented the door from opening inward.

One, two, three. With a deafening crash, the door fell onto the lower part of a stairwell, clanging against the metal handholds. Startled, the angel lifted his hand slightly. It was exactly what I had hoped for. I seized control of my energy and stepped through the doorway, releasing a lightning bolt into the angel's chest as I turned and ran up the stairs.

I could have stayed and fought him, but even if I'd won, I would have lost. I doubt the Ruling Council would look kindly on my killing an angel, regardless of whether it was self-defense or not. I could have summoned Gregory, used the protection of our bond to my advantage, but I didn't want to constantly be hiding behind an angel's skirts. I needed to be strong enough to do these things on my own, to become more than the lowly cockroach he believed me to be. Besides, there was always a chance he'd refuse to come, refuse to protect me. He hadn't exactly jumped to my defense when the demon Haagenti had me in his crosshairs, and I *had* been crying wolf lately, summoning him for all sorts of trumped up emergencies.

I shook off thoughts of my very complicated relationship with the angel and dashed up the stairs, swinging my way around the landings to keep speed. I heard pounding footsteps behind me, felt the swish of elven nets as they whisked by. The mage was in pursuit, and probably the angel too since I doubted my lightning bolt had done more than piss him off. I wasn't sure about wiry guy. He'd seemed rather disillusioned with his companions, and he may have taken the opportunity to break and run. Still, the two after me were more than enough to take me down.

Fourth floor and the footsteps clanging on the metal stairs behind me grew closer. Desperate, I burst through a door and into an office area, barreling into an employee and sending him flying against a copier. The door slammed against the wall once more, indicating that one or more of my pursuers were right on my heels. I didn't dare look back, instead weaving in and out of the walled cubicles like a frantic rat in a maze, trying to lose them long enough to find somewhere to hide.

The office employees screamed, some racing for the exit while others hid under their modular desks. Their panic gave me an idea: I lit fire to the contents of various trashcans as I ran past. Before long, curls of smoke rose toward the ceiling, setting off fire alarms and the building sprinkler system. The office dissolved into chaos, people running for the stairwells in a mass exit. I inserted myself into one crowd and searched for the mage or the angel as I tried to stuff myself through the fire door with the fifty other people fighting to get out. They were nowhere to be seen, which meant they'd probably be waiting for me somewhere.

We moved into the stairwell, and I paused on the landing as the people beside me hurried down the stairs. Up or down? Were the mage and angel still searching for me in the office? Were they waiting on one of the landings? Or had they exited the building? I raced through the options and decided they'd most likely be waiting for me on the street, expecting me to escape with the humans. With an angel to wipe the minds of all witnesses, they wouldn't think twice about grabbing me. Which left one way to go — up.

I climbed the additional three floors to the roof exit, trying to be as quiet on the metal stairs as I could. Even on tiptoes, each tread squawked with the weight of my foot. The roof door was even worse. I don't think it had been used in years. I struggled, finally managing to open it wide enough to squeeze out. The hinges were so rusty that the door remained ajar as I made my way across the roof, looking for a hiding place.

Huge boxes containing the air conditioning units hummed, blowing out scorching air as I walked by. There was the one entrance, a square with the door I'd come out of. Other than that, the air conditioning units were the only things up here. The roof had a slightly spongy, rubbery feel, and in spite of the slight angle for drainage, small puddles of water pooled from this morning's rain. The roof was edged in a low cement rim, about two feet high with holes attached to downspouts at the corners.

As I walked the perimeter, I kept my eye on the door, anxious that my pursuers might decide to do a thorough search of the building. I peered over the edge carefully, watching as the firemen cleared the building and began to usher the office workers back in.

"Nice view, isn't it?"

I jumped and spun around, narrowly avoiding toppling off the roof. The angel leaned casually against one of the massive air conditioning units. I'd been watching the only entrance. How the hell did he get up here? Fly? If so, he was definitely breaking the rules — angels might occasionally manifest wings in front of humans but flying around was frowned on. If he didn't care about those rules, he probably didn't care about the one that said he shouldn't kill the Iblis, a member of the Ruling Council.

"You might as well come with me." He strolled across the roof in my direction. "You're dead anyway, and what I have in mind would be far less painful than what you'll go through when one of the enforcers catches up to you."

He couldn't know who I was or he would realize no enforcers would dare mess with me. But what was it he had in mind? I was curious, even though death, painful or not, wasn't exactly on my agenda today.

"I'm surprised they're not here now with all the energy you've been throwing around." A faint tinge of blue surrounded him and snaked its way toward me, sent to sooth me into compliance.

"Maybe I'll take my chances with the enforcers," I told him as I thought furiously about how to escape. "Unless you're offering to treat me to a latte or buy me a puppy, that is."

He laughed. "Oh no, I plan to kill you, but you'll be in comfort and probably live for a week or two. Death by the enforcers will be excruciating, especially if the big guy comes to get you."

What the fuck did he plan to do with me that would take a week or two? If he were a demon, I'd expect a long, drawn-out torture, but angels didn't do that sort of thing. Plus, he said I'd be comfortable. I shook my head to clear it. Regardless of whatever sicko plan he had for me, I needed to concentrate on escape.

"Yeah, I'll take my chances with the enforcers."

He took a few more steps toward me, the blue stuff growing thick. "No, you're going to come with me. There's no way off this roof but down the stairs, and I'll be on you before you take five steps. Come quietly and I won't have to hurt you."

Yeah, I'd heard that one before. "I'm not coming with you."

He shrugged, edging closer. "Suit yourself. You really don't have any other choice."

"There's always another choice," I told him as I stepped backwards off the roof.

Frederick is not a city of lofty skyscrapers. This building was one of the tallest at seven stories, which didn't give me a lot of time between the top and the hard pavement rushing to meet me. I tucked my arms tight against my body and gained as much speed as I could, creating my wings in a flash, less than six feet from the ground. Muscles strained as I snapped the leathery wings to their full length, angled to adjust my momentum from downward to parallel with the street. Flapping furiously, I tried to regain the speed I'd lost in the transition and rise above the cars inches from my feet. People shouted and screamed. I heard the grind of metal on metal as vehicles swerved to avoid me and collided. Gregory would probably have my ass for this, but I wasn't about to go quietly with some homicidal angel to an inevitable death.

I'd jumped off the Patrick Street side of the building — a broad one-way street with parking on either side. Trendy eateries, coffee houses, and antique shops in historic brick row houses lined the street, all heavily populated with an early lunch crowd. Plenty of people saw my suicidal jump and my transformation to a winged being. I didn't care; I was too busy trying to gain altitude and avoid the parked cars. My wings were nearly thirty feet across and I felt them slap against the vehicle roofs as I slowly rose. I'd just made it past the library when a streak of white shot by me, barely missing one wing and turning half of a Mini Cooper to dust. The fucker was shooting at me! In a crowded downtown street!

Another blast knocked a minivan across the road, leaving a pothole the size of a sofa in the asphalt. My wings beat furiously, and I tilted to turn right on Market Street, grabbing a lamppost to slingshot myself around the corner and accelerate. Chunks of pavement filled the air behind me as another blast missed me. If I hadn't made the corner, he would have hit, and I wasn't sure how disabling or lethal whatever he was shooting would be. My one experience with angel energy blasts had nearly ended in my death, and I got the idea this guy wasn't using any less power.

Weaving side to side, I avoided two more blasts and darted left, the wrong way down Church Street, past the line of law firms, financial planning offices, and houses of worship. I'd been sacrificing vertical assent for speed, and one of my wings clipped a street sign, sending it flying through the window of an upscale cosmetology school. Judging from the sounds behind me, and the pulverized bits of debris in the air, downtown Frederick probably looked like a Word War II Spitfire had unloaded its machine gun through the city.

I banked hard to the right onto Court Street then negotiated the tight turns around City Hall that brought me back around onto Church. Angels were faster, more powerful than demons, but my leathery wings were far more maneuverable. I hoped to lose him by staying downtown and weaving in and out of the streets, keeping low and using the buildings to hide as I flew.

The bell tower chimed the hour as I turned right, onto Bentz, speeding to get past the open expanse of Baker Park and through the residential section beyond the old armory. The buildings here weren't more than two to three stories tall, and between the two parks surrounding the armory, there was plenty of open space for the angel to gain enough speed to flank me. I stayed low, turning down Third Street just as another blast streaked by. Desperate to loop around and return to the central area of downtown, I made a sharp left onto Klinehart's Alley and immediately realized my error. The alley was too narrow for my vast wings, and, without the space to maneuver, my speed slowed. I felt the angel gaining, felt the heat of his reckless stream of lethal white energy. Frantic, I darted right through the old Carmack Jay's parking lot and pulled on the red-purple that networked from my branding into my spirit-self to summon my angel, Gregory.

I left the parking lot as a blast seared the under-section of my wing and flew behind a tavern, weaving in and out of the backyards of residential row houses.

Now! I need you right now! I thought as I again summoned the angel. I was panicked. This guy was closing in on me fast, and I had a feeling his offer of a "comfortable" death would no longer be on the table.

Rolling, I avoided a clothesline full of linen, then angled right, barely missing a trellis full of early rosebuds, to plow into something rock-hard. I crashed to the ground on top of the obstacle and looked right into an angel's surprised black eyes. We skidded along the pavement, and I was briefly thankful that he'd be the one with road rash, not me.

Crumpling a wing painfully, we slammed sideways into a backyard fountain, and I felt his arms wrap around me, holding me steady. Time stood still as we stared into each other's eyes, and I felt a surge of emotion. He'd come. He'd come to rescue me. Yes, I was embarrassed that I'd needed to call him, that I was such a little cockroach that I'd needed his help, but still — he'd come.

Reaching a hand across my back, Gregory seized the waistband of my pants and flipped me up and over his head, leaping to his feet in front of me. I rolled over, dissolved my wings and got to my knees, peering between his legs to better see the expression on the angel's face when he rounded the corner and saw my formidable protector.

Nothing.

No angel came around the corner, no blasts of white energy came around the corner: nothing came around the corner. After a few minutes, Gregory turned to face me, his eyebrows raised, a quizzical look on his face.

"So, what's the crisis, cockroach? Do you need me to lift another sofa so you can clean under it? Is there another can of tomatoes in your cabinets that you can't reach?"

I felt my face heat. I missed him when he wasn't around and had taken to summoning him for all sorts of *important* household emergencies.

"It was an angel, trying to kill me."

His eyebrows went even higher.

"Seriously, an angel was after me," I sputtered. "Two humans accosted me in an alley, and there was a mage, then the angel came, so I set fire to an office building and had to jump off the roof. He was going to kill me."

He eyed me. "An angel? And a mage? What next, little cockroach? Have Martians invaded the planet? Are they trying to kill you too, or just shove an uncomfortably long, exploratory probe up your backside?"

I winced, regretting I'd ever told him that story. He hadn't believed that one either, but it had bought me a whole evening of his time watching *Invasion of the Body Snatchers* and *Men in Black*.

"I swear to you on all the souls I Own that there was an angel and a mage."

Gregory sighed. "Fine. Describe them."

"Well, the angel was either an effeminate guy, or a butch girl with blondish hair and pale skin." Not the best description, but many angels are difficult to tell apart appearance-wise. "The mage looked like Mr. Clean. He was super buff with a bald head and bushy, white eyebrows. He wasn't wearing a robe. He had on a black t-shirt and dark jeans. There was a gold ring on the middle finger of his right hand. It looked like a signet ring — onyx with an inscribed X and inverted triangle. It was magic."

Gregory slowly shook his head and I got the feeling that any credibility I'd earned had slipped away. "You killed another human just now. That's four since you've been the Iblis. Is this wild tale your way to get out of the reports, to shirk responsibility for the deaths? A fabricated story of a mage and an angel after you?"

"No! I'd ditched the mage, but the angel was going to kill me — to haul me off somewhere and make me comfortable for a couple of weeks while he slowly killed me. I'm not lying; I swear."

Black eyes searched my brown ones. "Everyone knows you are off limits. Plenty of my Grigori are anxious to see you dead, but they'd never go against my direct order and take matters into their own hands."

"He didn't seem to know I was the Iblis. I don't think he was one of your angels."

The angel hadn't been one of the Ruling Council either. I would have recognized his energy signature, even if I hadn't recognized his corporeal form. The only other angel I'd met was Althean last August, and he'd been reduced to a pile of sand.

Gregory frowned. "No angel would take it upon himself to randomly hunt demons as a vigilante. Perhaps it was another demon? Someone you've angered back in Hel that managed to assume a somewhat convincing angelic form?"

My shoulders slumped. It wasn't a demon: it was an angel. Feathery wings, white destructive energy, the ability to inhibit my own energy use with just a touch — an angel. I could see an angel coming after me as the Iblis, trying to take me out and cut the demons out of all Ruling Council decision-making. Maybe he had known I was the Iblis and just didn't care. Maybe one of Gregory's team decided to take matters into their own hands and end the life of a despised demon. Looking at the angel before me, over six feet tall with a powerful build and a forbidding countenance, I doubted it. He radiated vast power, and his age backed it up with knowledge and skill that few angels would challenge.

"One of the Ruling Council's households perhaps?" I suggested. "That Dopey guy hates me, maybe he sent one of his household to take me out?"

I knew as soon as I said it that I was wrong. As much as that angel hated me, I got the impression he wouldn't sully his hands to be involved in my murder. Plus, I really had a strong feeling this guy hadn't known I was the Iblis, hadn't known who I was beyond an Imp on the wrong side of the gates to Hel.

"Choir, not household," Gregory corrected. "And who is Dopey?"

"Gabriel. The one I hit in the face with a pastry at the last meeting."

Gregory's eyes lit with amusement, his lip twitching up. "I very much doubt that, little cockroach."

I sighed, running a hand through my hair. "I don't know, then. I swear, though, an angel was after me. He shot a trench down Market Street and blew up a few cars."

The angel considered my words then nodded. "Okay. Let's go see."

I led the way back to Market Street and up the three blocks to where I'd been flying for my life. Nothing. The roads were smooth, the cars intact and all in place. We continued down Patrick Street, past the library and the office building to the alley. Drug dealer guy still sprawled on the pavement, blood everywhere.

"This would be the human you killed?"

Of course it was. He knew; he could tell. I blew out a breath in exasperation. "I know this looks bad. You don't believe me, do you?"

I turned to face him, and once again his eyes searched mine. "A story of how an angel and a mage were after you? I'm sorry, cockroach, but I just can't fathom how that could be."

I looked around at the dank alleyway, the body, the fire door off its hinges. I hadn't imagined it, hadn't been hallucinating. An angel had tried to kill me. But he'd quickly backed off and covered his tracks once Gregory had appeared. He probably assumed I was dead by Gregory's hands. Regardless of why he'd been after me, what he'd intended to do with me, I could rest easy at this point. I was safe. This whole thing had to have been a fluke. That angel wouldn't be after me again.

~3~

"Mal, it's about time you got home."

Dar stood in my living room. My foster brother was in his favored form, a middle-aged man, stocky build with black hair, silvered at the temples. At his side stood a young, thin, blond woman with her eyes downcast. She trembled, her hands white-knuckled and fisted at her waist.

"You're not supposed to be here until tomorrow," I replied. Yes, I'd been delayed getting back from my rent collection, but Dar's early arrival was unexpected. He was bringing Wyatt's birthday present, and the party wasn't until tomorrow night.

"Yes, well, smuggling a human through a gate wasn't exactly easy. I took my best shot and went for it. How about a little gratitude here?"

Dar always came through, and he did deserve some appreciation. "Fuck off, asshole. Please tell me you didn't molest her on the way over."

He grinned, puffing out his chest. "I restrained myself. Wasn't easy keeping the others from her, though."

Yeah, I could imagine. Demons loved playing with humans. Unfortunately, playthings didn't last long when subjected to our enthusiastic attentions. I looked at the blond woman, checking her visually for any damage. Beyond her obvious terror, she seemed to be in good physical shape. Of course, that didn't mean she hadn't been subjected to mental or emotional abuse.

23

"Are you okay, sweetie?" I asked her softly. "Can I get you a drink, or something to eat?"

Her head jerked up, and I found myself staring into vivid blue eyes in a pale, drawn face. Her gaze registered a shock of recognition before a sort of wary fear edged back in.

"I am fine, thank you." The words came out dry and hoarse, as though she hadn't had a drink in days. I glared at Dar.

"I swear, Mal, no one harmed her in any way. I know how weird you are about humans and their feelings. I ensured everyone kept their distance."

I rubbed my forehead, thinking how I should handle this early arrival. I'd planned to have her here for Wyatt's party. Maybe have her jump out of a cake or something with a big "Happy Birthday! Love, Sam" sign glued to her chest. I had no idea where I could hide her. Decades ago I would have just stuck her in the basement, bound and gagged so she wouldn't make any noise. I knew better now. Humans don't particularly like that sort of thing, and this girl was already terrified. I doubted being hog-tied in a basement would do her mental state any good, and it would really suck if Wyatt's gift was in the middle of a panic attack when I presented her.

"Take her to the kitchen," I told Dar. I'd run over, get Wyatt and bring him over for his gift right now.

To Dar's credit, he was very gentle as he steered the woman around the bar area and to the back section of the kitchen, where a wall would hide them from view. Still, the girl jerked away from his touch, a small whimper escaping her. I wasn't sure what was causing her fear, but hopefully the presence of another human would help. She'd see that we hadn't killed or mutilated Wyatt and perhaps relax a bit.

I ran to the wine fridge and pulled out the champagne I'd been chilling for tomorrow's party. We'd just have it early. Wyatt would get his gift, then we could continue with our dinner plans and the movie I'd picked up. The girl might put a slight cramp in our romantic evening, but that was all right.

We had our whole life ahead for romance. Well, Wyatt's whole life, which would be a great deal shorter than mine. Either way, romance would have to take a back seat to other things. That was okay. Wyatt's happiness filled me with a joy of my own. It was weird how contagious feelings were when two people loved each other.

Wyatt's house was just down the road, visible from my front door. It was a bit of an eyesore — a Cape Cod crumbling to ruin from neglect. He still had plywood over the windows that were broken during demon attacks this past winter. At least he'd replaced his destroyed mattress, otherwise we would have been forced to sleep on the couch or only in my house.

I walked through the door, grateful that we'd finally had his protective barrier removed and I *could* walk through the door. Wyatt was sprawled on his sofa, happily shooting the dastardly zombies rushing him from the TV. He glanced up, relaxing his instinctive grip on the pistol beside him when he realized it was me.

"Sam, can you give me a shout or something and not sneak up on me like that? I was two seconds from putting a bullet through you."

I'd been shot by Wyatt before. It wasn't something I wanted to repeat.

"I'm not sneaking," I protested. "A frost giant could stomp his way through here and you wouldn't hear him with your damned video game up so loud."

Wyatt glared and paused the game. This isn't how I wanted our evening to go.

"I'm sorry." I plopped down next to him on the couch, folding my body against him as his arm came around my shoulders. "I had a lousy day. You have a right to be jumpy after what happened this winter, and I shouldn't have been snippy."

"It's okay." His lips brushed the top of my head and his arm tightened in a quick hug. "Did rents not go well? Did you have to get rough with someone?"

There was tightness in his voice as he said the last bit. Wyatt had been increasingly stern about my collection methods. He'd been increasingly stern about a lot of things lately.

"No. Rents went fine. I stayed a bit late and played with Angelo."

The hand resting on my shoulder caressed my arm. Wyatt approved of playing with Angelo. He also approved of me dragging poor Boomer to the local nursing home for "pet day", and slapping soup in a bowl for dirty, ungrateful humans to eat.

"A pack of humans accosted me in an alley, I assumed to rob me, but then one of them turned out to be a mage, and an angel showed up. They chased me through an office building and onto the roof. I jumped off and tried to fly away, but the fucking angel chased me all over downtown. He was damned close to killing me, so I called Gregory."

I deliberately left out the part about me killing one of the humans. That was not on Wyatt's "approved activity" list.

I felt him pull away. He lifted my chin with his thumb to meet my eyes with his.

"What are you talking about? A mob attacked you? Headed by an angel with a mage for back-up?"

It did sound pretty farfetched. "It's okay. I think they were some kind of rogue vigilante group. As soon as Gregory showed up, they vanished, leaving no trace. I'm sure they think he killed me."

Wyatt shook his head, confused. "Okay . . . what does Gregory think about all this?"

"He doesn't believe me." Not that I blamed him. I'd been summoning him all spring, and demons weren't particularly truthful. I should have just put the whole thing out of my mind, but something bothered me about the incident. An angel and a mage? It was too bizarre. It reminded me of the beginning of a bad joke — an angel, a mage, and a rabbi walk into a bar...

"Never mind," I told Wyatt, giving him a quick kiss. "I want you to come over to my house so I can show you something."

He grinned, and I knew right away where his mind had detoured. "Are we still grabbing dinner out later, or eating in?"

I had a vision of us naked in bed feeding sushi to each other. That fun would probably need to be on hold for another day, though. I led him to my house, pouring the champagne as soon as we walked through the door.

Wyatt gave me a quizzical look as I handed him a full glass of bubbly and wished him a happy early birthday.

"Party isn't until tomorrow I thought," he commented, taking an obligatory sip.

"I've got a special gift for you, but it arrived early. It's in the kitchen."

He grinned, and I followed him into the kitchen, nearly plowing into him as he came to an abrupt stop.

"Ta da!" I announced, pushing past so I could better see his reaction.

I wish I hadn't. He stared at the girl, his eyes darting back and forth between Dar and her terrified face. I'd hoped she would calm down a bit when she saw Wyatt, but if anything, she appeared even more confused and afraid.

"Ta da!" I repeated, gesturing in my best Vanna White impression.

"It's a girl," Wyatt said slowly. "A girl and your brother, standing in your kitchen."

"Yes, exactly. Although Dar isn't part of the present. Or my kitchen, either."

"You're giving me a girl for my birthday?" Wyatt's voice rose in anger.

"Well, yes. I know she's really scared now. It's got to be a bit of a shock for her, seeing you for the first time like this, but she'll come around. Dar promised me that no one harmed her. She's just a little nervous."

"A girl. You're giving me a human being as a slave?"

Wyatt was furious, his voice thunderous. The girl's eyes flickered between him and the floor, her trembling increasing. How could this have gone so wrong?

"No, no. Don't you recognize her? It's your sister, Wyatt. The human changeling. The one Amber replaced. I got her back from the elves and brought her home."

I'd thought this would make Wyatt ecstatic. I'd rescued his sister from a life of slavery and reunited them. Could it be he didn't recognize his own sibling? I thought humans would instinctively know their family, that their eyes would meet across my kitchen and they'd race to embrace each other in happy reunion.

He had no idea how difficult this had been. It had taken me months and considerable amounts of money and favors. In spite of his desire to get rid of Nyalla, it had been nearly impossible to broker a purchase from Aelswith. Demons tended to buy humans for only one purpose, and the elves were usually reluctant to turn over all but the worst of them to that kind of fate.

It wasn't just the rape, torture, and eventual Own that Nyalla's owner had objected to. It was me. No one in Cyelle was allowed to deal with me, speak to me, or any of my household, unless it was to drag me in and throw me in a dungeon. I'd needed to go through five households to broker the deal. And I'd needed to bribe heavy so the demons handling the transaction along the way didn't molest or terrorize the girl. I didn't think Wyatt would be as appreciative of my gift if she'd shown up broken and hysterical. Not that my precautions seemed to have helped. She was one step away from broken and hysterical as it was.

"Seriously? She's my sister? The one the elves stole and kept in slavery?"

"She's your sister, Wyatt. Her name is Nyalla. I brought her back to you."

Finally I saw what I'd hoped for in his face. With a sharp intake of breath, he turned to me, eyes shining with joy and grabbed me in a hug.

"I love you, Sam. Thank you."

"I love you too, Wyatt," I murmured. We'd had our challenges the past few months, all over his half-breed sister and my tendency to kill people first and ask questions later. I'd hoped this gesture on my part would finally make things right between us.

Wyatt pulled away and walked toward Nyalla, taking her hand.

"I'm your brother, Wyatt. I'm so happy to meet you, and I'll do everything I can to make this difficult transition work. I hope you enjoy life here as a free human."

Nyalla's blue eyes were huge, her face pale. She glanced at Dar and me, tugging her hand from Wyatt's grasp.

"Does she speak?" Wyatt asked in concern. "Did the elves make her a mute or something?"

I frowned at the girl. She'd spoken the last time I'd met her, or had she? I remember that Aelswith had answered all the questions on her behalf. Crap, maybe she couldn't speak, although I thought I remembered her replying to me earlier. Maybe she'd just shaken her head?

Wyatt crouched slightly to look into her downturned face. "It's okay. You don't need to be afraid. You're safe now. No one is going to hurt you."

She lifted her head, searching Wyatt's face with anxious eyes.

"What did he say?"

She spoke in Elvish, and suddenly her muteness made sense.

"He said that you're safe, and he's going to help you make a new life here with the other humans."

Her face turned to mine, a faint light of hope in the back of her eyes. "Am I not going back? Am I not going to be raped, tortured and killed by a group of demons?"

Hadn't Dar told her? I glared at him, and he shrugged.

"No! I brought you over here as a present for Wyatt."

"Am I his? Will he expect me to have sex with him, or just clean and do other tasks?" she asked, eyeing Wyatt with some apprehension.

I was pretty sure humans in general didn't have sex with their siblings, and I really didn't want Wyatt to be intimate with anyone but me. I began to tell her this, when Wyatt elbowed me, clearly wanting in on our conversation.

"You don't speak English? Do you know any human languages?" I asked her, although I was pretty sure of the answer.

Nyalla shook her head. "I was taken as an infant, and we are not allowed to associate with other humans until the age of puberty, when we are rendered infertile."

The elves neutered their humans? I glanced at Wyatt, thankful that he couldn't follow our conversation. "But after? Surely you had human friends? A boyfriend?"

"My low status prohibited me from social or sexual contact with other humans. Only those high in their households, or in the mage program, are allowed that privilege."

"She doesn't speak English," I told Wyatt. "She doesn't speak any human languages, only Elvish and possibly some Demon."

I didn't tell him the rest. That his sister, stolen from her crib and placed into slavery, had been rendered infertile and denied the company of her own race. That she'd been verbally abused, given solitary meaningless jobs. Was she a virgin, or had some elf had his way with her? It was unlikely, since they weren't attracted to humans, but after seeing an elf/demon hybrid, I didn't rule it out. I doubted she had been told to entertain a demon. She wouldn't have survived that.

I didn't have a chance to ask her, though, as Wyatt once again grabbed her hand.

"It will work out. You're smart; you'll learn quickly. Immersion is the best way to learn a language, I've been told. I'll pick up some software for you, too."

She looked at Wyatt in confusion, and, with some hesitation, took his hand and placed it on her breast. "I will do my best to please you, Master. I hope that you will allow me to prove my worth in your service."

Wyatt snatched his hand away in horror and looked at me. "What was that about? What did she say?"

Crap.

"He's not your master," I hastily told Nyalla. "He's your brother. Didn't Dar tell you? You're home. I've brought you home."

"My brother?" Nyalla reached out a tentative hand to touch Wyatt's. "Do I have other family? Parents?"

"Your mother still lives. And you have a step-sister, Amber. She is the changeling that took your place."

Nyalla looked confused. "But the elf changelings are dead. How did this happen that one lived? The elves would never have made such a mistake."

"Your sister is not all elf. Amber is an elf/demon hybrid."

Nyalla looked horrified. "Elves do not do that!"

31

"One did. And she smuggled her baby over here so it wouldn't be killed."

"An elf woman bore a hybrid child, and not only allowed it to live, but disguised it as a dead changeling baby so it would be safely raised in place of the human child. In trade, the human child got to be a slave to the elves." Her words were slow, a storm of emotion lurking on the horizon. I glanced back and forth between her and Wyatt, unsure how to approach this topic. I decided on honesty.

"Yes. But it's not the child's fault. It's not either child's fault. Elves do changeling swaps all the time. They kidnap older humans too."

A look of pain and anger crossed Nyalla's face. "She got to have my life, my childhood, while I was kicked, and scorned, and unloved. I have never known a loving touch because of her. She stole my life. I will never call her sister."

This really wasn't turning out like I'd expected.

Wyatt elbowed me. "What is she saying? What are you telling her?"

"I'm explaining who you are and about your family. She's confused about what's going on. Just let me talk with her a moment then I'll translate for you."

I turned back to Nyalla. "The elves stole your life, not Amber. She's as much a victim in this as you are."

Nyalla's eyes flashed, her jaw set with stubbornness that reminded me of Wyatt when he was digging his heels in about some less-than-savory project of mine. "Some victim. She got a life of love and I got . . . this."

"Yes, Amber," Wyatt interjected, speaking slowly and rather loud as humans do when talking to those who don't speak their language. "She's wonderful. You both will be best friends."

Uhhh, probably not.

"Yes, she has had an easy life, so far, compared to you. But you are now free to do and be whoever you want, while she is hunted. Elves will kill her. Demons will turn her over for the bounty. Vampires would attack her as an enemy. Werewolves and angels might also do her harm. She lives in constant fear that she'll encounter someone not human while pumping gas or doing yoga and it will be all over."

Nyalla glared. "Oh, poor little elf-girl! Indulged and pampered, kept safe for two decades, but now she might be snatched out of her golden life and killed. What do you think my life has been? Do you not think every day I worried that I would be killed? That Aelswith would one day put me down like a useless dog? When he sold me to the demons, I thought my worst fears had been realized."

I winced, sympathetic for the girl and the life she'd had. "But that hasn't happened, and now you have your whole life ahead of you. We'll help you, Wyatt and I, and Amber too."

The mulish look returned to Nyalla's face. "I do not want her help. I will not ever call her sister."

"Give her a chance." I frowned at the slight girl before me. "She'll embrace *you* as a sister. It would be best for you to put aside your anger and do the same. It's not her you should blame, but the elves who have made enslaving humans an acceptable practice."

She shook her head, obviously unwilling to forgive and forget. "So what am I supposed to do? I cannot communicate with these people; I know nothing of their world and culture. The only tasks I can do are menial housekeeping and sanitation. I will have the same life here as I did with the elves, only more isolated and scorned."

Kirby's words flashed across my memory: *What would I do? This is all I know. This is my life.*

I'd fucked this up. I wanted to show Wyatt I wasn't as bad as he thought, that I had somehow developed the ability to show compassion. I thought I'd done a good deed in freeing Nyalla, but maybe I hadn't. This was like when good-hearted people set laboratory animals loose in the wild, only to see them torn to shreds within minutes, or slowly starve over weeks because no one arrived with their food pellets.

I turned and looked at Wyatt, who was waiting impatiently by my side, trying to follow the obviously contentious conversation. He raised his eyebrows.

"Wyatt, I don't know what to do." I wasn't sure whether to reach out to him for comfort or not. "I thought this would be a happy homecoming, but she's confused. She's angry that Amber stole her life. She's been socially deprived, verbally abused her whole life. She's afraid she doesn't have the skills or abilities to make the transition and survive in this world."

Wyatt wrapped his arms around me, and I relaxed, putting my forehead on his shoulder. I'd been walking on eggshells around him ever since I'd gotten back from Hel and was grateful for each small touch. Were we okay or not? I was never really sure, and I was desperately worried this intended olive branch had backfired.

Wyatt ran a hand over my hair and pulled back, holding my shoulders. "She's in shock, Sam. It's like PTSD with prisoners of war. We'll get through it. I'm determined to make it work, and I know she'll come around with Amber. Everyone comes around with Amber."

I took a deep breath, but I still couldn't see this ending in anything but disaster.

"Maybe I should take her back. I've pulled in all my favors with the Wythyn side of Tlia-Myea's family, but maybe I can find a sympathetic elf to take her in. I'd leave her with my household, but someone would get overly excited one day and she'd wind up dead. Plus, she'd have the same dislocation issues that she has now."

"I'm not letting her go back there." Wyatt's jaw set in a masculine replica of his sister. "We'll take it easy and slow, get her some language skills first and introduce her to fun, enjoyable things. I'll make this work."

I sighed. "I screwed this up so bad. I'm sorry, Wyatt. So very sorry."

He gathered me close, his hand in my hair, his lips against my ear. "Don't be. This is the best birthday present ever. You did a wonderful thing, Sam. I know it wasn't easy. It's not just the difficulty in getting her away from the elves and across the gates that I appreciate, it's that you thought of it at all. I'm so happy you did something to benefit another human being."

Wyatt tugged my head back and kissed me, his lips firm against mine. Sliding a hand down, he cupped my rear and pulled me against him. I felt how very happy he was, pushing against my lower stomach.

"Oh, get a room!" Dar snickered.

We pulled apart and I gave Dar a happy look. I didn't care what he thought, or how un-demonic my display of affection was. I was just thrilled that Wyatt's and my relationship was starting to return to normal.

"I plan to get a room," I teased him.

"You? You and him?" Nyalla's voice was shrill with disbelief. "You have a human toy who is not a damaged slave? You and my brother are mated? But you are a demon. You should have killed him by now."

Yes, it was odd for a demon to have this sort of relationship with a human. It was odd for a demon to have this sort of relationship at all, but I wasn't exactly a demon anymore.

"Your brother is my boyfriend. I love him. I would never intentionally hurt him. That's why I bought you from your owner and smuggled you across the gates. I wanted to reunite him with the sister he lost."

Nyalla stared at me. "You're the Iblis, the voice of the demons, and you are in love with a human?"

Maybe that's one of the reasons I *was* the Iblis. Wyatt, as well as my friends, had somehow made me less of a demon and more of something else. Of course, that portion of the angel I'd grabbed and held might have something to do with it too.

"Yes. I have human and werewolf friends, and there's an angel that hangs out at my house all the time."

Nyalla began to laugh. Tears rolled down her face, and she wiped them away. "Well, I guess if you can somehow fit in over here, then I'll manage."

"You will. Wyatt is wonderful. He's loyal and loving. He'll help you. And I will too."

I turned to Wyatt. "I know we had plans for tonight, but perhaps you should take Nyalla to your house and get to know her a bit, one-on-one."

"Ask her. She may not want to be alone with me right away, and we can introduce her to television, Chinese take-out, and popcorn."

It was a good idea, but I wasn't sure how comfortable she'd be around me, either. I'd originally planned to have her stay with Wyatt, but perhaps we could all stay here and sleep on the couches. I turned to Nyalla and asked her.

The girl looked back and forth between Wyatt and I, then shot a nervous glance at Dar. "Will he be here too?"

"Nah, I'm leaving." Dar grinned. "I want to open up a couple of sinkholes over on South Street and maybe collapse the I-70 bridge before I head home."

Great. He was going to get me in so much trouble. Gregory held me accountable for all the actions of my household, and who knows how pissed he'd be over Dar's "activities".

"Just don't kill anyone," I warned. "I've got enough of those fucking reports to do as it is."

Nyalla took a deep breath. "Then I think I would like to participate in the mooo-vie and popcan."

I smiled at her awkward pronunciation. "Popcorn."

"Popcorn," she repeated, the beginning of a smile tugging at her lips. It lit up her whole face, and I saw even more resemblance between the thin, pale girl and her gorgeous brother.

"She'll stay," I told Wyatt. "Can you order the food? Just get a selection of everything, that way she can try a bite of it all."

Wyatt pulled a phone from his pocket while Nyalla watched, full of curiosity. I walked Dar to the door, again warning him not to kill any humans and to return back to Hel as quickly as possible.

"Spoilsport," he teased. "When's the last time you killed a human?"

"Today," I admitted. "But it was sort of self-defense. Two humans, a mage, and an angel attacked me in an alley."

Dar stared before he barked out a laugh. "Did they all walk into a bar with a Rabbi?"

I punched his shoulder. "I'm serious. The mage was worthless. The net he threw over me wouldn't hold a fucking rabbit, but the angel was a bit of a badass. He flew all over downtown after me, blowing up chunks of pavement along the way."

My foster brother laughed again. "Sounds like a fun afternoon to me, besides the angel, that is. Was he part of this Ruling Council? One of their flunkies, maybe?"

"I don't know." I ran a hand through my hair. "He didn't seem to know I was the Iblis. Maybe he was some kind of fallen angel and the others were his minions."

"Yeah, because angels are so weak they need to turn to a really bad mage and two humans for household members?"

"Choir," I corrected him. "I know it sounds ridiculous."

"Well that's the least of your problems right now, Mal. There's a reason I'm here a day early."

He pulled a small folded card from his pocket and handed it to me. "Ahriman's steward delivered this to yours last night. I'm just guessing here, but I'm thinking he's demanding an answer from you."

I grimaced. Killing Haagenti had spurred a whole new batch of breeding petitions from hopeful demon candidates. I hadn't even responded to the ones I'd received last fall. They were gathering dust on my dining room table. Ahriman's was on the top.

"I saw his petition, Mal. It's flattering; a great opportunity. Why don't you take it? It would benefit us all. I'd fucking jump for joy if he offered me half what he's offered you."

Bad things happened to demons that got their personal energy, their spirit selves, close to mine. Plus, Gregory had made it quite clear he was vehemently against my having any doings with Ahriman.

"I've been busy. And the terms aren't all that great. Yeah, the household would profit, but the exclusivity is a concern. One thousand years, Dar."

He tilted his head and grinned. "I've waited nearly a thousand years for you to accept my petition. I can stand to wait one thousand more."

I smiled and took a deep breath. Might as well get this over with. Breaking the seal on the card, I read the contents, which drove the smile right from my face.

"He's tired of my delays and insists on an immediate answer." What I didn't say was that Ahriman intended to pick off my household one at a time until I responded. I got the feeling "no" would not be considered an adequate response.

Dar shrugged. "So do it. I don't get why you're hesitating on this one."

Because Gregory would fucking kill me. And I had an odd dread over the prospect of anything to do with Ahriman. I'd never met him, but that demon had one hell of a ruthless reputation. My mind whirred. I could bring my household here, but there were nearly twenty. There was no way I could keep control over that many demons, and I'd be held accountable for all their actions. Plus, nothing would stop Ahriman from sending over a stream of hit men, as Haagenti had done, to kill them on this side of the gates. I couldn't protect them all.

I ran a finger down the skin parchment. It was a good offer. He'd even agreed to allow me to return here occasionally and visit the humans, so long as I returned when requested and satisfied the terms of the contract. Wasn't this part of being responsible? Being the Iblis? I had to put the needs of my household above my own selfish desires.

I took a breath and signed the card, burning my sigil into the parchment with my energy. At least he didn't expect me to present myself for another two months. That would give me enough time to make arrangements and hopefully figure out some way to explain this to Gregory—if I ever did explain it to him. Perhaps it would be best to just keep this little contract a secret.

"Thanks, Dar." I handed the card back. "And thanks for all your help in getting Nyalla here." I reached out and gave him a quick hug. He pulled back, yanking a chunk of my hair with a force that brought tears to my eyes.

"What the fuck, Mal? Are you treating me like one of your humans now?"

"Sorry. Fuck off, asshole. There, how's that? Better?"

"Much better," Dar said over his shoulder as he made his way to the rental car he'd already dented. He protested, but I got the feeling that deep down inside, he kind of liked the hug.

Brothers. Family. I thought of Dar and Leethu, of all the demons I had a strange affection for. I thought of Wyatt, of Amber and Nyalla, of Michelle and Candy. And I thought of that darned angel. They were all my family; mine. In spite of the earlier drama, the less than ideal situation with Nyalla, that I'd nearly gotten killed by some psychotic rebel angel, that I'd

just signed a deal with Ahriman, in spite of all that, I felt . . .
happy.

~4~

I was overcome with a sense of déjà vu as the angel plopped a human head on my dining room table.

"This better not take long," I warned him. I should have been used to these unplanned visits by now, and normally I was thrilled to see him, but today's appearance was especially inconvenient. Wyatt and I had stayed up into the wee hours of the morning watching movies and introducing Nyalla to earth culture and cuisine. He'd left just a few moments ago to pick up Amber from the airport, giving me precious little time to get ready for his party tonight.

"It's important." He motioned to the head.

It didn't look very important. The last time he'd shown up with a head at my door, he'd insisted it was a demon, only to retract his statement later, telling me it was a human who had been cryogenically frozen. Everyone makes mistakes — everyone except angels, that is. Gregory admitting to an error was fishy enough. This head on my table only confirmed my doubts.

"And there's a Ruling Council meeting tomorrow. I'll pick you up early in the morning."

His announcement distracted me from my perusal of the slightly decomposed head. I'd had little sleep last night, curled up with Wyatt on the couch keeping Nyalla company, and I intended for Wyatt and I to remain awake and active all night, celebrating his survival of yet another year. Humans didn't live very long, and I wanted each one I shared with Wyatt to count.

All that was going to make for a very rough time of it at the Ruling Council meeting tomorrow. Normally I wouldn't mind sleeping through it, but this one was all about me and my endless stream of four nine five reports.

"Is this the meeting for the report I'm protesting, or to go over the other ones?" I rubbed a crick in my neck, stiff from both a night on the couch and the prospect of six angels chewing my ass out.

"All of the above."

Shit. Well, no use fretting about what tomorrow might bring, especially when I had this lovely head on my dining room table. "So, what's up with this guy?" I poked a cheek with my finger. The skin was damp and cool with a waxy sheen.

"Do you know him?" Gregory asked.

Yes, definitely déjà vu. I reached for the head and ran a thorough scan. Empty. It appeared to be human, but oddly stripped. I looked at the facial features, but didn't recognize this as the Owned form of any demon I knew.

"Another cryogenically frozen human?" I turned to the angel, searching for the slightest reaction. "How are you finding these, and why are you bringing them to me?"

"I lied at the council meeting. The head I brought you this winter was a demon, and so is this one."

He lied? Not that angels seemed to be adverse to falsehood, but why would he have lied to his peers, the other angels on the council? What reason would he have to hide a demon death from them?

"So just mark it as a dead demon by unknown causes and move on. Why bother to lie? It's not like anyone would care about a dead demon." I certainly didn't care about a dead demon. I didn't know him.

His black eyes bored into mine. "This type of death is very similar to one I've encountered before, but there are differences. I suspect that this is not what it seems, that someone may be employing misdirection. If so, I don't want them to know I'm on to them until I figure out who is doing this, and why."

I frowned. I knew politics were convoluted up in Aaru, but Gregory seemed more suspicious than usual. "And you can't trust the Ruling Council? Do you suspect one of them?"

He shrugged. "In Aaru, you quickly learn to trust no one."

But he trusted me enough to tell me this much, at least. A demon. I shook my head at the absurdity of it all.

"Do you suspect an angel killed them?"

Gregory's eyes met mine. "I don't know. It seems implausible, but the manner of their death gives me cause for concern."

"Why do you care?" I asked softly. "It's just a demon. A demon who has clearly violated the treaty by his presence on this side of the gates. Dead is dead — by your hands or someone else's — it shouldn't matter to you."

His shoulders tightened as he clearly struggled to decide how much to confide in me. "There is no reason I can think of for an angel to cover up the execution of a demon, or to kill one in such a fashion, but if one is doing so, I need to know why."

My mind darted back to yesterday, to the angel so determined to kill me. But Gregory was right. There was no reason for an angel to cover up the execution of a demon like this.

"What if it's not an angel killing them? What if. . .." My voice trailed off as I remembered my conversation with Dar this winter. The hypothetical one where he'd casually mentioned a devouring spirit could erase demon energy to this degree. A devouring spirit like me.

"No matter who's killing them, you're the Iblis. It's your duty to assist me in the investigation and attempt to protect your people."

He obviously had a different job description for Iblis than I had. None of the demons outside of my own household recognized any increased authority with the title. And demons really don't give a flying crap about investigating murders. But I was beginning to wonder if I really was a demon anymore. Reaching over, I ran my hands down the side of the cool skin, picking the head up to examine it with my human senses.

"How can you tell they are demon corpses? How the heck are they brought to your attention?"

He stepped close to me, the heat from his power leak intensifying. "That is not something you need to know."

"This is the second one in less than six months. Are you sure you're catching them all? Is it possible this has happened to hundreds or thousands of demons, and you're only aware of these two?"

I saw him shift at my words, felt a discomfort from him. "I suspect there are many more we're not aware of, but I have no proof."

I stared at the head in my hands. It was just a head. A human head. I couldn't tell the cause of death, couldn't tell it was ever a demon. On impulse, I turned it to examine the severed portion of the neck, running my fingers along the edge of skin, which was beginning to dry and curl.

"Was he decapitated when you found him? Was that how he died?"

"No. It's easier to transport a head as opposed to a whole body, and that is where the majority of the energy signatures reside. There was no visible cause of death. He appeared to have been simply removed from his body."

I frowned. There was no "simply" about it. This sort of thing didn't just happen. Demons didn't die and leave absolutely no trace in their corporeal forms. I smoothed the dried, curled edges of skin and felt something . . . slippery. And familiar. Again I ran my fingers across the area, sending my personal energy into the flesh. There. A small spot on his neck. It felt like that silicone stuff the angels used to cover our raw energy to keep us from using it. The trace was too miniscule for me to determine if it was the same as what the angels used, or if it was a similarly effective magic taught to sorcerers by the elves. Either way, its presence sent chills down my spine. Without the use of raw energy, a demon would be as defenseless as a human.

"Next time, I need to see the whole body." I put the head on the table and turned to look at Gregory.

He nodded. "Difficult, but I will make every attempt. What do you think?"

I glanced back at the head. Slippery blocking stuff would be angel or sorcerer. The absolute lack of any energy signature at all would be devouring spirit, according to Dar. But neither of those made any sense.

"No fucking clue. I'm just thinking with more of the body, I might be able to pick something up."

He didn't reply. An awkward silence filled the room. Why was he still here? We'd discussed the head. He'd delivered the message about tomorrow's meeting. Was I supposed to invite him to stay for lunch?

"What did you find out from the elves? You said last time you thought it might be possible for a sorcerer to do this, and that you'd check it out."

I poked at the head, rocking it backward. "I didn't bother. You said at the council meeting you'd been mistaken, so I didn't think there was any need to inquire further."

That was a lie. I'd already asked Dar to check it out and he'd reported back to me. I'm not sure why I kept our conversation from Gregory. Perhaps because I had a feeling that he was holding back information from me and I was piqued. I'm a terrible liar. He glared at me, his jaw tightening.

"Cockroach, I know you better than that. You're a dog with a bone, and I know you 'bothered'. What did you find out?"

"Nothing important, really. Dar said he wasn't aware of any elf magic that could do this. He said it was probably a devouring spirit."

Gregory recoiled at my words. "I, too, had suspected a devouring spirit, but why would they leave the body behind? I've only seen them at the stage where they take everything."

I deliberately looked at the head on the table, keeping my face averted from his. It hurt to hear the coldness in his voice. "I . . . I've seen cases where they have left the physical form behind." Like when I devoured Haagenti. Like when I devoured my first breeding tutor so long ago.

"You've seen that?" Gregory made a noise back in his throat, like he was swallowing something bitter. "You've seen a devouring spirit? Watched one kill? That's disgusting, even for a demon." I couldn't help but flinch at the revulsion in his voice.

"Why? Why is it so disgusting?" I was angry. Demons thought devouring was perverted and icky, so I'm sure the angels thought even worse. Still, I had complicated feelings for this angel, and it hurt that he would think I was disgusting. It's not like I could help it.

"Grabbing another being and basically *eating* them? Seizing a portion or all of someone without their permission and keeping it, using it for selfish purposes? How is that *not* disgusting?"

His words ended abruptly and he stared at me in shock. "You? But you're an imp, you're not. . .."

"How do you think I killed Haagenti? There's no way I could have taken him out at my level otherwise. I devoured him."

Comprehension crossed his face. "That's what went wrong with the binding! No wonder you seized part of me and managed to keep it. If I'd have known you devoured, I would never have attempted it."

He would have just killed me. That was the unspoken end of his sentence. Pain lanced through me like a hot iron on every nerve ending. I knew he wanted to kill me when he first met me, but hearing this twisted something inside me. If he'd have known, I'd be dead. We'd never be where we were today. It would have all ended before it started.

"I didn't do it on purpose." The hurt managed to leak into my words, no matter how hard I tried to keep it out. "If I could give it back, I would."

"I know," he said, his outrage transforming into something gentle. "It's not like you can help it."

His eyes were drawn to the head on the table, and he frowned.

"I didn't do it. I didn't kill this demon, or the one you brought over this winter."

He looked back at me, assessing my words for truthfulness. "Devouring spirits are extremely rare, thankfully. I doubt there are any besides you on this side of the gates."

"I didn't do it," I insisted.

"If a devouring spirit is killing other demons, if there's no underlying plot or plan that would threaten the humans or angels, then I don't care. It's an internal issue to Hel, not of my concern."

I got the feeling that he was lying. That a devouring spirit, either in Hel or here, was very much something he cared about. But either way, he didn't believe me.

"It. Wasn't. Me. And it may not be a devouring spirit. Look here." I picked up the head and showed him the section of the neck with the tiny slippery spot. He ran his hands over it and tilted his head, perplexed. "I can't really tell from this small spot, but it seems the demon may have been restrained."

Restrained. As in what he did to me when he wanted to completely block my use of raw energy.

"Demons don't do this. And devouring spirits certainly don't do this. I won't rule out a devouring spirit, but this may have involved either an angel or sorcerer."

He examined it closer, a small smile on his mouth. I suddenly realized that in his sneaky way, he managed to get me to reveal everything I knew, everything I suspected.

"Okay, cockroach. I'll withhold judgment until we have further evidence."

Jerk. But I still wanted to ease the pain in my chest.

"Do you really think I'm disgusting?" Pathetic, but pride was never my sin.

He turned that devastating smile on me, the heat from his power increasing, his spirit-self reaching out to touch me.

"Yes. Psychotic, greedy, crass, unenlightened, and disgusting."

I smiled back. "Thank you. I think you're pretty awesome too."

There was a moment between us. A brief second of peace where we both recognized our differences and the attraction we felt in spite of them, or perhaps because of them.

"Tell no one else what you are," he said, a note of worry in the seductive tone. I brushed against his spirit self, missing this caress, the feel of him. It had been all business lately, and I'd worried that my relationship with Wyatt wasn't the only one teetering on the brink.

"It's a bit late for that. I announced it to a big crowd of demons after I killed Haagenti."

He pulled back, his lips in a tight line as he examined my face. "That's not good. Not good at all."

I got the feeling that was a gross understatement.

"They *saw* me kill Haagenti — saw me do it. I'm sure it's all over Hel right now, but it's not that big of a deal. Devouring is kind of twisted, even for a demon, but there are worse things."

"No, there are *not* worse things. If anyone confronts you about this, lie. Say they were mistaken, that it's a vicious rumor. Don't ever devour again. Ever."

"I don't exactly run around doing it on purpose!" Well, I had done it on purpose a few times, but that had been self-defense.

"No more," he insisted, taking my face in his hands. "No more, and don't tell a soul."

His face was close to mine, his thumbs brushing my cheekbones with a physical caress so unusual for him. I was breathless with him this close, my thoughts shifting to other, more pleasant activities. "Okay. I won't devour again, and I won't tell anyone."

I expected him to pull away, to break contact now that he'd gotten what he wanted, but his hands remained on my face, his spirit self reaching out to touch mine. I held still and closed my eyes, enjoying the heat of his power, the feel of him moving against me.

"Are you ready for the council meeting tomorrow?" he asked, that seductive note creeping back into his voice. "It's going to be a rough one. I have a premonition that you'll be spending quite a bit of time in Aaru being punished."

I shuddered. Naked and restrained wasn't as fun as it sounded. Maybe if I hit one of them in the face with a pastry again, I could manage to get the meeting adjourned. Probably not.

"Seriously? I mean, I know that Gabriel guy hates my guts, but the others might vote my way, right?"

His eyebrows shot up, practically disappearing into his copper curls. "I read your report, little cockroach. It's incomplete and flippant. I'm not sure even I can vote in your favor."

"You just want to punish me again," I complained. He seemed to get perverse joy out of dragging me up to Aaru and torturing me.

He smiled, and I felt his touch grow even more intimate. "Well, yes. I do."

In retaliation I withdrew from my flesh, pulling my spirit-self deep within and away from him.

"Nice," he told me. "Have you practiced animating your form while dead? Can you now reside within an inanimate object or energy?"

I moved away from him physically, extending my spirit-self fully back into my human form. So much for the prospect of angel sex. We were clearly back to business . . . again.

"No. I can't figure out how to move around dead. I just lay there."

He scowled. "And inanimate objects? Energy? Elements? I told you to practice these things!"

Yeah. And I always do what I'm told.

"Why the fuck would I want to live inside a rock or a chair? Or inside air molecules? That's just stupid."

I felt his anger, but also felt a sense of urgency within him, almost panic.

"You need to do this." He went silent, as if he were considering something.

"I want to take you somewhere. Show you something."

"Right now? I need to be back before tonight." Crap, before that even. I hadn't even begun to decorate. And Nyalla was upstairs, sleeping in one of my spare bedrooms. She might be alarmed to wake up and find herself alone in the house. "I can't. I really can't today. Maybe after the council meeting tomorrow, but not today."

He reached out and pulled me to him. "It will only take an hour at the most."

Before I could protest, he'd transported us in a disorienting jerk.

~5~

I could feel the heat all around me, stealing the air from my lungs and searing my skin. The angel pressed to me, smashing a furnace of power against my front, while the natural element of the forest fire raged against my back, squeezing me uncomfortably between them. I felt the threads of my clothing smolder, exposed skin beginning to blister. We were close, practically inside the blaze.

Pull back as you burn

I did as the angel said, distancing my spirit self from the flesh. I still was aware of the pain, but it was as if I watched another. Thick smoke blurred the angel who was inches from my face, and I closed my useless eyes. I burned.

There was a caress against me. I felt his admiration and his attraction. Whatever it was I was doing, I seemed to be doing it properly, according to him. Even with the distant pain, the edge of fear as my body died, I felt safe. He wouldn't let anything happen to me; I'd be okay as long as he was near.

My body failed, lungs choked with smoke, skin cells erupting. I tried to move an arm, but couldn't figure out how to do it without extending my spirit self dangerously into the dead flesh. Struggling a few seconds on my own, I turned to him, awaiting his instruction. This was a lesson, and I was an eager pupil in the arms of an angel who was older than the sun.

Let the body go. See without eyes. Hear without ears. Move without limbs.

I'd die. What did he want me to house my spirit self in, if not this burning flesh? I felt the physical form of the angel shift like molten lava, his spirit self still reassuring against mine. Did his flesh burn too?

Open your eyes and see.

I knew he didn't mean human eyes. Reaching out with my senses, as I did while in Aaru, I saw him, a smokeless fire before me, shielding my burnt body from total consumption by the inferno around us. What would happen if my body was completely destroyed by fire? I'd learned to exist safely inside a corpse, but had an uneasy feeling I'd die if the body no longer existed. He moved, as if to leave me to the fire, and I pressed against him in panic, my spirit self clinging to his for protection.

Let it go.

No fucking way. I couldn't think of any Owned form that would safely exist in the blaze around me. The only option left was to hold on to this angel as if my life depended on it. Because my life *did* depend on it.

Let it go. Trust yourself. Trust me. I'm here to catch you, like a safety net.

I was like a trapeze artist frozen at the apex of a swing, on the verge of releasing from the bar to fly free a moment before snatching another. Would I have the courage to let go, to trust I'd survive that moment of free-fall? Or would I swing back, clinging to incinerated flesh?

Let go. Become the flame.

But how? I felt his spirit self merge slightly with mine, two becoming one in a thin line of translucent white. Yes, I could create fire, but how could I house myself in a form of energy? The angel before me had, but I wasn't an angel. None of us demons were angels anymore. We'd devolved — perhaps too far for this sort of thing. I didn't trust that I could do it and live.

I have you. I won't let go, he insisted.

I didn't trust myself, but I did trust him. I jumped, feeling the remains of my human body fall away into flame and ash. There was the familiar stab of panic and joy, just like what I felt when I exploded out of my physical form and collapsed it back into a new one, converting the matter around me to my whim. For a second, I was free, a being of spirit unrestrained. I spread thin, stretched and on the verge of dissipating into nothingness. Fire of my doing burst around me, but I couldn't figure out how to make it cloak me. The stretching became painful, and I felt a tear at the edge of my being, where the scars from my fight with Haagenti would always remain.

I've got you.

And he had. My panic subsided, leaving me shaky and drained. I wouldn't be doing this again. No fucking way. I'd almost died. If he hadn't been here to catch me, I *would* have died. Whatever it was I was supposed to have learned, I hadn't. I'd failed, and I just wanted to go home, out of this fire, to where I could remain safely in a flesh form, as I had for centuries.

Try again. His voice was gentle, but I heard the firm command behind the softness.

No. I hated to disappoint him, didn't want to admit to my failure and my terrible fear to try again. I just couldn't. Couldn't. For a moment my panic returned. What if he forced me? Pulled away and threw me over the edge? There was nothing I could do to stop him.

Hush. I won't make you if you're not ready.

He rubbed against me, gently smoothing my new scars and shielding me from my surroundings. Feeling safe again, I opened my senses. I was gathered against him, joined in a strange combination of ecstasy and comfort. He felt like home — warm, powerful, and safe. I had a longing to join with him all the way, to swirl our spirit selves and make him part of me, but I was curious about the flame we shared. It wasn't truly fire. It was some kind of strange energy source I'd never seen before.

What are you? I asked.

An angel, he teased. *What are you?*

Your Cockroach.

It just came out of me, an involuntary response. The derogatory name he'd always called me had turned into a strange endearment, and I'd just formalized it, honoring him by making it part of my official name. Not only that, but I'd made it clear this was a private name. Only he could call me this, only he would know this name and its significance. I was *his* Cockroach.

I felt his surprise, and an explosion of emotion, like water bursting free from a dam. It was overwhelming, sweeping over me with its intensity. The humans always saw angels as a loving, happy bunch, dedicated to singing praises about the benevolence of their deity. Not the angels I'd met, and especially not Gregory. He always appeared to be serious, grim. He rarely laughed, and in the ten months I'd known him, he'd never seemed happy, but suddenly he was. He was more than happy.

He curled himself even closer to me, increasing the sections where we were joined, and stirring up all sorts of sensations. My thoughts blurred, all thought of the forest fire vanishing along with my fear of death. I relaxed and enjoyed the feel of him in and around me.

Give me magnesium, chlorine, oxygen, sulfur and carbon.

Huh? I shifted against him in confusion, and felt him brush against my store of raw energy.

Create it, and let me share it.

That was a new one. He'd asked me to create things before in what had become our private lesson time, but never when we were semi-joined like this.

How do you want them? And how much? This was important. Chlorine wasn't the most stable atom in the periodic table. This I knew from personal experience.

I felt him wince, as if he'd shared my rather explosive memory. *Four oxygen on one chlorine. The others standalone. A few ounces. I can dispose of any unused.*

Safe in his embrace, I used my raw energy to create a few ounces of each, carefully combining the chlorine atoms with the oxygen ones.

Without a physical form to hold it, I expected the chemicals to just drop to the forest floor, which, given the fire around us, would have been a rather violent disaster, but the angel held it aloft. His flame changed, and suddenly the lot ignited, in a sizzling ball. He launched it, and it exploded just above the tree line, sending fireworks of silver-white to the sky in a burst of light and color bright enough to penetrate the thick, dark smoke. I knew he watched for my reaction, and I felt his pleasure in my delight at his trick.

Calcium chloride this time instead of the magnesium.

How are you doing this without black powder? How are you propelling the stars? I'd explored human-made fireworks before. They were a dual-stage explosive, with initial propulsion, then a secondary, hotter ignition of chemicals. Magnesium had given his light show the silvery color, emitting light as it vibrated under heat. The worrisome chlorine and oxygen molecule created the heat needed, and the sulfur and carbon served as a reducer. But how was he getting the primary explosive?

I am not completely without talents. After all, fire is a skill of mine. His voice was teasing and affectionate.

I guess fire included explosives of all sorts. Nifty skill to have. I was downright envious.

Come on. I'm not getting any younger here.

Yeah, at six billion or more years old, he certainly wasn't. I obliged and saw orange sparks fly and explode like an immense marigold of fire as the calcium chloride heated to the exact temperature for maximum color. He continued to request chemical combinations, and our movements became synchronized as we worked together. Gregory instructed me, explaining the optimal ignition temperatures for each compound, and how the addition of chloride enhanced the shade. The shapes above us grew complex, a kaleidoscope of color. I relaxed, safe in his embrace and enjoying his skill and knowledge.

Your turn.

He separated his spirit being from mine, touching only a small part to reassure me that he was nearby. I felt him edge me to the outside of his form, to gently ease me on my own. I clung to his spirit self, desperately trying to merge us again.

You can do it. I'll catch you if you need. I'm right here.

I steadied myself, touching only that small portion of him. I was still inside his physical form, sharing it, and the prospect of attempting to do this on my own was terrifying. He nudged me again, and, in panic, I tried to grab a portion of his physical form, his flame, to steal and use as my own.

No. Greedy Cockroach. Make your own flame.

I could feel his amusement. He held firm against my grasping reach. Ignoring my fear, and concentrating, I created a mundane flame, far simpler than his unknown energy. Cautiously, I edged myself into it, like a swimmer at a January beach testing the waters. I was surprised to feel the flame support and cradle my being. I'd done it. I was fire. I could move. I could exist in a flame as long as there were appropriate conditions for combustion. I created a small amount of magnesium, along with the other elements, and sent it skyward in a flash of silver. Gregory renewed his contact with me, the touch turning seductive.

Nicely done, my Cockroach. Now try orange and blue.

Calcium chloride and copper chloride. Tricky, since copper required a lower temperature. I kept my fireworks on the ground, and our flames exploded in the colors that mirrored my spirit being. This was fun, but my concentration was beginning to falter with the press of him against me.

Giving up the pursuit of fireworks, I turned my attention to the angel and caressed him in return. I didn't have to ask twice. He snatched me from my flame and gathered me against him, my orange-blue an obscene splash of color against his red purple. We swirled together, and I lost track of everything except the feel of him all around me.

His spirit self explored every inch, giving wide berth to the massive amount of destructive raw energy I held. As he neared the scarred edges, still tender from the fight with Haagenti, I pulled back. He persisted, maneuvering me until he could again touch the damaged sections.

I'm still injured there.

I'm being very gentle. I just want to see.

It's not pretty. I was embarrassed. Yes, he had scars too, but his were old and knitted together, trophies from a time of war, while mine were still fresh and raw and had a less than glorious story behind them. I winced, remembering his disgust over my devouring nature. These must repulse him as well, a reminder of who and what I truly was.

I think otherwise.

I relaxed, sensing his sincerity. His careful touch actually felt good, soothing against the tender areas.

So I'm beautiful in spite of my scars, I teased.

No, you're beautiful because *of your scars.*

It was one of the nicest things he'd ever said to me. I felt a strange sensation of trust, a sense that perhaps this weird mismatch of opposites might actually turn into something beautiful, might reveal a future I'd never considered. I let myself free-fall into his embrace, and the soothing touch turned erotic. With a forest fire around us, a smokeless flame housing us, we merged sections, then pulled apart, always remaining safely attached to our shared corporeal form. I wanted so much more, and I knew he did too. Someday. Maybe someday we could do this all the way again, but for now, this strange exquisite torture of foreplay would have to do.

We continued to share one flame, caressing and exploring until we finally relaxed in a sort of cuddle. Reluctantly, I separated myself, creating a flame to house my being once again.

Sorry. I know that wasn't what either of us wanted. Wasn't enough.

He'd once told me it was dangerous for us to do this kind of thing here, that without our physical forms, we ran the risk of coming apart and dying. I couldn't help from wanting him in this way, in spite of the danger. Having him so close, stroking me, with the fireworks and the joy of sharing his knowledge and skill was more than a poor imp could resist. If he wanted to take the risk, as we'd done before, I wouldn't say "no".

I felt him smile, lost myself in his quick caress. *I'm very old. With age comes great patience. Things won't be this way forever, little Cockroach. Have some patience of your own. It's a good virtue to cultivate.*

I had no interest in virtues, especially one where I was expected to deny myself what I truly desired. Fun as this had been, I wanted more. And I wasn't convinced we'd ever be able to have more. Besides the horror of my punishments, the angels wouldn't allow me in Aaru, even as the Iblis, and there was nowhere else we could exist as beings of spirit. It seemed tragic that we could only tease each other or risk death.

Patience.

I saw through his mind's eye. He'd existed for billions of years. Waiting another millennium or two would be of no consequence to him. But I was not patient. I was a demon, an imp, and I wasn't even a thousand years old. I wanted him. All of him. Maybe if we couldn't do it his way, we could do it mine? An erotic fantasy of him sprouting physical genitals and plowing into me until I cried for mercy began to take hold. Why not? It was unlikely we'd ever be in Aaru together. Why not fulfill our needs, satisfy our significant attraction for each other in a different, non-angelic fashion? As if in agreement, he pressed firmly against me, locking my energy tightly within the embrace of his own.

Form your human body as I transport us so you don't burn your house down.

We were in my kitchen, which felt like it was spinning around me with the now-familiar sensation of vertigo. I'd just managed to create the human form I'd worn for the last forty years as my feet hit the floor. Gregory held me in his odd human form, instead of the flame. I reached down to his skin, pores solid, like marble with an odd glow, and stroked a finger along his arm. Angels could never manage to create true flesh, just this strange attempt at a copy.

I needed him. Needed more than his teasing. If we couldn't fuck like angels, I was determined to propose something else. Physical sensation was just as deep, as emotional as the angel joining I'd done with Gregory. We could share that and not risk death, not have to deal with my unwelcome presence in Aaru. I knew deep in my heart that he'd probably never consent to sex, but maybe we could bond in some way physically that we couldn't fully do spiritually. Did oral count as sex? No, I think that was an exception. But perhaps I should start with something a little less extreme. He was an angel, after all.

I used a stream of raw energy and adjusted the molecules in the wake of my finger, leaving him with a stripe of perfect human skin. He ignored it, so I continued, converting more of his skin and aligning all the nerve endings to provide maximum stimulation.

He winced. Not quite the reaction I'd hoped for. I went to run a light touch along the newly formed skin, to soothe and bring pleasure, when he pushed me away, instead caressing me with his spirit being as we had in the fire. I loved what we shared, but I was in human form, naked in my kitchen and pressed against him. The roughness of his shirt and jeans against very sensitive parts of my body were filling me with all sorts of ideas. Reciprocating his caress, I reached up to grab around the back of his head and pull him to me.

He'd kissed me before, but it had always been as a method to heal. I had something different in mind and merged his mouth with mine, transforming his lips into a more sensitive human form as they touched mine. He caught his breath, hands reaching up to grab my wrists as I held his head in place. Undeterred, I continued to move my lips against his, gently worrying a lower one between my teeth.

With a gasp, he pushed me away, shaking his head and grabbing his arm, clasping the tan skin.

"Don't. Don't ever do that."

"Why not? You teach me, show me your skills. I'm just sharing mine with you."

To me, sensation was sensation. That glorious feeling of closeness and affection was just as potent whether it was as a being of spirit, or of the flesh. Gregory had shown me the joys of the spirit; I was simply trying to share the exquisite sins of the flesh with him.

"I have no wish to experience your skills in human copulation techniques."

I rolled my eyes. Of course not. How foolish of me to assume he'd want to fuck like an animal. Bigot. Prude. Why was it always his way or the highway?

"All right, although that's not totally what I meant. Yes, I'd be happy to show you my extraordinary sexual abilities, but I was also talking about my skills in creating a more accurate representation of human flesh. Your form sucks. I'm trying to show you how to do better. Just like you show me."

"I don't need to do better." He snarled. "It's too much sensation. It endangers my vibration level, my evolution. I chose this manifestation on purpose, to avoid the temptation of sin."

That was probably the most honesty I'd ever heard from him. Still, it hurt that I'd come to value and respect his way of life, yet he didn't mine. "It was just a small strip of flesh on your arm and your lips. If your enlightenment can't hold up against such brief temptation, then it's not very solid, is it?"

He turned away and walked toward the table with its decapitated head centerpiece. "Tomorrow's meeting will be to address your appeal on the one four-nine-five report, as well as discussion on the two you've submitted, and the one from yesterday."

"Don't try and change the subject! Since we met, I've tried to understand your history, your philosophy, and point of view. I've trusted you. I've let you show me a small bit of what it's like to be an angel. But you won't give me the same trust, you stubborn, arrogant prick."

In a flash, he slammed me against the kitchen wall, his hands painfully digging into my shoulders.

"I have given you more trust than an angel has ever given one of your kind. I have protected you, lied for you, adjusted my entire life, risked my future because of you. But I *will not* budge on this. I won't fall from grace for your selfish whims. Do not tempt me again."

He vanished and I slid down the wall to sit with my arms around my knees, mourning the loss of our closeness in the fire. Just when I thought we had a connection, an understanding, he turned back into every stereotype I'd ever heard of angels.

~6~

I was grateful for Nyalla's help in party preparations because by the time Gregory had gotten me back from our forest fire excursion, I was way behind schedule. Somehow she'd managed to accept a cake delivery in my absence, even with the language barrier. In less than twenty-four hours, she managed to learn a variety of movie and food related words in English, and I'd just taught her the Happy Birthday song. She'd been singing it under her breath as she hung streamers, trying to commit it to memory, while I put together appetizer trays in the kitchen. My mind raced, full of thoughts about Gregory, my near escape from that killer angel, whether Nyalla and Amber would get along. I had a bad premonition that Wyatt's party was going to be ruined by a catfight of epic proportions. I'd enjoy that sort of thing, but I knew it would hurt Wyatt terribly to have his sisters break into a hair-pulling brawl.

A bloated sun devouring all in its wake

Nowhere to turn but the skies above

A choice between right and left

Where each path leads to sorrow.

That didn't exactly sound like the birthday song. It was in Elvish and quite a bit louder than Nyalla's previous melody.

"What are you singing?" I asked, coming around the kitchen to see the girl perched on a chair, carefully taping a streamer to the ceiling. She jumped at my words, nearly falling.

"I am so sorry. I know my voice is lacking in depth and melodic quality. I did not realize I had been singing that loud."

"There's nothing wrong with your voice," I cut her off with a wave of my hand. Every time the poor girl started to relax, began to get a bit of sparkle in her eyes, she'd yank herself back into a kind of wary stiffness. It was as if she was afraid to hope, afraid she'd suddenly wake up and find herself a slave again. She stood before me on the chair, shoulders hunched, eyes on the floor. Her whole body tensed, as if she were about to be struck. I cursed myself for my abrupt words, realizing I'd inadvertently sent her back to a world where no one was kind, at least, not to her.

"I'm sorry. I didn't mean to snap," I tried to keep my voice soft and gentle. "It's not you. I just get so angry when I think of how you've been treated by the elves, how all humans are treated by them. It pisses me off."

Nyalla glanced up under blond-tipped eyelashes and smiled slightly. "I wish that they could never take another human unwilling from this world. I wish that all the humans in Hel could be free, either to return here, or own property and be equal citizens there."

Me too, although I couldn't see how that could happen. The elves had been doing this for thousands of years and would be unlikely to stop unless forced. "How is life in Cyelle for the humans?" I asked. "I know your owner was not kind to you, but are others better off? Or worse?"

Nyalla shuddered. "Aelswith was cold and harsh in his words, but at least I was protected by law from extreme physical abuse. Other kingdoms do not have such laws. In Cyelle, humans could not be murdered, and all deaths were investigated. Wrongful deaths of humans would result in prosecution and punishment; the same with life-threatening physical abuse. No human starved or went without basic physical needs. Of course, accidents sometimes happened, but things are not so good in other kingdoms. In Wythyn, an elf can torture or kill his or her human without any repercussions."

I frowned, thinking of what they went through. They were like hamsters in a cage, unable to escape or protect themselves. Humans were valued depending on their usefulness, but even a sorcerer had nowhere to hide if he displeased the elves.

"Life is still hard, though. We are discouraged from any artistic expression, as we have no understanding of basic beauty and form. No painting, no poetry, no singing." A sly little smile crossed her face. "Although in private, many of us flout the rules."

The whole thing made me sad. I was glad I'd managed to get her out of there, give her a chance at a new life, but there were so many still in Hel. I yearned to save them all, but how? There was no possible way to change elven society. The best I could do was help Nyalla, protect her, and encourage her to make the most of her life.

"Well, your voice is beautiful — a charming human voice with nice range. Humans *value* distinctive inflection and individual expression in their arts."

Her nose wrinkled, and her eyes came up to meet mine. "That doesn't sound very beautiful. Should not those who practice the arts strive for perfection?"

I held out a roll of streamers and she hesitated a brief moment before taking it. "If you're an angel, then yes," I told her. "Elves desperately try to model themselves after the angels. Annoys the piss out of me. Angels are bad enough, wannabe angels are downright painful to be around."

I saw a smile lurk at the corner of her lips before she turned to tape another streamer. "You're not an elf; you're a human," I continued. "In my mind, that's a superior being. Not some pansy-ass fake angel."

"So if the elves model themselves after angels, do humans model themselves after demons?" she asked innocently. It was a good thing she wasn't facing me to see the shocked look on my face. "Demons value emotion and sensation above balance and perfection of order. Are you saying that humans do too?"

"Oh my," I breathed, trying to keep my voice calm. "Don't ever say that to an angel."

The future of the human race was in a precarious enough position without those assholes thinking they had a bunch of demon groupies on their hands. I could just see the Ruling Council now. There would be an order out for extinction before lunch was on the table.

"Yes, humans value emotion and sensation," I told her, trying to keep the visions of Armageddon from my mind. "But they also enjoy balance and strive for their own definition of perfection."

She turned to face me again. "Do *you* like elven music?"

"Many of us find elven songs to be technically beautiful but somewhat cold in execution."

Nyalla smiled, her posture relaxing fully. "Me too," she said softly, as if she were afraid to admit it.

Fucking elves. I swear if I ever managed to lay a hand on Aelswith, I was going to pop his head off his neck.

"I was just wondering what you were singing when I was in the kitchen. I've never heard it before." I commented, happy to see her looking more like Wyatt's sister and less like a cornered animal.

Nyalla looked puzzled as she climbed down from her chair. "Surely you have. It is the Exodus — one of the grand epics. The elves sing it at all their festivals and sometimes at small gatherings."

I shook my head. I hadn't remembered hearing it before, but then again, I usually wasn't paying much attention to their song lyrics with all the food, drink, and other entertainment offered.

"It is very long; a historical record of elven society before their home planet met its end. The beginning is beautiful — all about the magical place where life first began."

"But you were singing of loss, of an impossible choice, and devouring." I winced at the last word, remembering Gregory's insistence on keeping my unsavory habit under wraps.

"A devouring sun," Nyalla corrected. "Their planet was at the end, and the angels gave them a choice — to share Earth with the humans, share Hel with dwarves and goblins, or share Aerie with the other Fae races." Nyalla's mouth quirked up in a charming lopsided grin. "Elves are not good at sharing. There was no good choice as far as they were concerned."

I was astounded. "Why would they come to Hel? That had to have been the worst of all choices."

Nyalla shook her head and unrolled another length of red streamer. "Aerie was the worst choice. Elves *really* do not get along with fairies, pixies, water sprites, nymphs, or other fae. You should hear the songs they sing of them; they are very derogatory. They do not like dwarves, goblins, trolls, or the soil races either, but they all keep their distance and respect boundaries."

All this confirmed what I'd thought — that elves just didn't get along with *anybody*. Still, *demons*?

"Why Hel? Why not earth with the humans? They seem rather fond of humans, even if they're high-handed in their dealings with them."

Nyalla shot me a wry look before turning her back to tape the streamer. "And be under the constant thumb of the angels? When the war happened, they made their choice — the left hand over the right. Angels of Chaos over Angels of Order." She spun about to look at me, her eyes sweeping down my form with a perplexed frown. "Demons no longer seem to be the Angels of Chaos from legends, though. You have. . . changed."

"Devolved" was the word Gregory used. "The angels have changed too," I protested.

She nodded. "According to the epics, they became more rigid and unbending during the war, that's why the elves made the choice they did." Her eyes focused far away, with a haunted look. "And the elves changed too. They bear only slight resemblance to the wise, gracious creatures of the sagas."

I hated to see that look in her eyes. "Well, fuck the elves. And fuck the angels, too."

She grinned, eyes darting back to me before turning to her decorations. "I am not particularly interested in having sexual relations with either elves or angels," she giggled.

"Shit, I hope not! That's just gross!"

I was gratified to hear even more giggles. She faced me again, her hand covering her mouth, eyes dancing. I smiled at her, feeling oddly protective toward this girl. It wasn't just that she was Wyatt's sister, it was something else. I liked her. I cared about what happened to her. I wanted her to be happy — to see her eyes light up like this more often.

As if reading my mind, a more serious look swept over her face. She pulled her hand away from her mouth, and her eyes searched mine, as if she were trying to decide something.

"Do not trust the elves, Sam," she said, the informality of my name awkward on her tongue. "I have heard things, disturbing bits of information. There are some that mean to move against the demons."

I laughed. "One kingdom can't do shit against the demons, and elves would rather poke their eyes out than join together in any sort of strategic move. It's just talk, Nyalla. We have all sorts of complicated alliances with the elves. They need us far more than we need them."

She shook her head, approaching me and laying a tentative hand on my arm. "The elves are afraid of what the demons are becoming, and they seek a means with which they can control you."

She tugged on my arm, her expression urgent. "If what I overheard is true, one kingdom can control all of Hel. They plan to expand their reach with a new kind of magic."

Elves were more organized and better planners than demons, but they had enough on their plate trying to jockey for position amongst themselves. I couldn't see them ever bothering with us, let alone this farfetched idea that they would conquer us. And elven magic only went so far against demons. It was terribly ineffective against the top tiers of our hierarchy. Even the most skilled sorcerer lacked the 'umph' to fuel their spells to the degree needed to bring down a truly powerful demon.

"Some say they plan to eventually cross the gates," she continued. "To expand their reach to here. When Aaru falls, they'll make their move."

I wasn't sure what drunken elf conversations she'd overheard, but Aaru was not likely to fall. If we couldn't do it in the demon wars, then who would? I thought of Gregory with that cold anger of his that frightened me so, swinging his sword against anyone who would dare attack his heaven. Aaru would never fall as long as he lived. And the elves would never come to earth.

"Nyalla, the elves swore long ago they would never cross the gates, that they would never step foot in the land of the humans. Millions of years they've held fast to their vow. They're like angels that way too — once they've sworn something, they never retract. Never."

Nyalla raised an eyebrow, suddenly looking far older than her nineteen years. "Never is a long time. Circumstances change, and individuals sometimes find that they do things they swore never to do."

I opened my mouth to protest and again thought of Gregory. *I've changed my mind about a lot of things*, he'd once told me. And here we were, in some strange relationship together

— friendship, and a whole lot more. I doubt that was what he'd had in mind when he'd agreed to a complete split between our races two and a half million years ago. *Never* was indeed a long time.

Nyalla removed her hand from my arm, and with a shy smile, turned to pick up another roll of streamers.

"Anyhow, here is the end of the song:

The heavens shook with grief
Rent asunder with jagged rift
The right and left hand removed from their Source
Violence wrought
Each hand to die, ruined without its pair
As the goddess wept tears of blood.

I left the girl to her song and returned to my veggie trays, unable to shake the sorrow in my heart. The demons had changed — and not in a good way. We were devolving, losing what we'd been and becoming something horrible. The angels saw our plight and mocked us, feeling it was punishment for our sins. And if Nyalla was right, the elves, once sympathetic to our cause, now feared us enough that they planned offensive action. My people were on a downward-sliding evolutionary slope that would end when we were no more than creatures of base instinct. All because of a war so long ago, way before my birth.

Could we ever find our way, return to the angels that we'd once been? I sliced carrots, my mind clouded with thoughts of demons as animalistic monsters, the angelic race dying out due to their stubborn pride, the elves isolated bigots who preyed upon other races. Was there any hope that this story of so many races would have a happy ending?

We'd barely finished food prep and decorations before people started to arrive. Amber's plane had been delayed, so there was a celebratory group already half drunk at my house to meet Wyatt when he returned from the airport with her. I'd invited Michelle and Candy, as well as some of his gaming friends. Nyalla stiffened beside me as they walked into the room. I held my breath.

"She looks like an elf," the girl hissed.

She did. A demon adaptation hid the telltale pointed ears, but Amber's face was oddly symmetrical, her cobalt-blue eyes large, almond-shaped and slanted upward at the edges. Even her deportment was elf-like. She walked in with light grace, each step a ballet. Her eyes scanned the room before landing on Nyalla. She'd taken two steps toward us before her sister spun on her heels and dashed into the kitchen.

"Give her a moment," I told Amber. "She'll come around." Or maybe not.

The half-elf chewed her lip, a frown creasing between her brows. A faint curl of pheromone snaked from her — proof of her succubus half. It made her all the more attractive. No wonder Nyalla was resentful. It wasn't just the circumstances of Amber's childhood — the childhood that should have belonged to the human girl, it was the daunting perfection of this elf/demon hybrid. She had an unobtainable, ethereal look with her golden hair and flawless, creamy complexion. Grace, beauty, brains, and that succubus sexual lure — Amber was the kind of perfect girl everyone wanted to hate. That she was friendly and approachable made the bite of envy even sharper.

"Should I go in and talk to her?" Wyatt asked, casting a worried glance toward the kitchen.

"No. I've got a better idea." I walked to Candy and said a few quick words, grinning as she made her way to the kitchen. If anyone could snap Nyalla out of her sulk, it would be my werewolf friend.

Sure enough, I soon heard giggles coming from the kitchen, and less than ten minutes later, the pair appeared, arm-in-arm with half-empty glasses. I watched as Candy introduced the girl to Michelle, and she was soon ensconced in a welcoming group, all trying to teach her various words and communicate via gestures. By the time we sang Happy

Birthday, and Wyatt blew out the candles on his cake, Nyalla looked flushed with happiness, or possibly with wine.

"Thank you for taking care of her today while I went to the airport." Wyatt's breath stirred the hair around my ears and sent a happy tingle down my spine.

"What, no 'thank you' for the party?" I teased. Most of our guests had left, and I had been longing for a lovely evening, just Wyatt and I alone in my comfy bed.

"Thank you for that, too." His hand moved my hair aside, and his lips traced a feather-light line down my neck. Yes, it was definitely time for our guests to hit the road.

"But I especially appreciate your fussing over Nyalla, making sure she didn't feel out of place." His mouth moved to that sweet spot where my neck joins my shoulder, kissing and licking. Everyone needed to leave right now, or I was going to wind up a puddle on the floor. Hopefully a naked puddle on the floor with Wyatt on top of me.

"I'm going to take her to my house tonight and show her the language software I bought. I moved some stuff out of the other bedroom and set it up for her. We'll bond, do some brother/sister stuff."

What? My melting stopped. No! Brother/sister bonding? Not Wyatt/Sam bonding? I swallowed hard, pushing down my disappointment. Our intimate moments seemed to be getting farther and farther apart. I know that was normal with human relationships, but I'd thought somehow Wyatt and I would be on fire for each other forever, or at least until he reached an advanced elderly age when pharmaceutical remedies were a necessary daily supplement.

"That sounds wonderful." My voice choked with the lie. "I think she'll really enjoy that."

Wyatt pulled me to him for a frustratingly tempting kiss, then pulled back to ruffle my hair. "I knew you'd understand."

I did understand. But that didn't mean I liked it. This sister stuff was putting a cramp in my love life — first Amber with her "half the universe is gunning for me" genetic problem, then helpless Nyalla. When would Wyatt's attention turn back to me? *Would* his attention turn back to me? I shook my head, feeling guilty for my thoughts. I was being a selfish bitch. One of the things I adored about Wyatt was his giving nature. This was part of who he was. The human I loved was excited to have his sisters with him, to spend some precious time with them. If I really cared about him, I'd just have to learn to share, and not begrudge others his love and attention.

"She's a nice girl, Wyatt. I think she's going to be okay. Take as much time as you want to connect with her. You've both got a lot of lost time to make up for."

His smile made my day. "I love you."

He kissed me, and I got the feeling that my words and actions over the last two days had done more to repair the rent in our relationship than any amount of soup kitchen and nursing home volunteer work could do.

Slowly the party guests headed home, and the only people left in my house were a sexually frustrated imp, two humans, and an elf/demon hybrid. Amber stayed her distance, sending friendly, hopeful glances at her sister. Nyalla ignored her, turning her back to pick at a tray of crab puffs.

"Okay, this is bullshit." I strode over and grabbed Nyalla by the arm. "Snap out of it. This is your sister, Amber. She's very nice, and she wants to meet you." I dragged the unwilling girl toward her sister and yanked her until she was only three feet from the other woman.

"Hi." Amber's voice was soft and sweet, hesitant in a charming way. "I'm so glad to meet you. I want to take you out shopping, do some girl stuff with you — the kind of thing Wyatt wouldn't be good at. We'll get you some new clothes, have a spa day. It'll be fun."

I translated and saw Nyalla's head raise with interest when I mentioned clothes. She was wearing some borrowed items of mine, and although I was fairly slim, the outfits hung loose on her thin frame. For the first time, she truly examined the other girl, from the top of her golden head to the tip of her peep-toe pumps.

"You don't have many friends yet," I added, trying to tip things in Amber's favor. "Wyatt's great, but he's a guy. It would be a good thing for you to have another female to spend time with."

"What about that Candy woman? Or Michelle?"

"Candy is a werewolf, and she's not a young girl. I'll arrange for you to spend some time with Michelle, but Amber is the same age as you and can give you a good idea of what life is like for a girl your age here."

Nyalla looked skeptical. Once again, her eyes roamed over Amber, and she self-consciously reached up to tuck a loose hair back into her single braid, smoothing it down.

"Give it a shot," I continued. "And if you hate her guts, well, she's away at college most of the year anyway. You can pretend you didn't get her texts, or couldn't figure out the Facebook app or something."

Nyalla frowned. "She is so beautiful. I bet she has never had buvfish stuck in her teeth or sweat stains on her bodice wrap."

I nodded my head. "Probably not. But she does get pissed off and blow up trees on occasion." I put an arm around the girl's shoulder. "Look, I've got a sister too. Leethu is gorgeous. When she's around, I could be a fucking cocktail napkin for all anyone cares. It gets old, but Leethu is cool. She's fun, and I really like having her visit me. Maybe not living in my house for weeks, or anything, but a day here and there. Give it a shot. You need to start making friends, and here's your first chance."

"All right." Nyalla reached out and took Amber's hand in an awkward handshake she'd just learned this morning. "I will buy clothes and take a spa bath with her."

Close enough. I relayed the news, and Amber beamed.

Walking them to the door, I kissed Wyatt and watched as they strolled, happy and cheerful, down my driveway toward Wyatt's house. Crickets chirped in the warm June evening, the scent of honeysuckle filled the air. Amber's laughter danced across the breeze as they filed in through the front door of Wyatt's decrepit Cape Cod. Hesitating a few minutes, I reluctantly closed my front door and pressed my back against the solid wood. I was alone. Alone. It shouldn't have bothered me, but the very thought sent a chill down my spine.

~7~

"Four reports and you've not even been the Iblis for a year. That has to be some kind of record." Dopey's voice was snide as he paged through the stacks before him. Actually, it was three reports and one appeal, but I figured it was in my best interests not to correct him.

"Wow, you truly are the demon of death," Sleepy chimed in. I'd quickly realized this angel was as far up Dopey's ass as he could get. Grinding my teeth, I forced myself to remain silent. Dopey threw a few more barbs my way with Sleepy as back up before giving up and turning to my appeal.

"You claim you were visiting this Joseph Barakel to enquire about the location of a young woman. You believed he was in regular contact with her, and during your visit, he dropped dead of natural causes?" Happy asked.

I nodded. Yep. That summed it up. The six angels lined up before me stared in disbelief. Well, five of them. Gregory didn't appear to be paying attention. He'd heard the story before, so I'm sure whatever incredulity he originally had at my excuse, he was well able to hide by this point.

"Why were you seeking this young woman?" Sneezy asked.

Happy paged through the paperwork, looking for the answer. It wasn't there.

"Just some private detective work for her family." It wasn't really a lie. "She was last seen in the company of a man named Joseph Barakel, and I thought this might be the man."

Bashful looked up. "Was he?"

"No. Turns out he didn't know the woman at all."

Dopey pushed the papers aside. "You killed him. You obtained illegal entry into his house, jumped out at him when he arrived home as if you planned to do him harm. You pulled out your mean, threatened and bullied him. These 'natural causes' were the direct result of your presence."

"I didn't! I was polite and respectful. I even tried to revive him when I noticed he was having a medical emergency."

"His impact analysis doesn't reveal any issues," Happy said. "He killed a young child, committed several crimes. His golf scores were unremarkable."

"He had several unpaid parking tickets," I added helpfully. "And he had a predilection for elastic waist pants."

Happy nodded in sympathy, curling his lip at the mention of elastic waist pants.

"Let's just vote and move on," Dopey said. "We need to review the three four-nine-five reports, and I, for one, don't want to be here any longer than is absolutely necessary."

I sighed in relief. For once, I agreed with Dopey.

"All in agreement with the Iblis?"

Sneezy nodded. Happy nodded. Fuck. Fuck, fuck, fuck. Including me, that was three of seven, and I wasn't sure I got a vote. "All in agreement with the need for the report?"

Dopey. Bashful and Sleepy. Gregory gave me an absolutely wicked grin that sent a wave of heat right down between my legs. Then he nodded. Asshole. Guess he'd forgiven me my transgressions yesterday, as he was clearly flirting in his own way. In a Ruling Council meeting, too. He should be ashamed. He didn't look ashamed though, and my mind detoured from four-nine-five reports to visions of Gregory and I tumbling naked across the conference table.

"Any abstain?" As if there were any left. They'd all voted.

"Well." Dopey looked smug. "That's four against and two in favor. Four-nine-five report for Joseph Barakel due within forty-eight hours or punishment."

"Censure," I corrected.

"No, punishment. I think we're beyond the point of censure."

I looked at Gregory in mute appeal, but he refused to intervene. I knew he'd come to enjoy this whole punishment thing. Having me up in Aaru, without corporeal form and at his mercy for approximately thirty-six hours seemed to be an ideal scenario for him.

"So, let's review the report from the alleged serial killer this fall. Any questions or comments?"

The angels paged through their respective reports. Happy shook his head in disappointment, and my heart sank.

"I can empathize that this individual lacked artistic sensibility, but does that justify an early demise?" he asked.

"He did kill a large number of humans," Bashful commented.

Sleepy waved his hand. "Homeless people. Their impact analysis can't have revealed anything significant."

Bashful shot him an angry look. "An insignificant impact doesn't justify their murder. This man stole their lives, and would have stolen many more."

"That doesn't matter. Humans killing humans is part of their destiny. We're only concerned with otherworldly creatures who interfere with human lives."

The air crackled with power. Bashful was no lightweight, *and* she was pissed. "We may not deliver justice in human-on-human violence, but a pattern of demonic behavior in humans doesn't contribute to their positive evolution. I feel this man's death probably benefited the human race overall, even if his premature end was at the hands of the Iblis or her agent."

My agent. That would have been Boomer, my hellhound.

Sleepy snorted in derision, shoving his paper away. "Shall we vote then? All for the Iblis?"

Happy, Bashful, and Sneezy nodded. Crap. I searched my mind trying to think of what my punishment would be for killing a human without what the angels would consider to be proper justification. They surely couldn't put me to death for such a thing? What would they do to me?

"All against?"

Dopey and Sleepy nodded.

I held my breath as everyone turned to face Gregory. His vote would mean a tie, and I doubted I could serve as my own tie-breaker. What would they do to me?

"I abstain," he announced.

The others continued to stare at him, awaiting elaboration. Gregory remained silent, finally raising his eyebrows at the group. Shifting awkwardly in their seats, the five turned back to their papers. Wow. I guess it was good to be ancient and powerful.

Dopey's lip curled in disgust. "Fine. Matter resolved." He tossed the paper aside.

"And now Jacob Bara."

Moments passed, the silence only broken by the sound of turning pages. I held my breath.

"I don't comprehend this one," Bashful said, frowning down at her paper. "He *wanted* you to kill him? As a favor because he was too afraid to do it himself?

I squirmed. "Yes. I told him I didn't want to, but he begged me. What was I to do?"

Dopey snorted. "Say 'no'?"

Happy held his report closer to his face, as if reading tiny print. "He doesn't seem to have had any terminal illness, anything that would indicate he was in interminable pain and required a mercy death."

"What reason could he possibly have to wish for his own death?" Bashful said, echoing Happy's unspoken question.

Damn this whole situation. Amber was having fun with her siblings while I faced punishment, or worse, for protecting her, and I'd originally gotten into this mess by protecting Dar. Why was I paying for everyone's sins?

Six pairs of eyes turned to me. Well, five pairs. Gregory was oddly distracted, frowning as he gazed into the distance.

"Um, it was over a girl," I stammered. "A girl. He'd had his eye on her for nearly twenty years, and, well . . . he had to die. And he couldn't work up the nerve to do it himself, so he asked me. As a favor."

Crap. I was in so much trouble. I'd dodged one bullet tonight, but this one seemed to be speeding to its mark, right between my eyes.

"Unrequited love." Bashful sighed.

"Humans are so dramatic when it comes to affairs of the heart," Sneezy commented.

"Still, suicide is a sin. And so is murder." Dopey glared at me.

"I'm a demon. Sin is my middle name," I blurted out before I thought of the ramifications. Silence fell and they all looked at me, horrified. Great. My big mouth had probably cost me any sympathy votes.

"For the Iblis?" Dopey asked.

Bashful nodded. Fuck. I was sooo fucked.

"Against?"

Dopey indicated his vote.

"Abstain?"

The others raised their hands. Well, everyone but Gregory who was still frowning at the wall.

Dopey hissed, and the room sizzled with tension. Bashful ignored him, while the other three looked worried.

"Are you so afraid of her that you won't vote? This is clearly an unjustified kill. The man wished to commit a sin and she assisted! How is that a matter that warrants a supportive vote, let alone three abstains?"

I noticed they refused to call Gregory to task for his lack of vote and inattention to the matter.

"He clearly lived with his sorrow for an unacceptable period of time," Bashful protested. "Was he supposed to pine away for another ten years, depressed and in emotional pain?"

"Sin," Dopey shouted. "What part of 'sin' do you not understand?"

"So, is assuming an unacceptable level of risk to the point where death is a strong statistical probability a sin?" Happy asked, a very un-angelic smile lurking at the corner of his mouth. "Mountain climbers, space travelers, women who choose to get pregnant even though it endangers their life — are these suicides?"

"Don't be ridiculous. This man would have continued on his normal lifespan had the Iblis not interfered."

Bashful shook her head. "Don't discount the emotional pain of unrequited love. Would you deny someone who was suffering terribly from a disease the mercy of death? We've permitted this. Many human laws now permit this."

"Sin!" Dopey shouted. "I don't care how despondent he was over this woman, he wasn't at the edge of death, or in agonizing pain."

"We can heal virtually every human condition that exists. Does our refusal to do so constitute murder by failure to attend? Should we angels be brought up on charges for every human death?"

Dopey balled up his agenda and threw it at Bashful as he stood. I thought, for a second, there would be a fight, but he kicked his chair over and stomped from the conference room, slamming the door. Everyone looked around in an embarrassed fashion while Happy cleared his throat and straightened the papers before him.

"Well, let's move on to the last report, shall we?"

I breathed out a sigh of relief. It seemed that any tie vote would be in my favor. That was very welcome news.

"Tyrone Cochran."

The angels flipped through the report, tracing my writing with their fingers as if they were in some sort of synchronized dance.

"What exactly does 'involved in the sale of recreational substances' mean?" Sneezy asked.

"Drugs. I'm not sure what kind. Probably not pot as he didn't seem to be bulging with huge bags of leaf when I saw him. Probably heroine or crack. Oxy is popular, but that section of town usually goes straight for the hard stuff. The controlled-substance pills are more in the suburbs with the soccer moms."

Bashful wrinkled her nose in disgust. She and Happy were my aces in the hole. If I could sway them, I'd be good. I wasn't sure about Sneezy, and Sleepy seemed uncomfortable without the support of his buddy, Dopey. Gregory was still lost in thought. What the fuck was wrong with him?

"There are large sections that appear to have gibberish as answers," Sleepy mentioned, eyes darting in search of a powerful supporter to back him up. I wasn't about to let him sway the others.

"I'm sorry my handwriting is so poor," I tried to compose a regretful facial expression. "Which section are you referring to?"

Over half of the report was crap. With mine and Gregory's activities, and Wyatt's party, I'd had scant time to prepare this thing. And it's not like I knew anything about the asshole who'd assaulted me in an alley.

"The impact analysis," Sleepy said, pointing to his paper.

"Well, the Taco Bell burrito scale of immense magnitude returned an 'r' factor of point eight six. Then when I applied the nose-picking coefficient, I discovered a multivariate numeration of nine dot oh sixteen on the Richter scale."

Sleepy's eyes bulged; his mouth gaped. "That . . . that makes no sense whatsoever."

"Makes sense to me," Bashful said cheerfully. "All in favor?"

"Wait," Happy interjected. My heart sank. "I think we need to ask for a revision of this report. Some additional information is needed. I'm just not comfortable voting on it without documentation on the methodology regarding the Taco Bell burrito scale."

"If you didn't mean to kill him, why didn't you render medical attention after you blew his leg off?" Sneezy asked. Crap, I was rapidly losing my supporters. I hadn't mentioned the mage's net, figuring that bringing elves and their nefarious activities into the picture would do my cause nothing but harm. Likewise about the angel that chased me all over downtown Frederick.

"I'm not very good at fixing injuries. I can't heal. Demons don't have that skill."

Bashful nodded, but Sneezy looked unconvinced. "There's no reason you couldn't have provided a tourniquet."

"Well, I didn't have an opportunity to do so because someone else had engaged me in combat." I didn't tell them that 'someone' was an angel.

Sleepy shifted in his chair, looking at Sneezy and Bashful for support. "I find it difficult to believe that a demon could not extricate herself from a brawl without turning to lethal methods. Even with a gang of humans attacking her."

Humans, yes. Humans, a mage, and an angel, no. I tried to look pious. "I'm forbidden from Owning or killing by my master. What's a bound demon to do when she's attacked? I merely thought to deliver a flesh wound, not kill the man. I was acting in self-defense, using what I thought was minimal force. His death was purely accidental."

"I'm voting we ask for a revision of the report with a forty-eight hour delivery date," Happy announced.

"Agreed." Sleepy and Sneezy chimed in.

Happy glanced at a disengaged Gregory and grimaced. "Forty-eight hours it is."

Well, two out of four wasn't bad. I had two reports to write, and now that I'd had time to witness the convoluted internal politics of the Ruling Council, I could better make shit up that would get them off my case.

The angels vanished, leaving me with Gregory. I watched him for a second and wondered whether I should call for a taxi. What was he doing? He'd paid no attention to the majority of the meeting. What was so important that he'd check out in that fashion?

As if sensing my thoughts, his black eyes turned to me, the grim look on his face deepening into a scowl.

"Are you going to take me home?" I was uncertain what his expression meant. He'd been downright suggestive when we'd discussed my appeal. What happened?

Getting to his feet, the angel walked around the long conference table and, without a word, gathered me to his chest. He held me there, tight against him with his chin on the top of my head for a heartbeat before transporting us to my house. Once in my living room, he released me and paced the floor.

"Do you want. . .."

"An angel is dead," he interrupted.

I stared in disbelief, at a loss for words.

"Dead."

I wasn't sure what the appropriate sentiments were to express condolences to an angel, so I just repeated what I'd heard humans say over the decades. "I'm so very sorry for your loss. Was he a close friend? You must be devastated."

"I told you not to do it anymore, not to *ever* do it again. Are you so far gone that you can no longer control yourself?"

What did I do? Was he still talking about his dead buddy, or about something else? He was pacing the floor in a controlled rage, the tension in his voice conveying a worry and grief equal to his anger.

"Is this about Gabriel storming out?" I asked tentatively. "Because I think he was more pissed off at Bashful than at me."

Gregory grabbed me by my shoulders before I even saw him move, pressing me against the door, high enough off the ground that my feet dangled in the air.

"You killed an angel. An *angel!* Of all the careless, reckless, suicidal actions. Do you know what this means? What will happen?"

What the fuck was he talking about? I'd been in a Ruling Council meeting all day. Had Dopey stroked out in the lobby of the Marriott or something?

"I haven't killed an angel. Ever. I swear on all the souls I Own that I have never killed an angel."

Gregory's eyes searched mine.

"I swear. You were with me yesterday, then I was with humans and Candy the rest of the time...." my voice trailed off as I realized I'd been alone last night. All alone in my house with no alibi.

The angel kept a tight grip on my shoulders, but eased me down to stand on the floor. "An angel was murdered last night. Drained. Empty. There is nothing left but the corporeal form he'd inhabited."

I caught my breath. An angel had been killed in the same manner as the demons. A devouring spirit, and Gregory clearly suspected me.

"I didn't do it. I didn't kill those demons, and I have never, *ever*, killed an angel."

Gregory's hands tightened on my upper arms, digging painfully into the flesh. "You said yesterday you were chased by an angel, and today one is found dead. If he attacked you again and you defended yourself the only way you could, tell me. I'll try to help you if you tell me the truth."

I recognized the seriousness of the situation. "I am telling the truth. Maybe someone is trying to set me up. Twenty demons heard me announce I was a devouring spirit and I'm sure that juicy gossip spread all over Hel."

He frowned, considering my words. "Too convoluted. If someone wanted you dead, it would be easier just to kill you."

"But what if another angel wanted me dead? I'd like to think you'd have a bit of a problem with that, but if I were convicted of murdering an angel, there would be nothing you could do to protect me."

Gregory shook his head. "Angels don't have the ability to devour. If you didn't do it, there has to be another devouring spirit on the loose."

"It wasn't me. Please believe me. It wasn't me."

We remained motionless for what seemed an eternity, his fingers tight on my arms, his eyes boring into mine. Suddenly he yanked me to his chest, crushing me tight.

"We'll find this other demon. But you can tell no one. You must never again devour, and do not tell anyone that you ever have."

There was a noise behind us. We broke apart and whirled around to see Nyalla halfway down the stairs, her hair wet from the shower, her body hidden under my too-large clothing. She had that terrified look on her face again — the one Wyatt and I had worked for the last two days to try to erase.

"I didn't mean to listen. I don't understand much of your language. I won't repeat anything, I swear by the Goddess."

Nyalla's voice was barely a whisper, her eyes huge as they darted back and forth between me and the angel.

"Who are you?" Gregory thundered.

Elvish. She'd spoken in Elvish. I doubted Gregory had heard that language in over two million years. Regardless, I wasn't going to let him frighten Wyatt's sister to death, especially with all the progress we'd made.

"Stop it!" I smacked him as hard as I could across the arm, making sure I spoke in Elvish. I'm sure he barely felt it, but I didn't want to further scare Nyalla by throwing demon energy around my living room. "You're going to give the girl a heart attack. Calm the fuck down and be nice for once in your life."

Nyalla's mouth dropped open at my words, shock erasing some of her fear. "It's all right. He's an angel. He won't hurt you."

"Who are you?" Gregory asked again, in a well-modulated tone. "And how do you know Elvish? Your accent is perfect."

Nyalla stayed rooted on the stairs, her eyes anxious as she stared at the angel. "I've lived with the elves my whole life. They took me from my crib when I was a baby, kidnapped me."

The angel frowned, causing Nyalla to cringe. "Elves don't cross through the gates and they don't kidnap humans."

I blew out an exasperated breath. "How the fuck do you think they get humans to train in magic? You know about the sorcerers, know where they get their magical knowledge. Do you think the elves send audio courses over or something? They fucking kidnap humans."

Gregory turned his scowl toward me. "The humans have had the ability to open communication portals for millennia. Many humans skilled in magic gain their knowledge from the elves that way, and also by summoning demons."

I threw up my hands. "You think she's lying? She's spent her life with the elves. She can tell you what a bunch of douchebags they are."

"Perhaps demons have been kidnapping humans and taking them through the gates — either angel gates or the ones they create themselves, but elves are not doing this."

He was an idiot. "Elves *are* doing this! If a demon had kidnapped her, she wouldn't have lived long enough to make it through a gate. She's been raised with elves, lived her life with elves — not demons!"

The angel turned his back to me. "Well then, I guess we owe the elves a debt of gratitude for rescuing this child from the clutches of the demons."

Elves didn't rescue Nyalla, I did. Me. An imp, a demon. Me.

Gregory walked over to Nyalla as she stood rooted to the stairs. Her face paled at his approach. "I promise. I promise I won't say anything. You can remove my tongue if you want, wipe the last few hours of my mind, anything. Just please don't kill me. Please, please don't kill me."

Gregory stopped, his eyes widening. "Child, I have no intention of killing you. I'm an angel."

I snorted. Ah yes, the good guys. Riding in on a white horse to save the day.

Nyalla winced as his hand came toward her. "Don't you dare hurt her," I ordered.

Instead, the angel caressed her cheek and spoke a soft word. A glow lit the right side of her face before fading away. Again he spoke to her in whispered words too quiet for me to hear. She nodded then flashed me a quick smile before dashing back up the stairs.

"What did you do?" I demanded as Gregory turned around. "I swear on every being I Own that if you hurt her in any way, wiped her mind or rendered her mute, or anything, I'll fucking kill you."

The angel's lips twitched up in a wry smile as he took my arm and led me into the kitchen. "I did no harm to your new human, little Cockroach."

I watched him with suspicion as he positioned me by the stove and set about putting on a pot of coffee. He'd gotten quite good at this.

"Now," he said, once the smell of warm coffee filled the air, "we need to find this devouring spirit as quickly as possible. Your life depends on it."

I nodded. "Can you bring me the body of the angel? Maybe I can find something, some kind of clue if I scan it."

He shook his head, pulling a mug out of the cabinet and setting it before me. It said "World's Best Dad" on the side in faded red letters. Angelo had given it to me filled with jellybeans as an Easter gift, and I treasured it.

"It will raise suspicion. I'll try to bring you any other demon corpses that we find, but there's no way you'll be able to see the angel's body without putting your own life in jeopardy."

"Where was the angel's body found?" I wondered if it *was* the angel who'd been chasing me. I didn't think there were many of them flitting around the Frederick County area.

"Northern Mexico. Parral."

That wasn't exactly a stone's throw away. "Was he one of yours? An enforcer? A Grigori?"

"No." The angel slid the coffee pot from the burner and filled my cup. "He had no business being down here that I'm aware of. We're questioning his choir to find out what the purpose of his trip was, who he intended to meet, and why he didn't follow proper protocol in leaving Aaru."

I wasn't sure his reasons for walking the earth had any relationship with his death. Mexico. Demons aren't much for cleaning up their messes, so if his body was found in Mexico, that's where he was killed.

"Were the drained demons found in Mexico also?" I asked, sipping my coffee. It was always better when he made it.

"No. One in Damascus, one in Burlington, and one in New York City."

"Damascus? All the way in Syria?" Damn, that was a big geographic area. Demon's tended to stay on the continent where they came into from Hel. We didn't remain long enough for extended travel. If this devouring demon was jet-setting across the world, we'd have an even more difficult time tracking him down.

"Damascus, Maryland. Not Syria."

Ah, that made more sense. I could envision the line in my head. Vermont, New York, Maryland. Wait. Fuck. Damascus, Maryland? That was practically in my back yard.

"Was the first one Burlington?" The angel nodded. "Then he'd be close. The next should be down as far south as Danville or Raleigh." I calculated the distances, just to be sure.

Gregory lifted the coffee pot in an offer to top-up my cup. "So, we should begin looking for a swath of destruction, some evidence of erratic demon activity in a two-hundred-and-fifty to three-hundred mile radius south of here?"

"Yes." I held my cup out for a refill. "I'll ask Wyatt if he'll help. He may not, though."

Wyatt was refusing my requests lately unless I could show some positive charitable intent. I doubted dead demons and a dead angel would tug on his heartstrings enough to convince him to help. He might be swayed if I told him I would be blamed for the murders. Or not. And he was pretty busy with Amber and Nyalla right now.

"How much time elapsed between the demon deaths?" I wondered if he'd been making these kills all in one trip, or darting back and forth across a gate. Multiple trips would be risky, especially if he was using the same portal, but then again, so was any extended time here. I should know.

"I brought you the first in January. The second was found in May, and the latest, three days ago."

Could be multiple trips, but that close together led me to believe he'd been here the whole time.

"Why didn't you bring me the one you found in May? I only saw two."

His face settled into that bland, inscrutable expression. "I don't trust the one who found that body. I didn't want him to know that I was taking them to you, or that I suspected there was foul play."

He'd been covering it up for some reason. At that time he hadn't known the killer was a devouring spirit, hadn't known I was a devouring spirit. He couldn't have been protecting me — there was some other reason he'd not wanted anyone to know his suspicions, or that he was using my special expertise.

"One of your Grigori found it?" I asked. "You don't trust one of your own people? Aren't all the Grigori in your household?"

"Choir," he corrected. "No. Grigori are made up of selected angels across all choirs. They serve for a limited time then another takes their place. I'm the only constant."

"You don't trust one of your own Grigori?" I repeated.

His expression darkened. "No."

I sucked down the rest of my coffee with a long gulp. "What's going on? What aren't you telling me?"

His eyes, full of worry, met mine, and warmth spread through my chest. "That's a matter internal to Aaru. A matter very personal to me. It's best that you not know anything about it, that you not be involved in any way — for your own safety, little Cockroach."

He was worried about me, worried about my safety. He was protecting me.

"I protect you far more than you know, little Cockroach." His words were a caress. Our eyes met for a long moment until I broke our gaze to take a drink of my coffee. The cup was empty.

"Good?" he asked, indicating the mug.

"Always." I smiled, feeling rather unsettled at the intimacy of the moment and wanting to return to a lighter, more casual exchange. "If this Grigori thing doesn't work out, you could have a great career as a barista. I'll pick up some applications at Starbucks next time I'm there."

He smiled. "I'm glad you have such a high estimation of my abilities as head Grigori. It's nice to be appreciated."

He vanished, and I sat my empty mug in the sink. What was going on? Gregory not trusting some of his own staff? My imagination ran wild, and, for a brief moment, I felt a pang of worry. Then I laughed and shook my head. That angel was billions of years old. Nothing would ever happen to him. Nothing. And it sent something surging deep inside my core to think he worried about me, protected me. Dead demons, a dead angel, and me as the most likely suspect, yet he still protected me. Dead angel. A dead angel in Mexico.

I frowned. The dead angel was an outlier, far outside the line of the other killings. How had a devouring spirit made it to Mexico from Maryland in such a short time, and why had he changed directions? What happened that he encountered and killed an angel? A non-Grigori angel? Should I also be looking in a radius around Parral Mexico? The events couldn't possibly be unrelated. Two devouring spirits was improbable, three was approaching an impossible coincidence. Impossible.

~8~

Nyalla was oddly silent during dinner that night. I realized her English was still limited, and I'd been trying to translate for her as we showed her the culinary joys of Maryland seafood.

"Nyalla has been teaching me Elvish," Amber announced with a fond look at her sister. "She's drawn maps with the different kingdoms on them, and I'm learning all sorts of cultural stuff."

Side by side, there was scant resemblance between the two. Nyalla's hair was darker, more of an ash color, although her recent exposure to the sun was bringing out streaks of near white to frame a still-pale face. She looked like a slight, female version of Wyatt — attractive in a very human way. Amber, by contrast, eclipsed everyone in the room. It wasn't just her exotic elven looks. Amber had a presence about her, an odd combination of elf aloofness and succubi sex appeal.

"She's supposed to be learning from you," I scolded the hybrid. "You'll have millennia to learn about your mother's culture. Just concentrate right now on getting Nyalla up to speed so she's able to begin some sort of normal human life."

Amber looked up from her oysters in surprise. "Millennia? I thought…. I just assumed I'd have a normal human life expectancy." The girl frowned, a crease marring her perfect forehead. "I don't want to outlive my friends, my family. I don't want to watch them grow old while I remain young."

Yeah, I worried about that every day too. "Millennia. Concentrate on helping your sister, and you can bemoan your terrible fate later."

Amber nodded as she casually scooped a dollop of horseradish on her oyster and squeezed fresh lemon over it. I watched her for a moment, thinking that her acceptance of her extended lifespan, and the fact that she'd outlive all her family, was far too easy. Amber was good at hiding her emotions. She seemed fine, but I suspected this news had rocked her to the core. Vowing to spend some one-on-one time with the half-elf, I turned to Nyalla. The girl was wrestling with a crab claw, trying unsuccessfully to extract the meat from the shell.

"How are language lessons going?" I spoke in Elvish.

She smiled shyly. "Very well, thank you. And my most honored brother, Wyatt, has procured an identification card for me. He is going to teach me to navigate a human conveyance after sunrise tomorrow. I have already learned how to use the comp-pute-er, and how to spin a web on it. I can operate the cooking and personal hygiene systems, and now have a variety of suitable clothing. I am told I will be going to a spa bath with my elven sister after noon respite tomorrow."

Okay. Computer, Internet, household appliances and clothing — check. Driving lessons and make-over/bonding time tomorrow. Progress.

"My name is Nina Lewis," she announced in English with only the barest hint of accent.

"Very nice," I told her. "Should I call you 'Nina' now?"

She shook her head and flashed a mischievous smile. "Friends and family call me Nyalla." Once again, her accent was close to perfect. Her memory when it came to words and language structure was amazing, and she had a great ear for pronunciation.

"How did you learn my language?" She'd mentioned she knew a few words, and I was curious. It's not like she could have spent a lot of time among demons.

The girl shrugged. "Demons make terrible messes at parties, usually involving bodily fluids that elves and other humans do not want to clean up. I would stand in the corner, ready to take care of any unpleasantness. I heard them talk among themselves, and, over the years, picked up some words and sentences."

Wow. It was amazing that she could learn the basics of a language just by listening in at the occasional party. It was just as amazing that she would have bothered. Not many did.

My surprise must have shown on my face, because Nyalla gave me a quick grin. "I like to know what people are saying. Watching and listening to them helps me anticipate their wishes, and avoid punishment."

That familiar anger toward the elves stirred in me. Assholes. How many humans there felt the same? Slaves. I clenched my jaw and struggled to put the anger back. It's not like I could do anything about the situation, and I didn't want the girl beside me to think my fury had anything to do with her.

Nyalla turned her attention back to the crab claw, twisting off the lower portion and peering with despair at the meat, still trapped within the exoskeleton.

"Here, let me help," Wyatt reached across the table and took the claw from her, twisting it sharply in his hands. With a resounding crack, the shell split, freeing the pink flesh. He handed it back to her with a smile. "Dip it in the butter first."

I pointed to the butter and watched Nyalla as she tasted it.

"Oh, this is wonderful! So much better in taste than appearance."

Yes, so many things were.

"So are the oysters," I told her. "Better snag a few before Amber eats them all."

"She plans to go through the gate. I thought you should know."

Nyalla's tone was casual, as if we were discussing the weather, or the merits of the seafood before us. I stared at her. What gate? She couldn't possibly mean. . ..

"She has been having me draw maps, especially of Wythyn and Cyelle and has been asking me about how demons and elves transverse the angel gates. I suspect she intends to have revenge for her mother's death."

Nyalla continued to separate the crabmeat while I gaped at her like an imbecile.

"I do not want her to hate me for revealing her plans, but I also do not want her to get herself killed on some fool's quest." Her eyes turned to me, pleading. "I like her. You were right. In spite of everything, she is a kind and giving person, although she is very impulsive and reckless. She will not live for those millennia if she continues with her planned course of action."

I wiped my hands on a napkin and got to my feet. "Come on, Amber. Let's run over to Wyatt's and get his Xbox. We'll show Nyalla how to decimate an undead army."

Everyone looked at me like I was insane.

"You hate to play video games," Wyatt said. "And we can just go to my place and play if you want to."

I glared at him. "Nope. All the beer is here, and I've got four televisions. Come on, Amber."

She shrugged and flashed Wyatt a quick smile as she pushed back her chair. "Sounds fun. We'll be right back. Help Nyalla with the oysters, but save a few more for me."

We were barely five feet out my door before I turned on her. "You are not to cross those gates into Hel. Do you hear me? I'll chain you in my basement if you so much as step a toe in Columbia Mall."

"I love Columbia Mall. They've got a Sephora, and a Forever 21. Girl's gotta have her shopping."

She was definitely part demon. I jumped in front of her, halting our progress and forcing her to meet my eyes.

"I mean it. You'll die. I don't care how much Elvish you know, how many maps you've memorized, you'll die."

Her face set in that familiar mulish expression. Maybe it wasn't genetic after all.

"They put a price on my head. They killed my mother. What do you expect me to do?"

"I expect you not to throw your life away like an idiot. You're not even twenty. That's an infant in both demon and elf lifespans. Save revenge for a few centuries."

"I'm not going to be any more powerful no matter how long I wait," she snarled, frustration in every word. "I can occasionally do lightning, that's it. I haven't been able to do anything else you've tried to teach me. Nothing. I can't fix a paper cut, can't change anything about my appearance. I suck as a demon; I suck as an elf, and I'm not human. I live in constant dread that I'll run into the wrong person and I'll be dead before I can even try to defend myself. At least this way my death will have meaning."

I pulled out all the stops. "Your mother gave her life to protect you. Would you denigrate her sacrifice by throwing your life away? She wanted you to live, and you'd go and commit suicide? She risked everything for you — her reputation as well as her life. Ungrateful child."

Amber's eyes grew huge and filled with tears. Shuddering, she covered her face with delicate hands. "I don't belong anywhere! I feel like I'm a fraud with Wyatt and Nyalla. I'm not their sister, not really. I don't even have the power of a Low demon. The elves would kill me on sight. And now I find I'll outlive every single person I care about? Watch them grow old and die right before my eyes? What kind of life is this?"

I wrapped my arms around her and felt her shake with sobs; her tears wet my shoulder. "I know you're afraid of outliving your family, of being alone. I feel the same way. Don't you think that constantly goes through my mind too? That I'll have to watch Wyatt grow old and die while I live for thousands of years more? I know you're feeling alone, but I'm here. I won't leave you, and if the fates allow, I'll l be around far beyond even your long life expectancy."

Her sobs increased, and I rocked her slightly, holding her tight. "You're part of my family now. Don't throw your life away like this. The best revenge is to live well, and rub their noses in it when you're old and powerful."

She pulled away, rubbing red, swollen eyes, so vulnerable and unattractive in her usually perfect face. "I'll never be powerful. I'll just be a freak. A beautiful freak, constantly afraid that I'm going to be killed."

"You're just a baby," I assured her. "I couldn't do much more than lightning at your age either. Leethu formed you with great care. She speaks of you as her proudest creation. She'd never leave you defenseless."

Amber hiccupped and wiped her nose on a sleeve. "Will I ever meet her?"

"Someday." I smoothed her hair, gold and fine as a newborn's. "And someday you'll show the elves what a bunch of idiots they've been. Just be patient. Be patient and trust me to help you."

She smiled up at me, her eyes already beginning to lose their red puffiness. I hugged her once more and thought how twisted it was that I was advocating patience — the virtue I'd disdained when my angel had said those very words to me.

"Come on, you beautiful freak, you. Let's grab Wyatt's X-box and take out our frustrations on hoards of undead. Loser runs out for donuts in the morning?"

"That would be you, Sam." She laughed. "I've never known anyone so bad at video games."

We walked arm-in-arm to Wyatt's house and lugged the equipment back to mine. As Amber predicted, I lost terribly. Nyalla showed a surprising aptitude, coming in a close second to Wyatt. Video games led to movies, and by early morning, Amber was sprawled asleep on the floor, her hand half in a bowl of popcorn. Nyalla was huddled in a tiny ball at the end of a sofa, practically buried under a blanket.

"Wanna sneak upstairs?" Wyatt asked as I turned off the TV.

We were cuddled up on our own sofa, my head on his shoulder, my hand on his inner thigh, just mere inches from where I wished it was. I glanced over at the sleeping girls, longing to sneak upstairs to bed with my man.

"Can I talk to you in the kitchen first?" I whispered.

Wyatt followed me in, his eyebrows raised. "What's up?"

I took a deep breath. There was no easy way to say this. "I had a talk with Amber on the way to your house. She's got some crazy thought of running over to Hel and avenging her mother's death and her unfortunate circumstances."

Wyatt looked stunned. "But she seems fine. On spring break, when you were teaching her demon things, she was downright happy. Her grades are good, she's applying for an internship. She goes clubbing with friends, and on dates. How long has this been going on?"

"I don't know." I rubbed his arm soothingly. "I think her plan gained some immediacy after Nyalla arrived. Don't beat yourself up over it. I didn't realize what was going on either. Amber is very good at hiding what she's feeling and putting on a cheerful face. I think it's an elf thing."

"What can we do? I can't watch her all the time. She's a grown woman."

I thought for a moment. "I'll let the gate guardian at Columbia Mall know to watch out for her, and I'll have Dar keep his ears open, in case she slips through. Other than that, just let her know how much she's needed here, how family is more than blood."

Wyatt pulled away and put his hands on either side of the sink, his head lowered.

"I didn't want to worry you with this, but I know you'd never forgive me if something happened and I'd kept it from you."

He looked up at me and nodded. "Thank you." He sounded miserable.

I went to him again, wrapping my arms around him. We stood there for a few moments before he turned and reciprocated the hug.

"How did you find out?"

"Nyalla. She may have been hopeless at magic, but she's got great intuition."

"And she's good at killing zombies too," Wyatt commented in a lighter tone. "Maybe she has a future in special ops."

I chuckled and looked out of the kitchen, at the girl curled up under a blanket. "Or in intel."

"She sleeps better at your house." Wyatt rubbed his face against my hair. "That's no surprise; I sleep better at your house."

"Shall we go get some sleep then?" I ran a hand down his back and tucked it in the waistband of his pants.

"How about we not sleep?"

"Now, that's a plan." I tugged him toward the stairway.

~9~

"I'm not done yet. I've got twenty-four more hours," I said, my voice rising in panic. Gregory had appeared quite unexpectedly in my living room, his face serious as a heart attack. All I could think of was those four-nine-five reports hanging over my head like a sword of Damocles. I hadn't even started the damned things. Wyatt and I had enjoyed a sleepless night then I'd run out to get donuts while Nyalla proudly made coffee. I was planning a nice long nap, but from the look on the angel's face, I wasn't going to get it.

"I'm not here about the reports. There's another dead demon I need you to examine."

I was beginning to feel like a coroner.

"Okay. So where's the head?" He was usually dangling one by the hair when he arrived.

"You said you wanted to see the intact body. I'm not able to transport it here, so we need to go to it."

I glanced between the angel and the enormous stack of paperwork on the kitchen bar. "It better be a short trip."

Yes, I realized it would be in my best interests to find this devouring spirit before I became even further implicated, and especially before he killed another angel. Still, those damned reports had a deadline, and a terrible penalty for tardiness.

"I'll persuade the Ruling Council to give you an extension," he promised.

I shrugged, pushing aside the reports and walking over to the angel. He looked stern, worried. My skin prickled. When a six-billion-year-old angel is troubled, it's time to take notice.

"So where is it?" It had to be somewhere close — Virginia or North Carolina maybe. Or Mexico.

I stood in front of him, expecting the usual. He'd pull me to him, wrap his arms around me tightly and teleport us in a disorientating jolt. Instead, he stared down at me, his frown deepening.

"Seattle."

Seattle. I'd used that angel gate a lot when coming from Hel. It was the gate I went through forty years ago when I began my very long stay with the humans. A wave of nostalgia hit me. Seattle was a favorite place.

"Okay. Let's go."

I couldn't understand his hesitation. He continued to frown down at me, absently rubbing his chin with his hand.

"I can't. Can your horse teleport you?"

What the fuck was the problem? He was able to create inter-dimensional passageways; he could certainly pop us both at the other end of the continent.

"I've only had Diablo teleport small distances — usually line of sight. He's pretty unreliable, even then. There's no saying he wouldn't take off without me."

"Can you create your own gate there? Like the one you made into Aaru?"

Stupid angels. "I *told* you I didn't make that gate, or the one in Waynesboro. They're wild gates. Naturally occurring."

His expression clearly conveyed disbelief. "Fine. Then go back to Hel through the gate in Columbia and come back in through Seattle."

"This is such bullshit. Just gate me there, already. I'm not haring halfway across Hel, through four hostile elven kingdoms, because you've got the lazy bone going on."

Gregory shook his head, chestnut curls dropping across his forehead. "I can't. For that distance I'd need to jump you through Aaru, and you're not allowed."

Even with the Sword of the Iblis, most of the angels didn't recognize me as holding the title. And even the ones that did, didn't want me in their precious homeland. That's why we had to hold the Ruling Council meetings in a fricken Marriot. I did sneak into the forth circle every now and then through the wild gate and leave Gregory odd presents, but I think he exerted some influence to have those infractions overlooked.

Still, I didn't believe him. There was no reason to have to go through Aaru to get to the west coast. Why was he lying?

"Well then, I guess we better start walking. Or we could always manifest wings and fly."

It would be a ridiculously long flight, but I'd do it just to catch a glimpse of his wings. I wondered what they looked like, if the scars from his battle with the previous Iblis were noticeable.

His eyebrows shot up. I swear a light bulb appeared above his head.

"We'll fly. On a human airplane."

I stared, dumbstruck. Angels on a plane? It was like the beginning of a really bad movie. I'd flown commercial loads of times, but I was willing to bet Gregory would be the first angel to ever do so.

"Right. Just gate us. Explain the detour through Aaru to the other five dwarves later."

"There is no need to involve dwarves in this matter," he said, clearly not understanding my reference. "Book our flight, and we'll leave straight away."

This was getting ridiculous.

"Book your own flight. I'm not paying for two cross-country tickets because you don't feel like transporting me. Besides, you need to learn to do these things for yourself."

I felt the wave of power scorch me as his face darkened with anger. Black irises bled out to encompass the whites. I was pretty sure under those grim lips hid sharp piranha teeth.

Gregory could never hold his form when angry, and I'd evidently pissed him off by refusing to do his bidding.

"Do you know who I am? I am not about to do these menial human things myself. You will do this."

The compulsion thudded into me, only to slide right off. You would have thought he would have learned by now that sort of thing didn't work on me, bound to him or not.

"Is that the sin of pride I hear?" I mocked. "Better take that massive ego down a notch because I'm not doing it. I'm not one of your peons to order around."

He started to glow. Yeah, it probably wasn't the smartest thing to egg him on like this, but I got a rush out of driving him to lose control. Gregory in a rage was even sexier than when he was seductive.

"We have a short window here," he hissed. "I don't have time for your contrary behavior. Do it."

"Fuck off. If it's that urgent, then just gate me there. Or get your pansy ass gate guardian to do it."

He hesitated, considering my words. "Would she know how?"

I snorted. "Probably. She works all day in a mall. She's probably got every tech gadget sold there at this point."

"Good." He waved his hand at me. "Contact her, and have her make the arrangements."

I raised my eyes to the ceiling and shook my head. This angel had taken the art of delegation to an extreme. Still, I wasn't going to do it.

"No way. She works for you; call her yourself." I dug in my pocket and hit a speed-dial number. "You can use my phone, since I'm sure you don't have one."

He took it from me in astonishment. "She has a phone? You call each other?"

I motioned for him to put it to his ear. "Of course. We do lunch pretty regularly. Sometimes we buy shoes."

I heard the guardian's voice from the phone. Gregory put it up to his ear, looking as if he were afraid the phone might remove a section of his head.

"Get me two plane tickets to Seattle on the next flight," he ordered.

There was silence then I heard a shriek of laughter from the receiver. The angel got that furious look again. I slapped a hand over my mouth to cover my grin.

"Sam, knock it off. I'm wise to your pranks. You seriously owe me lunch for this one," I heard the guardian say.

"It's me, you worthless dreg of ether. Get me the tickets. Now!"

Well. That wasn't very angelic of him. The guardian laughed again, and Gregory exploded in anger. I mean *exploded*. There was a flash of light and heat that obliterated his physical form and stabbed my eyes with pain. I heard a sizzle, and the smell of burnt electronics filled my nose. Before I could react, Gregory had spun me around and grabbed me in a tight embrace as everything tilted away.

A second later, the world erupted into chaos. I heard screams and crashes. A voice in front of me wailed a frenzy of panicked apologies. I fixed my destroyed eyes and blinked, looking around to see where Gregory had taken me.

We were in a store, facing the huge glass panes and wide entrances to the mall area. Racks of brightly colored children's clothing lay before me, scattered to the side in a pile. A figure I recognized as the gate guardian groveled on the ground, screaming out for mercy and covering her head. The angel's arms were still around me, tightly holding me against his chest.

"What the fuck?" I struggled to break free from his arms, hearing the din of screaming voices behind us. They were so loud they drowned out the shrieks of the gate guardian. Normally, humans had a sort of bemused worshipful air about them when they saw Gregory. What the heck was going on?

He released me. I stumbled forward a few steps before turning around. Then I gawked, my mouth open. Before me stood an angel. A furious angel with an indistinct humanoid form that glowed with the light of a million watts. My eyes watered and I had to squint to properly focus. I heard humans screaming and crying from behind him, but I couldn't see anyone. His wings completely blocked my view.

Wings. Gorgeous, huge wings that reached from one wall of the store to the other. They were a sort of cream color, with a pattern of dove-grey across them and along the bottom edges of the feathers. And there were six of them. Three pairs. The main ones filled the store, but the other two sets appeared to be for embellishment rather than function. Two came from beneath the main wings in an elegant "S" shape that trailed along his legs to touch the floor. The other two were above the main wings, curling in an arch several feet above his head. They were beautiful, but so ridiculously frou-frou that I couldn't help but laugh.

Gregory was busy castigating the sniveling gate guardian as I took in his appearance. At my laughter, his wings beat in irritation, causing items of children's clothing to fly about the room. He turned his glare on me, and his glow intensified.

"Turn down the light," I complained. "You already burned up my retinas once. I don't want to have to keep fixing my eyes because you can't keep your temper in check."

"What is so funny?" he hissed.

"You and your pretty-boy wings." I laughed again. "Why the fuck do you have six wings? A little ostentatious, isn't it?"

"They reflect my level, my status," he snarled. "They are *not* ostentatious."

The gate guardian took this moment to crawl closer and rub her face against what should have been his feet. Sheesh. And I thought Eloa was a sycophant.

"Well, put your non-ostentatious wings away. You're trashing the place and scaring the humans behind you to death."

He turned to look at the panicked crowd trapped behind him. Unfortunately, his massive wings didn't allow for much maneuverability in the store. One sent another rack of clothing flying, the other knocked the cash register and display items off the check-out counter. Blue poured from him, and the humans at the rear of the store went silent. Even the gate guardian was affected. She stopped shouting apologies and wrapped herself around his ankles. I wasn't completely unaffected, either. The blue always calmed us demons, but when it came from him, it did more. I wanted to rub myself against him, fill myself with him in every way, rest forever in his embrace. It was hard enough to resist him without the blue stuff.

"I didn't know it was you. I thought it was the imp playing a prank. I'll do as you say; please don't banish me," the guardian begged, her face tight against the blurred glow of his legs.

He turned back to her, sending additional merchandise across the room.

"Two tickets to Seattle on the next available flight," he commanded.

"And an iPhone," I added.

The angel frowned at me.

"What? You melted mine; you owe me a replacement."

"And an iPhone," he confirmed to the guardian.

Her head bobbed. Gregory shifted slightly, nudging her away with one leg. He was starting to glow less, his voice returning to a more normal tone. The wings were still out, though. Those silly, beautiful wings. I walked closer to one, wondering if I could see the scars from his terrible battle two and a half million years ago. When our spirit selves were damaged, they never healed properly. Sometimes they didn't heal at all.

He twitched his wing away from my outstretched hand. "What are you doing? Don't touch them."

"You've got little girl's dresses and jumpers hooked on your wing. I'm just trying to get them off."

He pulled the wing around, nearly knocking me to the ground with the tip, and tried to reach the lilac ruffled pinafore dangling from it.

"Hold still," I ordered. "Let me do it."

He paused, in internal debate, then consented. "Don't bite me," he warned.

Now *that* was a tempting idea. I walked over and carefully removed a carnation-pink dress, allowing my fingers to caress the feathers. They were so unbelievably soft, the grey a slightly different texture than the cream color. I let my personal energy, my spirit self, extend out to feel him on a different level and closed my eyes to savor the experience. Never in all my life had I thought I would be touching an angel's wings. They felt smooth, powerful. The ridges of scarring like a pattern of lace throughout their form. Oddly, the scars were just as beautiful as the wings. They revealed history, told a story. I opened my eyes and trailed my fingers along the feathers as I reached for the lilac pinafore. Everything in the background faded away. The store, the humans in their stupor, the cowering gate guardian — it all vanished from my awareness. All I knew was the feel of his wings. I wanted to rub my face against them, breathe in their sweet scent, wrap them around me. . ..

"Hey!"

I landed flat on my back, knocked to the ground by that powerful wing. The lilac pinafore flew out of my hands and onto the floor.

"You licked me!"

Well, yeah. How could I help but lick him? I licked an angel's wing. I licked *my* angel's wing. And, oh, it tasted so wonderful.

"Settle down. It's not like I bit you. You didn't say anything about licking."

I got up and dusted myself off. Gregory's eyes were intense as they watched me. I felt the pull of attraction, the increased heat of the power he leaked. My eyes rose to meet his, and I longed for him to grab me, for us to merge together as we'd done months ago in my house. The atmosphere thickened around us, the air pulsing with desire. I didn't dare move, waiting for him to initiate contact in this oh-so-public place.

Dragging his gaze from mine, he rubbed a hand through his hair and shook his head to clear it. The wings vanished, and I finally saw behind him where a dozen women and two children sat, their eyes glazed and fixed in adoration upon the angel.

"Plane tickets and a new phone. Now," he ordered.

The gate guardian had been staring at me in shock, but Gregory's words jolted her into action. She bowed, practically scraping the floor with her head, and dashed out the front of the store.

"So do we wait here? Will she just courier the stuff to my house?" I asked. I also wondered what he was going to do about the trashed store and the enthralled humans. No one else had entered the store, or even walked past it, since we'd arrived. No doubt, he was keeping them away somehow.

"We'll wait at your house," he decided, reaching out and yanking me into his embrace. Lately he'd been waiting for me to walk into his arms for transport, but I kind of liked it when he took charge. It was fun.

We popped back into my living room. The angel held onto me until my vertigo settled, his chin resting on top of my head. I stayed a bit longer than necessary, enjoying the feel of him wrapped around me. Tentatively, I reached out with my spirit self to stroke against him.

"Not now, little Cockroach," he said, his voice full of regret. "I have too much to think about."

I pulled away, slightly embarrassed at the rejection.

"Should I call you when the tickets arrive? Let you know when we're leaving?"

He shook his head. "No. I'll stay here and wait. Hopefully we can fly out before nightfall."

~10~

The girls were off relaxing at a spa for the day, so I settled Gregory on my couch with paperbacks of *War and Peace* and *Atlas Shrugged*, thinking that might occupy him for all of five minutes. Then I jogged down to Wyatt's house, making sure I called his name loudly as I came in, so I wouldn't get shot.

"I thought you were going to take a nap," he commented, pausing his game and patting the cushion beside him. I moved the various cables, controller, and half eaten chip bags from the sofa and plopped down next to him.

"I was, but Gregory came by with an emergency, and now I'm waiting for our plane reservations to Seattle."

Wyatt stared, his face blank.

"I forgot to tell you yesterday, but someone has been killing demons, basically devouring them and draining all their energy — both their raw energy and their spirit selves. Now that an angel is dead in the same way . . . well, I'll be in some serious shit if we can't find out who is doing this and the fact that I'm a devouring spirit comes to light."

Still blank.

"There's a dead demon in Seattle, but Gregory has some trumped-up excuse why he can't just gate me there, so we're going to fly commercial. Can you imagine him on a plane? It's going to be hysterical."

"Are you in any danger?" Wyatt finally asked. "You seem rather cheerful about the whole thing."

"Right now I'm not a suspect, and I get the feeling Gregory is trying to protect me and keep this all under wraps until we find the killer."

"So it's a mystery?"

"Yeah, although we need to solve it pretty quickly, before it somehow manages to get pinned on me."

A long-suffering expression came over Wyatt's face. "And you need my help?"

I felt a moment of guilt, and of sadness. There was a time when Wyatt couldn't wait to help me out. Where was my partner in crime?

"I thought I might. The first three demons seemed to be in a pattern, and I thought it might be like what Althean was doing when you tracked him down for Candy and me. But the dead angel is out in northern Mexico, and this last demon is in Seattle. It breaks the pattern."

Wyatt frowned, and I could see him becoming intrigued by the whole thing. "Maybe one or more of the murders is a red herring, and there still is a pattern."

I shook my head. "If they were just stabbed, or blown up, I'd consider that, but these guys are all *drained*. There aren't many devouring spirits — I'm the only one I know of. And angels don't do this sort of thing."

I could see Wyatt thinking. I could practically see the scenarios run through his mind. "Then a devouring spirit. At first, he killed casually, along a normal journey for him, but something happened that made him take off to Mexico in a panic. There, he scraps it up with an angel and manages to kill him before fleeing north and killing another in Seattle."

"Possible. Demons don't usually go racing around like that unless they're panicked. The last one in the pattern was in Damascus, Maryland. Couple of days later there's a dead angel in Mexico."

"Was the angel on his trail?" Wyatt asked. "One of Gregory's guys?"

"Nope. He's not even supposed to be down here." I pivoted around on the sofa to better face Wyatt. "I'm pretty sure that angel who attacked me a few days back wasn't one of Gregory's. He had no idea who I was. Do you think there's a bunch of angels down here without permission? Maybe this other one tried to grab a demon too, and found himself with a devourer on his hands?"

"Could be. What are you supposed to do in Seattle? Can you determine something from the dead demon's body that will help lead you to the killer?"

"It's probably nothing," I confessed, reaching to grab one of the chip bags I'd moved and dig through the crumbs. "One of the dead demons had a faint trace of energy along his neck. It was like what Gregory uses when he blocks off my energy. That angel who chased me downtown did the same thing."

"That would implicate an angel," Wyatt said, pulling the bag from my hands and passing me a fresh one from his side. "Angel's don't devour, and demons don't have that blocking magic, so maybe it's a pair working together."

I nearly choked on a chip, laughing. "That is *not* happening! My weird relationship with Gregory aside, angels and demons never work together. Besides, their power to restrain us outside of Aaru goes away when they're not touching us. It wouldn't leave a signature like that. So it might not be angels. It might be a sorcerer. Elven magic mimics angels'; they could have come up with something similar that had a longer effect."

"So a sorcerer and a demon working together to devour a bunch of demons and an angel. I get how a devouring spirit might be motivated to do that, but what does the sorcerer get out of the deal?"

I licked the salt off of my fingers and shook my head. "I have no fucking idea. And all this is crazy conjecture at this point. We'll see what I can find after I look at this dead guy in Seattle, but honestly, I'm thinking this mystery is more in line with Gregory's skills than mine."

Wyatt gathered me close and kissed my forehead. "Either way, stay safe. Don't let any hungry demons gobble you up, and stay away from killer angels."

"I will." I handed back his game controller.

After watching him for a few moments, I headed to my house, unable to take much of the mind-numbing video game activity that fascinated Wyatt. My angel was being just as boring, disassembling my toaster and watching a show proving the existence of Bigfoot. Bored demons are never a good thing, so I threw on my bathing suit and headed out to grab some late afternoon sun by the pool.

Even this late, the sun beat down on me, warming my skin and radiating off the flagstone patio surrounding my pool. I closed my eyes and dozed, listening to the cicadas, the mockingbirds, and the buzz of a distant neighbor's mower.

"Here."

I looked up to see Nyalla wearing a bikini the size of a postage stamp. She had two beers, one extended toward me.

"Thanks." I took a swig from the beer and watched the girl sprawl onto the lounge next to mine. "Is that one of Amber's suits?"

She laughed. "No. I got it when we went shopping. Amber is appalled by how much skin it reveals. It is far more modest than what I wore with the elves, though."

"For an elf/demon hybrid, she's surprisingly repressed. You know she's part succubus?"

Nyalla shook her head. "Maybe that part of her personality will reveal itself later?"

"How did spa day go?" I leaned my head back and allowed the sun full access to my face.

"I had a wonderful time," she replied in careful English.

"Seriously?" I sat up to better see her expression.

Nyalla gave me a quick glance out of the corner of her eyes. "No. I do not understand the appeal of having others bathe your face and color your nails. They wanted to cut my hair. Can you imagine? My hair has never been cut. Why would someone do that?"

"Some women prefer a more easy-to-care-for style. And it's nice to be pampered and fawned over sometimes."

The girl snorted. "Here men cut their hair, women cut their hair. They look like they are on the way to their execution. And pampering from someone who loves you would be nice. When it is a stranger doing the care, it is just awkward."

I murmured in assent and relaxed back on the lounge. For a few moments, the only sounds were the bugs and birds, and the clink of our beer bottles as we lifted them and sat them back on the pavement.

"Can I stay here with you?" Nyalla asked.

"Tonight? Sure. Gregory's going to be here, but you can hide up in your room, if you like."

Your room. I'd already designated it to be her room. I wondered if I should go shopping when I got back from Seattle. Pick up some décor more trendy for a nineteen-year-old girl.

"No, forever. I mean, as long as I live, or as long as you would have me."

I turned again and studied the girl. "Nyalla, you are always welcome in my house. Call it your home, and stay as long as you like."

Her face lit up, and I saw the faint tension around her eyes melt away.

"But I have hopes that eventually you'll want a place of your own, or maybe find a special someone to love."

She considered my words. "Maybe. But I cannot see that far ahead. All I want now is to feel safe, and have time alone to explore and find myself." She sat up and leaned forward, toward me, her eyes soft and earnest. "I am very fond of my brother, and my step sister seems to be a good-hearted person, but they fill my every moment. I am not used to so much activity and attention. It worries me. It is very stressful."

"I can tell them to back off some. Have them give you some space."

"No! I do not want to hurt their feelings."

"Does Wyatt know you want to live here?"

She nodded. "He said he understood. He seemed relieved. I think Wyatt is also exhausted by all this activity."

I smiled. "You're more like him than you know. So what do you want to do tonight? Anything? Or nothing at all?"

"I would like to just chill," she replied in English. "Watch TV, or read. I may go for a walk with your dog."

"Your English is awesome! You just chill, and make sure you take Boomer if you go out, so you don't get lost."

She nodded and pulled a bottle from the cooler beside her. "Another beer?"

I took the beer and we settled back to enjoy the last rays of the day.

By the time the air turned cool and we ventured inside, Gregory had our flight information. Nyalla disappeared to enjoy her alone time, and I wrote down the flight schedule and details in Elvish on a notepad in case I missed seeing her again before I left.

I texted Wyatt to let him know what time our flight left then settled in to wait. When I woke up on the couch, Gregory was watching my four televisions with picture-in-picture on each and searching the Internet on both my laptop and a cell phone.

"Where'd you get that?" I rubbed the sleep from my eyes, impressed at his multitasking and amazed that he knew how to work any of the electronic devices.

"My gate guardian brought them by a few hours ago. Here. This one is yours."

I took the iPhone and looked at it in astonishment. "You set it up? How did you manage to set it up?"

"It does come with directions," he huffed out, insulted. "And these human tools are ridiculously simplistic."

"Is the other one a spare? In case you lose your temper again?"

He looked embarrassed. "No, that one is for me. I'm finding them rather useful."

"Yes, very useful for a simplistic tool," I teased. "What time is it?" I peered at the dining room clock.

He waved his new cell phone at me. "According to this device, five o'clock in the morning."

"Shit! Our flight leaves in three hours." I jumped up. "We need to get going! Do you have any idea how long the airport security lines are? We should be leaving right now. Grab your bags and meet me back here in ten."

I didn't wait for him to reply. I raced off, taking the stairs two at a time before cramming a handful of clothing and toiletries into a small roller bag while trying to text Wyatt with a free hand. He hadn't replied from my previous text, and I worried he wouldn't be up yet. I hated to leave without some kind of contact with him. He'd always been with me before. The fact that he wasn't coming along this time bothered me. Were we really okay? Lately all I'd done was worry and wonder.

Turning up the volume on my phone, I threw an extra set of clothes in the suitcase. I doubted we'd stay long. It would only take me seconds to scan the demon corpse, but we'd have travel time, and the return flight was probably the next day. Crap, I'll bet that angel forgot to make hotel reservations anywhere. Hopefully we could just walk in somewhere and get a room.

I ran down the stairs and found Gregory exactly where I'd left him — on the couch surfing the Internet and watching eight television shows simultaneously.

"Why do you not have any luggage?" I demanded. "I assume we're only staying overnight, but still. . .."

My voice trailed off. Did he need luggage? Unlike me, he could create clothing, although he seemed restricted to his jeans and signature polo shirt. What about toiletries? I wondered if angels had morning breath, or ever needed to shave.

Gregory frowned at the envelope holding our itinerary. "I only bought one way because I wasn't sure how long we would need to be there."

Fuck! What was he thinking? No one bought one-way tickets after nine-eleven.

"They are going to flag you as a terrorist flying one way to Seattle from Baltimore without even a carry-on bag. You're going to get pulled aside and strip-searched, and we'll never make our flight."

Wait, why was I telling him this and ruining my chance at seeing him seized and strip-searched?

"What would I put in this luggage?" he asked, perplexed.

"Well, a change of clothes for one thing. Do you plan on sleeping in jeans and a polo shirt, or naked? Are you going to wear the same damned thing for two days? How about a comb? Toothbrush?"

He looked blankly at me. Cursing him, I went back upstairs and grabbed another roll-on bag, throwing in some spare toiletries and random t-shirts and jeans. None of them would fit him, but at least he'd look like he'd actually packed for a trip.

I was cramming the bags in the car when I saw Wyatt jogging up my driveway. He was bare-chested with a pair of pajama bottoms on. My heart gave a lurch to see him sleep tousled in the morning — one of my favorite things in the world was waking up next to him.

"You're heading out now? Will you be back late tonight, or are you staying over?"

He rubbed his face, his voice groggy with sleep. I wanted to wrap myself around him, rub along his warm skin, feel his breath in my hair. I turned toward him, a pang of longing in my chest. I didn't want to go, didn't want to leave him here. I hadn't had much time alone with him lately. We never had time anymore, and it was killing me.

"Yeah. Gregory only got a one-way ticket. I can't see this taking too long, so we might be able to get a red eye back and get in early tomorrow. If not, we'll catch something the next day. I'll text you and let you know."

Wyatt frowned and reached out a hand to brush my arm. "I wish I was going with you. I'll miss you."

I turned away from him and busied myself adjusting the suitcases in the trunk. That pang in my chest was rapidly becoming a heavy lump.

"You'll probably miss me even more when I get back; the Ruling Council meeting didn't go too well and I may wind up back in 'punishment'."

"Sam! I forgot. What happened?"

Yes, definitely a big, heavy lump in my chest. I turned one of the suitcases over and pushed it to the other side. There was a saddle still in my trunk from months ago. Had it been that long? When was the last time Wyatt and I rode together? I shook my head, unable to reply as that lump moved up to my throat.

"Sam?"

I felt his arms around me, his face in my hair, and I struggled to regain composure. I was leaving in ten minutes. No way I was going to bawl my eyes out right before heading to the airport.

"Was it that bad? What are they going to do to you?"

I took a deep breath. "Two went in my favor. I have to do a report for the guy in Virginia, and re-do the one for the drug dealer that attacked me rent day."

Wyatt spun me around to face him. "Wait, do you mean the incident with the mage and the angel? You didn't tell me you killed someone. Why didn't you tell me?"

"Because you'd get that look on your face. The one where I think you're just going to walk away and never see me again. I feel like I can't tell you things anymore. I'm always worried you'll think bad of me, blame me, accuse me of being a horrible person. I hardly see you alone anymore as it is. If I tell you I had to kill a human in self-defense, you'll pull away even more." That came out angrier than I had intended. I was so hurt. And lonely.

Wyatt crushed me against him, pressing his lips against my ear. "I'm so sorry. I'm still trying to get my head around the fact that you're a demon. I don't always like everything you do, but I don't want you to hide things from me. I'm sorry you felt like you couldn't tell me this. I'm sorry I wasn't there for you."

I hugged him back, loving the feel of his muscular back under my hands. If only I weren't leaving. If only I had twenty quick minutes. Full of regret, I pulled away, running my hands down his arms to where he held my waist.

"I'll only be gone a day or two. Clear some time in your schedule and we'll go for a ride. Maybe have a picnic. We can send the girls to the mall or something for the day." Not Columbia Mall though. Amber was not going anywhere near that place.

"It's a date."

Wyatt bent his head to kiss me. I dug my hands through his hair and held on tight, loving the feel of his lips and tongue against mine. I'd missed him. I'd seen him every day, but I'd missed him.

"Play with your toy later. You insisted we had to leave right now. Let's go."

I pulled away from Wyatt and shot an irritated glance at the angel before turning back to my favorite human.

"I'll see you in a few days," I murmured.

"Call me. I love you."

I nodded. "Love you too."

I watched him in the rear view mirror as we drove away. We needed a date, desperately needed some alone time together, but here I was, crammed into an SUV with an angel, heading to the airport. This was absurd. Why couldn't he just gate me there in our usual fashion? It was clear he was just as unhappy about this method of transportation as I was.

~11~

It was obvious to the airport staff that Gregory had never gone through the commercial airline song and dance before. I confiscated the itinerary and rifled through it to see what airline we were on. United. First class, way cool. Two tickets for Samantha Martin, and . . . blank. What the fuck? How had that gate guardian managed to buy a ticket for someone with no name? Was his identification blank too? I thought of how confused the humans would be, how they'd react at security. I started laughing and actually had to sit down on the curb before I fell over.

"What?" the angel asked, trying to grab the paper out of my hand. "Is there something wrong? Did the gate guardian get them wrong?"

I wiped my eyes. "The gate guardian has great skill in making airline reservations. Evidently you have no name. I just hope your passport is blank too."

Gregory snatched the itinerary and looked at it, frowning. "She understands human travel customs." He handed the papers back to me. "I don't need a name to travel."

"Please tell me she provided you with a passport too. You're going to need ID to get through security. I don't care how much blue stuff you throw around, I don't think you can sweet talk your way around Homeland Security."

Gregory looked insulted. "I'm an angel. I certainly can 'sweet talk' my way around Homeland Security."

I snorted. "Fine. This is going to be loads of fun. Let's go, pretty boy."

I got our boarding passes, checked our luggage, which was really my luggage, and steered him toward security. It was a huge line snaking through twisting paths of webbed dividing tape. Tired and bored travelers inched along with glazed faces, dragging carry-on, roller-board luggage in their wake. We'd be here an hour at the least. I'd had the foresight to grab a latte before getting in line. It was always a gamble since I'd need to throw it away if I hadn't finished my drink by the time we made it to the scanners.

"How do you buy things like this, anyway?" I asked as we moved a few steps forward. "You don't really have a wage-earning job. Do you counterfeit the money? Do you compel the humans into giving you these things for free? Does the Vatican bankroll you? Give you a Visa platinum with a picture of the Pope on it?"

Demons were good at earning and stealing money, but angels were probably above that sort of thing. I'd been wondering for some time now who or what was funding them.

"Why is this taking so long?" Gregory ignored my question and looked around in annoyance. We'd moved about three feet in the last ten minutes.

"They never have enough machines and personnel to get people through quickly, so they just tell everyone to arrive two to three hours before their flight to stand in line here."

I excitedly instructed him in the convoluted methods of human travel, thinking he'd enjoy the rules and restrictions, so similar to all the Ruling Council nonsense. "Sometimes you hit it right and blow through this whole process in five minutes, other times you're here for an hour."

The angel huffed. "That's ridiculous. Why don't they open more lines? Buy more machines?"

"Oh, there's more," I added gleefully. "If you are flagged, or act up, then they pull you into a room and take incredible liberties with your possessions and physical being. We probably don't have enough time for that, regretfully. I highly recommend it."

He glared down at me. "Do not act up, little Cockroach. If your actions result in us being detained, I'll beat you to a bloody pulp."

Oooo, promises, promises. Gregory's temper was starting to flare. I loved it when that happened. His irritation with the whole process was stirring up my naughty side.

"Those people up there," I continued, pointing. "They look at your ID and your boarding pass and check that all out. Then you go up to that conveyer belt and grab a bunch of those grey tubs. You need to take off half your clothes, shoes, jewelry, empty your pockets, take computers out of cases, separate any liquid items out of your luggage then put them in a single layer in the grey bins. The bins go through the x-ray machine there and you walk through the scanner when the security guy tells you to."

"I'm not removing my clothing," Gregory announced. "And I am not going through a scanner either." He was starting to blur a bit around the edges. I grinned in delight.

"Those scanners there are just the typical metal detector kind. If you beep, they'll ask you to check your pockets again and go through a second time. If you fail a second time, you get patted down and they sweep you with a metal detecting wand. If you fail that, it's off to the naked-grope room for you. Those other scanners are a type of MRI machine that projects a lovely image of your naked body to some dude in a control room."

"That won't be happening," he snarled, far from the picture of angelic composure.

I looked over my angel, inching slowly along. Blurry glow aside, he was a total hottie. I'm sure the humans would be thrilled to pat him down. Fuck, I'd be thrilled to pat him down. And I'd pay good money to get a look at the MRI image of him. Thinking of what it would reveal, I was once again struck with a fit of uncontrollable laughing.

"What now?" he demanded as we shuffled a few feet.

"Naked body," I gasped, still laughing. "You need to make sure you have all your human parts, because if they see something unusual, it's going to be all over the airport in five seconds. There will probably be pictures on the internet before you're halfway to the gate."

He glared at me. "What are you talking about? I look human."

Right. He was taller than a good ninety percent of the humans in line, and built like a weightlifter. Add in his oddly textured skin, glow, black eyes, and he didn't look human at all. If he hadn't entranced everyone in a hundred yard radius, they would have all been freaking out. But it wasn't what showed that was making me laugh, it was what I was pretty sure he *didn't* have under his clothes.

I motioned him to lean down to me, because he was so fucking tall that I couldn't whisper in his ear otherwise. "The humans are all convinced you're some movie star or something. You've got your mojo working on them pretty well right now, but if you step in that machine and you're not wearing a penis and some balls, there is going to be an uproar. All the blue stuff in the world won't be enough to keep those pics off the Internet."

Gregory ground his teeth, his black irises spreading to envelop his eyes in darkness. "I won't be stepping in that machine, and there is no need for me to manifest human reproductive organs."

Probably not, but it would be a whole lot of fun if he did.

I should have just shut up, but I continued to egg him on. I loved annoying him into a physical reaction. An angel punching me across the airport might make us miss our flight, but duking it out with Gregory would be worth it.

"I don't know why I'm giving you advice here, but I'd suggest you make everything a rather normal size. Dick about four inches flaccid, six inches if you want to be seen sporting a woody. Do *not* go smaller, and don't exceed that by more than an inch or you'll cause a riot."

He snarled, shooting out a hand to grab my neck. I dodged to avoid him. "Balls around the size of walnuts in a decent-sized sack."

He lunged at me again, and I ducked under his arm, nearly knocking over a group of businessmen in suits. Teasing him was so much fun. I felt giddy, out of control and unable to heed any warning signs.

"Dude, I'm not only trying to protect your reputation here, I'm trying to protect mine. I don't want it said that I'm traveling in the accompaniment of a eunuch, or a less-than-averagely endowed man. I wouldn't mind the Ron Jeremy size, but I don't want to have to fight off every man and woman in this airport. You're attracting enough worshipful attention as it is without everyone trying to get a grope on your junk."

He managed to finally get his hands around my neck, choking me into silence as we continued to inch forward.

"I will not go through any machinery. I will not lower myself to human physical standards. You will be silent and behave yourself. Understand?"

I nodded, gasping and coughing as he released me. Not a single person had protested my mistreatment. Angels got away with everything.

I could feel his increasing irritation as we slowly moved in our line. With each step, his glow intensified. It was all I could do to remain silent and not bait him further. I hoped they flagged him for his lack of identification. I hoped even more that they hauled him off for a strip search. I couldn't wait.

Finally, we reached the document checking station. I gave them the boarding passes and my passport. Gregory, of course, gave them nothing. The woman glanced at the boarding passes and looked at us apologetically. "You both are first class. You didn't have to wait in this line, you could have gone right through the VIP line over there."

I could feel Gregory's fury coming off him in waves. It was funny.

"Wow, I did not know that," I told her kindly. "Goodness, honey, did you hear that? We'll need to remember that next time." I'm a terrible liar, and Gregory looked like he was ready to rip my head off and toss it through the painted girders on the ceiling.

"Do you have your ID, sir?" the woman asked nicely. She was smiling at him with all her might. *Ha, busted*, I thought, grinning with anticipation.

"You have it right there," the angel indicated gently, a cloud of blue coming from him.

Fucking bastard. It worked. If the woman had been besotted before, she was in rapture now. He'd gone from hottie movie star to avatar of her god. She didn't even look down at the paperwork. Didn't look anywhere but into his eyes with worshipful adoration.

"Of course, sir. Have a wonderful flight."

I-told-you-so was written all over his smug face as we walked to the pile of grey bins. Fine. This was war. Gregory stood there and watched me, tapping his foot as I stripped off shoes, belt, and necklace. Asshole. He didn't even remove his shoes. Glaring at him, I yanked my t-shirt off and threw it in the bin.

"Oh, you only have to take coats and jackets off, not your shirt," the security guy told my lacy, bra-clad breasts.

"Cockroach," Gregory warned. "Put your shirt back on and behave."

Nope. Not going to happen. I knew I was pushing too hard, that I was becoming annoying, like that drunk cousin at Grandma's birthday party. I couldn't help it, though. I was an imp, after all. So I ignored his command and kept right on baiting him.

"The shirt has metal threads. I don't want to set off the alarm." I turned to walk through the scanner and turned back. "Will my piercings set off the scanner?" I batted my eyes at the security guy. The innocent routine usually didn't work, but it's not like he was even looking at my face.

"Put your shirt back on, right now," a blond woman in a security uniform commanded.

I looked down at the shirt in my hand and up at Gregory, delaying just a moment as if I were considering noncompliance. I knew I was a breath away from a lengthy strip search and possible expulsion from the airport. As much as I wanted to piss Gregory off, some common sense rattled its way into my head. I did need to get out and examine this demon. And I didn't want this whole thing to be extended any longer than it had to.

"Cockroach, if you don't put your shirt back on right now, I will forcibly stuff you into it."

I paused, the shirt just above my head and sighed as I pulled it on. I really did want Gregory to "stuff me into it", but we didn't have the time for that sort of fun.

"Fine. Spoil sport."

"I'll send her through and wand her," the security woman announced.

While we were waiting for the scanner, Gregory had already walked right past and was waiting, bored, on the other side next to my pile of stuff. I assumed the position, and held still while the scanner whirred away. As I thought, the folks looking at the readout asked to have me patted down and gone over with the wand. I was surprised they didn't order a strip search with the interesting piercings I'd created just for this event.

"Where are you heading?" the blond security woman asked, her tone indicating this was some kind of terrorist screening question.

"Seattle," I told her. "I'm checking over a dead demon to see if I can find any clues to the killer and help track him down before the angels blame the whole mess on me."

"And I take it the big guy is your doctor?" she asked dryly. "Ensuring you're safely on your meds for the flight?"

I laughed. "Nope. He's an angel."

She looked longingly over at Gregory as she patted me down. "I'll say he is. He could be my angel any day."

"Not likely," I told her cheerfully. "He doesn't have the right parts for you. You'd be terribly disappointed."

She raised her eyebrows. "I'm sure we'd manage somehow. You're good to go. Have a good flight."

Gregory glared at me and paced as I put on the enormous quantity of accessories I'd removed for the security process. Although this game of annoy-the-angel was fun, I was quickly running out of ideas, and I was on a tightrope in regards to Gregory's temper. I would love for him to lose control and slam me around a bit, but I didn't want him so furious that I'd spend a seven hour flight stuffed in the overhead bins, or strapped to the wing.

One of us was going to have to give in. I knew it would have to be me. We made our way toward our gate, me sneaking quick glances at him as he walked, brooding, beside me.

"All right, all right. You win round one. With the blue stuff and your angelic magnetism you clearly can overcome any human security measure. I admit defeat and bow down to your superior skills."

Nothing. Actually, his scowl grew more menacing.

"Are we still friends?" I teased. "How long are you going to be mad at me?"

Nothing.

"Come on. How about I buy you a drink? A make-amends cocktail? Or a blow job? That always cheers Wyatt up."

He halted, grabbed my arm and yanked me around to face him. "I do not consume food or drink, and I have no need to experience human reproductive methods. When will you get that through your thick head?"

I didn't think it was a good time to mention that blow jobs had nothing to do with human reproduction, but I couldn't resist pushing him further.

"I'm an imp," I mocked. "I seize every opportunity to piss you off and cause trouble. When will you get that through *your* thick head."

I'd been teasing him horribly, and this was a sore spot I loved to dig into. I just couldn't help myself. The stupid Ruling Council reports, worrying over Nyalla and Amber, having hardly any time to spend with Wyatt — it was all a heavy weight crushing me. I had spent so much time lately tip-toeing around Wyatt, that this was a relief to act out, to be an imp. Plus, annoying him and having him react in such a way was fun, the only fun I seemed to be having in the last couple of days.

"You are in danger of being accused of killing an angel, being executed as punishment for his murder. Stop playing around and get serious."

I looked up at him. Serious. He wanted me to be serious. Gregory shook his head as if recognizing the absurdity of his command and ran a frustrated hand through his hair.

"Truce. But only if you stop this incessant nagging about sexual organs and attempts at physical stimulation. I have no desire to indulge in that sort of thing, and I'm annoyed that you won't let the topic rest."

I felt hurt . . . and somewhat angry.

"Too fucking bad. This is who I am. I'm a demon, an imp. I 'wallow in physical sensation like a pig'. I am annoying — a pain in the ass. Either like me the way I am, or not. Stop trying to pretend I'm a fallen angel you can bring back into the fold. It's insulting."

For a split second, he looked shocked, then that cold mask descended over his face. "Fine. I thought you had potential, but I can't drag you unwilling into the light. You just keep on being a demon, but don't expect me to join you. I'm not going to descend to that level — ever."

I deserved this. He was right — I needed to stop pestering him and start taking my duties more seriously, even though I was an imp. But it wasn't really the loss of my favorite topic that saddened me, it was the fact that whatever relationship we had would only be on his terms. He'd never share a cup of coffee with me, never kiss me. Never. My relationship with Wyatt was damaged because he couldn't fully accept who I was. Yes, we were still friends with benefits. Yes, we'd always love each other, but we were broken and it was killing me to see the scars and think about what we might have had. The same thing was happening with Gregory. I felt a wave of sadness. I should just go home, go back to Hel where I could be a demon and not have the people I love constantly trying to change me.

"Fine." My voice was barely audible, and I just couldn't look at him. I pulled away from his hands and turned to walk to the terminal. This was going to be a long flight, out and back. And all I wanted to do right now was curl up in my bed — alone.

~12~

Gregory directed me to leave the rental car a few blocks away from our destination. It was a beautiful summer day in Seattle. The Fremont area rocked with action, and a wave of nostalgia hit me. It had been so long since I'd been here. The neighborhood had always been a bit funky, but it had somehow turned hipster, upscale, over the years. Smart coffee shops and ethnic eateries flanked shops selling sculptures and original paintings. The smell of sandalwood and myrrh wafted from the open door of a shabby-chic gift shop. I longed to explore, familiarize myself with my old stomping grounds, but we had a dead body to examine, and Gregory was clearly in no mood for play.

"There is an angel standing guard," he told me as we turned right on N. 35th street. "I'm going to go in, relieve him of duty, then walk outside to question him about the demon while you sneak in. Make sure he doesn't see you."

I nodded. No one was supposed to know I was here, or that there was anything suspicious about this dead demon. Just a routine incident, with Gregory here to do the paperwork.

We turned onto Evanston, and I headed left at the next block so I could sneak down Dayton and come at the house from the other end of the block. As I peered around the corner, I saw Gregory stride out of sight with another angel. That was my cue. Trying to not look out of place, I strode down Evanston and up to the six-foot-high privacy fence.

Behind the gate, the yard was covered in wooden plank decking with a decorative array of potted flowers leading toward the 1900's era house

It was a smallish house, with artistically weathered, grey wood siding and a porch barely large enough for the white, wooden rocker. The neighboring houses were tightly wedged in their respective lots, a scant few feet away. Even with the close proximity, no neighbors seemed to notice a woman walking up to and through the front door.

The inside confirmed why this house would fetch over half a million on the market. Pristine cherry floors in the foyer led up a narrow staircase to the left. I opened the door to a downstairs powder room and found modern bathroom fixtures but no dead demons. To the right, the walls of what had been a segmented house had been knocked out to make one large room. Cherry floors continued into the main room where a modern dinette sat in front of a turn-of-the-century fireplace. Overstuffed sofas and loveseats created a living area, and an open doorway led to a quaint, modernized antique-style kitchen.

Enormous bay windows surrounded a breakfast nook next to the narrow kitchen with its 1950's replica stove and tiled countertops. The backyard out the bay windows was small, but between the six-foot-tall privacy fence, the yard was verdant and full of heirloom roses and irises. I loved this little house. If I hadn't been so attached to my home in Maryland and my life there, I would have been tempted to oust the current owner and snag it for my own. There was no demon in the backyard, so I turned my attention to the narrow, elegant kitchen extending the width of the house.

It was a beautiful kitchen, but it was a pigsty. A pot on the stove contained hardened noodles, empty beer bottles lay on the floor and spilled out of the garbage can, dishes in the sink were piled high. The floor was covered with muddy footprints and spills, and a sticky chair lay overturned by the doorway. I frowned, perplexed at the difference between the care that had been lavished on the rest of the house and the utter neglect of hygiene in the kitchen. Demons. They were downright weird.

I walked back through the living/dining area to make my way upstairs and saw the angels through the bay window. Damn. I didn't exactly want to crawl, but I had no choice. Luckily, the fabulous cherry floors were highly polished, and I managed to scoot under the windows and through the living room into the foyer.

I trotted up the stairs and smelled the deceased before I actually saw him. Blood has a special odor, especially in such a large quantity. As I walked into the first bedroom, I saw a decorative design of red covering the walls and floors. For a moment, I wondered if it were from the dead demon or one of his human playthings. Gregory had said the other demons hadn't shown any sign of injury, but perhaps this one was different. Could the devouring spirit now be torturing his victims? Or perhaps this one fought back.

Walking around the massive oak dresser, I saw a twisted body on the floor. Something stirred my memory to see him there, legs splayed and arms outstretched, his head half under the bed. What an undignified way to go. The room was unremarkable other than the blood on the walls and the body on the floor, so without further ado, I yanked him by his legs. Might as well get this over with and fly back home. As his head came into view, I stopped, frozen. Cold iced my veins and all sound receded into the distance. I knew this demon. I knew him well.

Baphomet. I dropped to my knees and ran my energy through him, but found nothing to confirm the demon he'd been before his death. But I knew. I recognized this human form all too well — it had been his favorite. We'd won and lost bets with each other over the centuries, trading items and favors as our luck came and went. Time and time again, I'd lost fireball launchers, bladed snares, and even Boomer to him, only to win them all back. My luck always returned, his evidently hadn't.

Grief washed over me in waves. Baphomet had been a good friend. Yes, he'd tried to kill me a few times, but I'd done the same to him. We'd had good times together, and, in a way, he'd been instrumental in beginning my whole extended vacation here among the humans. We used to connect regularly, run off to cause trouble every year or so, but over the decades, our times together grew further and further apart. I hadn't seen him in nearly five years, and the last time the differences between us were becoming clear. He was a demon, and I'd begun to turn into something else.

I ran my hands over the cold flesh, no longer the warm, dark brown I remembered. I touched his high cheekbones and short ebony hair. I mourned, not just for Baphomet, but for our friendship that had begun a slow death years ago. And I mourned for me, for the demon that I used to be. Life was so much easier then, when I didn't care. Now everything I did had a ripple effect. I was aware of the future my actions affected. It wasn't just the impact analysis required for the four-nine-five reports; I'd learned firsthand how much pain I could cause Wyatt and all the other beings I'd come to care for. Yes, life had been easier, more carefree as a demon, but I wasn't a demon anymore. There was no use crying over my past, and no use crying over this corpse before me. The only thing I could do for Baphomet right now was find his killer.

Who could have done this to him? We demons all have a host of enemies, but devouring wasn't a common skill. Each time I'd done it, I'd been defending myself against a far stronger foe. It has always been a last-ditch effort when all hope seemed lost. The only time I'd devoured as an unprovoked attack had been involuntary — when I was a child and had been learning to breed. It was one of the reasons I was so reluctant to procreate. I was terrified it would happen again — that I'd be seized with the urge to consume and wind up killing my partner.

Baphomet didn't look like he'd been locked in battle before his death. The blood on the walls didn't seem to have come from him. There wasn't a mark on him, not even a paper cut, let alone something significant enough to have caused his death. Even if he'd been torturing a Low, he should have little scrapes and cuts at the very least. If he'd been fighting a devouring demon, there should have been some visible injury.

That left the possibility of ambush. I couldn't imagine he'd be breeding outside of Hel. Could someone possibly be using devouring as an assassination technique? It would be very effective, but would require planning combined with ruthlessness — a combination uncommon among all but the highest demons.

Taking a deep breath, I scanned him as thoroughly as I could. There was no remnant of demon energy whatsoever in the corpse, but as with the last head, right at the front of the neck, I caught a faint trace of that slippery energy. I concentrated and extended myself into his cells, cataloging each one in detail as I traced the indistinct line that circled his neck. It was still active, slippery and blocking my energy as I explored it. I'd encountered this sort of thing before, but what the angels used and what I'd experienced at the hands of elves and sorcerers wasn't quite the same.

I sat back on my heels and frowned down at Baphomet. The energy was too faint to assign to any specific species, but that wasn't what perplexed me the most. It was the placement that had my mind in a whirl. Neck. The angels didn't fool around. They always went right to the source and coated our stash of energy deep inside to prohibit our usage of it. Elves employed a net technique, encasing our entire bodies and blocking physical attack as well as an energy one. Why neck?

Restrained at the neck, Baphomet might still be able to heal some internal injuries but not be able to convert his entire body into another form. He would have been like a dog on a leash, one with all his physical abilities still available. With demons, energy attacks are only part of the equation. We are just as dangerous with only the strength of our corporeal form, as I'd proven time and time again. An elf would never have just restrained a demon's neck. Neither would an angel. Unless. . ..

I searched again, every cell. I had no idea how long it took me, no sense of anything outside my focused examination. By the time I sat back, the shadows were long across the floor, and I sensed the presence of my angel behind me.

"Did you find anything?" His voice was soft and kind, as if he'd intuited my earlier grief.

"No." I lied. I'd found plenty, but none of it made any sense. Baphomet had been restrained at the wrists, ankles and neck, leaving his energy accessible through his core. I couldn't see any reason for it, and couldn't see any connection between those faded traces and the devouring spirit that had killed him. Perhaps the restrain marks were just a fluke, something unconnected with their deaths. Or perhaps the devouring demon had purchased this type of thing from the elves and used it to keep his victims from fighting back. None of it made sense.

"Sahiviel suspects there was a different demon that lived in this house. Neighbors say that the deceased demon would come here frequently to visit, and that the individual residing here left about a day or so before this one's time of death."

I stood and took one last look at Baphomet before turning to face Gregory.

"You okay?" he asked.

I nodded. "Do you want me to check the house for any hints of another demon?"

"Can you do that?"

I shrugged. "I wouldn't find any energy traces, but demons don't live exactly as humans do. Sometimes there are telltale signs."

I searched the house, but couldn't find anything to corroborate what the neighbors had claimed. The only thing I did find was a pocket mirror — a small communication device similar to the one I had at home. I'd been meaning to get a portable one to stay in better contact with Dar and my household, but hadn't gotten around to it. Checking to make sure Gregory was in the other room, I pocketed the mirror. If a demon had lived here, I'd try and contact his household through the device later and see what information I could glean from them. It was a long shot. Many households, mine included, didn't always know the details of what was happening on the other side of the gates.

I shook my head at Gregory as I walked back into the bedroom. I wondered what they'd do with Baphomet's body. Not that it really mattered. It just bothered me to see him there, lifeless and twisted on the floor.

"How confident is your angel buddy that there was a second demon? Does he have some way of tracking the guy? Because, otherwise, I think we're at another dead-end."

"We have a description, but unless he tries to go through a gate or goes on a killing spree, it's unlikely we'll run across him. There are only so many angels here, and you demons are good at blending in with the humans when you want to."

"So if he continues this one-off, demon here, demon there thing, we'll probably never catch him?" It was a depressing prospect. I looked again at Baphomet's body, wondering what I could do to find this guy before he killed again.

"He'll escalate." Gregory didn't sound too happy. "They always do."

"Escalate? You mean because he's a demon and we enjoy mass murder?" I had a bad feeling I didn't want to know the answer to my question.

"No, because he's a devouring spirit." Gregory looked down at me, and I could see the sorrow in his eyes — *feel* his sorrow in the red-purple of his spirit that networked through my own. "They reach a point where they can't control themselves. They'll begin to devour everything around them. Everything. Endless hunger."

I struggled to take a breath. "What . . . what do you mean, *everything*?"

His gaze grew intense. "All life, all matter, the entire universe if they're unchecked."

I felt like I was suffocating. "How many? How many have you angels killed over the ages?"

"Ten. Eight of them in the last millennium. Eventually there will be too many, and they'll come too fast for us to kill. One will slip through and herald in the apocalypse, devouring all creation."

"So there is no solution but to kill them? What did you all do when we lived in Aaru? Kill us at birth?" "Them" had become "us". I felt like lead weights were pressing on my chest. I devoured, but I had it under control. I couldn't believe that someday I'd snap and go on a rampage, that Gregory would be forced to kill me.

"There were no devouring spirits when you were in Aaru — you were Angels of Chaos then. Devouring spirits are an anomaly that seems to have occurred with the devolution of your species."

I stared at him, mute with dread at his words, and what I knew would come next.

"I should have killed you the moment I found out," he said, clearly miserable at the idea. "I'm putting my own selfish desires ahead of what's best for the entirety of creation."

"But I'm okay," I choked out. "I didn't kill those demons, or that angel. The universe is safe from me."

He shook his head, eyes still locked with mine. "One day you won't be. Something will happen, or you'll reach a certain age, and you'll snap. There won't be any warning, and who knows how much of the planet, or beyond, you'll consume before we manage to stop you. *If* we manage to stop you."

"Then why haven't you killed me? Why don't you just kill me right now?"

The angel's mouth was pressed into a grim line. Without a reply, he turned around and left — walked right out of the house. I heard the front door close behind him. I felt as empty as the demon on the floor beside me, and so alone.

~13~

"Hey, baby. How's it going?"

I was sitting on the hood of the rental car, eating a takeout falafel and talking to Wyatt. When Gregory hadn't returned to the house on Evanston, I locked up and headed out. I wasn't sure what to do with Baphomet's corpse, and I wasn't about to just hang out there, waiting for the angel to show up. If he needed me, he'd contact me.

"Not sure when we're heading back. Gregory's MIA at the moment, but I'm assuming we'll take the red eye back to Baltimore."

"Did you find anything out from the corpse?"

Wyatt was definitely intrigued. Good thing, since I'd probably need his special skills in the future. We were at a dead-end now, but Wyatt could find a needle in a haystack if only I could tell him what needle I was looking for.

"Not much. He was killed the same way. There were traces of restraints around his neck and all four limbs."

"Well, that's good." Wyatt's voice was encouraging. "That confirms your suspicions."

I snorted. "What suspicions? I'm just as flummoxed as before. Someone used angel or elven/sorcerer magic to tie this demon up then drain him dry. No idea who, or what, or why."

"Is there anything I can do?"

Now I felt guilty. I'd been having resentful thoughts about Wyatt and his unwillingness to get involved in my activities, and here he was offering to help. Maybe the problem in our relationship wasn't him; maybe it was me.

"I don't know how you can." I sighed and sat my half-eaten falafel on the hood of the car, suddenly not hungry. "I knew him, Wyatt. He was an old friend. We hadn't been in touch lately, and we'd sort of grown apart, but I hardly expected to arrive here and find him dead on a bedroom floor."

"Sam, I'm so sorry." Wyatt's voice was sympathetic. "When was the last time you saw him?"

"A couple of years ago." I thought back, remembering all the times we'd connected over the decades. Baphomet didn't like to stay as long as I did, but he tended to keep his real estate holdings and businesses in trust, so he could return to them later. I'd flown out two years ago to discuss a scheme to sell stolen body parts. I really hadn't wanted to get involved in black market kidneys and passed on the project. He'd left a message for me late last year about some other project, but I'd never called him back.

"Maybe there is something you can do for me," I said as the thought formed in my mind. "Baphomet was using the same human form he had been two years ago. Can you search property records, and anything else you can find for Anton Breskine? And also 3256 Edmonston in Freemont? Does he own that house?"

"Anton Breskine. I've got a Washington State driver's license — African American male, five-foot-eleven, one-ninety, thirty-five years old?"

"That's him." Baphomet had been using that form for the past sixty years. He'd had to forge a birth certificate every decade or so to keep himself within that magic mid-thirties window. I could modify my human forms to a variety of ages, but most demons, Baphomet included, could only recreate the physical being at the same age they'd Owned them.

"I'll send you the address from his license. It's a place on Eastlake."

Eastlake? I remembered him buying a place there about five years back. He'd been really thrilled with the purchase, although he'd said some of the neighbors were a bit weird. I'd flown out to see it, because weird to Baphomet would have been really extreme. The house had been beautiful, the neighbors disappointingly normal.

"The house on Edmonston is owned by a Paul Yong."

I didn't recognize that name, but Baphomet may have Owned other humans since I'd seen him last. The neighbors had told the angels that someone else had lived there, but that didn't mean Baphomet wasn't connected somehow. He may have been renting it out to a human or another demon.

"Anything else?"

"Looks like Anton Breskine owns the house on his license and has for the last five years. Nothing else in Washington. Do you want me to check another state?"

"California," I said on impulse. "Specifically in the LA area."

"Hmmm, a couple of businesses, one with considerable unpaid tax debt."

Yeah, that would be Baphomet. I wondered about the lack of businesses in Washington. Baphomet was pretty predictable in his interests and liked to live a lavish lifestyle. How was he funding it all with only those few dried-up places in LA?

"Thanks," I told him. I really meant it too. "How are the girls? Are you ready to run screaming yet?"

He sighed. "Nyalla is holed up in your house reading magazines and working on her language software. She meets us for dinner and movies but seems to want to be on her own a lot."

"And how's Amber?"

"She's . . . Amber. I don't know, Sam. Same as always. Charming, understanding, caring. She pops over and we spend hours together, but when she leaves, I realize I don't know anything about her life or how she really feels. She talks about her fall class schedule, various friends, a part-time job as if everything is just normal and perfect. Every time I try to dig and find out how *she's* coping with all this, she redirects me."

Amber was very good at redirecting. "I'll call her."

The half-elf actually called me as I drove to the address on Eastlake. As Wyatt said, she rambled on about activities in a superficial way while I waited. Amber never called me unless she needed something that only I could give her.

"Sam, I think I need to get laid."

I pulled over to the side of the road, because I was on the verge of crashing the rental car.

"Well, nineteen-year-old human girls generally do seem to enjoy regular sexual intercourse," I told her, feeling flustered at the awkward conversation. I was a demon; this shouldn't bother me, but somehow having a sex-ed type discussion with Amber turned me into a blushing prude.

"Yeah, but I stopped when, you know, when I found out I wasn't human. What if birth control doesn't work on half-elf freaks?"

"Your body is human," I assured her. She wasn't fully in control of her demon abilities. As her powers began to mature, she'd be able to change her physical make-up, including the effects that drugs, alcohol, and poisons had on her physical form. That was probably a long, long way off though.

"Okay, but what if my demon side goes crazy and I kill my partner?"

That was always a possibility, although succubi and incubi were not anywhere near as violent as other demons. They tended toward pleasure, not pain. Leethu could happily

143

dole out anything her partner desired, but she'd never been willing to participate in anything non-consensual.

"You don't kill Wyatt when you have sex with him. What sort of things do you do? How do you keep your violent urges in check? Does he let you tie him up and stuff? Or maybe he ties you up, so you can't hurt him?"

I made a choked noise and held the phone away from my ear, staring at it in horror. I was *not* going to discuss Wyatt's and my sex life with his sister!

"Ummm, maybe abstinence is a good course of action for you," I finally replied.

The irony of my recommending abstinence was not lost on me. I'd once taken a whole stack of church youth group pamphlets promoting teen celibacy and altered them to include graphic drawings and cheerful commands to "Go Forth And Fuck!".

"I'm trying, but I don't feel well. I feel brittle, like I'm on the verge of snapping. And I'm tired, like I'm getting a cold. I never get colds."

"Vitamin C," I urged. "And maybe a nap."

"I tried exercise," she continued, ignoring my suggestions. "But at the gym yesterday, there was this class instructor and I could hardly control myself. What made it worse was that he was clearly interested, eager even, to get it on in the locker room."

"Wait. Raoul? That zumba instructor?" I'd been trying to get in that guy's pants for the past year. He was a Latin god of a man. Every woman at the gym lusted after him. Sadly, in spite of his flirting, he was always resolutely professional.

"Yes. He gave me his number and somehow managed to find mine through the membership database. He's called me three times begging to see me."

Was he stalking her? A flash of anger sparked through me. No one fucked with my little family and lived to tell the tale. Although there wasn't much I could do right now from Seattle.

"Call the police." I urged. "Report him to the gym."

"I'd rather throw him in the back seat of my car and ride him until he collapses from exhaustion. I'm just afraid he'll wind up dead, with or without a smile on his face."

Oh. My. Not a visual I thought I'd get from Wyatt's little sister. Was this normal human crazy hormone stuff, or something else?

"Can you restrain yourself?" I needed to get a hold of Leethu and see what advice the succubus could possibly give her randy daughter. The sun was low on the horizon, and I'd hoped to check out this potential house of Baphomet's before Gregory and I headed back to the east coast. I didn't have a portable mirror to reach my household right now, anyway. Hopefully Amber could take a bunch of cold showers and keep from fucking anyone to death until I got back to Maryland and could contact Leethu.

"Yeah, I guess I can just use a vibrator, or that. . .."

"That's a great idea," I cut her off. Now I had images of Amber masturbating running through my head. "Just hang in there and let me check some info. I'll be home in the morning. We can talk then."

~14~

The sun was sending its last rays over the water as I stood in the Eastlake house and surveyed my surroundings. It was just as beautiful as I remembered — across the road from the famous floating houses on Lake Union. The place cost a fortune, even when Baphomet had originally bought it. Not that sufficient capital was ever a problem for us demons. Amoral beings tend to generate wealth at an astonishing rate. The house wasn't necessarily a mansion, but in Seattle, location was king. And Eastlake was primo.

Baphomet's residence was not as trendy as the other demon's. Most demons moved every few months, but Baphomet had been here five years. That was practically unheard of, even though this was a house any of us would want to keep a tight hold on. Baphomet *was* particularly fond of his real estate purchases. I think he still had that place in London from three hundred years ago. And he'd had an absolute meltdown when his house in Sardinia had burned to the ground.

Except for myself, demons usually maxed out their stays at no more than three years. Baphomet had done an extended vacation before. We'd had a bet going on, and he'd been determined to win. Since then, he'd never stayed long, always expressing disdain for any visit more than two months. Why had he remained so long?

The only thing unusual my brief search revealed was a stack of papers on the table — some of them posters railing against demonic possession, and others letters filled with tiny handwriting. The letters all accused the reader of heinous acts and promised both banishment and an infernal afterlife. For a moment I thought I'd found some kind of clue to the killer, but then I realized the incoherent rambling was more likely that of a mentally ill person. They often recognized us demons and took especial delight in outing us to the rest of the public. Luckily, their accusations were usually just considered to be a symptom of their mental condition.

Another dead-end. This whole trip had been a bust so far. I hadn't found anything on Baphomet's corpse that would help me identify who had killed him, why, and where he might be. The restraint marks and traces didn't make sense at all. Maybe if I spent more time in Baphomet's house, searched it further, I could find something, but it was more likely I'd only find random information about his various business interests and demonic hobbies. Maybe there was no big plot. Maybe Baphomet and all the other victims had just been in the wrong place at the wrong time.

Sighing, I glanced over at the huge communication mirror on the wall, so like my own at home. Baphomet had been my friend, and I owed it to his household to let them know about his death.

"Baal, I'm so relieved. We've been trying. . .." his steward's voice trailed off as he realized this was not his master on the line.

"It's me, Az. Baphomet is dead."

It probably wasn't the most gentle death notification call in the history of the world, but we demons are not very good at this sort of thing. I heard his sharp intake of breath.

"Angels? I told him not to stay so long, told him it was insanity, but he said he would be safe. That he knew someone."

I snorted. No one was safe from the angels except me and my household. Probably not me either, I thought, remembering the chase down Market Street.

"I'm sorry for your loss," I told him, uncertain what to say. I assumed as the Iblis, I needed to do this sort of thing. And Baphomet had been my friend. Well, as much a friend as any demon could be.

"Iblis, I humbly ask that you accept us into your esteemed household," the steward said without missing a beat. A household without a master wasn't safe. They'd be picked off quickly without protection. I wasn't much better than any other demon, in spite of my Iblis title, but I was the first available, and more likely to take them due to my friendship with the deceased.

"Sure." I might as well. I seemed to be taking in every stray around lately. Thankfully I'd scored Haagenti's funds when I'd killed him, or I'd be facing poverty with a household this size. It was a funny situation. Rich here among the humans, destitute in Hel.

"We're grateful for your protection, Iblis. Is there anything I can do to assist you?"

An idea bloomed. "Yeah. How long was Baphomet here this time? And was there a demon he came over with? Somebody he mentioned living near him that he was friendly with?"

"Our former master had been on the other side of the gates for nearly seven years. He traveled over with Raim, and last I spoke with him, they were working together on a project of significance. I believe they'd become partners."

Raim. I knew of him, although we'd never crossed paths. In Hel, he preferred an avian form — a sort of crow shape. He'd become somewhat legendary as a thief and made a hobby out of blowing up buildings. I hadn't heard of any unexpected demolition in the last seven years, but that didn't mean he hadn't been causing chaos in some other fashion.

"Can you contact Raim's household? Inquire as to his whereabouts?"

"Yes, of course, Iblis, but the last I spoke with them, they had not heard from Raim. I inquired when I was unable to reach our former master, thinking they might have news of him. They too were concerned."

Households got nervous when their heads remained away for extended periods. Could Raim also be dead? Gregory's words echoed in my head, and I wondered if he'd snapped and began a devouring spree that would only end with his death.

"Did . . . did Raim devour? Were there any rumors?" It was like asking if a human were a serial rapist. Not many demons would admit to devouring. The line remained silent, and I felt the steward's discomfort.

"There were rumors, Iblis, but no one has confirmed. I'm sure they are vicious lies told by his enemies. I've heard the same lies about you."

Those lies about me were true. They were probably true about Raim too.

"Will you be continuing our prior master's project, Iblis? Would you like me to continue sending Lows, or higher-level demons?"

I opened my mouth, but before I could ask the steward what he was talking about, the world lurched around me. With a wave of vertigo, I found myself dizzy and disorientated, being hauled along by a strong arm around my waist.

"What the fuck?"

"Your flight leaves in ten minutes," Gregory announced. "I'm having the plane held."

My eyesight cleared, and I saw us hustling right past the security line and the scanners, everyone ignoring the angel half dragging an imp.

"You didn't have to summon me out of the blue like that," I complained, trying to get my feet under me to halt our breakneck pace. "I'm sure there's another plane in the morning."

"We have a lead on the killer. You're going home on this plane." The angel hauled me past the gate desk and onto the jetway.

He had a lead? Excitement poured through me. A lead! Finally, after such a discouraging afternoon. There was no way I was going to go home now. No way. I grabbed the edge of a wall, recessed to allow the walkway to collapse, and held on with all my might, nearly wrenching my shoulder from its socket.

"I'm not getting on that plane. I'm coming with you."

"You're getting on the plane." He stopped and tried to pry my fingers off the ledge.

"Fuck you," I snarled. "I'll crash the plane, jump out the window, blow a hole through the fuselage. I'm not getting on that plane."

That gave him pause. He stood before me, his eyes completely black, his form shimmering with indistinct edges as he took a calming breath. "Little Cockroach, you need to go home to your human and stay there. I'll go and confront the devouring sprit."

"Like hell. I'm coming with you. This is personal. I'll wind up being implicated; I'm in danger of being blamed for this whole thing. I'm going to make sure it gets resolved."

I saw him waver, saw the conflict in his eyes — his need to keep me safe versus his understanding of how I must find this guy before someone decided I was the culprit.

"I knew him. I knew this last demon. He was an old friend of mine, and although he was a bit of a bastard, he didn't deserve this." At least I didn't think he did. With Baphomet, one never really knew.

He paused, running a finger across my cheek and along a loose tendril of hair. "I know, Cockroach. I felt your sorrow about his death. I'm sorry you're grieving, and I understand your need for closure and vengeance, but you will be safer at home. If this demon killed your friend, managed to overpower an angel, I fear he'll do the same to you."

I could tell he wasn't going to budge, that my personal safety outweighed any need to deliver personal judgment in his mind. He was an angel, though, and there was one thing I knew he was a stickler for — duty.

"As the Iblis, it's my responsibility to investigate these deaths and bring the murderer to justice." I had no idea if that last part was true, but I knew it would make my case stronger in the eyes of an angel.

A warm light came into his eyes, and once again he caressed my face. "He is very strong. I fear you might need to resort to something unsavory if you face him."

I understood the unspoken words. I was only an imp. And who knows if encountering another devouring spirit would set me off on my own course of destruction. Gregory had always been hands-off when it came to most threats to my person. The only time he'd intervened had been when an angel had caused me harm. This sudden protectiveness was both flattering, insulting, and rather suffocating.

"I am the Iblis. You are always lecturing me about duty and responsibility; well here I am, ready to step up to the plate. He's killed at least four demons. That makes his justice my responsibility."

"He's killed an angel. That makes his justice my responsibility."

I faced him, seeing the resolve in his face. It wouldn't matter. He could tie me up and stuff me on a plane, but I'd keep coming back. He'd never been able to control me, never been able to get rid of me. And from the look in his eyes, he knew it.

"It seems we have a disagreement about jurisdiction. I propose we work together since we both want the same outcome." It was an angelic solution. Normally I'd rant and rave, physically assault him and demand I get my way, but I'd found things went better when I played on Gregory's terms. His eyes returned to normal, his form solidified as he considered my proposal.

"We'll be more likely to find him working together," I added. "And the quicker we find him, the less likely he is to do massive amounts of damage."

"Your argument is a sound one." Reaching out a hand, the angel took a lock of my hair and rubbed it between his thumb and forefinger, sending a tendril of his personal energy in to caress mine. "Don't devour, little Cockroach. Promise me you won't devour."

I promised. I didn't swear it, though. Because if the shit really hit the fan, devouring might be the only option left open to me. And I was determined that this killer, whether or not he was Raim, wouldn't get away.

"So where is he?" I wondered how we'd get there since Gregory was refusing to gate me, although summoning me must be a whole different scenario. My presence would definitely put a cramp in his plans if I had to travel by human methods.

"He tried to get through the gate in Seattle, to return to Hel. I need to question the gate guardian, then we can begin to track him."

"Well, the gate is down by the water, our rental car is up in Eastlake, and we're probably an hour or so by taxi."

"You get a taxi, and I'll meet you there."

"Oh, hell no! I'm in this too. We travel together."

The angel was starting to glow again. This whole trip wasn't doing much for his temper. None of this was doing much for his temper.

"Just transport me with you, stupid, stubborn angel. Surely you won't need to move me through Aaru this short a distance. What's the big deal?"

I'd caught him in his lie, and he knew it. "No one can know you're here, on this side of the coast with me. If I gate you anywhere, there's a chance someone will notice. I can't risk that someone will even think of you in connection with these killings — especially the murder of an angel."

He was probably right. He usually was. And if the murderer was trying to get back to Hel, he only had so many options. If we worked quickly, I might still be home by late tomorrow.

"Okay. You rush off and question your guardian, and I'll meet you somewhere after, so you can brief me and we can track this fucker."

He looked both surprised and relieved at my acquiescence before he vanished in a flash of light, leaving me in a jetway in the middle of an airport. I knew where the gate was, I'd certainly used it enough times, but I had no idea where I was supposed to meet him. Figuring I'd hang out at the waterfront and wait for him to find me, I headed out of the airport and toward the taxi stand.

~15~

By the time I'd reached the waterfront, I'd changed my mind. I was an imp. It was my prerogative. The taxi driver, who'd channeled his inner Mario Andretti when I'd waved a Ben Franklin in his face, gladly detoured and dropped me at First and Union, not a block away from the gate to Hel.

It had taken me nearly an hour to get there, even with our breakneck speed. Gregory was still there, talking to the gate guardian who looked like a cross between a homeless guy and a street musician. He'd never had a wide range of corporeal forms, and I'd seen this one many times over the last century. With my energy held tightly inside, I walked along the opposite side of the street, head down. Even with my precautions, I saw Gregory's hand clench and knew he'd sensed me and was pissed at my presence.

Taking that as a sign that I was close to detection, I casually walked to a front door and slipped through the narrow passageway between two buildings, looping around behind the buildings and the gate. I'd planned to skirt the immediate area around the gate guardian and lurk a block or so away, but halted when I saw the hole.

It's not like I could miss it. Nearly four feet across, the edges were a jagged tear, as if someone had taken a giant bite out of the concrete parking area. Cautiously peering over the edge, I saw water fill the hole about three feet down. It was obviously not made by a man-made digging machine, and I hadn't seen any rock-eating monsters nearby. A troll could have done this, but the ones who'd slipped through the wild gates and established territory among the humans were all in Scandinavia. At least, they had been the last time I'd seen them. They didn't generally like urban areas, and although there was a lovely statue of one up in Fremont, I doubted any were gobbling up rock and mortar here in the Pacific Northwest.

Curious, I got onto my hands and knees and scooted around the jagged edge, examining it as carefully as I could. Bits of cement broke off under the weight of my hands and splashed in a rain of pebbles and dust into the water below. It was dark, edging close to midnight. The security lights in the parking area behind the building were strong enough to cast faint shadows along the ground, but not strong enough to pick out colors. Still, I couldn't mistake the dark red along a twisted piece of the rebar grid that poked out from the concrete. It was human. Which didn't always mean the being that spilled it was human. Faint traces of demon energy lined the edge of the hole.

A demon had torn up this chunk of a parking lot, so very close to one of the major angel gates. What kind of idiot would do that? The energy it would take to convert the section of the parking lot into raw energy would be like a beacon call to the angels. If he'd had any plans to slip through the gate undetected, this would put a big dent in them. Unless he'd done it after his unsuccessful attempt? I rubbed a crumbling edge with my finger. If he'd been caught by the gate guardian, driven back behind the buildings, if he'd found himself without enough raw energy for defense, he would have needed to convert matter into energy quickly. He would have used whatever was at hand.

I frowned. Matter to energy conversion was inefficient, even for us demons. We always tried to store up as much as we could before leaving Hel, replenishing it slowly from the scant resources of earth while here. This dramatic hole would have resulted in barely enough raw energy to kill a Low, although it was probably enough to give a gate guardian second thoughts about pursuit.

Had he cut himself? Was he wounded by the gate guardian and bleeding? I touched the blood and rubbed it between my fingers. Odd. It should be dry by this point, not thick, wet, and slippery. Slippery. It coated my fingers and dove down to the personal energy within them, touching my spirit self with a silicone-like glaze. I'd felt it on the necks of the devoured demons, felt it on Baphomet's neck, wrists, and legs, and now I felt it in this demon's blood. What did this stuff have to do with a devouring spirit, and a bunch of dead demons? If only I'd been able to get to the dead angel — did he have it too?

Perplexed, I left the hole and headed to the end of the parking lot, walking face first into Gregory's polo-shirt-covered chest as I rounded the corner. He grabbed me in an oh-so-familiar move and began slamming me against a nearby wall.

"What were you thinking? I take all these precautions, and you waltz right on by us on the street?"

He pinned me firmly against the building, his fingers digging into my shoulders as I caught my breath. "I held my energy tight inside," I protested. "There's no way he could have detected me. No way."

"I *saw* you! What if he recognized your human form? And although you had admirable control at that moment, twenty seconds out of sight and you splay your spirit self all over the place."

Crap. When I'd examined the hole, I'd forgotten and revealed myself. I bit my lip and looked up at the angel in what I hoped was an apologetic fashion.

"What were you thinking?" he repeated, giving me a few more whacks against the building.

"There. Was. A. Hole," I choked out in rhythm with my back hitting the brick behind me.

Gregory let go and I slid down a few feet, catching myself before I hit the ground.

"The demon," I gasped. "He must be low on raw energy, because he converted a big chunk out of the parking lot."

The angel frowned, turning his head to look toward the vast expanse of pavement. "How big? It would have to be a hole the size of two city blocks to produce enough energy to defend against an angel."

Standing upright, I wiggled past Gregory to lead him to the spot. "Yeah. I don't get it. It's dangerous to convert this close to a gate — suicide practically. And if he were being chased and defending himself, he would have needed to convert twenty times this much matter."

We stood and stared down at the hole, like two insurance adjusters contemplating the potential repair costs.

"The guardian didn't pursue the demon." Gregory's voice was slow, measured. "He blocked the demon's passage, and when the demon attempted to devour him, he let him go."

I raised my eyebrows. Let him go? This guardian took his job seriously. He'd once chased me three blocks in an attempt to take me out. I couldn't imagine him letting *any* demon go.

"I don't blame him," Gregory said, squatting to better examine the hole. "There are legends about devouring spirits, and guardians are ill-equipped to deal with that sort of thing."

"So why the hole?"

The angel traced along the edge with a finger, just as I had done. "Maybe he wasn't converting. Maybe he was devouring."

I couldn't help the small sound of disbelief that escaped me. Cement? A section of dirt and parking lot? Why the fuck would *anyone* devour that?

Gregory looked up at me, and I could see his eyes, a solid black, even in the dim light "If he's snapped, then he can't help it. We need to find him now, before he completely loses control, before he manages to make it through a gate."

I didn't believe it. If he'd snapped, there would have been a devoured gate guardian, and half the waterfront missing. This wasn't the beginning of a devouring spree, it was something else. "I think he wanted to create a diversion. Bring the guardian running, then slip through the gate."

Gregory looked at me like I was an idiot. I know he preferred his own theory, but I'd done this a million times. Guardians were easily distracted, any bit of demon energy, magical activity, or a half-price sale at Macy's and they were off and running. It was a piece of cake to loop back around and sneak through. I hated to give the angels our secrets, but I suspected Gregory might be putting too much into this. Sometimes a hole was just a hole.

"He's snapped," the angel repeated slowly, as if to drive the fact into my thick head. "He's devoured countless demons, an angel, your friend up in Fremont, and just tried to devour my gate guardian. He's snapped."

Fine. We'd go with that, since Gregory was clearly not interested in hearing about demon distraction techniques.

"Wouldn't it be easier for you guys to just let him go back to Hel? He'd be our problem then." In fact, his presence in Hel would be a plus to the angels. Who knows how many hundreds of demons he'd devour before someone managed to take him out. Less demons they'd need to worry about coming over here and causing problems.

Gregory stood and walked slowly around the circumference of the hole. "Devouring is a problem for all of creation. Yes, it might be beneficial to turn this weapon against our enemies, but if the demons in Hel could not eliminate him, if he managed to overpower the elves, he'd be unchecked. Plus, there's a chance he could be controlled if he fell into the wrong hands. A truly powerful demon, an ancient, could compel a devouring spirit and target him like a weapon."

I laughed. "Yeah, like me. We all know how well compulsion has worked on me. If *you* can't manage to do it, no one can."

"Few devouring spirits are imps," he replied. "Only the strongest can compel them under normal circumstances. Your being an imp makes you practically immune."

"But this guy probably isn't an imp," I mused.

"Weapon of a powerful demon or an uncontrolled devouring spirit in Hel, by the time he reached a realm that we had a presence in, he'd be too powerful to stop."

"He'd devour all of creation," I added softly.

Gregory's head came up, his eyes meeting mine in a stoic sorrow. "Exactly. I do not think this particular devouring spirit is the one to bring about the end, but it pays to be safe when the stakes are so high."

I looked down at the rebar, at the red blood with the telltale magic. Regardless of whatever magic was used to restrain these demons, this guy had to be stopped. I didn't want to muddy the waters with misdirection, and I just couldn't see how the slippery stuff I'd found on each corpse and in this blood tied in with a devouring spirit gone mad.

"I need to see the dead angel," I told him. Something nagging in the back of my mind told me there was a missing piece to the puzzle.

"Why? What could you possibly discover from the corpse of an angel that you've been unable to find on four dead demons?"

I opened my mouth to tell him, but he cut me off with a wave of his hand. "No. I cannot do it. There will be all sorts of questions. I can't see that the benefit would outweigh the risk."

"So what do we do now?"

The angel walked toward me, wiping the concrete dust from his hands. "He's desperate to get through a gate. He's so low on energy that devouring is all he has left, and he appears to be injured. He needs to go home."

"So we stake out a gate? Which one will he head for?"

Gregory was silent, his eyes searching me for something. "What?" I asked.

"How do you know where the gates are? Do you know every one of the angel gates, or just a few?"

I laughed, quickly cutting off the sound with my hand over my mouth. "Sorry. It's just . . . these gates have been in the same place for millions of years. There are seven main gates to Hel and forty-nine sub-gates. Everyone knows them. It's not that hard to memorize fifty-six locations."

"Yes, but some are mobile. The one in Columbia could be anywhere in or around the mall. How do you find it?"

"I just do. I can feel them nearby. I can't pinpoint exactly where they are until I'm pretty close to eyesight distance, but I can feel them."

"How close," he urged. "How near Columbia are you when you feel the presence of the gate."

I shrugged. Where was he going with all this? "I don't know. The parking lot maybe? I know there's one there, so I'm not actively trying to sense it. I doubt I could feel it much beyond the exit off 29, tops."

He blew out a puff of air. "That's a relief."

"So he's coming back here, right? He'll try for Seattle again?"

"Yes, probably. If he can't sense them beyond a few miles, he'll most likely try for this one again."

I peered at him in the dim parking lot lighting, trying to see if he was making a joke. "It doesn't matter if he can sense them or not. We know where all the angel gates are. If he's injured, I'd doubt he's in any condition to head for the east coast, and that's the nearest major gate to this one."

"Name the seven main gates to Hel," the angel commanded, ignoring my comment.

I smirked. This was like a quiz show. I wondered what the prize would be. Knowing angels, It would probably be something I'd hate.

"Columbia, Seattle, Dakar, Bangkok, Copenhagen, Bogota, and that stupid one off northern Russia. Why the fuck would you put a gate nearly two and a half miles up in the air over an island? Fine for those of us with wings, but I can't tell you how many demons plunged to their death through that damned thing. Nobody uses it anymore. Not in the last eight decades. . .." I frowned, remembering something I'd read.

"It's gone. Well, not totally gone, but so damaged we had to disable it."

My mouth fell open. "The *Tsar Bomba*. Holy shit on a stick, the humans blew up an angel gate!"

Gregory looked grim. "Novaya Zemlya is the island, and the bomb was a fifty megaton RDS-220, to be exact. There were a lot of very angry angels over that one. Many were advocating extermination of the human race, citing they'd acquired power they were ill-equipped to handle."

"They didn't do it on purpose," I sputtered. "How the fuck were they to know you put a gate to Hel two and a half miles up in the air. It's not like they even know about the angel gates."

"It's not the loss of the gate, it's that they have a weapon with enough power to damage one that is concerning to us."

I shrugged. "Could be worse. I don't blame them for trying. They're like children, exploring their world."

Gregory grimaced. "Children destroying their world. How fair is that to the other life forms that inhabit it? These are gifts they are too unevolved to handle. Gifts they should not have received for another million years. Hopefully they've put that nonsense behind them and learned their lesson."

"I think you underestimate the appeal of blowing shit up."

"Well, don't tell that to the others on the Ruling Council. It was a rough couple of decades, and I don't want to stir it all up again."

I nodded, wondering what all this had to do with a devouring spirit, injured and desperate to get home.

"That makes six gates," Gregory commented. "Six is a very inauspicious number."

Ah yes, the number of the beast. The angels preferred seven. "So where is the new gate?"

Gregory shook his head. "I don't want that knowledge to get out right now. If you all have no real way of sensing them outside a certain distance, then it's not germane to the issue at hand."

"So, it's in a weird, remote location where you can't easily put a guardian, and you don't want the word to spread that it's an easy spot for demons to cross over," I intuited.

"Something like that." He shifted, looking around the parking lot. "He's in no condition to head toward Baltimore or further, so he's bound to come back here."

"Or not. Some demons have a far greater sensory range than I do. I'm just an imp, after all."

He looked at me in dread. "How far?"

I smiled. "Dar can sense a gate over two-thousand miles away. Even the wild and elf gates. It's a skill many demons have. I suck, and I'm lucky if I can sense a minor gate at over fifty yards. With other gates, my range is pretty much less than fifty feet."

I could tell by his expression that this shiny, new angel gate was well within Dar's range. "Vancouver?" I guessed. "Missoula?"

He looked up at the night sky, as if gauging the time until dawn. "Juneau."

~16~

We were scheduled to be the first morning flight into Juneau, taking off pre-dawn in our hijacked G6. The owner of this luxury aircraft was happily riding in the seat beside me. He'd initially been a bit pissed about its theft, but became starry-eyed the moment he'd caught a glimpse of Gregory. I was amused to see that angelic laws or ethics didn't seem to encompass personal property rights.

Gregory had exploded all over the airport in a temper over our travel logistics. The last direct flight to Juneau had long left Seattle by the time we'd reached the airport, and the next flight out included a seven-hour layover in Anchorage. He'd been on his spanking-new iPhone with the gate guardian back home, barking out orders for water passage, but that option encompassed over two days of travel. Even a charter plane was out of the question since Juneau airport locked down at midnight to incoming flights.

At least the delay had allowed us to take a very uncomfortable taxi ride back to Baphomet's house to retrieve our rental car and my luggage. Originally Gregory had insisted we abandon it all in a mad dash to Alaska, but with nearly four hours to kill, he finally agreed. I had no idea who would have ended up paying for the never-returned rental car, but I wanted my suitcases and their contents. I'd managed to convince him to stop for a bite to eat at an all-night diner on our way back to the airport. I ate; he didn't.

I glanced over at the brooding angel across from me and sighed, shifting uncomfortably in my seat. Something in my pocket dug a sharp edge into my leg, and I realized I'd forgotten the pocket-sized mirror I'd lifted from the house in Fremont. The house had been registered to Paul Yong. I looked at the communications device, a much smaller and simpler version of the one at Baphomet's house. Had Baphomet kept this one as a back-up? Or had it belonged to some other demon?

Shrugging, I punched the clear stone on the rim and waited. Even at ten-thousand feet, the mirror should work. When no one replied, I left a vague message about how I'd found the mirror and was trying to find out who it belonged to before stuffing it back into my pocket.

It was going to be a long flight. Gregory had been on edge since he'd discovered the murdered angel, and the airplane owner was cheerfully enthralled, so I wasn't expecting stimulating conversation from either of them. I looked out the window at the rippled sheet of cloud-cover below us, just becoming visible in the early dawn light. I'd called Wyatt before we had flown out, woke him up at what had to have been four in the morning Maryland time, to tell him not to expect me for a few days at least. I'd need to call him again when we landed since there was a good chance he might not remember our conversation. Then I needed to call Nyalla and see how she was doing, solo, in my house. Then Amber, to make sure she hadn't gone all praying-mantis-meets-black-widow on the neighborhood boys.

My pocket sent a shock into my leg, and I jumped, quickly pulling out the mirror before it could zap me again.

"Uh, hello?" I wasn't sure how to answer the thing, not knowing who was on the other side.

"Mal? *Mal?* What the fuck are you doing with this mirror?"

I recognized that voice. "Dar? What the fuck are *you* doing with this mirror? I found it in a house with Baphomet's dead body, and I wasn't sure if it was his or not."

"Baphomet's really dead?" he exclaimed. "His household showed up yesterday saying they were now under your protection. Your steward was ready to toss them out, but we were all good friends back in the day, so I figured they were probably telling the truth."

"Yeah, he's dead." That sadness came over me like a fog again. One more piece of my past, gone forever.

"Angels? Was it that fucker you said chased you a few days back?"

"I don't know." I wasn't sure how much to tell Dar. He knew I devoured. He'd known it for centuries. As much as I trusted my foster brother, I knew he'd not be able to keep juicy rumors about Baphomet's method of death to himself.

"Keep this line, Dar. I'm away from my house for a few days. You can use this one of Baphomet's to contact me until I get home."

"Will do," he said cheerfully. "It's not Baphomet's mirror, though. It's some other guy's. Rain, Raim, or something. His household showed up right after Baphomet's with the same story. I don't know this guy, so we stole all of their stuff and tossed them out."

"Raim? It's his mirror?" The fact that I felt sympathetic toward the displaced household showed just how far from my demon roots I'd come.

"Yeah, Raim. I've never met the guy, but your steward said there were some unsavory rumors floating around about him."

"Can you go find them? Bring them into my household, and have their steward call me on this line." Maybe if I spoke with the guy, I could find out more about Baphomet's partner, and whether he was the devouring spirit we were searching for.

"For fuck sake, Mal! How many more demons are you going to take in under your wing? We're squeezed in like sardines, and even with Haagenti's funds, you're going to run short. We don't know this Raim guy, and we don't owe him or his household anything. Let them rot in the gutter."

"No, Dar," I insisted, my voice firm. "I need them. Do as I say or you'll rot in a gutter."

"Bitch." It was a term of affection for him, and I caught myself smiling. "Anything else I can do for you? Rip off your scales? Poke sticks in your eyes?"

"Is Leethu there? Can you have her call me on this line?" I had a mirror, might as well kill several birds with one stone.

"She's right here, actually. I'll put her on."

Even through the communication device, I felt Leethu's seductive aura wind its way around me.

"Ni-ni, what can I do for you?"

"I need your advice." I jumped right into the topic, explaining Amber's self-imposed celibacy and my concerns that her urges were more than just teen-girl hormones.

"Oh, she is a precocious little thing!" Leethu exclaimed, her voice full of proud admiration. "I too started early. Do you remember?"

Yes, I did. Even at my young age, I'd fallen in line with the others, trailing about after the succubus, pining away for a glance, a touch, or possibly more. She'd been sent off for training soon after all that had started, and the whole sibling group had protested her absence loudly for several days before something else caught our interest.

"She's not even twenty yet. Isn't that a bit young to be getting these kinds of skills?"

Leethu's laugh rang like wind chimes. "Having to masquerade as a human has speeded things up a bit. Of course, she'll not be anywhere near as powerful as a full succubus."

Phew, that was a relief. Amber had enough issues to face without hoards of insane admirers hounding her everywhere she went.

"So she's okay? She can bonk this guy at the gym? She's really worried she'll kill someone."

"Oh, that is always a strong possibility." Leethu didn't seem too disturbed about that fact. "Heart attacks, aneurisms, they all happen pretty regularly, and sometimes humans don't realize how fragile they are when they request the truly kinky stuff."

Fuck. For once, I was glad I was just an imp. "So, if she stays vanilla, and her partner gets a medical evaluation first, she should be okay? It's going to really do a number on her if she kills someone, Leethu. I don't want that to happen."

"Well . . . I can't guarantee she won't lose a partner or two. She's young, and it will be hard for her to know how to control her pheromones and aura. It's not a big deal. It happens."

"It is a big deal, Leethu. How does she keep from killing someone?"

"She could fuck vampires. Personally that's not my thing, but many of us enjoy them. They're pretty sturdy, but always non-consenting. They get kind of bitey when they're pissed off, so she may need to yank their fangs first. Werewolves are fun, but they sometimes get carried away, and I've had to kill a few in self-defense."

I shook my head in frustration and glanced over to see Gregory watching me, obviously listening in.

"She can't fuck a vampire. Because . . . well, you know, they would probably eat her. Plus I doubt she'd go for the whole rape thing. And werewolves aren't allowed to have sex with *humans* per their existence contract." I hoped Gregory wasn't putting two and two together here. I wasn't sure how much he'd heard of the conversation, and I didn't know how the angels would feel about their beloved elves breeding with a succubus. Amber had enough races gunning for her without adding angels into the mix.

"I could send a demon over for her. An experienced incubus to give her some guidance." Leethu offered. "Does she prefer men? Irix owes me a favor. And he's a good tutor."

I hesitated, sneaking a quick glance at Gregory out of the corner of my eyes. I didn't want to foist this guy on Amber, but she should have the opportunity to consider him as an option. At least until she felt confident enough to have normal human relationships again.

"Okay. I'll grant him safe passage. I don't want him throwing his influence around though. If Amber agrees, then fine. If not, he goes home without stirring her or any of my friends into a crazed orgy. Got it?"

"I have got it," Leethu replied, ending her connection.

"You're setting up your boyfriend's sister with a sex demon," Gregory drawled. I was half afraid to look at him and see his expression. "Don't you think Wyatt is going to have a bit of a problem with that? And why is she so worried about killing human sexual partners. That rarely happens without homicidal intent, you know."

I squirmed. "It's a long story. And no, Wyatt probably wouldn't approve. If she says 'no', then this Irix will go home and no harm done. If she likes him, well, I'll find a way to explain it to Wyatt."

Gregory made a noise of disbelief. "You're going to explain to Wyatt that you've procured a paid sexual partner for his sister? A sexual partner that will probably occupy her thoughts and set the standards for her relationships the rest of her life. You do realize how succubi and incubi work, don't you? They're power is through positive sexual memory and the emotion it generates."

"Yes, yes," I glared up at him and was a bit surprised to see he was actually amused. "She's not really human. She'll be okay, trust me. Amber is more immune than you'd think."

"Ah, so she's a hybrid." His tone was just as amused as his expression. "Cockroach, your family has more twists and drama than those soap operas I saw at your house on the Spanish language channel."

It truly did. I looked back at him and took a deep breath. "I need to provide safe passage through the Columbia gate for this Irix demon."

His eyebrows raised toward his hairline, lips twitching with a hint of a smile. "I don't believe he is part of your household, although the size of your household does seem to be reaching astronomical proportions. He's not performing duties that fall under the responsibilities of your title either. No, I don't think he will receive safe passage."

"Please," I begged. This had become a ritual, and I pretty much knew his next words before he spoke them.

"I would grant this in return for a favor."

Damn it all. He'd been racking up favors like crazy for the past six months and had never redeemed a one. Everything I asked lately seemed to require a favor in return. Even getting the can of tomatoes off the top shelf had cost a favor. This one was number twelve.

"Fine. You have another favor," I snapped.

He smiled benevolently and pulled out his cell phone.

"Hey, you can't use that on the plane. You'll fuck up the computer stuff and we'll crash."

He shook his head, and dialed. "I'm an angel. I get to break the rules."

It was so unfair. I broke the rules too, but he always got away with it. I turned to the bemused plane owner beside me. "He's using a cell phone on your plane," I told him.

He smiled , his eyes shining with happiness. "He can do anything he wants."

That pretty much summed it up. I slumped down in my seat and resigned myself to the unfairness of it all as Gregory made arrangements for the safe passage of Amber's sexual tutor.

~17~

The wheels of our plane touched down in Juneau at an unseemly hour of the morning. As soon as the plane door opened, I gasped in wonderment. It wasn't just the stunning landscape that amazed me, it was the huge quantity of tiny wild gates. Miniscule rents in the air, they sparkled like prisms. Beside the gates were thin sections, as if they were on the verge of becoming. I wondered how long it would take them to reach more than their current few inches and longed to explore them further.

"What?" Gregory asked, squinting into the distance in the general direction I faced.

I remembered his and the other angels' disbelief when I'd told them about the existence of the gates.

"Nothing. The mountains are very pretty," I lied. No sense in getting into a huge argument about this, although it would be funny if Gregory accidently stuck his foot through one.

Occupied by fantasies where Gregory fell into a wild gate and wound up somewhere in Hel, I dragged the two bags down the staircase, onto the tarmac. I was wheeling our luggage toward the airport rental counter, when Gregory took my arm and detoured me to baggage claim.

"I've got a present for you," he announced, hauling me past the conveyor belts, circling with their drab-colored baggage, and through a set of doors clearly marked "authorized access only".

"Stay here," he commanded.

I remained where indicated while he spoke with another angel who was guarding a large box. The angel craned his neck to send curious looks in my direction around Gregory's advancing form. As my angel spoke, he stopped trying to eyeball me and replied with a deferential posture. After a few seconds, he darted another quick look at me before vanishing.

"Come here, Cockroach."

I walked toward him. "I guess that was an angel you trusted? Because he clearly saw me, and I wasn't exactly being stealthy. He might have thought I was a human, but I doubt it."

"I trust him. That's Nisroc, and he's the gate guardian up here. He's allowed more leeway in terms of distance from the gate, due to its remote location."

I approached the box and Gregory waved his hand at it. "I asked him to do me a special favor. The fact that he managed to accomplish it, just further proves his worth."

Ahh, a protégé. A warmth spread over me. I could empathize; I'd begun to feel the same about Amber, and even Nyalla, of late.

"So, what's in the box? Flowers? Diamonds? A body part from my enemy?" We demons had particular ideas of what constituted "presents".

Gregory pushed the lid aside, and I peered down at the corpse of an angel. This would truly be a gift to make any demon swoon with joy, but I doubted he'd meant it to be *that* sort of present.

"This is the angel that was murdered. The one who was found in northern Mexico. I'm still trying to determine why he was here among the humans. There's a disturbing lack of cooperation among his choir at the moment."

I shivered. I would truly hate to be an angel in that particular choir. I loved Gregory in a towering rage. His temper totally turned me on, but this cold anger of his did nothing but frighten me and remind me how very ancient and powerful he really was.

The corpse hardly looked human. It seemed more statue than flesh, with pore-less skin devoid of color. With some dread, I lay my hands on its flesh and sent my personal energy within. I'd never examined an angel's corporeal form in this way. Gregory and I had always been intimate as beings of spirit, and he staunchly resisted any more than cursory physical closeness. Every now and then, he'd slip and caress my face, or rub my hair between his fingers, but any move on my part was quickly rebuffed. This was the first time I'd ever really been able to see how angels put together their physical bodies. It baffled me. Nerve endings were intact for function, but disconnected from pleasure and pain receptors in the brain. Hearing, smell, taste, and vision were dulled. The odd skin texture helped block all but the most vital sensory input. I shook my head, thinking this was a terrible waste.

"Well?" I could sense Gregory's impatience.

I hesitated, reluctant to disclose what I still didn't understand. It wasn't what the angel's body revealed that perplexed me, it was what it didn't. There were none of the restraint marks that the demons' had had. None. He seemed healthy and hale, not a mark on him. There were no indications he'd been in a battle when he'd died. In fact, the expression on his face looked . . . shocked. Like his death had come out of nowhere and surprised him. He was drained, devoured right out of his corporeal form, but his death had differences when compared to the others. They had been stripped clean, even some of their physical form rendered oddly sterile. This angel had traces remaining. It was as if his death had been a quick, desperate action, with little time for a thorough job. Maybe it was a different killer. Or maybe the killer just hadn't had a lot of time for this one.

"Cockroach, there are things you aren't telling me." Gregory's voice held a warning note.

I threw up my hands. "I don't know. It's different than the demons. Perhaps the killer was in a hurry with this one, or nervous, because he was an angel."

"Or maybe a different killer," Gregory mused, echoing my thoughts.

Once again I explored the corpse, taking especial care to examine the faint traces of angel energy that remained. His removal had been incomplete, and there was enough of him probably for the angels to positively identify. There were bits along his torso, and one good-sized chunk at his hand.

I paused, sucking in a breath. Because there, on the piece of him left in his hand, was a scar. A recent scar, barely a day old when he'd been killed. It hadn't healed, hadn't even begun to close over. And I recognized this scar.

"What?" Gregory asked, seeing my startled expression.

"This angel . . . it's the same one that chased me through Frederick. The one I told you about. The one I summoned you in a panic over."

He came to stand over my shoulder, the heat from his power leak searing along my back. "This is not good, little Cockroach. It further implicates you in these devourings."

I winced. "Yeah, I get that."

"How can you tell it was the same angel? He was devoured. Nothing remains."

I shook my head. "It was sloppy, hurried. There are parts of him still here, and this part I'd damaged when he grabbed me in the alley. It can't be a coincidence. It's in the same place, and it was small enough that he might not have bothered to fast track any healing before he died."

"That attack on you happened right after the demon was found in Damascus." His words were right next to my ear. "So close. I could see there might be a connection, but why would his body have been found in Mexico?"

I turned to face him and caught my breath at how near we were. "Demons don't bother to move bodies. We don't bother to cover things up, or hide murders. We'll deny it, blame it on someone else, but we don't move bodies."

So either something important took the angel immediately to Mexico, where he was killed, or he was killed in Maryland and there was a specific reason to move the body.

"Who would care to move an angel killed by a devouring spirit?" I asked. And why would they bother?

He looked over my head, focusing into the distance as he thought, but his hand reached up to rub a lock of my hair rhythmically between his fingers. It was a strange habit of his, and I loved it.

"His choir, maybe? Perhaps there were activities occurring in the Maryland area and they didn't want him to be associated with them."

"What activities were there in Maryland besides a devoured demon?" I asked, knowing his logic was headed down the same path as mine.

He shook his head and looked down, his eyes meeting mine. "None. I keep a close eye on that area, as I have a particularly troublesome Cockroach to look after."

"So his choir, or whoever moved the body, didn't want him connected with the devouring demon that killed him?" I asked, ignoring the thrill I felt at his comment.

Gregory shrugged. "Or he wasn't killed in Maryland. Perhaps his involvement with the devoured demons found along the east of the continent led to a trip west."

I let out an exasperated breath. "We keep uncovering more questions and no answers. How does any of this make sense?"

The angel's eyes narrowed and I felt a shiver down my spine. "I have an idea. But first, we must stop this devouring spirit before he becomes any more powerful. I want to find answers as badly as you do, little Cockroach, but we can't let our quest for the truth blind us to the crisis before us."

I wasn't as convinced of this crisis as he was, but I agreed. Something bothered me, but regardless of that nagging intuition, I knew I needed to find Baphomet's killer and bring about justice. It wasn't very demonic of me, but I felt I owed it to my friend to avenge his untimely death.

~18~

We'd snagged a rental SUV toward the city. I was driving, as Gregory lacked both the skill and the desire to do so. The city of Juneau was about seven miles to the south, along a narrow strip of coast between the channel to the west and the massive ice field and mountain ranges to the east. I was a bit bummed we didn't have the time to head a tiny bit north toward the Mendenhall glacier. I longed to see it before the massive ice formation melted into the ever-increasing lake.

We were driving along a typical throughway—straight and narrow, with trees and various buildings to one side, an expanse of floodplain and marsh to the other. Thick, grey clouds hung low over the horizon, covering the tips of the impressive mountain range we'd seen when we'd flown in. A light mist clouded the windshield and forced me to turn on the wipers. I knew Juneau got more than its fair share of rain, but I'd hoped for more pleasant weather than this chilly wetness. June was far more "summery" back in Maryland.

This part of Alaska was strange. The groups of the tiny wild gates revealed themselves every half mile or so, and the rest of the atmosphere seemed thin, as if it were on the verge of becoming a giant passageway. Aside from the supernatural, Juneau seemed to be little bits and chunks of habitable land separated by vertical rock, thick forest, and huge bodies of water. The humans had done their best, carving small sections of usable territory from a harsh and brutal nature. The actual city of Juneau was small — smaller than many of the quaint towns back in Maryland. There were no hundred-story high-rises, no ornate monuments to mankind's hubris. Everything seemed to realize it existed on a razor's edge, at the fickle whim of Mother Nature.

As we pulled into the north end of the city, where a harbor full of boats lined the channel to our right, I jumped to feel the jolt of electricity through my thigh. With an apologetic look at Gregory, I pulled the SUV over and yanked the mirror from my pocket.

"Iblis." The voice over the device trembled with relief and gratitude. "We are forever in your debt. We've lost five since you initially turned us away. The remaining ten of us would not be alive if not for your generous protection."

I felt a stab of guilt. Damn Dar for turning them back. I needed to have a serious conversation with him about this.

"Are you Raim's steward? The head of his household?" I needed to make sure I was getting my information from the closest source.

"Yes, my former master was the demon known as Raim. If we can do anything for you, Iblis, please name it. Anything."

Again I felt that twinge of guilt. But there was a murderer on the loose, and I didn't have much time to find out what was going on before Gregory took matters into his own hands. "Did he devour? I know there are rumors, but I need to know if you have any knowledge beyond gossip."

There was a lengthy pause. Gratitude was one thing, but betraying a past master, even one you thought was dead, was a matter for careful consideration.

"Once. Just the once that I am aware of." The steward sighed, and I could feel his anxiety. "Raim was a strong demon; he had no need to resort to such disgusting methods in the normal course of things. Once, when he found himself in fear for his life, he devoured his attacker. I've never known him to do that before or after. He may have had the ability and the inclination, but he clearly had the fortitude to keep his perversions in check."

I winced. Perversions. Ouch.

I'd devoured more demons than Raim. Had he just been good at hiding it, or had something set him off? Or were we completely going down the wrong path?

"Do you know anything about the project he was doing with Baphomet?"

Again the steward hesitated. "Baphomet approached our master, needing some particular skills of his for this project. At first he wasn't interested, but Baphomet made it worth Raim's while to partner with him. I believe they were bringing low-level demons across the gates for some gain. The details, I do not know."

Baphomet's steward had indicated the same. Was this all a red herring? Perhaps Raim's "perversions" had nothing to do with the demon deaths and Baphomet's murder. Perhaps he'd also been caught in this whole mess as a victim, and was being implicated simply because he had the ability to devour. Or perhaps I was desperately trying to make excuses for this demon, unwilling to admit to something that could very well be my own future.

"When is the last time you heard from Raim? Do you know what human form and identity he was using at the moment?"

"Paul Yong," the steward replied promptly. "About a week ago, he contacted us to say he was becoming bored with the project he was doing and was concerned that one of the partners was not completely trustworthy. He planned to return to Hel this week after the last batch of demons came over to them. We never heard from him after that. He wasn't the sort of master who communicated frequently, so we didn't become concerned until a few days ago. When Baphomet's steward contacted us yesterday with the news of their master's demise, we knew the worst had occurred."

"Thank you for your honesty."

"Iblis, we are so very grateful for your protection. If there is anything we can do for you, any activity you wish us to undertake, we will do so without hesitation."

I shifted uncomfortably. Maybe I'd been here, living the life of a human for too long, but his offer made me feel oddly guilty, like I was some kind of slave master.

"Just relax and take some time to adjust. I value your contributions to our household and will definitely let you know how you and the others can be useful in the future."

I disconnected the line and glanced over to find Gregory regarding me with a rather sappy look. It was even more unsettling than the steward's professions of service and loyalty.

"What? What the fuck is that look for?"

"I think my little Cockroach protests too much," he said with a grin. "Could it be that I sit beside an angel after all?"

"Fuck you," I told him, pulling the SUV back onto the freeway.

We drove a few moments in silence. I felt his amusement, his smug satisfaction, and it grated like sandpaper on my emotions. He'd overheard way too many personal conversation in the last few hours, and he'd clearly gotten the wrong idea about me. I'd set him straight earlier about my unwillingness to rehabilitate to his angelic standards. I didn't want him reviving that particular project. It was time for us to get back to the business at hand.

. "So where in Juneau is this gate? When should we expect Raim to get here? Are you angels somehow tracking his progress, or guessing?"

Gregory looked at me with an intense stare. "So, this Raim you've been talking about is our devouring spirit? I overheard his choir say he devoured once, but is that rumor? The demon who tried to get through the gate in Seattle may not be him — it may be a different demon."

"Well, I'm making some assumptions. He came over with Baphomet, and they seemed to have had a partnership of sorts. There are rumors he devoured. I can't believe there are three of us here. That's too much of a coincidence, even for me to swallow."

Gregory shook his head. "So the dead demon in Seattle, your friend, this Baphomet, was in partnership with our suspected killer. The devouring spirit snapped, and your friend somehow got caught in the crossfire?"

"I don't know," I tried to think through the various angles. "He was only known to devour that once. Why would he leave Seattle to go munch up a bunch of demons on the east coast, then return to devour an angel and his former partner? It doesn't make sense. If he'd snapped, he would have started with Baphomet and worked his way around the Seattle area."

"Perhaps their project involved work on the east coast and that is where he began to devour. Or perhaps their project involved using his devouring abilities for some gain, and he lost control and turned on his partner."

I caught my breath at the last theory, taking my eyes off the road to glance at Gregory. Would that be me someday? Only devouring as need, then turning on someone I cared about, taking them by surprise? Would it be Dar? Leethu? Or even the angel beside me?

"That is why you cannot devour again," Gregory replied, reading my thoughts. "The more you devour, the greater the likelihood that you will lose control. It's a slippery slope, little Cockroach."

The air was heavy with thoughts of my bad habit and my probable future.

I finally broke the silence. "I don't know if the killer is Raim or not. You work on trying to secure the gate and catch whoever it was that tried to get through in Seattle, and I'll track down Raim. If these two are one in the same, then our efforts will double the chance of catching him. If not, then Raim may shed further light on what happened."

He considered my words, but I felt a worry coming from him, concern for my wellbeing.

"Agreed," he finally replied.

"So where is the gate? How do we know when the demon is arriving? Or is he already here?"

Gregory tried to scoot further back, but the seat was as far as it could go. An American SUV had tons of legroom, but not as much as a six-and-a-half-foot-tall angel needed. His knees were absurdly close to his face. He looked uncomfortable, and I got a perverse pleasure seeing him folded up like an accordion in the front seat.

"There is one major airport, one seaplane base, and four helipads in Juneau. That doesn't count any of the small, unofficial landing areas. Juneau may not have land access, but there are a million ways this demon can arrive via air or water."

I took my eyes off the road to give him a reproving glance. He was an angel. I'd expected more from him. "So you have no fucking idea when he's arriving or how he's getting here?"

The angel shifted in his too-small seat. "No."

I yanked the car over to the side of the road and pulled the emergency break, stepping out as I dialed Wyatt's number.

"Hey babe, you in Alaska yet?" His voice was cheerful and affectionate, and I felt a surge of longing. I was on the opposite end of the continent, but if I closed my eyes, I could still feel his skin against mine, smell warmth, man, Wyatt.

"Yeah, finally." My voice was full of regret. "Gregory stole a private plane, so we made it in first thing. How are you? How are the girls?"

"They're off at the mall, then lunch somewhere. Nyalla now has a cell phone and actually ordered dinner last night while we were out. Her English has gotten really good — she's smart and seems to have a knack for languages."

I could hear his pride, but couldn't help a quick stab of worry. "Which mall?"

"Tyson's corner. Don't worry, I told Amber she wasn't to set foot in Columbia Mall." I took a deep breath in relief. There wasn't much I could do from Alaska if the half-elf tried to get through a gate to Hel.

"Can you research something for me?" I asked, longing to wrap this whole thing up and get home. I missed him, missed my dog, missed my horses and my rental properties, missed the hot wings at the Eastside Tavern.

"Of course," he said cheerfully. "Whatcha got?"

"Raim, aka Paul Yong, may be our guy. We're not sure, but either way, he's a demon of interest, and I'd like to talk to him. His household hasn't heard from him in ages. Can you see if there's anything on him in the last couple of days? Hits on his credit report, possibly cell phone calls?"

"Sure. I'll see if I can hack into any of his credit card accounts for recent activity, too. I take it location is important?"

"Yeah. He could be anywhere. If he's our guy, though, he'll probably be either in Seattle, or heading up here to Alaska."

I heard Wyatt typing. "Do you also want me to check all flights yesterday and today into Juneau from Seattle?"

"From Anchorage, Ketichikan, Skagway, and Vancouver too. That should cover air travel unless he flies a small plane into a private airport."

"I'll check into water travel from Skagway and Ketchikan also. I doubt he would have taken a boat from any further than that. Do you want me to scan for stolen planes? Yong didn't have a pilot's license, but other humans the demon Owned may have known how to fly."

Wyatt knew us so well. I loved working with him on these projects. His mind flew alongside mine almost as though we were one in thought.

"Yes, but I don't think the killer knows we're on his tail right now. He got away from the gate guardian in Seattle, and we think he's just heading for the next closest major gate to Hel. I doubt he'll expect to encounter any angels until he gets to the gate, unless he's so far gone that he's recklessly throwing energy around."

"Are there any other suspects you want me to track? If a different demon is the killer, you'll have no way to track his arrival."

My heart sank. "No. Part of me hopes Raim isn't the killer, but it would be so much simpler if he was. Any ideas on how to find a devouring demon that we don't know?"

Wyatt made a noise in agreement. "How about I scan breaking news along the northwest passage for any disasters, murders, or stolen planes? Seems the most likely thing for a desperate demon to do."

He was the best — my partner in crime, even if it wasn't really crime anymore.

"Thank you, Wyatt. Love you."

"Yeah, I love you too. Just make sure you come back in one piece. And don't go killing anyone."

I hung up, because there was no sense in giving Wyatt false assurances, and turned to see Gregory out of the car and staring at me with a rather peculiar look on his face.

"Got him. Or at least we will get him if it's truly this Raim guy. Wyatt is very thorough, when I can convince him to help me out."

"I remember how useful he was last summer, when tracking Althean. I'll have to remember his talents for any future issues."

Yeah. I couldn't see Wyatt agreeing to work for Gregory. He didn't often agree to help me out anymore, and his feelings for the angel were pretty far into the negative category. I climbed into the rental car and headed toward our hotel, confident that Wyatt would call as soon as he had a solid lead.

I turned inland, heading for the bed and breakfast address Gregory had given me when we left the airport. We climbed steadily, navigating the switchbacks of city streets that were thick with trees and foliage springing from the sides of roads, narrow medians, and yards. Everything was overgrown. Outside of the more industrial, government-type buildings, the dwellings were hidden deep in a field of green. Finally, high above the city, we pulled in front of a three-story home. A placard outside read *Wolf's Den Inn*.

The view of the downtown and waterfront from the inn's mountain-side perch was spectacular. Wisps of low-hanging clouds danced across the channel below, giving the vista an air of magic. Everything in Juneau seemed to be right on the edge of the mountain range, right on the edge of the inlet, or right on the edge of a glacier, and this inn was no different. It was as if nature grudgingly granted limited space for human residence, hogging the rest for herself.

The house appeared to have been built in the early twentieth century, with wooden German siding that had been painted cream, and dark-green trim around the more modern windows and doors. A huge wooden porch spanned the front of the house, filled with an assortment of rockers, small tables, and terracotta planters bright with geraniums. As I lugged my bags up the steps, I noticed various water-resistant board games on the tables, and a small antique metal cooler next to a rocker.

"You check in and get settled," Gregory said as I reached out a hand to open the screen door. "I've got something I need to do."

Before I could protest, he vanished. I was a little grumpy that he'd left me to use my credit card instead of his angelic charm, but cheered up once I was inside.

The remodel on the house had clearly been done with an eye to preserving the feel of history. Wainscot covered the lower half of the walls, and the floral wallpaper above reminded me of a century ago. A cheerful fire in the large stone fireplace drove the damp chill away. The chairs were full of needlepoint pillows and crocheted throws. It was warm and cozy, and I immediately felt at home.

"Welcome to the Wolf's Den Inn." The woman that greeted me at the front desk eyed me carefully but seemed pleasant enough.

"Thanks. I'm checking in. Reservation for . . ." I hesitated then remembered Gregory's plane ticket with a blank space where the name should have been. "Samantha Martin."

The woman glanced at her records, then up again. Her gaze was non-offensive, but shrewd and knowing. She reminded me a bit of Candy, and I found myself wondering if the name of her inn was more personal in nature.

"Yes. The Klondike room. I have your paperwork here."

I approached the desk and dug my credit card out of my pocket.

"Just one?" She took the card, frowning slightly and flaring her nostrils. I was convinced she was a werewolf at this point and was tempted to ask her if she thought I smelt like burnt chocolate.

"No, I'm traveling with someone, although I'm not sure he'll actually be staying here. It's not like he sleeps or anything, but I guess I should get him a room key anyway."

She nodded, scrutinizing me over the top of her reading glasses. I returned the favor. She looked to be mid-fifties, a wiry figure in a pair of blue jeans and a yellow button-down shirt. Her hair was light-brown, pulled up into one of those bun-like ponytails.

"Do you want to leave one of the keycards at the desk for him to pick up?" she asked after I'd signed for incidentals.

"Ah, no. I'll just take it." Gregory was liable to just pop into the room without a key. And it's not like I knew what name to leave it under.

She hesitated before coming out from behind the desk and taking one of my roller bags.

"I'll give you a quick tour on the way to your room. This front room has two computers for guest use, and a fax machine. There's Wi-Fi throughout the inn, but the connection is better in the front part of the house."

We left the vast front room and walked through a smaller library and on to the dining room. Antiques occupied places of honor throughout. A handsome silver coffee urn sat in the library on a leather-inlaid hunt table, sturdy china with an ivy pattern beside it. Plates filled with cookies seemed to occupy every end table. The dining room held a large mahogany dining set, already prepped for breakfast with jade milk glass plates and bowls.

"You've missed breakfast this morning," she apologized. "I can send something up for you, though. We pride ourselves that no guest goes hungry."

I smiled. Werewolves and their obsession with food. "I'd love that. Anything you have would be welcome. My traveling partner doesn't eat, and he frequently forgets that I do."

"We have a full breakfast each morning at eight. It might tempt even your friend. Salmon, pan-fried halibut, smoked ham and bacon, omelets, the occasional duck or goose. There's always plenty."

I doubted any of that would temp an angel, but my stomach growled at the thought. "That's a whole lot of meat. You guys must have a pretty solid digestion," I mentioned casually.

"Carnivores," she confirmed. "Although we also have sourdough French toast, and fresh berries when in season. Just to be civilized, you know."

I nodded as we looked out the glass bay window into the rain-soaked gardens behind the house. Everything burst with color in spite of the gloomy weather. I liked it here. And I already liked this werewolf innkeeper. My tour guide led the way back to the front of the house and up a sweeping staircase to the third floor.

The room was adorable. A braided yarn rug covered the old pine floors, and the quilted bedspreads were appropriately themed with bears and other wildlife trotting across the squares. A sitting area, beside the king-sized bed, consisted of a round table, two cushioned armchairs, and a small couch.

"I'm Gina. Please let me know if you need anything." The woman placed my bags off to the side before slipping quietly out the door.

She'd barely been gone thirty seconds when the reality of my situation hit me. I was in a rainy, chilly city wedged between a deep-water channel, miles of ice, and a massive mountain range, waiting for an angel. Nothing to do but wait. Wait for Gregory to come back. Wait for Wyatt to call me with any info on Raim. Wait for something interesting to happen. Bored. I was so bored. Normally I'd explore my surroundings and stir up trouble, but I didn't want to call attention to the area and possibly scare off our killer.

I plopped down on the sofa and contemplated my options. Watch TV, nap, read the tourism brochures artfully fanned out on the coffee table, or . . .. I looked out the window at the town below, at the Gastineau Channel beyond. Who knows how long Gregory would be? I was reluctant to summon him — he could be in the middle of something important. Although, if he went off solo to capture this murderer, I was going to be royally pissed. I leafed through the brochures and finally threw my jacket back on and headed downstairs. I wasn't about to waste my time curled up under a quilt, no matter how fluffy and warm.

~19~

Gina was back at the desk in the front room, frowning over a stack of what appeared to be invoices. The werewolf typed a few things into the computer, then ran both hands over her face, sighing as she picked up another paper to scrutinize. I coughed lightly as I came into the room. Werewolves weren't easy to surprise, but this one seemed engrossed in the depressingly large stack of bills. She glanced up, her eyes wary as I approached.

"I'm not sure when my friend is going to get here, and, as nice as your place is, I'm going a bit crazy with boredom."

The werewolf's eyes widened. A bored demon was never a good thing. She had a valid reason to be concerned.

"Anyway, can you recommend something to do? I've read all the tour brochures. Zip line? Whale watching in the bay? Fly fishing?" Or perhaps I could cover City Hall with moose musk and sit back and watch the fun.

Gina took a deep breath. "Look. I've got nothing against demons, and you seem to be a bit more under control than ones I've come across in the past. Normally it's just the gate guardian up here, but I've heard through the pack that there's an enforcer sniffing around. As worried as I am for the safety of my inn, you're better off lying low here than causing trouble in town. If that enforcer guy catches wind of you, you're dead."

I couldn't believe she was warning me. Candy aside, most werewolves don't give a shit about what happens to us.

Vampires try to stay on our good side, to walk that thin line of alliance, but werewolves just like to keep their distance.

"I'm not sure your credit card will accept the charges posthumously," she added, dropping her head to sort through the stack of papers. "Can't have you dying and stiffing me on the room. And it's not like the angels are going to cover my losses."

"That enforcer sniffing around is the guy I'm here with. If you see him, please send him my way."

"Mm-hmm." Gina's face registered disbelief. "Well, you're not going to find any zip line or outdoor adventuring activities at this point. They all head out early in the morning."

"Gold rush museum?" I asked, desperate to get out and do something. I couldn't stay in this adorable little inn one more moment without setting it on fire or digging large holes in the plaster. "Whorehouse? Illegal gambling? Frat party with a rousing game of pong?"

She shook her head. I'm sure there were those activities in Juneau, and she was just reluctant to point me in their direction.

"There's a nice bar downtown. They serve the local beer, and sometimes the guys will have a pick up poker game."

She pulled out a little fold-out map of Juneau with cartoon pictures depicting popular businesses and key locations — such as the hospital and the office for hunting licenses. With a highlighter, the werewolf marked the streets from the inn to the Northern Lights Taproom.

"What's this one?" I pointed to a small graphic—a fish with "x's" on its eyes, holding a bottle with one fin. The tiny label said "Fjords Landing".

Every muscle in her body tensed. "No. You don't want to go there. Lots of religious people. They're probably holding a revival right now and singing hymns."

I bit back a smile. She didn't know demons very well if she thought that threat would steer us away. Imps, in particular, loved disrupting religious festivities. Still, I was trying to keep a low profile, and shouting out death metal tunes in the middle of Amazing Grace, or rasping pew benches into pointy, splinter-laden seats wouldn't keep my presence a secret. I sighed with regret and took the map, hoping the Northern Lights Taproom had a history of drunken bar fights.

It seemed only about ten blocks on the little map, and the rain had slowed to a fine mist, so I walked. I soon realized that ten blocks on the map was more like twenty in reality because most of the city was perched on a vertical slope. I was halfway there, sweating in the chill damp of the afternoon, when a number registering as "unknown" texted me.

Dear Sam, This is Nyalla sending you a text message, which Wyatt informs me all young humans do. He has given me this phone, and I am pleased to be contacting you and telling you how much I am enjoying your hospitality and your home. The men bringing pizza last night requested that I inquire when your sister will be returning. Also, you are out of beer. Yours sincerely, Nyalla.

For a moment I was stunned at the oddly formal, lengthy text, then my mind immediately jumped to the more important message. How the fuck was I out of beer? I'd had four cases of the stuff before I'd left. Had she become an alcoholic? Been hosting parties in my absence? Decided to water the plants with it?

"Hi, Sam. How is Alaska?" Nyalla's voice was cheerful over the phone, and she was clearly proud of her English. I didn't want there to be any misunderstandings, so I switched to Elvish.

"What happened to all the beer?" I had to use a phonetic Elvish version of the Dwarven word for the beverage, as elves did not brew or consume beer.

There was silence on the other end of the phone, and I got the feeling my abrupt words had hurt her. Damn it, I wasn't used to being so careful around someone. She'd been treated so poorly, spoken to so roughly during her life with the elves that I needed to think before I blurted something out.

"It's okay. I'm not mad or anything, I'm just wondering what the fuck — heck, I mean heck happened to all that beer?"

More silence, then a reproving voice said "Well, you did not leave me with enough. Not that it is your fault — you only expected to be gone one day. I tried to purchase more, but the identification card Wyatt made for me is not the right kind for purchasing alcoholic beverages."

I slapped a hand to my forehead. She was nineteen, and she'd tried to buy beer. It's a wonder Wyatt wasn't bailing her out of jail. It's a wonder I didn't have a warrant for my arrest for contributing to the delinquency of a minor. Four cases, for fuck sake!

"Nyalla, it's actually against the law for you to be consuming alcoholic beverages. I'm not exactly the law-abiding type, and I'm okay with you having the occasional beer, but please be discrete."

"But Amber drinks beer," she protested. "And it was not for me. I only had that one when we were by the pool before you left. How am I supposed to provide beer for others when you are not here and I am not allowed to purchase it?"

I knew it! She'd been hosting wild parties in my house the moment I left. They'd drank all my beer, probably raided my vodka stash, most likely ate all my hot wings too. I sputtered, trying to control my indignation enough to speak to the girl without scaring her half to death.

"What am I supposed to give Boomer with his food?" she continued. "I gave him the remaining amount for dinner tonight, and had none left for the horses."

All I could do was make incoherent noises into the phone for a few seconds. "Nyalla." I took a deep breath, trying to remain as calm as possible. "Boomer and the horses should not have beer. Wyatt takes care the horses when I'm gone and

Boomer . . . he takes care of himself." I wasn't about to go into gory details about Boomer's preferred diet.

"Are you sure?" Nyalla sounded skeptical, as if she thought I was pulling a prank on her. "They all seem to enjoy it."

I'll bet they did. Good thing the beer wasn't particularly high in alcohol, or that she'd been giving them the vodka instead.

"Positive. I'm not mad. It's okay, but please check stuff out before you do it next time."

"I did," she argued. "I looked it up on the internet. Many people give their animals alcohol. I saw the pictures."

I winced. Some of those pictures were probably me, back in the day, getting animals drunk to barf all over their owner's carpets and sofas. Nyalla wasn't a demon though.

"Check with Wyatt next time. Or Amber." Wait. Amber was half demon, maybe she shouldn't check with her. "Actually, just check with Wyatt."

"I will," the girl sounded hurt. "But I am trying to do these things on my own."

"I know, honey. Just hang tight. I'll be home soon. I miss you all."

"I miss you too, Sam."

I hung up and stared at the phone in disbelief. Here I was giving advice to a young girl, counseling her to *not* do all the impish things I loved to do. If I wasn't careful, I'd wind up on one of those after-school-special programs. Shoving the phone in my pocket, I walked into the taproom. I needed a drink.

~20~

I felt like I'd stepped back into an old western movie. Northern Lights Taproom was a three-story row house complete with balconies along the front and a creaky wooden porch. A front door with two swinging shutters would have completed the image, but even without, the inside matched the tone of the building's exterior. The wooden floors had been hand-hewn back in the early twentieth century and the gaps between the boards were filled with dust and debris collected throughout the last hundred years. Thick, sturdy round wood tables and straight-back chairs filled the vast room. Along the left, a bar spanned the length of the building, brass fittings accenting the heavily varnished, dark-stained oak top.

Outside, the sky was gray and heavy, but the lighting inside was so dim I needed to pause to allow my eyes to adjust. The taproom could probably accommodate nearly two hundred on the main floor, and another fifty along the edges of the second floor balcony encircling the room. I assumed the third floor was apartments, or some leased space, since the large staircase only led up one story. For a moment, I fantasized that during its early days, the upper floor had held rooms for all sorts of naughty activities with for-hire female companions.

There were four occupied tables, and two at the bar for a total of twelve in the place — embarrassingly vacant from the maximum capacity of the room. I sat at the bar and was promptly ignored by everyone. There was no staff to be seen, so, after ten minutes, I gave up and wandered behind the bar to survey the offerings. I'd tossed a bottle of vodka into the ice bin and grabbed a cold beer when I heard a door squeak and saw a youngish man emerge from a room behind the bar.

Damn. Busted helping myself to the booze. I stood awkwardly with a beer in one hand and a shot glass for my chilling vodka in another. The man stared at me with blank eyes.

"They said it was a self-service kind of establishment," I lied, motioning to the two guys at the bar. Neither one had tried to stop me, or said anything to deter me. Clearly they were accessories to the crime.

"Good," the bartender slurred. "If I'd a knowed youse didn't need me none, I wounna botered commin outta."

Wow. The guy was hammered. And it wasn't even lunchtime yet. I was starting to like Alaska a whole lot.

"Dude. What are you drinking? Sit down and I'll pour you one."

The man sat hard on a stool behind the bar, nearly sending it backward into the lower rail of hard liquor. Bottles rocked, clinking together. Thankfully none fell off. "My ssshift started at eight, cause of all these peoplesh ins shere off da cruise shipt."

His hand waved around, encompassing the huge room. I didn't see how twelve patrons were "all these people", but was willing to allow that he might have had a rush of customers earlier. I poured him a shot of cheap whiskey, figuring he was too far gone to waste the good stuff on and climbed over top of the bar, beer and shot glass in hand. This place was pretty dead. No wonder the guy drank.

"You guys play cards?" I asked the other two at the bar, making an attempt to look friendly and not like I'd try and cheat them out of every cent. They ignored me.

"Hey, is there a more happening place around here?" I asked the bartender. His head was beginning to loll around, his eyes fluttering shut briefly before he jerked awake and upright on the stool. Any moment he was going to fall face down on the floor. I foresaw stitches in his future.

"Fuck this," I said, downing my beer and reaching over the bar to grab the bottle of vodka out of the ice bin. "I'm going to head over to the revival at Fijords Landing. Maybe I'll spike the holy water."

Once outside, I pulled out my little map, cradling the bottle of vodka under my arm and peering up at the street signs. Three miles of walking and I found myself standing outside a ramshackle, one-story building that didn't quite look residential, but didn't quite look commercial. I'd had to practically climb up the side of a mountain and hack my way through a forest of bushes to get here. Nearly half my vodka was gone, but the sign beside the door clearly said Fijords Landing.

It didn't look like a church. Although I'd seen plenty of churches use a fish symbol as their logo, I'd never seen one with x's in his eyes holding a bottle with a fin. It didn't sound much like a church, either. I didn't hear any hymns. The only noise coming through the thin walls was laughing, shouting, and stamping of feet. I shrugged, thinking this must be a special kind of Alaskan church, and waltzed up the steps and through the front door.

"Is this the revival?" I shouted to be heard over the din. "Cause I'm here for some saving."

Silence crashed over the room and every pair of eyes turned to me. It was then I realized my mistake. This wasn't a church; it was a drinking establishment, and it was full to the brim with werewolves.

If I'd been in a biker bar in the lower forty-eight, I would have just held my energy tight inside and played the I'm-a-human-woman card, but no matter how good I was, I couldn't hide my smell. Every wolf in this place knew exactly what I was. Candy had told me long ago, demons were easy to pick out a mile upwind, and that weres tried to keep their distance.

This time there was no avoiding me as I'd crashed their gathering in the middle of the day.

There was that typical moment of assessment among predators, where the atmosphere grew thick with tension and we all calculated our odds and potential next moves. One or two I could take. Possibly a few more now that Gregory's protection allowed me to use demonic means to defend myself, but there had to have been over thirty wolves in this building, and every one of them was itching for a fight.

I love to scrap it up, but didn't really want to wind up dead and didn't want to draw unnecessary attention to my presence by fighting hard enough to *not* wind up dead. So I hesitated, tensed and ready to run away, hit one over the head with my half-empty vodka bottle, or possibly pull their fur while they chewed me to bits.

They hesitated, too, and it puzzled me. This amount of adrenaline in one room just needed a spark to kick off a berserker-style fight, and I was plenty of spark. I could tell they wanted to jump me and rip me limb from limb, but something held them back. An attractive woman with glossy, black hair stepped forward and placed a calming hand on the forearm of the largest wolf.

"Angels," she breathed out in warning.

I frowned, thinking they'd welcome the angels to come and haul my troublesome ass off. Then I realized their dilemma. There were thirty of them, and Candy had told me once that werewolves needed special license to gather in groups of ten or greater. I was willing to bet they did not have that license, and I knew the angels were ruthless. Especially when it came to enforcing the restrictive existence contract that the werewolves were forced to abide by.

"I won't tell if you don't." Not that I would be in any trouble if Gregory found me here, but it was best to let them think we both had a lot to lose.

The big guy snarled. "Or we just kill you and you don't tell. That way we don't worry about you blackmailing us."

The woman's hand on his arm tightened, and I was surprised to see him hesitate, turning to her for guidance. Candy aside, I always thought the werewolves were rather chauvinistic, with males in the lead positions. Seems I was wrong.

"A cornered fox does more than bare his teeth," she told him in a low voice. "We could kill her, but not before she brought notice. There has been an enforcer spotted nearby today."

Gregory. Seems news of his presence had spread quicker than gossip at the county fair. I wondered who had ratted him out? Gina at the inn had known he was around even though she hadn't seen him. The only people who had seen him were the airport and car rental humans, and they were too entranced to say anything. Whoever spread the rumor had noticed him pretty much upon arrival and sent out the word right away. But as much as I admired their intel network, that did nothing to diffuse the volatile situation I found myself in.

"Look, I don't want any trouble with the local pack. I thought this was a church revival and just came for some fun. I'll even leave my vodka, if it will make you happy."

The big male narrowed his eyes, then turned to the younger woman beside him.

"Who am I gonna tell?" I continued, trying to convince them not to kill me. "It's not like I'm cozy with any angels. I'm a demon, after all."

The woman gave a nearly unperceivable nod and slid her hand down the male wolf's arm to his hand.

"Get out," he snapped. "And take your vodka with you."

I spun about and dashed out the door, happy to be leaving with my alcohol and body intact. This town sucked. The inn was adorable, but boring. The taproom was boring. This place was interesting, but I wasn't so eager to face the terrible odds. There was nothing fun in Juneau. I contemplated heading into the woods to see if there was a bear somewhere I could wrestle. A bear I could handle, thirty werewolves, I couldn't.

I was so deep in my depression that I nearly walked into a pedestrian. When I looked up to apologize, I recognized the gate guardian from the airport. He looked agitated, and immediately my mind thought of the worst scenario.

"Where is my angel?" I demanded in a panic. "Is he okay?" I frantically felt through the red purple networked throughout me to see if I could somehow sense his emotions or his state of health. I could when he was near, but who knows where the fuck he'd gone.

Nisroc took a step backward in surprise. "The Ancient Revered One? I thought he was with you."

I breathed a sigh of relief, then moved on to the other potential emergency situation. "The demon, the one we're hunting, did he make it through the gate? Did he slip through?"

The guardian looked confused. "No. I was just up there. I've been up there since you left the airport. No one has gone through."

I had another moment of panic, worried that he'd left the gate unattended and even now the demon could be sneaking through. "Then what?" I shouted. "What has happened?"

Nisroc turned bright red and looked around us, as if someone might notice him talking with a very agitated imp. "Where is the Ancient Revered One? Was he with you this evening? When did he leave your side?"

I was going to have a stroke if this stupid angel didn't get to the point. "He left this morning when we got to the inn. Said he had something to do. I haven't seen him since. Is he in trouble? For fuck sake, tell me what's going on!"

He closed his eyes and breathed out. "So you didn't tell him about Fijords Landing."

"No." I shook my head. "Why the fuck would I tell him . . . oh."

It suddenly all made sense. He was protecting the werewolves, covering up for them. Here Gregory was proudly putting him forward as a protégé and Nisroc was warning the local werewolves of his presence so they could lock their misdeeds firmly in the closet. Not that any of this bothered me. I covered up Candy's misdeeds all the time. I hated the whole one-sided existence contract. Nephilim or not, the werewolves had as much right to an autonomous life as any other being on this planet.

The gate guardian turned to the side and motioned for me to walk with him. I fell in beside him, and we strolled for a bit in silence, the sun still fairly high on the horizon.

"I found them when we first began construction on the gate. Right after the other portal was destroyed. They didn't want a gate to Hel in their backyard. They knew it would bring angels to an area of the world they hadn't frequented before."

I looked around at the stunning landscape. It was sparsely populated, and demons liked to be where the humans were. "No demons, no angels," I commented.

He glanced over at my perceptive comment. "Exactly. Once the demons figured out the location of the new gate, all that would change. The werewolves made my life very difficult for a few decades. Some are especially talented."

I made a sympathetic noise. "So you made a deal? Overlook some infractions, give them an early alert, and they let you do your job?"

Nisroc sighed. "Not all of us are in favor of the restrictions placed upon these people. I'm merely a gate guardian, not even technically an angel in status. My opinion would carry no weight with the Ruling Council. Still, I do what I can to ease their lives, even if it means I may lose my wings."

I shuddered. "That's quite a price to pay. Are they worth it? These people you hardly even know?"

He halted and faced me again. "I've come to know them quite a bit over the last fifty years. And there are principals that are worth paying the ultimate price for. If I didn't, I'd be no better than a dem. . . an animal. I'd be no better than an animal."

I nodded, and walked forward, ignoring his slip. "There are an awful lot of werewolves here. The existence contact regulates how many are allowed to live in what areas and tends to put larger populations in urban settings. It's odd that so many are here in such a wild setting. Odd that they received permission."

He stiffened, and I heard him take a shaky breath. "There are not so many," he said hastily. "Some are visiting; they get permission for that."

As a member of the Ruling Council, I had a copy of the existence contract. It was somewhere in my house, all six thousand pages of it. I'd not read it, but I was willing to bet it allowed no more than five werewolves in Juneau and the surrounding area. And I'm sure it did not allow for that many visitors. I got the feeling those thirty werewolves in Fijords Landing were just the tip of the iceberg.

"Umm," I replied in a noncommittal tone.

"Iblis, I respectfully ask that you not mention this to the Ruling Council, or to the Ancient Revered One."

I let him squirm a bit. I might be somewhat reformed, but I was still a demon.

"So you're asking me to lie? Lie as a member of the Ruling Council, and lie to the angel I'm bound to?"

His distress was palatable. "Then blame it on me. Say I exceeded my authority and gave them permission. Please, I beg of you not to let the children suffer any more than they already have."

Gregory kept stuff from me all the time, and I did the same to him. I'd become rather fond of Candy, and sympathized with the plight of her people. Plus anything that might annoy the Ruling Council of Dickheads was all right in my book.

"I won't mention it to him, or to the Ruling Council. I'll keep their secret, and yours too."

Nisroc sagged in relief. "Thank you, Iblis. I owe you a great debt of gratitude."

~21~

Gina was uncharacteristically nervous at breakfast, her hand shaking a bit as she flipped French toast on the portable griddle and put out massive plates of meat and fish. I was one of seven guests. Two were human tourists cheerfully pouring over guidebooks and discussing their planned hike around the Mendenhall Glacier. The other four were werewolves, there for breakfast and supposedly to protect Gina from my infernal presence.

"Sorry," I murmured to her as I went up, plate in hand, for French toast.

Her head jerked up in surprise, eyes meeting mine. I knew the other werewolves were listening, with their stupidly acute hearing, but it didn't matter.

"I hope I didn't get you into trouble. If I'd known the place was some sort of Elks Club for werewolves, I wouldn't have burst in like that. A good friend of mine leads the pack back home. We jog all the time together, sometimes on four feet. I'm not your enemy."

She shook her head in disbelief. "And that angel friend of yours is going to show up at any minute. Right."

She plopped a generous helping of French toast on my plate and dismissed me with a wave of her spatula.

The other werewolves managed to devour a large quantity of food while sending me menacing looks and waving their knives threateningly in my direction. The human couple rose, thanking Gina for the marvelous breakfast before heading out for their adventure. She gave them a genuine smile and I could tell she enjoyed running this inn, even with the depressing stack of bills next to the computer on the front desk. I hoped these four werewolves were actually paying her for breakfast and not mooching on her hospitality. Thinking of her precarious finances, I glared back at them, raising the tension in the room considerably.

"Stop!" Gina scolded, smacking her spatula on the griddle and causing us all to jump. "Knock it off right now. I can't afford to have you all trashing my place."

The four wolves looked guiltily at their plates, practically licked clean, as Gina continued, waving the spatula at them for emphasis. I could see her as a school teacher, bringing her rowdy students into line with a wave of her ruler.

"You four, it's fifteen each for breakfast. Pay up and get out. I can guard my own den, and I'm willing to accept consequences for my actions if it comes to that."

I watched, shocked, as the four hulking men shuffled out of their seats and began counting out money.

"And you," she waved the spatula at me, and I looked at her, wide-eyed and respectful. "You get out of here and go cause trouble somewhere else. I don't want to see you back here until after lunch. Got it?"

"Yes ma'am," I replied, backing out of the room and heading upstairs to change.

The best way to explore a new place was on foot, and I was sorely out of shape. Candy and I hadn't had much time for our regular jogs, and I needed to re-build my stamina if I had any intention of keeping up with her once I returned to Maryland. I threw on workout clothes, tied on my running shoes, and headed out the door, hoping I could find something interesting in this town. Gregory was still MIA (where the fuck was he?), and I'd still had no news from Wyatt. Waiting was not a strong skill of mine, but a good jog might serve to pass the time.

About half an hour into my run, my phone rang.

"Hello," I wheezed at Wyatt. I could barely even manage that.

"Sam? You okay? You sound like you're dying."

I paused and tried to catch my breath. "I am. This fucking city is practically on the side of a cliff. I swear, less than a quarter mile of it is flat."

"Well, I've got news, but it's not exactly good."

Great. When was I going to get some good news?

"Paul Yong tried to get on a plane this morning around nine o'clock. He was buying a one-way ticket, had injuries and seemed very nervous, so they tried to detain him. He took off."

Crap. "Any idea where he took off to?"

Wyatt's voice was smug. "I thought you'd never ask. He caught the train to Vancouver. Small plane from Vancouver to Ketichikan. There he chartered a seaplane to Juneau. He's due to arrive in an hour."

Fuck! I hung up the phone, adrenaline spiking with the thought that I might miss my chance to nab this guy. Where had Gina said the seaplane base was? I looked at the sky, but no planes were visible, so I started jogging, only to halt and dial Wyatt back.

"Wait. You said he was injured? Injured how?" A demon should have been able to fix any injury. There had been blood around the hole in Seattle, and Gregory had said the demon had been injured at the gate. I'd just assumed it was due to his fight with the gate guardian. But he should have fixed himself by the time he got to the airport. It had been over twenty-four hours. Was he that low on raw energy that he couldn't repair injuries, even slowly?

"There's a video on YouTube from someone's cell phone. I'll send you the link. Evidently he made quite an impression at the airport. Dirty, torn clothing, limping from a bad gash to the right leg. He looks like someone beat the snot out of him too."

"Thanks, Sweetie. I gotta run. I think the seaplane port is on the other end of the city, by the cruise ship docks, so I gotta haul ass."

"Be careful, Sam. If this guy is hurt and desperate, he won't think twice about using lethal force on anyone, Iblis or not. He wasn't exactly sympathetic in the airport video."

I ran, cursing the rolling terrain even in this relatively flat section of town as I headed south through back streets, past pizza places, office buildings, and various outfitters. I turned toward the Channel, putting on a burst of speed as I saw a small plane on the horizon. By the time I'd made it to the port, I was on the verge of a heart attack. But I'd made it.

The Cessna landed like a water skipper on the surface of the inlet the pontoons barely creasing the surface. It darted past the port, turning about once it had landed and slowed sufficiently. I struggled to catch my breath, hunched over with the worst side stitch in the history of the world. This fucker better be on the plane or I was going to have to yield to the urge to blow something up.

There was only one guy on the plane except for the pilot, thankfully, since I hadn't had a chance to look at the YouTube video and didn't know what the human form Raim was using looked like. He must have changed clothing. Tan pants and shirt were wrinkled, but didn't seem like he'd been wearing them for an extended period or been fighting an angel in them. He walked down the dock, eyes darting around as if he expected an assassin at every signpost. He was clearly afraid, so I decided to take a cautious approach.

"Raim!" I shouted, waving at him from the parking lot at the end of the pier.

He jumped backward, his eyes narrowing.

"Dude! Bout time you got here. There's an awesome fish place right up on the corner. Let's grab some halibut and a cold one."

He glared at me, clearly undecided whether to walk forward, run for it, or launch an attack. I took his hesitance for a good sign.

"Your household is frantic. Another demon saw you almost get dusted, down in Seattle, and told them you were trying to get home. They asked me to help you out."

His body relaxed slightly, but he clearly didn't fully trust me or want to drop his guard entirely at this point.

"Who the fuck are you?" He snarled, making an odd movement with his head, as if trying to crack his neck.

"Az." I gave him one of my demon names, figuring he might recognize it.

His face remained wary, but he took a tentative step toward me. "How did you find me? How could you have known I was here?"

It was a valid point. "I'm the Iblis. There's a sword, and it's magical, and I can locate demons." It was total bullshit, but I'm not good at making stuff up on the fly.

"That's a crock of shit. You're an imp. There's no fucking way you're the Iblis. How did you find me?"

I sighed, and put on my most suffering expression. "You haven't exactly been stealthy. There's a YouTube video of you at the airport all over the fucking Internet, and all your credit card activity is easily traceable. Dude, it's the twenty-first century; you can't take a shit anymore without someone putting it on your credit report and tagging you on Facebook."

He took another step toward me. "I could take you with one claw tied behind my back. I guess if they wanted me dead, they would have sent something better than a piece-of-shit imp to take me out."

I was a little insulted, but if it helped him drop his guard, I'd go along with it. "I'm just supposed to help you out. That's all."

He began to walk purposefully toward me, still making that odd movement with his head. The wary look had been replaced with a sneer.

"I need you to get me home. Right now, before they find me and take me back." This demon was an arrogant ass. Less than five minutes and he was already ordering me around like I was part of his household.

"I *know*. You've come to the right place. This gate is virtually unguarded. Easy passage. Let's get you some food and a cold beer, then I'll help you get back home." I hoped he didn't ask me where exactly this gate was because I hadn't a fucking clue.

I caught my breath as Raim drew near and tried not to stare. He was a wreck. His clothes hung off a gaunt frame, his eyes were fierce in bloodshot whites, greasy hair stuck to his head, clotted in places from some unknown liquid. Worse was his neck. It was torn and bloody, as if he'd dug something from it. Thick red caked his skin from chin to below his shirt collar. As he approached, he jerked his head to the side, making a clawing movement with a hand toward the bloodied area. What the hell had happened to him? Neither Baphomet nor the angel had shown this much physical damage. Raim wasn't exactly a lightweight. Had the gate guardian done this to him? The humans in the airport? Had he burst into a bar with thirty werewolves?

"I want to go back to Hel. I don't have any fucking time for food. I need to go home right now."

"I know you do." I tried for a servile tone. "The gate's heavily guarded right now. We need to wait an hour. The guardian will head off for a lunch break, then we'll make a break for it. We might as well eat while we're waiting. You look like you haven't eaten in weeks."

"They didn't feed us," he snapped, as if it were my fault.

Who was "they"? There had been plenty of food in Baphomet's house, and the Fremont place registered to Raim had shown signs of food preparation in the not so distant past. I shook my head. If he was the devouring spirit, maybe he had snapped, as Gregory had said, and was hallucinating.

There was a little seafood place four blocks down. I maneuvered him in that direction, thinking we could talk. I wasn't fully convinced he was the murderer, the devouring spirit we were looking for. Just because he devoured, didn't automatically make him guilty. Plus, something wasn't right with this whole thing. He looked like he'd had the crap beat out of him, like he'd been half starved to death. Neither his house nor Baphomet's seemed to have seen any kind of battle. Baphomet hadn't had a mark on him, but Raim was in bad shape.

"Baphomet didn't feed you?" I thought they were partners, but maybe something had gone sour and Raim had been imprisoned. Maybe Baphomet had deserved his demise.

"No, you stupid fucking imp. Baphomet was starving too. If I'd known it was going to go down like this, I never would have done it. I never would have agreed to help. That asshole Baphomet, it was all his fault. I knew I shouldn't have trusted him. This fucking crap is all because of him."

Yeah, they all said that. When things turned to shit, it was always best to blame someone else, or claim you had no idea what you were doing. It didn't work very often, but playing the innocent participant sometimes paid off.

"Did you kill that angel they found down in Mexico?" I asked admiringly. Killing an angel was a big deal. He'd be a superstar back home, and playing to his ego might get me a bit of the truth. This was the money shot. If he admitted to it, then Gregory was right. If not, well, then I'd need to find out some way around this whole thing.

He puffed up slightly then glared, again clawing at his neck. "Of course I did! I had to. He was going to kill me. Everything was in such an uproar after I killed him that I was able to escape." His eyes narrowed, his mouth creasing to a bitter line. "Not that I can claim it or any status for it. You know . . . the manner of his death and all."

Yeah, devouring didn't carry the same cache as popping an angel's head off or drowning him in a river of blood. I nodded sympathetically and cast him another admiring glance.

"And all the demons found dead and drained . . .?" I left the question hanging.

He laughed. "They were a bunch of stupid Lows. Lows and imps. Not like they mattered. Not like anyone even noticed they were gone. Baphomet orchestrated the whole thing, but he clearly fucked it up. I mean, look at me!"

My heart sank. Somehow I'd hoped that Raim was an innocent victim. Not that I relished being back to square one with no suspects, but I had hoped to find less of a psychopath. Raim hadn't seemed to have snapped, but whatever his little project was with Baphomet, it involved thoughtlessly killing a slew of demons, and even an angel. He was strong enough to take down an angel and didn't care to reign in his devouring urges. How many had he devoured? I didn't even want to contemplate it.

The demon paused at the door of the eatery, his face resolute. "If the angels find me, they'll take me back. They'll kill me."

"Yeah," I agreed softly. "You devoured an angel. You're in a lot of shit."

"I'm in a lot of shit anyway," he said, his face grim. "They broke me. I'm damaged, dying. I'm broken and I can't fix myself. Maybe if I get home I'll be okay. I've got to get through that gate."

Unexpected sympathy lit through me. I pushed it away. Broken and dying didn't excuse what he'd done, or his callous attitude toward the deaths of at least four demons. I might feel sorry for his damaged state, but that didn't keep me from realizing what he'd become if he were allowed to return to

Hel. There was no way I was letting this guy through that gate. He'd killed countless demons, killed an angel, and killed Baphomet. He'd leave a swath of death in his wake throughout Hel then devour all creation. I'd buy him a sandwich, lead him out of town into the wilderness, supposedly toward the gate, and then fight him in an unpopulated area. I reached up to my hair and felt the comforting hum of the feather barrette holding my hair back. Raim was far more powerful than I was, and I'd been forbidden from devouring. He hadn't. I'd need an advantage to take him out, and my weapon, my symbol of office, was it. I'd lead him as far away as I could before I transformed the barrette into a lethal weapon to kill him, then shoot his head off. That way, no humans would get hurt in the crossfire. I had enough four-nine-five reports on my to-do list without adding more.

"Fix yourself and we'll grab a quick bite to eat." There was no way they'd let him in looking like a botched guillotine execution victim.

"I can't. I fucking told you — I'm broken." Raim's eyes became glassy and unfocused, and he snarled once more, clawing at himself.

Crap, this was bad. This guy was more unstable than I'd thought. I needed to get him out of the harbor area right now before he lost it and launched himself at me or some passing tourist.

"Okay, okay," I tried to calm him. "We'll head for the gate. I'm sure the guardian has left by now."

I led him across Franklin Street and into a densely wooded area. My map hadn't indicated any houses up here, and I hoped to get him a bit away from the populated area before I blew his head off.

"How are you broken?" Why couldn't he fix himself? And he seemed pretty mentally and emotionally unstable, even for a demon.

"I told you. They tried to kill me." He choked, his words coming out in pained gasps as he clawed at his neck. I stepped up the pace, moving as quickly up the steep terrain as I could.

"The angel?" I remembered the white stuff Althean had shot at me last summer. If Gregory hadn't been there to heal me, I would have died. Had the same thing happened to Raim? If so, no wonder he was so terribly injured.

"Two angels, and the others. We had a deal, but I should have known better. You can never trust an angel."

"A deal? With an angel?" The guy was clearly deranged. He was a devouring spirit who'd killed off a bunch of demons, managed to get the upper hand in a fight with an angel, and was now seriously, if not mortally, wounded and on the run. I was beginning to think "broken" extended to his memory and cognitive process.

"You have no fucking idea what kind of bad shit went down. We were betrayed, not that I ever trusted this wild scheme of Baphomet's. Did he make it home?"

What was he talking about? He'd killed Baphomet — devoured him. I turned around to face him, wondering if he was truly insane, or if there was something behind his ramblings.

Before I could inform him of his partner's demise and question him further, Raim halted, a look of pure fury and hate coming over his face.

"You bitch! You sold me out!"

I heard a familiar hiss behind me and jumped to the side as a streak of white energy flashed past, exploding a good-sized clump of trees and scrub brush. Raim dove out of the way and the blast blew a hole in the ground, sending the demon tumbling in a spray of dirt and pulverized wood. With a scream, the earth trembled around us. I felt oddly unbalanced, as if the very ground were crumbling to nothingness under my feet, then Gregory snatched me, turning me toward his chest. Hard bits of earth pelted my back and legs while I buried my face safely into the angel's polo shirt and shielded my head. The blast quickly subsided into silence, and I lifted my face to peer questioningly into Gregory's grim face.

Nearly twenty feet behind him was the dense forest, but as I turned my head, I saw a blasted clearing instead of foliage, and a hole where I'd been standing just seconds before. Unlike in Seattle, this hole was nearly fifty feet across and at least twenty feet deep.

"Where is he?" I demanded, twisting around to try and see. I didn't exactly want the angel to let me fall into the deep hole of dirt and rock, but neither of us could successfully mount either an attack or a defense intertwined in this position.

The angel moved backwards, and I realized his wings were visible. The decorative ones remained stationary, while the massive main wings beat silently, maintaining our hovering position as we cleared the edges of the hole. Gregory descended, gently setting me down before hiding his wings.

"He's gone. I couldn't tell if he teleported or used the cover of the blast to slip away."

"You let him get away?" I snarled. "I had him. *Had* him. Now we'll never find him again."

Gregory huffed, his hands roaming quickly over me to check for damage. "Sorry. I was more concerned about keeping you from being blasted into tiny particles, or devoured. I guess I should have left you to your fate and just worried about catching the murderer."

Last year he would have. And he wouldn't have thought twice about it. I was grateful for his quick actions, but if he hadn't shown up in the first place, they wouldn't have been needed.

"Where were you?" I pounded his chest with my fist. "You're gone for over a day, then come swooping in at exactly the wrong time. Where the fuck have you been?"

He glared down at me. "I had things to do — personal, private things that I'm not about to discuss. I got news last night that the killer had once again tried for the Seattle gate, had been seriously injured by one of my enforcers and had taken off."

"Personal, private things," I shouted at him. "You're off doing personal, private things with a killer on the loose? And you have the nerve to question my priorities."

His form shimmered in anger. "Yes. And I do question your priorities, as well as your motives. I come back, thinking you're just out hiking, and find you with him. Were you helping him? Were you going to hide him from me and sneak him through the gate?"

"I don't even know where the fucking gate is." By this point I was screaming at him, wanting desperately to punch a hole through the middle of his thick head. "I'm *not* helping him, I'm trying to catch him. I had him ready to come with me willingly. He thought his household sent me to help him get back home. I was trying to get him further away from the humans before I tried to take him out with my Iblis weapon. Now he'll never trust me again; I'll never be able to get near enough to him. You fucked this all up."

"You're ill-equipped to take out this demon, even with your sword, or shotgun, or whatever you're using it as now. Stay at the inn, handle the information gathering, and leave the rest to me."

"Fuck you!" I shouted. "I'm the Iblis. I killed Haagenti and a bunch of demons far above my level. I can certainly 'take out' this guy without any help from you."

"He devours," Gregory shouted back. "I don't want him to send you over the edge. I can't risk you losing control."

"I'm fine. I'm not going to go crazy and eat the universe."

The angel took several deep breaths, his anger fading. "You will, eventually. Hopefully in the very distant future. If I can help delay the process in any way, I will. And I really don't care whether you like it or not."

He vanished, leaving me sweaty beside what appeared to be a giant sinkhole at the edge of the woods. I knew what he meant, but I wasn't going to live my life counting the moments until I went over the brink. If it ever happened, fine. But until then, I was the Iblis; I was Az; I was Samantha Martin, and I wasn't going to go easily to could be my end.

~22~

I didn't see any reason to rush back to the hotel, especially since I needed to burn off some of my temper before I took it out on Gina's adorable B&B. So I explored Juneau, blending in with the cruise ship tourist crowd looking at whale-themed shot glasses and t-shirts, all made in China. Making my way north into the working part of the city, I discovered a little fish shop tucked away behind an insurance agency near the waterfront. The staff was more than happy to provide me with samples, and seemed oddly delighted by my willingness to try anything they had in its fresh, raw state. By the time I left, I had nearly five pounds of wrapped bundles under my arm. By the time I arrived back at the inn, at least one pound was already happily in my stomach.

"Do you have a fridge to store these in?" I asked Gina. She glanced at the labeled packages, pausing in surprise and lifting the nearly empty one closer to her nose to sniff.

"Seal? Not exactly the first choice of visitors to Alaska."

"You should try it. It's chewy and dipped in this greasy oil. I think it's one of my favorite things."

Her eyebrows nearly hit her hairline. "Most people cook it first."

That sounded good too, but at the rate I was going through it, I doubted there would be any left to cook.

"Demons." She said under her breath, as if we were completely beyond her comprehension.

I went to go upstairs when she halted me, an odd look on her face.

"There's an angel up there. He didn't seem like he was planning to lay in wait to kill you, but just in case, can you please not bleed on the quilt? It's handmade."

I paused, one foot hovering above the step, and stared at her in astonishment. She was warning me. Yeah, I know she was concerned about her quilts, but that wasn't her only motivation.

"He caught up with me in town. He's the guy I told you about, the one I came here with."

She shrugged, gathering up the packages of fish in her arms. "Suit yourself. I'll go ahead and charge your credit card, just in case."

I could hear Gregory in the bedroom talking on his phone when I came in. It was bizarre, how quickly he'd taken to human technology. I wondered if one day I'd come home to find him and Wyatt duking it out on the Xbox.

Taking my cue from him, I dialed Wyatt to give him the bad news. "He got away. I almost had him, but he blew a chunk out of a forest and managed to give us the slip. I don't know how we're going to find him now."

Wyatt made a sympathetic noise. "I can track his credit card usage, but there's a delay in posting — he could be long gone by the time you get there. If I freeze his accounts with a fraud, I can find out real-time, but it would tip him off."

"He's already tipped off." I looked toward Gregory. "I think we're probably going to have to stake out the gate up here. He's got nothing left. It's his last chance, and he's going to have to go for it."

"He'll be desperate, with nothing to lose," Wyatt warned. "Let Gregory deal with him. You just stay safe."

I felt a wave of irritation. Why was everyone suddenly wanting me to play it safe? When did an imp ever play it safe?

"I'll let you know what's going on," I promised. "Love you."

"Love you, too."

"Do you really?" an angel's voice said from behind me.

"Really what?" I turned to face him. Gregory always looked the same in his jeans and polo shirt, so far from the stereotypical angelic attire. He had his arms crossed at his chest, his expression unreadable.

"Do you really love Wyatt?"

It was one of the few times I could recall him calling Wyatt by his name, instead of toy, or some other derogative title.

"Yes. He's fun; he's kind and giving, honest and smart. He sees me for who I really am, and while he's not always thrilled with what he sees, he loves me anyway."

Gregory stood before me, staring with that inscrutable air about him.

"You need to let your Owned souls go, little Cockroach. It's twisted and sick to do such a thing to another being."

Where had this come from?

"Worse than devouring?" I teased.

He scowled. "I am very serious. When you were angels, you didn't do such things. Those souls trapped inside you hinder your positive evolution; they will be your downfall. You must let them go."

"We're not angels. We're demons. We Own, and some of us devour. I know you don't like it, but you didn't seem to have liked us much when we were angels up in Aaru either."

He winced, but ignored my barb. "I see your potential, the possibility of redemption for you if you change your path. It's true that Angels of Chaos were always different, always difficult to understand and appreciate, but they were still angels. You *are* still angels, somewhere deep inside. This, I know."

"Why are you always trying to redeem me?" I snapped. He'd hit a sore spot, something that had been chewing away at me for a long time. Why couldn't he come to care for me as the demon I was?

"Because that's the only thing that will keep you alive," he snapped back. "You stupid imp. Do you not think I see lines of possibility for you too? I see probable futures before you and I fear for you."

His omnipotence. But even an ancient angel wasn't infallible in predicting impending doom — mine or anyone's.

"You only have a thirty-percent accuracy," I reminded him. "Even with your super-duper special algorithms."

"I don't like the thirty percent I see," he hissed.

I shrugged in my best "whatever" attitude and whirled around to storm out of the room. I made it two steps before he grabbed my arm and spun me around against him.

"I'm calling in my favors," he told me between clenched teeth.

Fuck. He had quite a few.

"Twelve. Twelve favors for twelve souls."

I made a choked noise. He couldn't be serious?

"I'm very serious. And I get to pick which twelve souls."

I had two-hundred-and-twenty-eight Owned human souls. The loss of twelve wouldn't be a big deal, but I got the feeling this would go on until I had none left. Gregory was very good at racking up the favors, and I was forbidden from Owning any further humans. It might take a few decades, but eventually, he'd insist I free them all.

"You are such an asshole," I snarled. "I refuse to grant you this favor."

I knew I had to do it, that my little tantrum would do no good in the end. He knew it too from the smile that flitted across his face. He leaned down and put his forehead against mine, looking stern.

"Twelve souls."

I ground my teeth as he named them one at a time. Did he know every being I Owned? Was there anything this angel didn't know? With each name, I freed a soul, setting it loose to disburse wherever the dead go. At eleven he paused, and I waited.

"Samantha Martin."

I caught my breath, feeling tears spring to my eyes. Not her! Not the woman I'd been for so long. I searched, feeling her panic and anger as I struggled to pry her loose from my being.

"I can't."

He gripped my arms painfully, giving me a brief shake. "You must. I'm calling in a favor."

"No, I can't. She won't go. I don't . . . I don't really Own her."

This was embarrassing. Almost as bad as being a devouring spirit. What other failings would this angel discover about me? How could I possibly think we could have something between us? He was an angel, ancient and powerful. I was a lowly imp, a devouring spirit, and now this.

"You don't Own her?" he asked, confused.

"Not really." I squirmed. "It's kind of like devouring, only the soul isn't destroyed. It is assimilated. She's not fully assimilated, only partial."

"What are you talking about?"

"We made a deal. How do you think I masqueraded as a human for so long undetected? I had to *be* a human to do that. I gave her the life she really wanted, the life she felt she should have had, and she gave me her humanity."

"Partially. You said you didn't fully assimilate her, so you should be able to let her go."

"She won't go! I tried, and she won't leave. A willing partner must also agree to leave, or the deal continues."

He stared at me, dumbstruck.

"I tried. I know I must grant you the favor, but she does not recognize your authority over her contract with me."

He shook his head. "Fine. Let Antonio Scarletti go."

I released him, and breathed a sigh of relief. I'd need to be very careful in the future with my favors.

"I want you to promise me you will never Own your human toy. That you'll walk away from Wyatt and let him live his life in peace."

"Sorry dude, you're out of favors." The funny thing was, I'd already vowed that I would never Own Wyatt, and the sexual part of our relationship seemed to be maturing into something quite different from what I'd ever experienced before.

"Leave him alone." The hands tightened on my arms once more.

Asshole. He'd gotten me to give up twelve souls, be he wasn't going to dictate my relationships.

"Why do you care what I do with Wyatt? He put a bullet through your head. A really big fucking bullet, too. I would have thought you'd be happy to see him an Owned soul."

"It's wrong what you do to him. You know exactly where his weaknesses are, where he is lonely and empty. One day he'll look back and wish he'd been like his own kind, partnered with an equal, had children, had someone to grow old with."

I looked down at his hands, white knuckled on my biceps. He was right. I'd thought those same thoughts many times, but been too selfish to let Wyatt go. But now? Wyatt was free to make his own choices, whether it was to stay with me or choose someone else. I loved him. I'd always love him, no matter what he chose. And I knew he felt the same. Whether our relationship cooled, changed or deepened into something different, he'd always remain important to me as long as I lived.

"I swear to you that I will not Own him. I will not force him to remain with me. If he asks to leave, wants to end our relationship, I will allow him to do so."

I felt the weight of his stare. It pressed on me, urging me to more. Fuck him. Not doing it.

"Humans make such poor choices," he said softly. "Their lives are short, and their vision even shorter. Their souls are so intertwined with their physical beings that they act from emotion, from what they feel at the moment. Pain, euphoria, sadness. These things unduly influence them. It is not right to engage them in emotional relationships when they don't fully understand what they do."

"I love Wyatt. I'm not taking advantage of him. This isn't one-sided, this thing between us."

He continued to press, wanting more. We stood in silence, and I finally made myself look up and meet his eyes. They looked normal, human. Dark, dark eyes. They didn't command. They weren't forceful. They had sadness, a gentle pleading in them. Very gentle. As if he knew he was asking for so much more than he could ever expect me to give.

"Why do you care?" I asked, bewildered. "He's human. You don't even like him. You're not asking for this out of any concern for him."

The angel frowned. "All humans are important. Every one. It doesn't matter about my fallible personal feelings toward any one of them. They all deserve grace."

"Bullshit. Let me tell you a story about a girl, because there was no grace for her. When she was eight, Daddy left and never came back." I choked a bit, because I had pulled up all the feelings and emotions of Samantha Martin. They were powerful feelings.

"She continually attached herself to boys who would hurt her and abandon her because, if her love could be strong enough to make them stay, maybe her love was finally strong enough to bring her Daddy back. At sixteen, she was a drug addict runaway, dating a string of junkies until she finally caught the attention of a local two-bit dealer. He said he loved her, said he needed her, and she thought finally her love would save them both. Instead, he ran out of drugs and begged her to prostitute herself to his supplier for more. If she loved him, he argued, she'd help him, save him. She did it, but he left her there, and it wasn't just the supplier; it was him plus five dealers, and various junkies. They gang raped her, beat her, cut her, left her lying in blood and semen while they went out. She knew they'd do it again when they got back. And again, and again, until they killed her. She'd given up hope, lost her faith in everyone, including herself. She was going to die, alone, unloved, a failure at the one thing she'd needed to do in her life."

I paused, ensuring that the angel truly understood the agony this human girl had suffered, the sheer hopelessness of her life.

"That's where I found her. I promised her freedom, I promised her that the men that did this to her would die fearing her, I promised her an eternity where no one takes her love and gives pain in return.

"Did any angel notice her? Bother to do anything to help her? Relieve her suffering? Bring her some remembrance of past happiness?"

He stared at me, his dark eyes reflecting my pain, my outrage. Fucking angels with their talk of grace and redemption. It was easy for them to denigrate the sins of humanity but when did they ever bother to *help*?

"She was one of the fortunate ones. There are a million worse off than her, starving, diseased, tortured souls who have no hope left at all. Wyatt is happy, healthy, enjoying his life. Go save those millions. Go feed the hungry, smite the tyrants, cure AIDS. Leave Wyatt alone. Leave me and the things I love alone."

"We've interfered enough in the lives of humans; both angels and demons." His voice was soft, sad. "If I could turn back time, undo the things that were done, I would jump at the chance. I'd make different choices."

"Make different choices in regards to granting humans the gifts of Aaru, or in fighting the demon wars?" I asked.

He released my arms and traced a soft finger along my cheek. "Humans. For as much as I long to have my brother by my side again, I couldn't bear to think I might have never known you had things been different."

All the anger fell away from me. The most horrible event in his entire life, and yet he'd suffer through it to know me. It was a heady thought.

"I long for your redemption, little Cockroach, but I think it is I who has already been redeemed."

I leaned against him, touching him both with my physical and my spirit self. I knew he was attracted to me, that we were bound together, but this was sounding very much like a declaration of some sort.

"I love Wyatt. Love him enough to give him space and time to reconnect with his sisters and deal with all the supernatural shit he's faced this past year. I'll honor his decisions, but he's helped make me the demon I am today. And if you have any care for me, you'll acknowledge the part he has played in my life and trust that I'll respect his wishes."

The angel sighed, cupping my face in his hands. "Fair enough."

Then he kissed me. I was so shocked that I just stood there like a statue.

For a being that shunned physical sensation, he was a damned good kisser. Heat tore through me like a flare, consolidating in low, increasingly moist places as the first gentle touch of his lips grew demanding. His fingers skimmed along my jaw and down my neck; his tongue brushed mine, stinging me with sharp needles. Need spasmed through me, and my shock vanished, replaced with images of me splayed across the bed naked with his glorious tongue tasting me everywhere. I acted on that image, pulling my mouth away and arching my neck in invitation. Surprisingly, he went for it, nipping down the sensitive flesh with his pointed teeth, sweeping his hands down my arms to my waist and yanking me against him.

Oh my. I was thrilled to find he'd completely ignored my advice from the airport. When this angel fell, he evidently fell hard. And big. Was he really willing to take this all the way?

As he moved his mouth moved back up to claim my lips once again, his spirit self equally busy in its exploration of my personal energy. I was overloaded with sensations, physical and otherwise. My spirit leapt to his, merging as much as I dared while still remaining partially within my form.

"Slow down," he murmured, allowing me a moment for breath. "Patience."

I had no patience, especially with his spirit lighting me up, his lips on mine, his hands busy underneath my shirt, and the promise of more, pressing very firmly against my stomach. I felt the sharp bite of his teeth against my lower lip. Where the fuck had he learned all this? He continued, doing things with his mouth that I never would have imagined. If he kept this up much longer, I was going to come. Orgasm from kissing and angel fucking. I'd never be the same.

I saw a flash out of the corner of my eye.

"Ancient Revered One, I . . .." The words trailed off into a squeak.

Whoever that was, I was going to fucking kill him.

Gregory continued to kiss me for a few moments, giving me one last caress before lifting his head to look down at me, ignoring the gate guardian standing open-mouthed a few feet away.

"Make him go away," I whispered. Or let him stay. I really didn't care if he watched, I just wanted to continue on down this road we were on.

My angel chuckled and kissed the tip of my nose. "Patience. We have a killer to catch, and all of eternity to wallow in sin with each other."

I caught my breath at the implication. An eternity with him. . .and sin.

He drew me close, pressed against his chest with one hand buried in my hair, rubbing my scalp and smoothing the brown locks. I was breathless. I couldn't think, couldn't move. Visions of a future with him bloomed before me, lighting me up with sensation and emotion. My angel. Mine.

"Nisroc, stay clear of the gate. We'll handle this one."

The guardian nodded, shooting me a terrified look from the corner of his eyes before he disappeared.

Gregory gave me a brief, hard kiss, digging his hands deeper into my hair. "Dress for wilderness hiking, little Cockroach. The Juneau gate is at Devil's Paw."

~23~

Wilderness hiking, my ass. I'd packed for Seattle in summer, not tromping across an ice field. The best I could come up with was a plaid, flannel shirt that I'd borrowed from Gina to wear over my tank top, and jeans. I was going to fucking freeze. Stupid fucking Alaska. I should be home by the pool, in a bathing suit, with beer and hot wings, and a naked Wyatt rubbing oil on my body. Yeah.

But I wasn't. I was in Alaska, and I was going to be hiking through the Juneau ice fields to Devil's Paw. The serendipity of the name didn't escape me.

The easy method of getting there would have involved a helicopter dropping us off in the ice fields less than a half-day's hike to the mountain. Actually, the easy way would be to have Gregory just gate me there, right on top of the fucking mountain. Instead, we'd taken a helicopter up to Taku Inlet, then a boat along the river to Twin Glacier Lake. The river went deep through the mountains, all the way into Canada, but it would have put us too far south on a mountain range with nearly impassable vertical cliffs. Looking up at the impressive peaks ten miles away from our spot on the glacier, I longed to manifest wings and just fly there. I'll bet the views were spectacular from some of those heights.

"Come on, Cockroach. We've got a long hike."

Yeah, a twelve-hour hike. Devil's Paw was only fifteen or so miles as the crow flew, but we weren't flying, and depending on the condition of the ice field, our trip would be

227

agonizingly slow. I wasn't sure how Raim planned to get up there. At least I was fairly certain we were ahead of him.

"Why Devil's Paw?" I asked, struggling along the lumpy surface of the glacier. At its base, the ice ended in huge waves. I could clearly see both sides where the ice terminated and cedars lined the edges. Rocks protruded from the line of trees, splashed like paint with lichen patches. Juneau was a coastal rainforest with lush foliage, even at this northern latitude, but here, vegetation was more limited. Even so, in small sheltered areas that faced south, I could see a burst of color — heather and lupine in summer bloom. It was such an incongruity against the thick ice.

"You'll see." I could hear the gentle amusement in his voice. "I like Devil's Paw. It reminds me of Aaru in some ways."

Great. I fucking hated Aaru. Devil's Paw was the highest peak in the Juneau ice field area at 8584 feet. The ice field itself rose 4200 feet about the city of Juneau, making the impressive mountains in the distance seem deceptively mid-sized.

"This is just as stupid as the gate two and a half miles up in the air. It's on the top of a jagged mountain peak. Anyone who comes through it is going to face a three-thousand-foot drop, a treacherous climb down, then a frozen wilderness hike for days into Juneau."

"Exactly. When we made them, millions of years ago, all the gates were this remote. The landscape has changed as the humans have taken over the planet. Not many gates are as we originally designed."

I huffed beside him, out of breath. He didn't seem to have any problems hiking this rough terrain.

"I thought you made them so the elves could come back if they wanted to? No elf is going to want to step through a gate only to plunge to his or her death."

He looked back at me, a strange smile on his face. "They'll manage. Maybe you demons can post a warning sign, or provide climbing gear on your side of the gate."

I snorted and conserved further breath for climbing.

The twin bands of ice that descended to this lake fronted the massive Taku glacier, which backed against the enormous Juneau ice field. Sections of the ice had suffered summer melt — ablation. The snow covering had vanished, leaving the brownish-blue lumps of ice, and small pockets of brilliant royal-blue pools of water. Summer travel across the ice field would be hazardous. Snow bridges hid deep crevasses. Water flowed above and below the ice, creating areas of instability. Rock falls and avalanches were a reality, as were sudden storms and whiteout conditions. I really wanted to be on a beach in Aruba. Or by my pool. Or eating seal meat in Juneau.

A mile into our hike, I was ready to keel over. "Holy fuck," I gasped. "It's June, and there's ice and snow everywhere. At this rate, it's going to take us six months to get to that gate. Not that we need to hurry. Raim will never make it. He'll be frozen into the ice field, or up to his ears in snow."

Gregory plodded on ahead. I could tell he was slowing down to keep me from falling even further behind him.

"What were you guys thinking? Who the fuck puts a gate to Hel up here? What next? Are you going to shut down the one in Columbia Mall and stick it in Antarctica, twenty feet under the ice? Close Seattle and put it in the middle of an active volcano?"

Gregory paused at the top of the glacier, and I hustled to join him. Once there, I took a sharp breath as I looked over the vast stretch of white before me. Ice field was a gross understatement. The white went on forever, up and down as it met an equally white sky. Wisps of fog caressed the ground. In the distance, storm clouds hovered, trapped in the embrace of knife-like peaks. The only break in the field of white was the occasional jagged black rock rising like a monolith to the sky. I suddenly saw the comparison with Aaru. Cold and impersonal, a blank canvas of monochrome where any color or sound would be amplified. I shivered, feeling both the beauty and the moral ambiguity of nature at its core.

"This isn't going to work," Gregory's voice was grim. "It will take us days at this pace to get there. We'll have to fly."

"But he'll see us!" We'd stick out against the stark landscape, two huge objects moving at speed on a white background.

"The ice field is like a plateau with canyons, narrow valleys and crevasses — some of them wide. We can't see them from here, but they break out from the mountain range. If we fly down inside them, we'll be better hidden."

"How wide is wide?" I asked, thinking of his huge wingspan. "And I'm assuming they don't run the entire length of the range in a continuous fashion. We'll need to pop out and hop from one to another."

"It's that or spend days struggling with you through this to the gate. I don't know how fast this demon is traveling, and I want to ensure we arrive before him."

I looked out over the ice field, wishing we had cross-country skis, although, with the suncups covering the surface, skiing would have been near impossible. Flying was the quickest mode of travel. Fast and relatively safe — unless Raim spotted us and blasted us out of the air.

"Where's the nearest fissure?" I tried to gauge the timing, wondering how long we'd be exposed.

"There's one to the left of us, just past the glacier about a hundred feet. It starts to veer west after around five-thousand feet, so we'll need to come out of it and fly east, to one closer to the mountains."

"All righty then."

With a burst of energy, I created my wings, trying to keep to a thirty-foot or less wingspan. Gregory's were closer to fifty feet across, and he continued to have the two extra sets, much to my amusement. His feathers, cream and gray, brushed against the mottled rusty red membranes of my wings.

"Ready?"

I nodded and followed him as he took flight into the ice field, heading northeast and trying to remain as low to the ground as possible. I skimmed along, my feet barely off the surface of the ice, trying to stay near the angel. There were no thermals or updrafts to ride in this low altitude, and Gregory's massive wings beat their full range to keep him airborne. My lighter structure and wing design meant I had less trouble so low to the ground, but the air displacement cause by the angel's wings rocked me from side to side. I tried various positions, and finally had to fly slightly above him and to the rear. It put me at greater risk of being seen, but also afforded a magnificent view of the fifteen hundred square miles of the Juneau ice fields.

I squinted at the intense light reflected off the snow. Bands of jagged rocks broke the flat white ice, and a spider web of crevasses spread out from the mountain range to the east and parallel to the black spires. Ice hid under to deepening snow in the north west, covering the glacier formations with a deceptively sturdy surface. Looking out into the distance of the ice field, I couldn't see anything that might be another demon, but it was impossible to tell what was rock and what might be something else.

Gregory dropped over the edge of a fissure. I followed him down, amazed to see the depth and bold structure of the rocky walls. His wings brushed the sides of the canyon, and he angled them to avoid causing a landslide. My wing structure was far more maneuverable, and I delighted in darting around from side to side, up and down the narrowing opening. After a few hundred feet, we popped out from the tight confines and across a short stretch of ice before dipping back into a larger canyon further east. I caught my breath to see the bottom, far below with sides narrowed dramatically. A fall from the edge would be fatal.

After two miles, the ravine veered to the west, forcing us up and onto the ice. The fog had cleared, and the landscape was blinding in the sun. As we neared the mountains, the ice field began to buckle like a snowy blanket over a bed of giant golf balls before transforming into a smooth surface of snow. We'd reached higher elevations, but the safety of the snow was deceptive. Narrow crevasses, nearly sixty feet deep, scarred the ice field, and I knew many of them would be hidden under a fragile few feet of loose snow. I was glad for our as-the-crow-flies method of travel. Traversing that on foot would have been treacherous.

Almost immediately, this canyon began to veer west as the others had. Gregory pulled up to face me, his wings beating in strong tempo to hold him steady in mid-air. Snow ledges on the east side of the canyon crumbled under the buffeting wind of his wings and plunged down in a mini avalanche.

"There's one more. It's a good stretch ahead, and we won't be in long before we'll need to come out and fly over the surface the last leg to the mountains. Once we're there, we can shelter in the cliffs until we reach the summit."

Summit. Of course they'd put the darned gate right on top. Where else would they put it?

We rose onto the ice field, and flew the nearly two miles without incident. We were only in that crevasse for a few hundred feet before we began our mad mile and a half dash to the mountains. There was a bowl carved out of the snowy field, melted in a cone shape around a dark rock that had fallen in a landslide. We dipped down into it for a few hundred feet, and as we rose out of its shelter, I caught my breath at the brutal beauty before me. The mountain peaks were rough horns, narrow and sharp, formed long ago by glacier erosion. There was a harshness about them, an amoral power that impressed me beyond anything I'd ever seen on this planet. I knew at once why they'd named it Devil's Paw, and why

Gregory was so fond of it that he'd graced it with an angel's gate.

We angled left and flew into the mountain range, slowing down to maneuver the sharp twists and turns of the cliff faces. At times we burst back into sight of the ice field, but Gregory negotiated the mountain range like he'd been born here. Climbing, we headed toward a flat section midway up what I assume was Devil's Paw. Two knife-edged horns rose above the ledge, arêtes rising to the sky. As we swept in to land on the outcropping of rock and snow, I saw Raim — saw him right before he saw us.

I shrieked and plowed into Gregory, knocking him off the side of the mountain as Raim devoured the ledge under our feet. The angel grabbed me and twisted, catching the air with his wings and halting our descent while I pulled my own in tight so as to not hinder him. Circling a section of black rock, Gregory dumped me ten feet onto another ledge, where I landed hard on my rear, crumpling one wing uncomfortably in the process.

"Stay here. I'll take care of him. You. Stay. Here. And if the ground starts vanishing around you, fly as fast and as far as you can."

He flew away with unnatural speed before I could open my mouth to protest. Seriously? He seriously thought I was going to sit on my ass and do nothing? At the very least, I was going to watch him pummel Raim into oblivion. Thinking I might need it, I summoned my sword, the weapon that was the symbol of office. It didn't appear, either in sword, or shotgun form, so I dug my hand through my hair to see if it was somehow tangled there in the barrette shape I used to transport it. Gone. Had I left it back in the inn? It should come whenever I called, no matter where it was, but the thing was sentient and had a mind of its own when it came to my use of it.

I didn't have time to beg and plead the stupid weapon to come to me, so I leapt off the ledge, bare-handed, and flew back toward where we'd last seen Raim. He was still a good climb from the gate, and as far as I knew, he didn't have any raw energy left to sprout wings and fly there. He'd need to take the hard way up. I heard the blasts of battle as I quietly climbed a side section of the mountain, using my wings for balance and creating a set of claws to serve as crampons holding me to the cliff face. I first saw Raim, directly converting the matter around him to fuel his attack. It takes a lot of matter to produce enough energy to do any damage, and the mountain range was suffering. Huge sections vanished, enormous holes appeared in the ice field below. Careful to leave the ground beneath his feet intact, he had no problem dissolving any earth near the angel in an attempt to pitch him off the mountain.

Gregory shot a stream of pure white energy at the demon, and Raim did the impossible. He grabbed it and pulled, devouring and yanking the angel toward him. I screamed in rage, furious that anyone would dare attack Gregory and seek to devour *my* angel. Raim's hold faltered at my shout, and he turned to me.

As the demon's eyes met mine, time stood still. Raim's corporeal self was dissolving, and I could see the horrific mess that was his spirit being. He was injured, damaged beyond repair. He clearly had no raw energy reserves, and the damaged parts would keep him from holding or containing any. He was a dead demon walking. As his form dissolved, he'd be unable to recreate it, unable to fix any wounds. The devouring, the direct conversion of matter to energy was like a death rattle — a last ditch effort to survive, even though he surely knew his death would soon follow. I saw beneath the fading form to the mortal wounds that spread throughout his spirit self. I saw the fear and desperation in his eyes. And I saw a collar of shining silver wrapped tightly around his neck.

"You bitch. You angel-loving bitch."

It was true. I wouldn't allow him to hurt Gregory, and this demon hadn't long to live anyway. Reaching out, I snapped his connection to the angel and pulled.

Raim may have been facing an unavoidable death, but he wasn't going to go down easy. He, too was a devouring spirit, above me in power and skill. He was cornered, fearing for his life. With a high-pitched shriek, Raim frantically converted vast sections of the mountain range and glacier below, sending it all at me as a stream of energy. I absorbed it, storing it inside. Of course, his massive attack meant I was too busy converting and storing his blasts of energy to do anything offensive.

I felt Gregory continue to fight, to launch his white energy at the demon, but Raim continued to absorb it just as I was absorbing the blasts directed at me. The angel was clearly reluctant to bring out anything more lethal with the pair of us demons connected and struggling for the upper hand on the side of a cliff face.

Raim held steady, skillfully attacking both of us and succeeding in defending against the angel's strikes. It seemed a stalemate that would only be won by the being that managed to outlast the others. My money was on Gregory. Raim was on the edge of death, and although he was strong and desperate, if we kept the pressure on, he'd eventually buckle.

As we struggled, pulling through the connection we'd established with each other like a lethal game of tug-of-war, the demon suddenly lost all control. On the verge of death, he began to blindly discharge his raw energy in a swath of destruction, only Raim had no raw energy storage to discharge. I lost track of what he was devouring and converting, had no time to pay attention to whatever remained of the mountain ranges or glaciers. I couldn't even tell if the mountainside I clung to remained. All I could do was frantically absorb the energy. I went far beyond what I'd ever stored before, and began to feel strange, like I was floating in air with a misty body around me. The pain and discomfort vanished, and I blindly took everything the demon sent my way with an increasing nonchalance. I saw him fall to shaking knees, a hatred and fury in his eyes as he clawed desperately at the silver collar. His attack sputtered, and I reached out to him and pulled, devouring the other demon. Time slowed, and I saw his spirit self stretch and elongate, winding into me like thread on a spool.

Gone. This time not even his body remained. Strange. I'd never done that before. It didn't concern me, though. Nothing concerned me. I looked around, seeing with some vision beyond eyesight and was vaguely aware that nothing remained. Devil's Paw, the mountains surrounding it, the Juneau ice field. Everything was gone. The peaks above, ground below — it was no more. I wondered vaguely if there had been human villages nearby with casualties. But I didn't care. I cared about nothing. There was nothing in the world that mattered. It was all just an assortment of atoms that needed to be collected, combined, and eventually released.

I turned again, realizing that I was floating in the air, my body a blurred and indistinct form. An angel hovered nearby, his wings holding him aloft. A sword appeared in his hands, a long blade with angel wings curved into a guard at the hilt. It didn't matter. The angel, the sword, they were all just particles for me to condense within myself. *Condense, release, condense, release.* Like the beat of a heart.

The angel raised his sword and paused before lowering it.

"I can't," he said. His sword vanished, and he regarded me with acceptance and resignation.

His words resonated, spearing through the emotionless haze to something down deep inside me. Red purple burst to life within the confines of my spirit self, igniting a shred of consciousness. I thought of Devil's Paw, its twin horns rising to the sky in sharp ebony, like twisted fingers toward the heavens. I felt it all within me, the glory of the ice fields with their treacherous crevasses, the suncups, the deep, wide fissures, the harsh beauty of it all. I spread my arms and let the raw energy pour out of me in a wave of creation, instinctively recreating molecules and formations both above and below.

By the time I was done, I was sorely depleted and feeling rather nauseous as I stood on a ledge across from my angel. My physical form had returned to its solid state, minus the wings and clothing. I shivered, naked in the chill of the mountains, exhausted from the effort it took to create an entire section of the coastal mountains and glaciers.

"Did you see that?" I asked Gregory as I walked toward him, motioning with my hands to indicate the spires and snow around us. "I fucking rock."

He stared at me, astounded, but before I could comment further, my stomach seized and I spewed all over his feet, blacking out, facedown, on the rocky ledge.

~24~

At least I didn't feel cold, I thought as my mind fought its way up from the fog. I opened my eyes and saw that I was bundled up on a bed with a big blanket over me. The angel sat in a chair, facing me — an unreadable look on his face. This was the second time I'd been tucked in to sleep by an angel. What was next? Would he read me a bedtime story and bring me hot cocoa?

"I think I should be calling you Mighty Cockroach," he said, his voice tired. "That was some display out there."

"Yeah. I can projectile vomit with the best of them."

He laughed. The sound set my heart to racing. "It's a good thing I don't consume food or I'd be put off sushi for all eternity."

"Thanks for cleaning me up, by the way," I told him, noting that I was squeaky clean of puke. I also noticed that I had a huge polo shirt on that hung down past my knees. It seemed his clothing manufacturing skills were rather limited. Humph. And he had the nerve to criticize me.

"It was hard enough walking through town while carrying a partially naked, comatose woman, let alone one covered with half-digested bits of seal. Why seal? Of all the things to be eating; you must have gorged yourself silly on it."

"It's soooo good," I confessed, sitting up. Wincing, I felt around my head and found a lump on the back that seemed to be causing my splitting headache. I must have wacked myself when I passed out, although I had thought I went face

238

down. I also felt the feather-shaped barrette, my Sword of the Iblis. Fucker. I could have used it on the mountain, but at least it was handy now, pressed right against that massive lump on my skull.

A fleeting look of guilt crossed Gregory's face. "Sorry. I flew us off the summit and I accidently hit your head on some ice."

Yeah, accident. I'll bet he took advantage of my weakened state to get some licks in. Because he'd hardly have the courage to face me at full strength. I explored this fantasy a bit while rubbing the bump.

His expression grew serious. "I nearly killed you."

I continued to massage my head. "Nah, it's not that bad. Just a headache. Not like my brains are hanging out the back of my skull or anything."

Gregory walked closer, ignoring my deliberate attempt to change the topic and lighten things up.

"You were gone. Nothing of you remained except a great black hole of need in a semi-human shell. That thing on the mountain wasn't you anymore. I held the future of all life in my hands, and I chose death."

He was fretting over this; bothered that he'd made an irrational, emotional decision in the face of billions of years of careful actions in keeping with his convoluted morals and ethics. I, on the other hand, made these choices all the time — instinct over logic, throwing my future into the care of luck and fate. I knew it was a big deal to him, a life-changing moment, but to me it was business as usual.

"Next time you can kill me," I teased. "Don't worry, you'll get another chance to lop my head off."

In a flash I was off the bed, pinned against a wall. This was getting to be a habit with him. Any moment I expected him to start bashing me against the off-white plaster, but, instead, he gathered me in his arms, crushing the breath from my lungs.

"Stop it. I know there will be a next time, and I don't want to contemplate it." Pulling back, he looked down at me. "No more devouring, little Cockroach. No more. Let this future be a million years away, not next week."

I nodded, wincing as my head throbbed with the motion. "Will you heal me?" I could easily fix myself, but I wanted him to do it, to reestablish our connection after the dramatic events on the mountain.

A smile flitted across his face. "It will cost you a favor."

I hesitated. The loss of one soul for a kiss. It was a fair trade. "Done."

I released the soul he named, as he dipped his head and put his mouth on mine. The warm humming of his healing poured into me, and I held still, letting him determine the extent of physical sensation. My head now back to its usual pain-free state, I expected him to pull away and break contact, but, instead, he deepened the kiss, pressing me against the wall with his body and extending his spirit being to caress mine. I struggled to hold back, wanting to run my tongue around the inside of his mouth, to brush against the pointed, jagged teeth and the sharp hot needles in the tip of his tongue. I wanted so much more, but I held back. This was forbidden territory for him, and I knew it had to happen at his pace. We had time, a whole eternity to move this forward. I could practice a little patience for once in my life and let things progress as they may.

By the time he pulled away, I was struggling to breathe. He seemed completely unaffected, but I knew better. His spirit self still stroked mine, and I could feel his need. We stood there, silent, for a few minutes, savoring the closeness and connection before returning to the business at hand.

"He was dying," I told Gregory as he reluctantly stepped away from me and turned to sort through some papers on a desk. "Raim. There were huge parts of him missing. Even if he did get back to Hel, he didn't have long."

I don't know why I didn't tell him about the silver collar, the restraint marks on the other demons that hadn't been on the dead angel. Did it have something to do with Raim's injuries? Or was he just a devouring spirit and the collar was completely unrelated?

"Even so, he could have done enormous damage before his demise. Were you aware of what he'd done to the area surrounding us? He could have destroyed entire planets in the time he had left."

I'd been aware. In some tiny part of myself, I'd been aware. I just hadn't cared. Hadn't cared about anything.

Gregory looked up at me and shook his head. "What happened up there, little Cockroach? You were gone, ready to devour all of creation, but you stopped."

I shrugged. "I don't know. It was the strangest sensation. I was completely beyond any emotional response. I don't know what made me turn back."

He was still regarding me with a speculative look. "You could have just dumped all that raw energy and random particles all over the place, but you didn't. You rebuilt the entire ridge and ice field, right down to the molecule. You even repaired the rent in the atmosphere to a detail. Very precise, very careful work."

It was strange. I hadn't even known I could create on that scale, with that level of detail. And I'd done it all automatically, without any conscious thought.

"I'd love to be the hero here, but I honestly didn't have any burning desire to save the planet. I don't even recycle. It was like I was on auto-pilot or something."

Condense, release. Condense, release. Like the beat of a heart.

"Why?" he pressed, his eyes locked on mine. "You're a devouring spirit. Why would you restore that ruined landscape?"

I squirmed, not wanting to explore the answer to that particular question any further. "How could I allow a ridge named Devil's Paw to be destroyed? Total sacrilege. It would be like defiling my own temple. Besides, who the fuck knows where else you'd put that gate to Hel. Probably the moon or something."

He didn't look convinced, but thankfully he switched the topic. "You've killed the devouring spirit, repaired the major damage he'd done."

And now I'm going to Disneyland?

"And now you need to finish those four-nine-five reports."

My heart sank. Stupid fucking reports. I'd rather go to Disneyland.

"How did you get me the extension?" I wasn't sure I'd like the answer.

"I told the other members of the Ruling Council that I had some pressing business and would not have the time to punish you properly. They agreed, but insisted that the punishment be twice as long if you did not have the reports completed by the time I came to collect them."

Fuck. No, I really didn't like that answer. "And when are you coming to collect them," I asked, a feeling of dread lodged in my middle.

He smiled, his eyes dancing with anticipation. "Seventy-two hours. Which should be plenty of time."

For an angel, maybe. For an imp, no. I sighed, realizing I'd probably be spending nearly three days holed up in Aaru. Wyatt, hot wings, horseback rides would all have to wait.

He turned back to the desk. "I have your plane tickets. Hopefully you can enjoy yourself in Juneau today without turning the place on its head since the first flight I could get you was tomorrow morning. That plane will take you to Seattle, and you'll have a direct flight from there to Baltimore."

I frowned. "You're not coming with me?"

"No, I have some personal, private things to do right now."

What was it with the personal, private things all of a sudden? What the fuck was he so busy with?

"I booked you first class as a hopeful bribe that you won't get into too much trouble. Can you please try to not blow anything up, or cause a riot on the plane, or get arrested by airport security as a belligerent suspected terrorist? Or anything similar to that?"

I stared at him blankly, and he sighed at the futility of it all. "Okay, but I'm going to be too busy to swoop in and rescue you, so if you wind up in Guantanamo Bay or incinerated in a plane crash, you'll have to call Wyatt."

He paused and rifled awkwardly through the travel itinerary, obviously not wanting to meet my eyes. "I will see you soon. Get those reports done, and try to stay out of trouble." Not turning around to look at me or even say goodbye, he gated away.

I changed out of the ridiculously huge polo shirt and into more suitable clothing then went downstairs. Gina was in the dining room, setting the green, milk-glass settings on the lace tablecloth.

"I'll grab you some food from breakfast. You must be starving." she glanced up at me before darting off to, what I assumed, was the kitchen.

My stomach growled in response and I collapsed into the nearest chair.

"How long was I gone? It's late morning, I assume?" I asked as she came back in, arms laden with trays of meats and cheeses.

"You left yesterday morning and came back early this morning." She put a tray of food in front of me and sat in the chair to my left, scooting it close. "I wasn't sure what to think when that angel came banging through the front door with you half naked in his arms."

I nodded. "Thought he killed me, huh?" I mumbled, my mouth full of food.

The werewolf leaned toward me. "No, it was the sexiest thing I've ever seen. Like something on the cover of those novels Ahia is always reading."

I stared at her, food momentarily forgotten.

"I never thought I'd see the day. Never. I grew up in LA and have seen plenty of demons meet their end. I never thought I'd see an angel come through my door cradling one like she was the love of his life."

I cleared my throat, my mouth suddenly very dry. "It's weird, this thing we have between us."

Weird was a gross understatement. He was a total asshole, but he protected me, lied for me. He'd gone against his tightly held ethical principles for me. He should have killed me on that mountaintop, but he couldn't do it. He shouldn't be kissing me, but he had. Twice.

Gina watched me intently. "He's no lightweight. I thought it was just a random enforcer here, but he's one of the Ruling Council, one of the archangels. His opinion carries great weight."

I nodded. "I'm on the Ruling Council too. I represent the demons in the governance of . . . stuff." I wasn't sure how to describe what we did. Fuck, I didn't even understand what we did. Meetings, stacks of paperwork, debates over stupid finer points of nonsense.

"How do you weigh in on the werewolves? On the existence contract? Are you of the opinion we're Nephilim?"

This wolf didn't beat around the bush. She pushed a plate of salmon toward me, and I helped myself. As a demon, I was happy to take any bribes this lobbyist wanted to present me with.

"I'm the Iblis. I present the opposing viewpoint and shake things up. That's my role as the Adversary on the

Council. What I say or how I feel has no impact on the outcome. There's one of me, and six of them."

She nudged the slabs of applewood smoked bacon toward me. They were thick-cut and crispy, just how I liked them.

"But you have a powerful angel at your feet. That's two. And some people's two is bigger than other people's five."

I understood what she meant, but I wasn't sure Gregory would support me in this. His bending the rules might only extend to his direct dealings with me. He'd not had any compunction about opposing me on other issues.

"I think you're underestimating the forces at play in Aaru. It's a hotbed of Machiavellian intrigue." I snorted. "They call *us* demons. You should see the backstabbing that goes on in that place."

"But you. Can we count on your support? When issues come up affecting the werewolves, will you stand by our side?"

I hesitated. A vow was binding, and that was the direction she was clearly heading with this. Even so, I counted Candy as one of my best friends. She was devious, sneaky, and a brilliant planner. I'd do just about anything for that wolf. Still. . ..

"I can only vow to follow my own inclinations," I told her cautiously. "In the past, I have acted in support of the werewolf race, and there are many things in heaven I don't agree with. If I feel strongly about an issue regarding your kind, I won't hesitate to act on it. I can't give you any further promises than that."

She sighed, swapping out the empty plate of salmon with one stacked high with thinly sliced duck. "I left LA twenty years ago. I'd been petitioning to move to Montana for ten years, and realized my request would never be granted. The city is no place for a wolf. I was going crazy. I wasn't able to bond with my pack; I had no peace in my heart. I didn't belong there."

"You're illegal," I said softly. She nodded, brushing a quick hand over one eye.

"I couldn't go to the pack in Montana that I'd wanted to join. That's the first place the angels would have looked. So I came here and hid in the parklands north of Anchorage for a few years, before making my way down to the southern coastline."

She drew a deep, shaky breath, and I resisted the urge to put my hand on top of hers. "You were a lone wolf?"

"Yes. It's not a good thing — especially for us females. When I couldn't take it anymore, I made my presence known to the local pack. They nearly killed me. It wasn't just that I was a stray wolf, an outsider in their territory; it was the risk I brought to the pack. There are many here living off the radar, so to speak. If the angels came looking for me, a runaway, the whole pack would be in danger."

They were right. And as ruthless as it sounded, the good of the pack would outweigh the needs of one lone wolf, a stranger to them.

Gina looked up, a lopsided smile on her face. "A fifteen-year-old girl saved me. Can you believe it? She came forward and asked them to let me live, to bring me into the pack, and they did."

I stared at her, confused. Why would the pack jeopardize their entire group on the whim of a teenager? What sort of governance was that?

Gina's smile grew broader. "And, someday, if we're not cleansed from the face of the earth, you'll learn the secrets we keep."

With that, she stood up, collected the empty plates and vanished into the kitchen.

~25~

I left the inn and headed toward the waterfront, relishing the warm sun that shone on Juneau. The pockets of wild gates danced like prisms and the air shimmered. It was perfect. We'd won, defeated the murderer before he could cause damage on a massive scale. I'd recreated the stretch of ice field and coastal mountain range he'd destroyed, and it was a rare sunny day. But I still couldn't get the thought of that shining silver collar out of my mind.

"Hi babe." Wyatt's voice was a welcome sound through my phone. "I was getting worried."

"Sorry. It took us a while to get to the gate, then I passed out after the battle and didn't wake up until this morning."

"So? Bad guy dead, I take it, and you heading home soon?"

Bad guy. I frowned. Raim had been an arrogant jerk, but I still couldn't quite slap the label of bad guy on him. Behind all his nasty bravado, he'd seemed rather sympathetic, which was a ridiculous train of thought. He'd admitted to devouring demons. He'd devoured an angel. He'd eaten chunks of land in Seattle and by the seaplane base and destroyed miles of Alaska. He'd attacked both Gregory and I twice, with intent to kill. He *was* a bad guy. So why did I feel so guilty?

"My flight heads out in the morning." I hesitated, but of everyone I knew, Wyatt surely would understand. "I don't feel right about this, Wyatt. He admitted that he killed all those demons, wasn't at all remorseful about it. He admitted to killing the angel. He attacked us on the mountainside, was attempting to devour Gregory. If I hadn't killed him . . . well, he'd already destroyed miles of land. I think half the continent would have been lost before he died."

Wyatt's voice was soft and sympathetic. "Sounds like a bad guy to me. You did the right thing, Sam. If you hadn't killed him, so many more innocent people would have died."

He was right, but it still didn't sit well in my gut.

"Raim was injured, Wyatt. Mortally wounded, and I can't figure out why."

"Maybe the gate guardian in Seattle?" he suggested. "You said he went back and tried again to get through the gate. He looks pretty beat up in the airport video, and it looks recent, like he didn't have a chance to fix himself."

"He *couldn't* fix himself. It wasn't just injuries to his physical form, he was dying. Whatever happened to him seriously damaged his spirit self. He couldn't store energy, couldn't repair his form. When we caught up to him on the mountain, he was beginning to dissolve. He didn't have more than a few hours left before he would have come apart and died."

"What could do that?"

Another devouring spirit that didn't complete the job? "I've got no idea."

"Sam, sweetheart, I know you feel bad for this guy. There's no victory in winning against an injured and dying opponent, but he needed to be stopped. Think of how much worse things would have been had he gotten to Hel."

Very true. "I was lucky he was so damaged and weakened. If he'd been at full strength, he would have beaten me. My Iblis shotgun was nowhere to be found, so I had to fight him as another devouring spirit. His power levels were much higher than mine, and his skill was greater. Thankfully he didn't have enough power to back it up yesterday."

"I'm glad you're okay, Sam. I wish you were here."

"Me too. I'm going to try and forget about all this and have some fun in Juneau today. I'll call you when I change planes in Seattle."

"Sounds good. I'll be waiting here for you. And, Sam? You did good. I'm proud of you."

It warmed my heart to hear him say that. There was a time when I never thought he'd have praise for my actions again. "Love you, see you soon."

"Love you, too."

I did have fun in Juneau the rest of the day. I went whale watching on a small boat excursion where we saw a group of humpback whales arching their backs and flipping their tails above the water's surface as they dove for food. The scenery was beautiful, even more so from my point of view since my senses picked up the pouring streams of energy and power rushing like rivulets from a melting glacier into this realm from the tiny wild gates that rent the landscape. Harbor seals fought for a sunny spot on top of a channel buoy, and I contemplated changing my form and eating a couple of them before I left Alaska behind. Instead, I headed back to town to lunch on halibut and drink beer for the afternoon. Before I left, I made sure to order some salmon and halibut to be shipped fresh in a few weeks to my home. I tried, but they wouldn't ship me a live harbor seal. I did convince the owner to mislabel a few pounds of seal meat as cod and ship it to me with my order.

The next morning I was in my hotel room, packing to leave, when I heard a knock on the door. Gina held out a box. It was one of those refrigerated packs, and I wondered if they had gotten my fish shipment mixed up and sent it to the hotel instead of home, to Maryland.

"It's probably my halibut," I told her, pondering if I should eat it raw or try somehow to carry it on my flight. Wondering how long the ice packs would last through Seattle and across the continent, I opened the box and found a hand inside. A severed human hand.

"Doesn't look like halibut," she commented with admirable calm, her nose twitching as she peered into the box. "Looks like a mafia threat to me. Have you gotten on the wrong side of some godfather?"

I reached in to pick up the hand and saw the ring. On the middle finger was a gold ring surrounding an onyx stone inscribed with an X and an inverted triangle. I gasped and an emotion I'd never felt before flooded through me. I recognized that ring, and diving my personal energy into the flesh surrounding the ring, I realized that I recognized that hand. It was the mage. The mage who had attacked me back in Frederick on rent day.

"It's a ring of power," Gina commented. "Although I don't know exactly what it does."

"What? You recognize it?"

The werewolf looked a bit embarrassed. "Back in the seventies, you know. I was young and experimenting with some questionable metaphysical philosophies."

I stared at her blankly. "What does that have to do with the ring?"

She squirmed. "We did all kinds of crazy stuff. Sat in pyramids made of copper piping, smoked freeze-dried lettuce. I was reading a lot of books on alchemy and magic, and there was a sorcerer in one of them that had a ring like that."

This was turning into a shaggy dog story, and I couldn't figure out her point. "So. . .?"

"Nothing. The ring just looks the same. Basilius something. He never did get that alchemy thing to work, but there were suspicions it was all a front for something else."

I shook my head. None of that mattered. What did matter was that my angel had killed off the mage who'd threatened me, lopped off his hand and sent it in a box as a gift. I pulled it from the box and rooted around to see if there was anything else in there, like the note at the bottom.

Trust no one

Angelic script. Gregory's handwriting. He'd believed me. Gregory had believed me about the angel, the humans, and a mage attacking me downtown after rent day. He'd believed me, and he'd taken it upon himself to hunt down my attacker. How had he found the guy?

I admired my gift. For it really was a gift — a tribute. Gregory had delivered up my enemy to me, sent me a trophy. If that wasn't a declaration of his feelings, then I didn't know what was.

"This is the best present anyone has ever given me." I ran my fingers over the severed hand and felt his energy, the angel's energy like a signature, like a kiss. I wasn't sure how I was going to get the hand past airport security and home, but the ring I could keep as a symbol of an angel's love. I pulled it off the clammy, cold finger and shoved it onto my warm, live one. It was a bit loose, but I could fix that.

"All righty then," the werewolf said, eyeing the ring with a smirk. "I hope you've enjoyed your stay here with us in Juneau. Be sure to come back soon."

~26~

I should have been working on my four-nine-five reports as I flew into Seattle, but the only thing occupying my mind was the nagging sense that I was missing something. I could believe that Raim devoured Baphomet, but he'd not seemed to even know he was dead. If Raim didn't kill Baphomet, who had? And why would the devouring demon have jetted across the country to kill three demons on the east side of the U.S.? There were plenty of demons on the west coast to devour. Why was he down in Mexico, where he killed the angel? Raim said he had devoured the angel in self-defense. He'd obviously protect himself if he was under attack, but Gregory had said the angel wasn't one of his enforcers. Why was a random angel walking around among the humans, and what had gone on between him and Raim?

We were betrayed.

Raim's words surfaced. What in the fuck had he and Baphomet been up to? Baphomet's steward had said something about sending Lows and other demons over. I'd assumed they were for Raim to devour, but how would that have benefited the other demon? I didn't know what kind of scheme they'd been working, but I was beginning to think there was a third partner — a third partner who was conspicuously absent.

I stood before the gate to my connecting flight, staring at the arrivals and departures board in indecision. This wasn't my problem. The devouring spirit was dead, my name was free

Devil's Paw

and clear of any possible accusation in the angel's death, Gregory was sending me little love gifts, and Wyatt waited for me at the other end of this long flight. I had shit to do; four-nine-five reports to complete and horse manure to dump on the cars parked on Third Street. Let the angels deal with it. Let someone else deal with it.

"I need to change my flight," I told the woman at the gate counter. "Is there anything in . . . say four or five hours?"

I really wanted to go home, but I had a bad premonition that if I didn't keep digging and find out what was really going on between Raim, Baphomet, and this third demon, it would come back to bite me hard. And I was sick and tired of things biting me hard. So I scooped up my new tickets and headed out of the Seattle airport to rent a car for four hours. And I called Wyatt.

"Hey babe." I smiled to hear the warmth in his voice. "I've got a bottle of vodka in the freezer for tonight. Call me when your plane lands in Baltimore and I'll make sure I'm ready and waiting."

Damn. The idea of Wyatt 'ready and waiting' was causing all sorts of titillating, naughty thoughts to race through my head. Damn, damn, damn I wanted to go home. "Flight delay," I told him. "I'll probably be on the last flight in to BWI."

Wyatt laughed. "Hey, it's not like I go to bed at nine o'clock or anything. I'll wait. I miss you. I can't wait to see you."

A wave of longing hit me. "I miss you too. What are you doing with the girls tonight? Are they slumming it at your house while you spend the night with me?" I hoped so. I didn't want to have to worry about Nyalla hearing what I anticipated would be our exuberant love making.

"They're at Mom's."

Ugh. Wyatt's mom hated me. That I appeared to be an older, wealthy, cougar-type was bad enough, but add the fact

253

that I was Ha-satan into the mix and she was predestined to hate me.

"Amber told her Nyalla was a college friend from Finland who couldn't afford to go home for the summer. Mom welcomed her with open arms."

Well, at least someone got the open arm treatment. I grumbled under my breath, jealous that Nyalla was fitting in so well while I still struggled occasionally with humans. I missed the girls though. I'd been making plans to take them to a wine festival this weekend, and maybe hit up some of the museums. I wondered if Nyalla rode? I could put her on Piper and teach her. It would be fun.

"So, do you think you can go? We've hardly had any time together. We'll stay an extra day or two."

"Huh?" I'd been lost in daydreams of girlfriend time, of jogging with Candy, of falling asleep in Wyatt's arms.

"Vegas."

"Your horse?" I asked, confused.

"No, Las Vegas. Next week. The gaming company interview I told you about?"

Vegas. It had been a while. I was sure they'd forgotten by now. Either way, I'd need to play it safe and avoid Caesars Palace. "Sure. Sounds fun."

I thought about my call with Wyatt as I drove from the airport to the waterfront. I'd avoided telling him exactly why my arrival in Baltimore was delayed. He'd approve. Wyatt always loved a good mystery, was obsessed about tying up all the loose ends and working out the details. I wasn't sure why I kept it from him. This whole thing with Baphomet and the devouring spirit just seemed personal. Their project might have nothing to do with the deaths, but I wouldn't rest easy until I'd found out.

The gate guardian was cross-legged on the sidewalk, guitar case open for donations as he serenaded passerby with a suspiciously expensive guitar. An array of Chinese food containers sat beside him, the telltale stain of sweet and sour sauce along the edges. He sprang to his feet when he saw me, only to sit back down as I showed him my brand.

"Figures," he grumbled. "Nearly half a century you've managed to avoid me, and now you're off limits."

"Do you know I'm also the Iblis?" I squatted down next to him on the pavement.

He nodded. "What are you doing here? I thought you were out by the Baltimore gate."

"I'm investigating the deaths of some demons."

He looked shocked. I didn't blame him. Demons didn't usually give a crap about murders and deaths, even among their own.

"I need to ask you some questions about the demon you stopped from going through the gate — the devouring spirit."

A wary expression descended over his face. "I already spoke to my boss about that. He's got my report."

"He's dead, you know." His eyes grew wide, and I hastily clarified my statement. "The demon, I mean, not your boss."

"That's good news." He sighed in relief. "That guy almost killed me. I wasn't expecting that sort of thing — not a devouring spirit. Took me off guard. And then he came back a second time. If the boss hadn't posted one of his enforcers as a guard, I would have wound up a red smear on the pavement."

"The first time he came though, you said he was desperate? Injured? Do you remember what his injuries were? Anything he said?"

The gate guardian picked up one of the food containers and peered into it, a thoughtful expression on his face. "He wasn't saying anything coherent — just a lot of yelling and screaming. He tried to launch an energy attack, but it wouldn't come out. I don't know if he was completely depleted or if the part of him that transforms raw energy was damaged."

"His spirit self?"

He nibbled on a piece of pork, generously coated with thick red sauce. "Parts of him were missing." The guardian shuddered. "It was like he tried to eat himself. Or maybe someone else tried to eat him."

I'd also wondered if it was self-inflicted, but Raim hadn't seemed that insane to begin devouring his own spirit-self. Impossible as it sounded, could there be a third devouring spirit here, among the humans? Was it possibly this other partner of Raim's and Baphomet's?

"And the second time?"

The gate guardian paused, meeting my eyes. "That's the weird thing. He was just as damaged the second time. Not just the spirit-self injuries, I know those don't heal, I mean his flesh. He had scrapes and cuts, and his neck was a bloody mess. I don't understand why he didn't fix all that right away. Unless the fixing part of him was broken too."

Raim claimed it was. He'd said he couldn't repair his form, and I'd seen first hand the terrible injuries his spirit self had sustained. What had happened to him?

"So you didn't cause his injuries? The enforcer didn't?"

He shook his head. "He was that way when he got here."

Who, or what, could have caused that kind of damage? *We were betrayed.* Could it have been this third partner? If so, he packed one hell of a wallop to do that to Raim.

"Kept saying he needed to go home," the guardian continued, returning his attention to the Chinese food. "Kept saying that he'd be fine if he could just get back to Hel."

I frowned. His corporeal form was disintegrating. The only place he could exist without a physical form would be Aaru, which wasn't an option for him. How would returning to Hel do him any good?

"What about the collar?"

The guardian started, dropping a chunk from the chopsticks back into the container. "A collar? Like we use on bound demons up in Aaru? No one uses those anymore. No one binds demons anymore." He glanced at my arm. "Well, up until recently, anyway. I didn't notice a collar on him, but his neck was a bloody mess. Couldn't see anything past all the ooze and scabs."

I was striking out here. Searching my mind, I remembered Baphomet's steward's question to me.

"Have you been especially busy lately? Lots of demons, Lows even, attempting to cross?"

He squirmed, looking back down in the container. "No more than usual," he mumbled.

He lied.

"It's okay. I know you're busy. Hell, I've kept you busy myself over the last half-century or so. I know you guys lack resources, aren't given proper training or support. I know you all are just dumped here, and that asshole-angel doesn't want to hear excuses. I'm not going to rat you out, I just want to know if there have been a lot of demons lately. Perhaps ones that come and never go back?"

He squirmed even more, practically burying his face in the container. "No. Just the usual amount."

I looked down at the vast supply of sweet and sour sauce and thought about the gate guardian at home. How often had I bribed her away for lunch while Dar or another demon crossed the gates? Glancing over, I caught sight of the guitar. It was nice. Expensive.

"The Chinese food place is four blocks from here. I doubt they deliver to a homeless guy on a street corner."

His head jerked up, fearful eyes met mine. "I'm very quick. And an angel watches the gate for me while I'm gone."

An *angel*? Still, I doubted an angel watched it every time. There had to be some unattended moments. "One of the other enforcers?" I asked. "He's in this area?"

The guardian broke eye contact, his gaze darting around the streets as if he feared we'd be seen or overheard. "He's not an enforcer," he grudgingly admitted. "Sometimes angels slip over for other reasons. I'm not in a position to question — there are many things in Aaru beyond my level that I'm unaware of. I don't know who he is, but he's a nice guy. Friendly."

And kind enough to talk to a lowly gate guardian, to watch his post while he slips out for some coveted treats.

"When is the last time you saw him?" I wondered if this same angel was the one found dead in Mexico.

The gate guardian shot a guilty look at his containers of Chinese food. "I don't know. A couple weeks ago maybe?"

Again, he lied. The containers were still warm, condensation on the lids. They weren't a couple of weeks old, and from his nervous glance, he was covering for his friend.

Two angels working together, one dead and one still alive and busy? Or perhaps this one was just a nice guy doing a lonely gate guardian a favor?

Feeling like I'd reached a dead-end with this guy, I left. I wasn't done, though. There was more to this than a devouring spirit — I felt it in my bones. I needed to get to that North Lake house in Seattle, where Baphomet had been living, and search it top to bottom. And if I found something, I'd summon Gregory and spill everything to him. If I found anything, I'd enlist his help in finding out whoever was really behind these deaths.

~27~

I had a mere two hours to search Baphomet's house before I had to head back to the airport, so I started at the top and worked my way down. Unlike Raim's house, Baphomet's showed the careless clutter usually found in the places demons lived. Baphomet's was amplified by the fact that he held onto his properties through multiple trips, and he tended to collect things. He'd been the same back in Hel — hoarding tons of weaponry, artwork, and basically anything that sparkled. There must have been twenty boxes of cheap dime-store jewelry in his bedroom, several decades of shoe fashion lined the hallway, and there was a perplexing amount of craft supplies, neatly organized in plastic tubs in a spare bedroom. Unfortunately, nothing hinted at what Baphomet might have been doing that would have gotten him killed. I doubted it was plastic canvas Kleenex holders, or crochet prayer shawls.

After rooting through the kitchen and helping myself to a cold beer from a fridge full of spoiled food, I sat at a desk and began to go through Baphomet's paperwork. Demons don't like the human bill-paying song and dance, but most of us have learned to play enough by the rules so we don't get our electricity cut off. Hundreds of years ago, it was easy to steal, or threaten the locals into supplying the basic necessities for free. Giant corporations don't take well to threats of evisceration, though. Extortion letters wind up in the "loony" pile, ignored. If a demon shows up in person, they just call the cops to haul him off. Escalating only results in more force from the humans, which leads to either a prison stay or a mad dash to the gate to avoid the angels who sense the slew of law enforcement deaths by demonic energy and come running. I'd learned all this the hard way, and had grown to enjoy the fun things an imp could do in the human penal system.

Baphomet reluctantly paid his bills. There were some past-due notices for a variety of cell phone accounts under different names, and it seemed he was running a few credit card scams. Pushing the piles aside, I picked up a notebook and leafed through it. It was a log with groups of numbers, each noted with a date of arrival, shortly followed by another date of transfer. The batches had between three and five numbers, each unique. I flipped the page and saw that the following batch was marked "Low", and the one after "Level 2".

I frowned, a chill running through me. Here were the batches of demons that Baphomet's steward said he was sending over. No names, just numbers, as if their identities didn't matter, as if they were just cattle in a feedlot. The steward had said Baphomet had been requesting higher-level demons, so I assumed that was when he began to note their level designation on the log. They arrived as a batch, and were transferred as a batch — but transferred to whom?

I looked back, carefully going through each entry. It was standard paperwork, just as I would have done for transfer of property back in Hel. We're not the most organized creatures in the universe, but it pays to keep track of your stuff, especially if you tend to gamble or trade items back and forth. This log was the same format I would have used. It even showed the sigils of the demons enacting the exchange. Many transactions were strictly verbal with our vow as a binding contract, but in deals with multiple shipments and/or many items exchanging hands, it was best to put it all in writing and have appropriate sign-offs. I recognized Baphomet's mark. I didn't recognize the one next to his. Could it be Raim? It worked with our original theory — the one where Baphomet provided Raim with a supply of demons to devour. Maybe the whole thing was over and there was no mystery to solve.

Maybe there wasn't a third partner. Maybe Baphomet had been gathering demons to feed to Raim, but he'd snapped and killed them all before running off to Alaska.

Paging through the entries, I saw that the receiving signature was always the same, but occasionally Baphomet's was replaced with another. So there *was* a third partner! Had this guy been one of the bodies Gregory had found, or was he still out there?

I continued to flip through the notebook, although everything was blank beyond the first few pages. About to toss it aside, I noticed a bit of loose paper stuck between two sheets. Tugging it out, I unfolded a piece of parchment, similar to what we used for contracts back in Hel. It *was* a contract — one outlining a partnership between Baphomet and Raim for a period of seven years. The terms were rather vague. Raim was to assist in an unnamed project and provide "protection using special skills and any means necessary." Baphomet was more than capable of defending himself, so I wasn't quite sure why he thought having Raim as a bodyguard would afford him any advantage. In return for his services, Raim was to receive some monetary compensation, and a few magical items. Baphomet also had offered three of his household for a period of two centuries to serve Raim. It was a typical contract, nothing unusual in either content or terms.

I folded the contract to return it to the notebook and happened to glance at the signatures. There was Baphomet's familiar sigil, and one that must have been Raim's. I caught my breath and quickly flipped to the front pages of the log, to compare what I now knew to be Raim's sigil with the ones there. Sure enough, Raim had occasionally signed to transfer the demons in place of Baphomet. The sigil for the one receiving the demons was always the same, and the identity of that demon was a mystery. I'd never seen his sigil before; it could be anyone.

I sat back and pondered it all. Batches of Low and minimally skilled demons. Baphomet and Raim would have had to coordinate the shipment with their households, ensure the group got past the gate guardian then somehow manage to contain them until their transfer. So the demons weren't for Raim after all. They had all gone to someone else.

Who? And what the fuck did he want with a bunch of lower-level demons? How did any of this tie in with the dead angel, Baphomet, and the other demons, all devoured? Who had torn up Raim so badly? I had a feeling all my answers lay with this third partner. My finger traced over the sigil, and I felt the faint echo of his energy signature, just as unknown to me as the mark on the page.

I glanced at my phone for the time and realized I really needed to make a move if I wanted to make my flight home. All this would have to wait for later. I'd mull it over on the plane and run it by Wyatt in the morning over coffee. Sticking the log and contract in my bag, I headed for the door and nearly collided with a human as I threw it open. He had a piece of paper in one hand, suspended by a nail, and a hammer in the other.

"Is that an eviction notice?" I asked. I'd done this many times, but the ruled notebook paper he held in his hands didn't look like an official notice to vacate.

He shoved the paper at me, pocketing the nail and holding the hammer defensively. He'd not met my eyes; instead, he stared intently at my shoes. Shrugging, I read the paper and noted it was much the same as the ones I'd found on Baphomet's table. This one was even more explicit about the grisly eternity the reader would face.

"Do you live nearby?" It was a long shot, but I had an idea that this guy might have some information for me. Of course, getting a mentally ill person to voluntarily give information to a demon would be quite a feat.

He looked up in surprise, careful not to meet my eyes directly. "You're a different one. How many of you are there? This neighborhood is zoned single family, and you're violating the law having all these different demons live here."

"The demon that lived here is dead, and so is his friend. I'm the Iblis."

"Will you be living here?" His shoulders tensed, his mouth a tight line.

"No. I'll be leaving as soon as I gather some information. If you can tell me all you know about the demons and other beings who came and went to this house, I'll leave right now."

He hesitated, gripping the hammer with white knuckles.

"I will promise you, swear on all the souls I Own that there will be no further demons in this house, but I need to know some information. Otherwise I can't track down all the demons and others who've been here and ensure they keep away."

With his free hand, he opened a messenger bag draped across one shoulder and pointed to a stack of papers inside. "I have drawings and notes on all the nefarious goings-on in this house. You can't keep them, but I will let you look at them."

I ushered him inside and was surprised when he pulled a shiny bowl from his bag and plopped it on his head. "I know better than to enter the house of Satan unprepared, so don't even think of attacking me or stealing my soul. I have defenses that will melt you to a pool of liquid."

Okaaaay.

Still avoiding my eyes and clutching his hammer, the man pulled out the stack of papers and handed them to me. I recognized Baphomet, identified as the primary resident, and Raim, who had been labeled his infernal lover. They were decent drawings. The man had some talent.

"He'd been over nearly every night in the last six years, four months, and twenty six days," the man said, pointing at the drawing of Raim.

Other drawings showed a variety of demons, indicating that they had only been here a day or two at the most. I knew they were demons because the artist had added a pair of horns to each one and labeled them in capital letters. Two of them looked similar to the heads Gregory had brought to my house.

"They didn't stay long before the angel took them."

Ice ran through my veins. An *angel* took the demons?

"An angel? An angel came and took the other demons away?"

The man looked irritated. "Yes. I'd hoped at first he was here to kill them all, cleanse this home of their presence, but more demons kept arriving. I don't think he was a particularly righteous angel."

Demons weren't the only ones who used sigils. Angels did too. We were all angels once, and things like our language, our naming conventions, and our signatures had remained virtually unaltered for the nearly three million years, since the split. I didn't know every demon's sigil, but the one on the page could just as easily have been an angel. Impossible as it sounded, I believed the third partner in Baphomet and Raim's scheme had been an angel. He'd been the one who had received delivery of the demons. But was this angel still alive, or had he been the one found dead and drained in Mexico.

Angels. There were too many unexplained angels running around in this scenario. I'd had one chase me with intent to kill, one helpfully watched the Seattle gate while the guardian ran off for dinner. Were they all one and the same? Was I dealing with two or three, or more of the things? Why would Baphomet have cooperated with an angel, and what in the world was an angel doing that he needed a steady stream of demons to kill?

"Do you have a picture of the angel?"

He nodded, paging through the papers to pull one out of the stack. "There were two angels. One I only saw about a week ago. The one who usually came to pick up the demons was by this past Monday. He left with the guy who lived here and his buddy. I haven't seen any of them since."

Two angels. Well that answered a pressing question. One, perhaps, dead in Mexico, and another at large? I squinted at the pictures. They weren't drawn as well as the demon ones, and I wasn't able to determine if either of the angels was the one who'd attacked me.

"Do you have any idea where they were taking the demons?"

He shook his head. "I didn't care where they went as long as they didn't come back."

"They went willingly with this angel?" The house didn't appear to have seen any huge fights. Lows didn't have much power, but there would have been at least some scorch marks on the walls.

"Yes. With the glowing necklaces, they behave. Even the two main ones."

I caught my breath, remembering the silver collar around Raim's bloody neck. "Baphomet and Raim were led away by an angel? With glowing necklaces on?"

He nodded happily, the metal bowl sliding around on top of his head. "Yes. I was glad to see them go. I don't like angels much, but at least he finally got all of the devils out of my neighborhood."

I felt a headache coming on. What the heck had Baphomet been doing? Whatever it was, it clearly hadn't ended well for either him or Raim.

"Thanks." I handed the papers back to the man and watched him stuff them into his bag. "As promised, I swear to you that no other demons will be residing in or visiting this house."

"Not that wizard guy either," he said over his shoulder as he made his way to the door. "He spelled me so I get horrible diarrhea if I eat dairy products. Then he threatened me. Told me he'd lock me up on Oak Island with the others if I didn't stay away."

"Wait! What wizard?" I ran after the man who was halfway down the porch steps by the time I'd caught up.

He paused and pulled a paper out of his messenger bag. "This one."

A human. Well, a human with an absurd pointy hat. From the picture, he looked to be about fifty with dark skin and a black, neatly trimmed, curly beard. He was bald around the edges of the hat, and his eyes looked fierce as they shot little flames across the page. Clearly the man had taken some artistic liberties with this one. Either way, I recognized a human depiction of a mage when I saw one. Demons making deals with angels. Angels and mages.

A human, an angel and a mage walked into a bar. . ..

That last demon had been found practically in my back yard, and I'd been chased soon thereafter by a gang of humans, a mage and an angel, all working together. Suddenly major pieces began to click. I wondered if all the devoured demons had been offered the same "comfortable two-week-long death" that I had been. Either way, I had a feeling I might need to delay my flight yet again. Maybe there was more to be found in Raim's house.

"Do you know anything about a house in Fremont? This other demon, the 'lover' of the one who lived here, had a place in Fremont."

He gave me a wary look, fingering the metal bowl still on his head before putting the picture away and pulling out a scrap of paper. He wrote a name and an address on it and thrust it toward me.

"Here. Wayne keeps track of all the evil in the Fremont area. This is where you can find him. If there's a demon in Fremont, he'll know about it. And he might talk to you if you promise to get rid of the thing for him."

I watched him walk down the sidewalk and across the street toward the floating houses, before I turned to lock the door. Outside of Baphomet's log, there was nothing here that could help me further. With any luck this Wayne guy had seen who'd been coming and going at Raim's house. I hoped his information would provide more clarity.

~28~

Demons, mages, and angels working together? I mused over the concept as I drove my little rental car toward Fremont. It fit together, but I couldn't see what an angel or a mage would get out of that scheme. Why would they want a bunch of demons?

I pulled up to the crossroads in Freemont that had been written on my slip of paper and looked around for the kebab place. I was only two blocks from Raim's house. If this Wayne guy was half the neighborhood watch the other guy had been, I'd be ecstatic. Of course, he'd have to actually agree to speak to me.

I walked behind the kebab place and peered in the spot between the dumpster and a large cardboard box. "Are you Wayne?" I asked the man huddled there. He stared at me, his eyes huge, before spitting and pelting me with stale corn chips. I backed away, frantically swatting.

"I banish you to whence you came, foul demon! Return to your infernal home."

"That would be Maryland," I replied, shielding my face from further attack. "And I'd be happy to return there if you'd only answer a few questions I have about a nearby house and the demon who lived there."

"He's gone!" Wayne shouted. I felt more chips bounce off my arm. They stung with their sharp points and salt-encrusted edges. "I hope he's dead. I hope he never walks the earth again. You and your kind belong in hell."

"Yes. He's dead. Would you stop with the fucking corn chips for a moment and let me talk. I'm not going to hurt you. I just want to find out some information about who came and went in the demon's house before he left."

I peeked over my arm and saw a young man, beard practically covering his entire face, glaring at me from beside the cardboard box. Brown eyes bored into mine from a tanned background. He fingered another chip menacingly.

"I vow on all the souls I Own that the demon is dead. I promise you no other demons will be coming to that house as long as I get the information I need."

He hesitated, his beard bouncing as he chewed on a lip. "All right. But you stand over there, by the fence. Come any closer and I'm going to be forced to use my magic."

I tried to look properly intimidated as I backed up until my rear end hit the chain-link fence. He crawled out from his hidey-hole, watching me the entire time.

"That demon wasn't there all too much." He waved a chip at me. "He'd come in every few days then leave again. Haven't seen him for weeks. Another demon went there twice in the last year to see him, but never stayed long. They usually left together."

I nodded. "There was a dead demon found there a few days ago. Do you know what happened? Was there a fight?"

He barked out a short laugh, showing a general lack of front teeth. "Nah. That was the visitor demon. Some angel dumped his body and took off."

I stared, my mouth hanging open. An angel dumped Baphomet's body in Raim's house? What the fuck was going on? Had the angel killed Baphomet? I'd originally thought Raim was lying or delusional when he'd claimed to think Baphomet was still alive, now I wondered if he wasn't telling the truth. A sick feeling filled me — had I killed the wrong guy? Raim was an asshole, and he'd admitted to killing the one angel, and having a part in the death of the other demons, but

I was beginning to think there was an angel behind this whole thing.

We were betrayed.

Raim and Baphomet were taken out by the angel or angels they'd worked with. Baphomet was killed, and Raim seriously wounded before he managed to kill the one angel and get away. I'd killed him. He'd be a victim — although a rather un-innocent one — and I'd killed him. Guilt washed over me. I needed to find a way to make this right. But how? I had no idea where to find this other angel, or even who the fuck he was. And I wasn't sure I could involve Gregory at this point. Everything I had was too flimsy. He'd shit a brick to find out angels were running some kind of scheme in partnership with demons, but I needed to have more proof before I went to him.

"Do you have any idea what this angel looked like?"

He shook his head. "Blond, kinda shimmery. You, know — an angel."

Great. I thanked Wayne for his time and headed back to my car. I'd just need to puzzle this all out from home. All the major players were dead, and I doubted this guy would make a move anytime soon. Plenty of time to figure it out before he managed to obtain other demon partners, if that was his goal. Everything made sense except for the motive. Why would an angel want a bunch of demons? And why would he be working with demons and a mage?

If I hustled, I could still make my flight into Baltimore. I picked up the pace and headed toward my rental, answering my cell phone as it rang. A high-pitched shriek filled my ear, oddly echoed by an equally high-pitched shriek from the background.

"Sam! Sam! Get over here! There's a demon outside my mother's house trying to get in!"

Amber. My adrenaline spiked, remembering all the demon hit-men Haagenti had sent to Wyatt's house in the not-so-distant past. Shit! Amber was in Maryland at her mother's house for the evening with Nyalla. They were under attack, and here I was, on the opposite end of the country and completely unable to help.

"Call Wyatt," I shouted to be heard over the screaming. "Have him come shoot it."

The screaming increased, reaching a note that I'm certain only dogs could hear. "No, Mom! Don't let him in! Don't let him in!"

I paced, the girls' panic sending my own into overdrive. Wyatt's sisters, my girls, mine! They were helpless, facing a demon attacker, and I could do nothing to help.

"Blast it with your lightning. Aim for the head."

I heard a distant female voice calling Amber and entreating her to come down for her date with this Irix man.

Irix. Holy shit on a stick; I'd forgotten to tell Amber about the Incubus that Leethu was sending over.

"Wait, wait," I shouted. "Don't shoot him."

Too late. I heard a riot of thumping sounds that could only be Amber's foosteps on the stairs, then a quick intake of breath.

"Wow, that is truly the most attractive demon I have ever seen." Nyalla's voice was breathless on Amber's cell phone. The half-elf must have shoved the phone at her before charging down the steps.

"Tell her not to shoot. Don't shoot." I was shouting, but all I could hear from the phone was a sizzle of electricity, a yelp, and a masculine curse followed by more high-pitched screaming.

"What's happened?" I asked Nyalla. "Is Amber okay?"

"Oh my. He grabbed her by the wrists and has her across his shoulders, pinning her knees to his chest. She is kicking him in the side, but cannot seem to produce more lightning.

The demon is looking . . . irritated. Should I do something to help?"

"No, just stay out of the way and tell Amber to calm down. It's all a misunderstanding. Her demon sire, Leethu, sent Irix over to give her some training."

"Amber! Sam is telling that you must lower your temper and submit to lessons."

In the background I heard Amber's shriek of rage, followed by a chain of imaginative curse words. There was a laugh then a deep male voice.

"You may look like an elf, but you've got a mouth on you worse than the oldest demon." I heard him catch his breath in a pained grunt. "Kick me there again, girl, and I'll chain you to the wall and turn my pheromones up to eleven."

Shit; although, the proposed idea was somewhat turning me on. "Nyalla, what is going on? Can't you get Amber to calm down? Where the fuck is her mother?"

"Mrs. Lowry looks rather like she wishes she were the one across the demon's shoulders." The girl's voice was breathy and light. "You know, I think I might like to be the one across this demon's shoulders, too."

Irix's incubus skills were clearly working on Nyalla and the girls' mother, but would they work on Amber? I personally felt the pull of attraction from sex demons, but elves seemed to be resistant, and I could never tell if succubi or incubi attraction was as powerful toward each other.

"Nyalla? Can you get close enough to hold the phone up to Amber? So I can talk to her?"

"Gladly," the girl replied, her words beginning to slur.

"Amber? It's probably a little late for introductions, but this is Irix. Leethu sent him over to help you with the problem we discussed. He's an incubus and can be trusted to keep your secret. He's going to train you to control your succubus side."

"I'm not having sex with this asshole," Amber snarled. "The only thing I want to do to him is place his head in a blender and turn it on puree."

I smiled a bit in pride at this rare glimpse of Amber's demon half. Still, in spite of her bravado, the words seemed more like an offer of foreplay than a threat of execution.

"Maybe he can give you a few pointers from a safe distance across the room then," I suggested. "This may be the only chance you have to get some assistance from a sex demon. I'm not really qualified to help you with this sort of thing. Give the guy an hour, and send him packing if you feel like it. Okay?"

"Okay," Amber said grudgingly. "But I'm not letting him touch me."

"I'm already touching you," the male voice replied, full of amusement.

I heard a shuffle, like a heavy object being shifted, then a gasp from Amber, followed by the noise of the cell phone transferring hands.

"Iblis, if I did not owe Leethu a significant favor, I'd punish this little half breed and go straight back to Hel. But I'm willing this once to overlook being shot with a bolt of lightning and kicked in the balls."

"Thank you, Irix. I appreciate your restraint," I told him over the noise of Amber's renewed protests.

I heard him hand the phone off, then another shuffling noise.

"Sam? Will you still be coming home tonight?" Nyalla's voice was cheerful in spite of her sister's continued outburst of temper.

"Yes, I'm heading to the airport now." I could hear Amber in the background vowing that she would rather slit her own throat than say "please" to an arrogant Neanderthal of a demon. Irix was offering to procure a knife.

"Good. We need you home, Sam. And I miss you."

"I miss you too, Nyalla." I really wanted to stay on the line and hear what was shaping up to be a wrestling match of epic proportions, but I needed to hustle up or I'd miss my plane.

~29~

I headed though the airport toward my gate and debated whether I should summon Gregory now and let him know what I'd found out or wait until I got home. I wasn't sure what the fuck I *had* found out. A bunch of demons, two angels, and a mage had been coming and going in Baphomet's house, as told to me by a mentally ill neighbor? A gate guardian who snuck off for Chinese food and let an angel watch the gate for him? That I suspected this angel let demons cross but that I had absolutely no proof at all? At least two angels and one mage were taking a steady stream of demons to their death, but I had no idea why and no motive. Baphomet and Raim might have been betrayed by an angel that I thought they were in partnership with, and Baphomet's body had been dumped in Raim's house by an angel as told to me by another mentally ill person. It wasn't enough for Gregory to do anything with. It wasn't enough for me to do anything with.

I stopped by a magazine stand near the gate and browsed the selections. Another pregnant celebrity, some politician caught with a prostitute. I grabbed an interesting tabloid with headlines warning me about alien abduction and checked out the local tourist guides while waiting for the cashier. Ghosts and legends of Seattle, Native American tribes of the Pacific Northwest, a guide to camping the islands in the Strait of Georgia. Frowning, I picked it up. San Juan, Waldron Island, Patos Island, Oak Island.

Oak Island. Where the wizard had threatened to take Baphomet's neighbor. Hadn't he alleged that the demons had

275

been taken there too? Ditching the tabloid, I paid for the camping book, and for the second time that day, headed out of the airport.

"Wyatt, I'm so sorry, but I'm probably not going to be home until tomorrow," I told him, from another rental car.

There was a moment of silence. "Sam, what's going on? There are no flight delays. What are you doing that you're not telling me."

There was an accusation in his voice, as though he thought I was holding back on activities he'd not approve of, like mass murder or torture. I didn't want him to think that of me.

"Remember I told you about the angel and mage that chased me through downtown? Well I think they're somehow connected to what's been going on out here. I still have a feeling there's more behind it then the devouring spirit Gregory and I took out up in Alaska."

"You think a mage and an angel are involved in killing demons? Isn't that what angels do?"

"Well, under normal circumstances, yes. But I think the angel was in some kind of partnership with the two demons. I have no idea what they were doing, but I know this isn't just some devouring spirit gone crazy."

It sounded ridiculous, even to me. I was glad I hadn't summoned Gregory and babbled all this to him.

"Sooo, where are you going now?"

"About an hour and a half north of Seattle to check out a lead. By the time I get back, I will have missed the red eye to BWI. I'll catch the first plane in the morning, I promise."

"Okay." Wyatt sounded disappointed. I was too. "Let me know when you're boarding, and I'll make some plans for us."

I promised I'd call him with my new itinerary in the morning and hung up, hoping that his plans involved some naked action between the sheets. Heck, by this point, I'd be happy for a good snuggle.

The traffic on the bypass around Seattle was flowing easily. Clear of the city, I jumped back on Route 5 north, crossing over inlets and rivers until I reached the long inland stretch north of Marysville. It wasn't the most scenic or exciting drive I'd ever taken, but I was choosing my route for speed, not beauty. Finally the highway veered west after curving around Lake Samish, angling toward the coast and into the city of Bellingham.

The Alaska ferry departed from Bellingham, and the ports along the deepwater bay were impressive. I headed for the closest marina with an adjoining yacht club and was astounded by the hundreds of boats docked there — all completely beyond my ability to pilot. Should I steal one and hope I didn't wind up capsized or lost at sea? I had no idea of water navigation, and the little guidebook I'd bought didn't come with detailed directions. I eyed my iPhone, wondering if the GPS would get me to the right island, or land me sideways on a sandbar.

"Can I charter a boat to Oak Island," I asked an official-looking guy at the marina office. He looked at me strangely.

"Oak Island? If it's small island camping you're looking for, I'd suggest Patos or Sucia instead. There's nothing on Oak Island."

He was large, and it was clear that at some point he'd been even larger. Huge jowls hung down on either side of his mouth, swinging slightly as he spoke. It was hard to keep from staring at them. He looked like a well-shaved Bloodhound.

"Oak Island," I insisted, trying to keep my eyes on his watery blue ones and not on the loose skin in motion. "I'm not camping. I just want someone to take me there for an hour or so, and then bring me back."

Now the guy really was looking at me like I was an escaped mental patient. I had a sudden urge to put a metal bowl on my head and complete the image.

"There's no one today. I can probably get someone to take you there tomorrow."

Tomorrow I planned on being on a plane. After which, I would be wrapped in Wyatt's arms.

"Where can someone take me right now?" Maybe there was an island within swimming distance from Oak Island, or I could jet ski over.

The man frowned and fiddled nervously with his pen. He seemed like a friendly sort of guy, but I could tell he really wanted me out of his office, and probably out of the marina. Maybe it was closing time and he wanted to get home to hot meatloaf and mashed potatoes. Maybe he was worried I was a psycho with my obsessive interest in Oak Island.

"Let me make some calls. Come back tomorrow, and I'll see what I can do. It's high fishing season but someone might be able to squeeze you in before the weekend."

I recognized that dismissive tone. Purchasing a more detailed map of the area, I headed toward the door and again contemplated stealing a boat. It's not like I could swim there from the city. Or maybe I could. I thought about changing into my tiger shark form, but once I'd reached the island, I'd be forced to choose between exploring as a mammal without opposable thumbs, or a naked human — both less than ideal, especially if I encountered any hostile demons, angels, and mages.

"Hey," guy called as I was about to leave. "Hang on a moment. I'll call Skip real quick. I've got his cell number, and I know he's been doing a bunch of trips out to Oak Island, for some kinda corporate-retreat folks this summer. He might be able to fit you in."

I checked the maps on the wall that depicted water depths and the location of various shoals while the marina guy talked to Skip, giving him an unsettling amount of detail about my approximate age, physical attributes, and whether I was wearing a black suit and a pair of mirrored sunglasses or not. I had no idea these charter boat folks screened their clients so thoroughly. Whatever Skip's criteria, I seemed to have passed, because the marina guy hung up and informed me that I'd leave promptly at six in the morning from slip twenty, dock four.

"Skip has a couple of fishermen he's taking out with him, but he can swing by Oak Island and drop you off for a few hours, then come back to pick you up."

I frowned. Six in the morning. I'd hoped to be on a plane home by then, and if he had a fishing charter, I'd probably not be able to make the airport in Seattle until late. Those things usually ran at least four hours.

"Is there anything tonight? I just need a quick peek at the island. I'm willing to pay double the rate."

Marina guy looked rather hungry at my offer, but shook his head. "Nah. Everyone goes out in the morning. You'll not find anyone available this late in the day without prior reservation. Wish my boat wasn't dry-docked for repairs, or I'd take you myself."

I sighed, thinking Wyatt was going to get pissed at my constant rescheduling. I was thinking of telling him I'd be another three days then surprise him when I came home early. It wasn't just Wyatt, though, those damned four-nine-five reports were due in a couple days and there's no way I'd meet the deadline now. Any more delay here and Gregory would be summoning me out of the plane, forty thousand feet over Des Moines, for my punishment.

"Is there a hotel nearby?"

I settled into the little economy motel that reminded me of the one Candy, Wyatt, and I had stayed at in Gettysburg when we were tracking Althean — minus the vibrating bed. Wyatt wasn't happy about the change of plans, but was understanding of my need to tie up loose ends. I told him I'd call him when I was on my way, that if this island held another lead that I needed to check out, I may not make a flight tomorrow. In the back of my mind, I was well aware that it might be a week until I saw Wyatt again. The three-day punishment in Aaru was looking like a definite possibility, especially with my chasing all over Washington State taking precedence over the horrible reports.

The alarm woke me at five, after a fitful night alone on a lumpy mattress. Half asleep while driving to the marina, I parked in the vacant lot and threw my bag in the trunk. Just as I was about to head over to the docks, I looked down and saw the signet ring on my finger. Whatever was going on, I really didn't want to be caught sporting a magical ring that a mage had been wearing prior to his death. As a precaution, I removed it and stashed it under the front seat, next to my wallet. With the car locked and the key stowed under the wheel well, I grabbed my all-night gas station coffee and headed over to dock four.

The fishing-charter guys were there before me, and I grumbled under my breath about how much I disliked early birds. Fishing and all other activities should take place after ten in the morning. Except for sex. That was good anytime.

Skip was easy to identify as the man hopping on and off the boat, loading ice into the huge fish coolers, and beer into the equally large cooler by the cockpit. A ball cap hid his hair, but his short beard was brown on a tanned face. The boat had at one time been a stunning beauty but was beginning to show its age. It was good quality — a Grady White thirty-three-foot fishing boat with an outrigger kit sporting a series of pricy fishing rods, and a nice casting platform. I'm guessing in 2008, it had cost more than most people's homes, and, even now, the upkeep was probably higher than a monthly mortgage payment. Boats were money pits, especially as they aged. I eyed the brand new twin F350 motors on the back and winced. Those had to have set Skip back a pretty penny. No wonder he was willing to detour his fishing charter to take a crazy woman out and back to a tiny island.

"I appreciate you doing this last minute," I told Skip, extending my hand. "I'm Samantha Martin."

He looked startled and reluctantly shook my hand, avoiding eye contact. He was oddly nervous, and I wondered if he was always this edgy, or if he had some deferred boat maintenance he was praying didn't come to light during our trip.

"It's two fifty," he said gruffly.

Steep, but this was an inconvenience, and I was honing in on a private fishing charter. His tips might suffer due to this little side excursion. I handed him the cash. He pocked it, all the while avoiding my curious gaze. Giving up on engaging conversation with Skip, I balanced my coffee in one hand and jumped onto the boat to greet the two fishermen, who were also studiously ignoring me. They looked like the kind of guys who would charter a fishing trip — neat clothing, athletic builds. One had a shock of light brown hair, like a plush carpet, on his head. It was too long for a buzz cut, but too short to require gel to achieve its upright position. The other was completely shaved bald. I hoped he'd applied plenty of sunscreen on that head or it was going to look like a traffic flare by the time this trip was over.

"Hey, guys. What are you hoping to catch today?"

I was no angler, but I'd gotten quite a taste for the local fish up in Alaska, and I'd spent a lot of time in this area a few decades ago. If they caught something good, maybe I could buy it off them and eat it during my ride back to the airport.

The two exchanged looks, one mumbling something under his breath, the other shrugging. "Rockfish," he replied, turning his back on me to grab a beer out of the cooler.

I frowned. The rockfish population around here was really low. Most people went for salmon. With the Fraser River emptying into the Strait, salmon was available all year around. They could easily reel in a ten to thirty-pound catch.

The two guys made their way to the front of the boat. In spite of their decent sea legs, they really did look like yuppies on vacation. Tan, neatly creased shorts, and crisp polo shirts contrasted with Skip's worn, multi-pocketed pants and bait-shop t-shirt. Moneyed tourists, no doubt.

Skip fired up the engines, while I helped untie the boat, tossing the ropes to the dock. The water was choppy as we pulled away, but not overly rough. Leaving the marina, we hugged the edges of the bay, traveling south around the tip of Lumm Island before picking up speed northward, into open water. I counted the islands on my left until I'd reached five, then we veered around for a landing on the tiny bit of green that must be Oak Island. According to the map I had stashed in the trunk of my rental car, we were over the Saltish Sea, approximately twenty miles from Bellingham.

Oak Island was smaller than all the islands we'd passed, a mere strip of land oddly placed in the middle of vast water. The dark-blue sea became greenish-brown as our boat approached the island, indicating the decreasing depth of the water. Narrow sandy beaches rimmed the flat land that otherwise seemed to be bursting with thick tree cover. We pulled up to a small wooden dock, paint peeling on the splintered boards and posts.

According to the guidebook, Oak Island was about one hundred acres, which wouldn't have been difficult to explore except for the dense forest. I calculated how much I could get done in the half-day charter the fishing guys had paid for. If someone were using this island, they'd have to land a boat somewhere, and this dock was probably the only one. A small skiff could land right on the beach, but transporting goods, and demons, would require some kind of road or path. I strained my eyes as we looped past the dock to cut around so we could pull alongside the pier. There appeared to be a small deer track leading into the woods, but nothing significant. My heart sank. Perhaps the mage's threat to Baphomet's crazy neighbor had just been a joke. I hated the thought that I'd delayed my trip home, wasted my time on a wild goose chase. I was here, though. Might as well spend a few hours exploring the island just to put this one to rest. I'd paid for this charter. It would take me probably all of thirty minutes to walk the whole thing. I guessed I could relax on the beach and work on my tan until Skip came back to pick me up.

Skip pulled the boat in nose front. I frowned, perplexed. The boat would be more stable tied to the dock front and back at the side. I was no expert, so when he motioned for me to disembark from the front of the boat, I just shrugged and walked forward to squeeze my way past the two fishermen. That's when all hell broke loose.

I felt the brush of something against my hair and instinctively ducked, slamming a shoulder into hairless guy. Before I could apologies, I felt the touch of something cold on my neck and the slippery sensation dipping below my skin toward my stash of raw energy. My quick movement had kept the collar from fully encircling my neck and connecting. Before carpet head could rectify that, I kicked out with one foot, missing his knee, but nailing him hard in the shin.

He stumbled backwards, tripping over the beer cooler and landing on the deck. Yanking off the partially attached collar, I threw it overboard and launched myself at hairless.

"Hey, not on my boat. Not on my boat!" Skip protested. I saw him out of the corner of my eye, scrambling toward the back and away from the fray.

Hairless was stronger than he looked. He braced himself against the back of one of the cockpit seats and absorbed my rush, slamming a fist into my kidneys before wrapping his arms around me in a tight hold.

"Collar her," he shouted to carpet head.

It was probably at the bottom of the sea, and I was hoping they only had the one. My limited options raced through my head. With no collar, my demon skills were still available. I could easily overpower these guys, but Skip didn't seem to be running to my aid. Three dead humans was a whole lot of four-nine-five reports, and I wasn't sure I could pilot this boat, let alone figure out my way back to Bellingham. I could ditch them and transform into something small, swift, and four-legged once on the island. It was my best option. Escape, transform into a tiger shark, swim east until I hit land then wander around as a naked human until I found the marina and my car. It sucked, but it was better than the prospect of having to justify their deaths to the Ruling Council.

The split-second it took to make my decision gave carpet head time to get me in a choke hold with one arm, and slam my side with his other fist. I was being squashed between the two guys, with Skip distraught over his boat, looking on. I poured a low-level burst of electricity from every pore, happy to hear both men yelp in pain and shock. Carpet head let go, so I smashed my newly released head into hairless, hearing a satisfying crunch as it hit his nose.

Free. I elbowed carpet head, who was behind me, sending him overboard with a splash, and vaulted the cabin, leaping off the front of the boat and onto the dock as the pair shouted. There was no time to change forms, so I sprinted for the deer path, only a few feet away from the narrow beach. I hit the edge of the woods and spun about as something invisible slammed into me. There was a flash. By the time my eyes cleared, I'd stumbled into what, from the beach, appeared to be dense forest. It wasn't. Like an idiot, I stood and gawked, my mad dash to safety forgotten. Before me was a compound spanning at least four acres. The buildings were no more than three stories. A dozen dirt bikes were parked out to the side along with a utility vehicle and a pick-up truck — all hidden by the false vision of foliage.

I had only a second to stare in astonishment before I realized that I'd probably triggered some kind of security alarm when I breached the perimeter. And the guys from the boat were probably right on my tail or had contacted everyone at the compound to let them know I was on the island, I dashed toward the motorbikes, thinking this would be the fastest way to outpace them. I jumped on one and frantically tried to determine how to start the damned thing.

Three figures, holding guns, ran from one of the buildings just as I got the bike running and into gear.

I headed for the road and the forest beyond, thinking I could transform into something native to the island as soon as I got far enough away. I briefly wondered why the men with guns weren't shooting, as I felt a series of wires snatch me backwards off the bike and slam me into the ground. A mage. I probed the edges of the net and realized that this one was of far better construction than the one that had nabbed me in downtown Frederick. Not a mage; a sorcerer. No wonder the guys hadn't bothered shooting.

Thrashing blindly in the net, I heard the elvish chant that swirled in my head and numbed my mind. In the last seconds before unconsciousness, I called for the Sword of the Iblis to come to me. I'd broken a sorcerer's net before with it, and as much as I hated to use the ancient artifact here where I might accidently shoot and kill the humans, I knew I didn't want to get caught by these guys.

Nothing appeared.

I pulled on the red-purple that networked through me and tried to summon Gregory while struggling to remain conscious and tugging at the net. He didn't come. My head buzzed and lolled to the side, my hands numb and useless.

"This one is really strong, and she came to us. The angel will be very pleased." It was the last thing I heard before darkness overtook me.

~30~

I came to consciousness naked and chained to huge metal rings embedded in a concrete floor. Naked was unsettling enough without the damp, dungeon-like surroundings. Why the hell had they removed my clothing? And chained? As a demon, I could easily turn the metal into any substance of my choosing. Wet noodles was my choice today.

Reaching within, to my store of raw energy, I encountered the slippery stuff angels use to block our powers. There was no angel touching me at the moment, so, with a sense of dread, I reached up to my neck. My fingers felt a collar. The thin band of energy surrounded more than my skin; it sunk down into my spirit being and denied all attempts to pull from my stash of energy.

"You won't be able to get it off," a raspy voice said. "And you won't be able to fix any injuries you sustain while trying."

"Why am I naked? Did they do this to you too, or am I special?"

I heard a gritty chuckle. "Me too. Someone told me one of the first demons tore up his clothing and passed the strips around for weapons. They attacked the guards, using them as whips and nooses, so now everyone that comes in here is naked."

I squinted into the darkness at a shape off to my left. "I'm Az."

The shape moved and I made out a gaunt face, streaks of what I assumed to be blood trailing from his neck down over a bony chest.

"I'm Stab." The face inched closer until the chains holding the demon were stretched full length. "Are you the imp? The one with the sword? The one that devou . . . I mean, killed Haagenti?"

"That's me." Once again I tried to summon my sword, tried to summon Gregory, to no avail.

Stab shook his head. "There's no hope for me if they've managed to ensnare you. I'm next, anyway. The last one here."

"How many others were there?"

He sighed. "Three in the group I came with. From what I hear, there have been hundreds. All dead except for the one that escaped."

"Who escaped?"

"Said his name was Raim." The demon laughed, a hoarse sound that echoed from the walls of our cell. "Caused quite a stir. Turns out he devoured. He killed one of the angels and managed to use the little bit of energy that had somehow escaped the collar to get off the island."

I felt the stirring of hope in my chest. If Raim managed to make it out of here, perhaps I could too.

"They locked down security tight after that." Stab's eyes glowed as he turned toward me. "But they're really nervous about devouring spirits. Might be of help to you. If the rumors are true, that is."

"No. The rumors are not true," I lied. Gregory had forbidden me from devouring, but it might be my only way out. There were always exceptions to every rule, always circumstances when even supposedly vile acts were justified.

"Shame." The demon looked around the dim room. "They killed off the guy who was bringing us over from Hel and ended their supply. Until they find a new demon to partner with, we're all they've got."

"What are they doing with us?"

"I don't know. I just know we don't come back," Stab whispered, fear in his voice.

I again tried to summon either my sword or my angel, struggled to find even the slightest bit of raw energy I could access. The desperation in Stab's voice, his utter despair had me on the edge of panic.

"Did you get a good look at the compound and the layout when they brought you in? Do you know where we are in this building and where an exit might be?" I'd only briefly seen the exteriors before they'd knocked me out. If there was even a slim chance of escape, I'd be better positioned to take it knowing which direction to run.

"We're in a big block building in the center of the compound. I remember four sets of stairs down, then a right into this room. I think we're pretty far underground."

That made sense from the dampness on the walls. We were on an island at sea level. The fact that they'd managed to get a structure this deep, a compound this complex without anyone noticing, was impressive. I'd seen the elves demonstrate amazing architectural feats, so I wouldn't put it past the group to be employing magical means beyond the illusion of forest.

"I came over for a vacation, a bit of fun." Stab turned to me again, his fear contagious, snaking its way inside me. "I'm not very strong — almost a Low. Whatever they have planned for me, I know I won't survive it."

I turned away before he could see the tears in my eyes. I had no words to comfort him with. I couldn't even manage to get myself out of this mess, let alone try and save someone else. There had to be something, some tiny little detail our captors had missed, something I could exploit. I just needed to find it. Slumping to the floor, I ran my hands carefully over its surface as far as my chains allowed, trying to find an object, anything I could use to free myself physically. The floor was cement. It felt like it had been poured and raked, the expected smooth surface grooved in lines. There were no loose bits, no stones to pry from the surface. I crawled back and forth in a grid pattern, wincing as the grooves in the floor tore at the skin of my knees. Nothing.

I carefully felt each link of my chains with my hands and found them solid, thick metal. The rings were embedded deep into the floor. I wouldn't be surprised if they were connected to something stronger beneath the concrete. Wanting to cover every option, I felt along the wall, noting that some areas had small rivulets of water running from the ceiling far out of my reach to the floor below. There must be drains somewhere or we'd be in standing water. I hoped the wet walls didn't mean the whole thing was on the verge of collapse. With the collar around my neck, I wouldn't be able to change form, or escape a flooding room. I'd drown, or be buried by the building above. It would be a sad way for a demon to die, but it probably wasn't any better than what waited on the other side of that door.

There was only one way I was going to get out of here. I carefully prodded the slippery energy coating my own, searching for a weakness. Even as powerful as Gregory was, he couldn't contain my huge store of energy outside of Aaru. If he'd left gaps, then somewhere, this angel had too. If I could just find a gap, no matter how tiny, I might be able to pull enough energy aside to get myself out of this fix. Hopefully I'd have the days it would take to accumulate enough. Even if I found a hole, it would take me time to amass any kind of usable energy. If they came for me in a few hours, I probably wouldn't have enough to light a match.

*****

I'd lost track of time in our dark cell. I wondered if Wyatt was looking for me, if Gregory had come for my four-nine-five reports and found me missing. There must be some kind of barrier around this place that limited my communications with him. Any attempts to summon him resulted in nothing. I'm sure it was the same on his end. I suspected that might be the issue with my Iblis sword too, but it hadn't come to me on the mountain when I was fighting Raim either.

But Wyatt . . . he had to be looking by now. With my link to Gregory blocked, he would be the most skilled at finding me. Didn't those rental cars have some kind of tracking GPS in them? I envisioned him jumping on a plane and swooping in on a speedboat to rescue me, guns a-blazing. Then I worried. Hopefully he'd bring Gregory with him. Wyatt sometimes became overconfident when it came to his ability to take down supernatural creatures. I'd definitely want him to have angelic back-up for this one.

None of our captors came for us, which was a mixed blessing. The only sounds besides ours were the drip of water in a corner of the room, and the scurry of some elusive animal. My eyes had adjusted enough to see a slim crack of light coming through what must have been a doorjamb. That was it. No windows; nothing but solid cement reinforced by rebar in a grid on the walls. I wasn't sure how deep the rings holding us to the floor went, but it was beyond my capability to bend or pull them up. I kept trying, but without food or water, my physical body was beginning to feel weak. I'd taken to licking the water from the walls, but there was nothing I could do about the lack of food. Stab, beside me, looked worse. He seldom sat up anymore. I worried that even if I managed to free us, he'd never be able to walk out of here — not unless I somehow managed to free him from the collar that limited his abilities to that of a human.

There was a gap in my collar. It had taken me nearly a day, but I'd found it and begun pulling tiny bits of energy free. It wasn't much. I'd probably only have one solid shot before it was gone. Over time, I might be able to manage to free a decent amount, but if they didn't feed us soon, we wouldn't have much time.

I was propped up against one of the walls, in that twilight zone between wake and sleep when the door swung open on silent hinges. Light filled the room, blinding my eyes that had become used to the darkness.

I recognized the mage that walked through the door even though he didn't have the pointy hat and flaming eyes of the drawing. I didn't recognize the man that hovered behind him in the doorway, holding a rifle. Stab lay unmoving, the rise and fall of his chest the only indication that he was still alive. I carefully crouched, awaiting the perfect moment to make my move.

"Guess we'll take this one," the mage said, waving a hand toward Stab. "I doubt he'll last much longer."

Rifle man continued to guard the door as the mage carefully approached Stab. Realizing they'd come for him, the demon scrabbled toward me on all fours, his eyes wide with terror.

"Don't let them take me," he begged.

I'd thought about using the energy I'd squirreled away to kill the mage, but then I'd have none left. Instead, I used a portion to dissolve the attachment of my chains to the floor and tried to look beaten down and weak as the mage approached Stab. The demon continued to scoot toward me as far as his chains allowed, which left him about three feet from me at their full extension. The mage reached out a staff toward his neck, and with a flash of light, the collar connected to the staff. It reminded me of the poles and loops humans use to lasso crocodiles and bring them in.

"Got him," the mage announced.

Rifle man slung the weapon over his shoulder and walked over, unhooking Stab's chains from the rings on the floor while the mage half dragged him, keeping him at a safe distance. Nobody looked at me. Nobody noticed me until I lunged at the mage and wrapped the chains connecting my arms around his thick neck. He dropped the staff and frantically clawed at his neck.

I jerked the mage around so he was between me and rifle man, and Stab was safely behind us. In an enviously smooth motion, the guard had his gun aimed and ready.

"Can you walk? Get up and stay behind me."

I heard Stab shuffle behind me, felt his hands as he steadied himself on my body. At the same time I heard a whisper from the mage, and yanked the chain tight against his windpipe.

"If you even start to cast a spell, I'll pop your head off," I growled.

In reality, I was stuck. I had no idea how the fuck we were going to get out of here. Would the mage be a valuable enough hostage that we could make it to the edge of the forest? I had a bad feeling the answer was "no". And even if he were, attempting to negotiate the halls of whatever building we were in while trying to keep my human shield between me and multiple armed attackers was going to be impossible. Add in the fact that Stab could barely stand and was dragging a five-foot staff, and my little escape plan was doomed. Still, I had to try.

Stab clung to me, and I edged around, sidestepping my way to the door while I kept one eye on the rifle and the other on the open doorway. I figured if we could get out into the hallway, Stab could shut the door, locking the dude with the gun inside and we'd have one less problem to worry about. Rifle man must have been thinking along the same lines. As Stab peered out the doorway to make sure all was clear, he rushed me. I jumped backwards, knocking the other demon into the hall and dragging the mage by his neck, managing to get out in time and slam the door, but not before the guard unloaded a few rounds. He was either a good shot or very lucky because both bullets tore through my right shoulder.

I grimaced, slightly pulling myself back from the injury to better concentrate. I couldn't risk using any of the energy I'd collected to fix myself. There were potentially far worse things ahead of me than two bleeding holes in my shoulder.

"Are you okay?" I asked over my shoulder, hearing Stab struggle to get up off the floor.

"You go on without me. I'm just going to slow you down, and I'm not going to make it much longer anyway. If I don't get some food and water soon, or if I can't manage to fix myself, this form will die."

"Pull back," I urged, turning my head to look at him. "Consolidate yourself within the form if it dies and you'll survive. You can exist within any matter, doesn't have to be alive. I'll carry you out if I have to, just hang on."

He stared at me as if I'd gone insane.

"Go on without me."

I shook my head and transferred my chains to my left hand, sacrificing valuable energy breaking the cuffs that linked them to my right and stooping to pick up the stick attacked to Stab's collar. I had no idea how to unhook it, but at least I could urge him on and yank him out of the way if needed. Of course that meant I had to extend my spirit self back down into the shoulder that was now throbbing in agony.

"I'm not leaving here without you. Come on. If we make it to the beach, we can swim for it. I've got an Orca that I Own. You can ride on my back.

He looked skeptical. I didn't blame him. I hardly had any energy left that was accessible. I might be able to manage a full-body conversion, but then I'd be completely drained.

"I know an angel that can help get these collars removed," I told Stab, urging him forward. "If only we can get off the island and back to the mainland."

"But the angel brought us here," he protested, limping down the hall beside me.

"Another angel. A real badass angel. He'll wipe the floor with these guys. He'll shred them to bits and send me their body parts as tributes. He's ancient and powerful, and he's gonna be pissed as all fuck when he finds out what's going on here."

Again, I got the skeptical, "this imp is insane" look from Stab.

About twenty feet from the door, our hallway ended in a "T". I held the pair back and leaned out into the intersection, my shoulder screaming at the extension.

"I don't know whether to go left or right," I whispered. In reply I heard a muffled scream. I spun around, dropping the stick and pulling the mage in front of me as a shield. Stab was huddled on the floor, struggling under a sorcerer's net, and before me was the caster, eyes narrowed as he contemplated his next move. I was so fucked. I wasn't leaving here without Stab. I'd promised him, and I wouldn't break my vow.

"Let him go or I'm killing your mage," I announced, again tightening the chain around the man's neck.

"Or maybe not." A hand touched my un-injured shoulder and I felt the compulsion slam into me and bounce off.

Compulsion was the least of my worries. The remaining bit of energy I'd managed to pull away from the restraint rebounded into the rest, and I was left with nothing. Stab was powerless and in a net, I had no energy to use, nothing to fight an angel. The compulsion hadn't worked though, and one less bad guy was good enough for me. I yanked on the chain with all my might and heard a satisfying crunch as I snapped the mage's neck.

The sorcerer screamed in anger, and the angel grabbed me, smashing my head against the hallway wall. The grey cement block whirled around my head, and I collapsed to the floor as everything went black.

~31~

I woke to find myself back in the dark cell, my chains once again firmly connected to the floor. In addition to the collar on my neck, I now had one around each wrist and ankle. I'd need to find a weakness in five different restraints in order to pull any of my energy free. I could do it, but I doubted I had the time to amass any useful amount.

"Are you okay?" a weak voice asked to my left.

Stab. He was still alive, although, by the sound of his voice, he didn't have much more than a day or so left.

"Yeah. My head is killing me and I've got two gunshot wounds in my shoulder, but other than that, I'm just peachy."

I felt bad the moment I'd said it. He was worse, far worse, than me.

"That sorcerer was livid when you snapped his mage's neck. He wanted to kill you right then and there, but the angel wouldn't let him."

"Wish I could have done more. I'm sorry Stab. I tried to get us out of here."

I heard the rustle of him moving closer. "I know. I appreciate it. You're the only demon who's ever done anything for me."

That didn't make me feel any better. It only made me sad.

"The sorcerer doesn't have any more mages, just an apprentice. You killed the one, and he was shouting about how the other one was found dead a few days ago. He was shredded to bits, and his hand was missing."

I smirked, hoping that was the one Gregory had killed, the one whose hand he had sent to me up in Juneau. The only bright spot in this whole nightmare was the thought that he wouldn't rest until he'd tracked down and punished my killers. They'd never get away with it, and if they thought they could avoid that particular angel's wrath, they were sadly mistaken.

My mind churned, thinking of any possible way I could get us out of here. If I'd had use of my huge store of energy, I could easily take on the humans. Heck I could probably defeat the angel and the sorcerer too.

"How long have you been here, Stab?" I asked as I continued to look for gaps in the restraints that would be big enough to pull even the smallest bit of energy through.

"Two weeks, I think. Not exactly a great vacation, huh?"

He wasn't going to make it. He'd either die, or they'd come for him, and there was nothing I could do about it. I redoubled my efforts to search for cracks in the collars.

"I'm the Iblis. We'll get out and you can be part of my household. That means you can come and go through the gates with some minor behavior restrictions. You can visit me at my house in Maryland. We'll relax by the pool, grab some beer and hot wings, then go blow shit up downtown."

He sighed, the sound a hollow rattle. "I'll hold you to that, you know."

"I vow it on all the souls I Own."

We sat, the only sound the rustle of Stab's body against the floor as he shifted, trying to find a more comfortable position. My heart ached.

After a few hours, the door opened. This time I saw the sorcerer shadowed against the bright light, two guards by his side. He walked into the room, and the two guards took point at each side of the door. As the sorcerer approached Stab, I saw the angel waiting outside, his arms crossed before his chest.

"Touch him and you'll meet the same fate as your mage," I threatened.

The sorcerer jumped back, his eyes darting to me with a mix of anger and fear. The angel laughed.

"Not likely. Don't worry, we're going to take you too, just to make sure you've not slipped your shackles again."

The sorcerer employed the same stick-as-a-leash technique as the mage had, and a guard stepped forward to release Stab's chains while the other guard continued to keep his rifle trained on my head. Stab was handed off to the guard, clearly too weak to be much of a threat, and it was my turn to be connected to a pole. The sorcerer practically hyperventilated while the guard holding Stab released my chains one handed. The angel spun about, leading the way, followed by the sorcerer pulling me along, then the guard with Stab. The guard with the rifle was our caboose.

My mind considered and disregarded options. I was truly trapped, but I wasn't going down without a fight. I might be a dead imp walking, but I was going to ensure a few of these fuckers went to their deaths before I did. Pulling back, I made the sorcerer yank me along as we navigated the labyrinth of hallways. About three minutes into our walk, I lunged forward, taking him off guard. The pole slipped from his hands and I grabbed it, giving the sorcerer a solid whack across his head and turning to do the same to the guard holding Stab. My shoulder screamed, and I felt fluid leak from the bullet holes. Adrenaline and desperation does wonderful things to a human body, and I managed to keep a solid grip on the stick.

"Run," I told the demon, hitting the rifle held by the rear guard just as he shot. The bullets slammed into the wall, and I reversed, hitting him as hard as I could on my backswing.

Stab staggered down the hall the way we'd come, dragging his pole behind him, while I spun about. I'd need to face the angel, and without the use of my energy I'd surely lose. Hopefully I'd give Stab enough time to either escape, or hide in the facility. The angel was blocking the hallway before me, his arms again across his chest, his lips turned up in an amused smile.

"Nicely done. It's about time I got a real demon in here. You might be just the one I've been waiting for."

The sorcerer clutched his bleeding head and crawled behind the angel for protection while I stood sideways, trying to keep the unconscious guards in view as well as the angel.

"I want my money back. I was promised a comfortable two weeks stay before my death, and I've been far from comfortable the last few days. What kind of facility are you all running here?"

The angel laughed and walked toward me. I held the staff attached to my collar with both hands, swinging it in an arc to determine the exact extent of its range of motion. It rotated easy on the collar, but my shoulder was the weak link in my fighting strategy. The initial adrenaline burst was receding, and my arm was beginning to feel numb just as the throbbing in my shoulder moved into the realm of agony.

"I don't honor whatever promises the demons made to get you over here. Perhaps your anticipated vacation will await you in the afterlife."

He lunged at me, lightning fast, but I was fast too. I parried his attack with my pole, knocking his hand aside and stepping sideways. Rubbing his wrist, he watched me carefully, mirroring his moves to mine as we danced about the narrow hallway. He was toying with me, dragging the fight out by keeping it purely physical. One blast and I'd be on the ground, unable to protect myself from more than fists and feet. I'd done this too — dragging a fight out to give a victim false hope, only to revel in seeing that hope die in his eyes. Knowing what he was doing didn't make it any less effective, though. My heart raced with the misplaced idea that I might actually win this and escape.

Again, the angel lunged, feinting as I reacted and sending me off balance from an unconnected swing of my pole. Nearly blacking out from the stab of pain in my shoulder, I staggered slightly. He dove in to grab my arm, his grip wrenching downward, separating my shoulder from the socket. Great. With both injuries, the shoulder was useless. Grimacing in pain, I pulled backward, further disconnecting my shoulder from the joint and snapped a kick at his knee. It connected, but the angel jumped back, avoiding full impact.

"I think I'm in love." The angel laughed. "It's been nearly three million years since I've had the pleasure of a fight like this."

I could no longer see Stab down the hallway. The two guards were still out for the count, and the sorcerer cowered to my left. I went on the offensive, ignoring the waves of pain and swinging wildly as I advanced on my opponent. He easily stepped around me, but with his eyes on the pole, he completely missed the foot that hooked around his ankle and pulled him off balance. He threw out a hand to catch himself against the wall and I jabbed with the pole, hitting him right under his ribs.

The angel doubled over, but he also managed to grab the pole with both hands. Yanking backwards, I tried to slide it from his grasp, but his grip was firm and my leverage horrible with the damaged shoulder. The angel took advantage of my movement to launch forward. I fell backwards just as he pivoted, sending me sideways onto the floor.

"Got you, you stinking little cockroach."

Fury flared up inside me. Only one being was allowed to call me that. Spinning around on my back, I looped my legs around his and twisted, sending him crashing to the floor. Unfortunately, he fell right on top of me, crushing the breath from my lungs and enabling him to get a grip on my collar. With a flash of light it tightened, choking the breath from my throat. Once again, the world swam before my eyes.

"Yes, you'll do very well indeed."

It was the last thing I heard before consciousness slipped away.

~32~

This time I woke staring into a blinding florescent light on a ceiling. I was on my back, bolted to some sort of table by my hands and feet, my neck also attached through the collar. The special restraints were still on each of my limbs. I once again began the tedious process of trying to find a series of gaps to access my energy stores.

Everything hurt. I closed my eyes, trying to pinpoint the location and severity of my injuries. The repeated blows to the head made me feel like I was ready to puke my guts out. Not that there was anything in my stomach to come up. The gunshot wounds burned, hot and swollen. They felt infected, and I had no way to counteract the raging fever that would soon follow. Not that I'd live long enough for the fever to take hold. Worse than the gunshot wounds, the dislocated joint screamed in agony. With metal stakes driven through my hands and feet, to secure me to the table, I was in a world of pain. I got the impression this wasn't a usual means of restraint, that the special method was just for me.

It wasn't all that difficult to hammer a pike through hands and feet, but it took immense strength to slam them through the table. I gritted my teeth and wiggled my extremities slightly. There was a flat end keeping me from pulling my hands and feet off the stakes, and they felt like they'd been bent as they exited the table to keep them attached. I could probably rip my hands and feet free, given enough time and pain tolerance, but then I'd need to somehow deal with the one holding my collar to the table.

The collar only allowed me to turn my head a limited amount, but when I opened my eyes, what I saw alarmed me. I appeared to be in some sort of laboratory. Other metal tables were on either side of mine, complete with straps and what appeared to be a sort of drainage system of grooves. Large teardrop-shaped globes stood on stands along one wall, long tubes roped on a hook by their sides, like a drip. A sort of portable electronic console sat nearby. I couldn't see or hear Stab anywhere, which gave me hope. Maybe he'd gotten away. Maybe he'd found a way out and was safely heading back to the mainland.

My stomach had stopped growling days ago, and my mouth was like a wad of cotton. Whatever they had planned for me was obviously imminent. If I couldn't manage to gather enough raw energy to launch another attack, I wouldn't have any hope.

I heard the swish of a door opening. Out of the corner of my eye, I saw two armed guards and the sorcerer.

"Seriously? Two guards?" My voice sounded harsh, like I'd been smoking four packs a day for half a century. "You've got me bolted to a table. What do you expect me to do, spit on you?"

The guards stood at either end of the room. They looked rather bored from what I could see. The sorcerer, on the other hand, was practically shaking with nerves. He wasn't a young guy. I'm sure all this business with the angel and a bunch of demons wasn't doing his blood pressure any good.

"Your name wouldn't happen to be Gareth, would it?" I asked. It would be downright poetic if the runaway sorcerer I had refused to go after wound up being the instrument of my death.

His fear vanished and he glared at me. "No, I'm Pash. Gareth refused this assignment and ran away."

He turned back to the console, muttering something under his breath about how he should have been smart enough to run away himself.

"You're Feille's guy then?" Pash ignored me, but his shoulders tensed somewhat. The guy was clearly in a no-win situation. Feille was a rat bastard, angels were assholes, and the alternative was to run and be torn to bits by a bounty hunter demon. Not that any of this particularly endeared me to the man.

So why did Feille want a bunch of demons drained to an empty shell? That elf did nothing without a solid plan. Clearly he wanted something from us, something our energy stores or spirit beings contained. I frowned, remembering something I'd heard about elven magic and its increased limitations here, among human technology. It had its limitations against us, too. Really strong demons, old ones could shrug off the magic, and some spells only had a limited duration when used against demons. It really sucked when your life's work fell short of its goal in terms of power.

"Enhancing your magical abilities with demon energy as a catalyst," I guessed. "Nice. You guys would be a force to be reckoned with in Hel. You could subdue all your elven neighbors, enslave nearly all the demons."

A glass shattered at my conjecture and my blood felt like ice. Feille was fucking nuts if he thought he could get away with that one. All the demon energy in the world wouldn't save him from a high-level demon. Or would it? I'd underestimated elven magic too many times before. I'd be stupid to do it again.

But what were the angels getting out of all this? There had to be something more.

I heard the swish of the door again, then a heap of dirty flesh slid beside me along the floor.

"Hello, darling." The angel's voice was full of good cheer. "I've found your little friend. He was hiding in a storeroom only a few hundred feet from the exit. So sad that he didn't make an escape, isn't it?"

I turned my head, trying to see Stab, but all I could manage to view was a lump on the floor and a bare foot.

"You, hook him to that table over there," The angel instructed. "And you turn this little imp's table upright, so she can watch the fun."

I had no desire to watch the "fun". I didn't want to see what they were going to do to Stab, to watch helpless as the light went out of his eyes. I'd promised him I'd get him out of here—I'd promised—and now I had to see him die.

One of the guards raised my tabletop vertical, which meant I was suspended by the stakes through my limbs and my neck collar. I tried to hold myself upright, to take the pressure off my impaled hands and feet, but my one shoulder wasn't up to the task. Gravity took hold, and I felt my diaphragm condense as my weight sagged on the metal spikes, my breathing further compromised by the pressure on my neck from the restraint there. I had to tense all my muscles and try to hold myself up by pushing against the stakes through my feet, which wasn't easy in my weakened, starved state. Muscles shook, and I found myself constantly slipping and choking.

Stab didn't look any more comfortable. They hadn't bothered with the silver energy-blocking restraints on his wrists and ankles, but the thin chains binding him to the table cut deep into his flesh. Blood welled up from the cuts, thick and sluggish, illustrating how terribly dehydrated the demon was. He turned his head to me, and I saw he'd been battered by a hard object. His nose was smashed flat to his face, and both lips were torn.

"I'm sorry," he whispered.

"You gave it a good shot. I wish I could have bought you more time." I wish I could have killed this fucking angel and his sorcerer too. Then gone after Feille and mounted his sorry-ass head on a pike to parade through the streets. Fuckers.

Stab smiled. It was a gruesome sight with his torn mouth and mashed nose. "Hot wings sounded fun. Sorry I won't be able to make it."

My eyes burned. Fuck, I was *not* going to cry. Not in front of this angel. "Rest assured, this sorcerer is going to die. The angel too. And it won't be an easy or quick death."

Stab's smile was fleeting, and I heard a laugh from the being that had quickly climbed to the top of my "want-to-kill" list.

"You're in no position to kill me, sweetheart, but you keep on with your little fantasy."

I snarled, feeling all the rage of the past few days rise up. The sorcerer hesitated, an odd, glowing tube in hand, and gave a quick glance toward the angel.

"Maybe not, but you'll still die. Did you not notice I'm bound? He's going to come after you and take you apart one tiny little bit at a time. You'll never escape him, and you're a fool if you think you can best him in a fight."

The angel chuckled, taking the tube from Pash and slamming it into the center of Stab's chest. The demon gasped, rising off the table as far as he could before collapsing down.

"I see who has bound you. I have no idea why he'd bind a nasty demon instead of just killing you as always. No doubt he's got some job for you to do. He can't summon you from here with all the shielding in place, and centuries from now, when he finally gets around to it, he'll just think you died. Don't flatter yourself that you matter at all to him, or to any angel. You're all no more than a smudge of dirt on our wings to be washed off."

He didn't know. Didn't know who I was, or that Gregory's bond with me went far beyond the traditional one. He must have been down here with the humans for over a year without communication with Aaru, or surely he would have known. Angels love gossip as much as we do, and I'd been the subject of much gossip over the last year.

"Don't bet on it. He's the one who killed your other mage. Hunted him down and shredded him like coleslaw. Cut off his hand and sent it to me in a freezer box as a gift. Your fate will be worse."

The sorcerer had backed away, his face gray, his hands over his mouth. He looked terrified, like he was about to puke.

The angel shot an irritated glance at him. "Don't let her get to you. She's lying. Demons do. You should know that by now."

"Your mage had a ring on the middle finger of his right hand. A gold ring with a black onyx stone inscribed with an inverted triangle and an 'x'. I know. I've seen the ring, held it in my hand. I've held his severed hand in my hand. The angel is looking for you right now. I told people where I was going."

The sorcerer gagged, and the angel waved a hand at him to come help with Stab. "Get on with this. If he was looking for her, he would have been here by now. She's lying."

Pash edged over to the table, keeping one wide eye on me as he placed his hands over the glowing tube and began to chant. The lights dimmed and a bright white began to fill the large glass teardrop-shaped bottle off to the side. It must have been some substance other than glass, had to have been magically enhanced. Raw energy can only be held inside a demon. Once it is released, it has to become something — usually something terribly explosive, but somehow it remained in its neutral state within the glass.

Stab was still alive and breathing, and he didn't look to be in terrible pain as the energy flowed out the tube and into the vessel. He'd been telling the truth about not being a particularly powerful being. The glass jar was not even a quarter of the way full when the glow faded from the tube.

"Disappointing," the sorcerer murmured.

"Let's see if the rest of him is any more interesting," the angel commented as Pash removed the tube. The flesh glistened around the wound, knitting and closing to leave nothing but smooth, unscarred flesh.

Stab's eyes remained fixed on the ceiling, his jaw beginning to tremble. We can survive just fine without raw energy. We can't fix injuries, or defend ourselves beyond physical abilities, but we don't die. What came next would kill Stab. The dead demons had all been drained from their bodies, just as if a devouring spirit had taken them. I now realized that outside of the dead angel, Raim hadn't drained any of them.

The sorcerer wheeled the glass container off to the side and picked up what appeared to be an amulet and a metal box. He handed the box to the angel, who opened it and removed a rod that pulsed with crimson light. Stab closed his eyes and clenched his fists as the sorcerer placed the amulet on his forehead and murmured a string of words in Elvish. Stab jolted, and a deep indigo mist rose from his mouth, spiraling as it rose to the rod. With increasing speed, the mist coalesced inside the rod, swirling into a purple light that churned with a life of its own.

Stab was clearly dead on the table, and I worried that his soul was trapped inside that glowing rod. The angel smiled at me as the sorcerer began to tidy up the equipment.

"I'm off to go see if this one will work. We've been adjusting the methodology, but I don't have much hope for this particular experiment. I'm thinking these demons are far too low in status. No matter. If this one fails, we'll try again with you."

With a flash of light the angel vanished, leaving me to wonder what experiment he was doing with a demon's spirit being and where he needed to go. The only use I'd ever known for our personal energy was breeding, when we separated off a portion of ourselves and passed it to another for the formation of new demon life.

Oh fuck. Unlike demons, angels couldn't interbreed. They needed a demon for the process, and the war had divided us, taking away any opportunity for procreation among them. But it wouldn't be as easy as yanking us out of our bodies. In angel/demon pairings, the demon needs to do the formation. Without a willing demon, an angel could never breed — unless they'd somehow managed to figure out a way to employ a surrogate.

I glanced over at the sorcerer and realized that was the symbiotic relationship between them. The angels gave technology to the elves that would allow them to better control demons, to contain their raw energy for their own uses, and the elves assisted them in finding a baby mama method of procreation. I could only imagine how much that would divide the angelic host. Those who were desperate to have offspring, but not kiss and make nice with the demons, would jump at this chance while the purists held firm to their vows. It would be a turning factor that divided Aaru in two.

One of the guards lowered my table into a horizontal position. I gasped, feeling the pressure off my feet and the pain return to all the places that had gone numb. Stab was dead and I'd be next. My mind swam in agony and I felt a moment of despair. My corporeal form was badly damaged. I couldn't fix it, couldn't create another. I couldn't fight as a demon, and I sure as fuck couldn't fight as a human with the injuries this body held. Sleep would be good right now, but I worried that sleep might drift into forever.

Pash finished tidying up and walked out with the two guards, leaving me in the well-lit room with Stab's corpse and the creepy laboratory equipment. I craned my neck to see the glass containers. Three were full, one had that small amount of energy Stab had unwillingly contributed, and two more were empty. Lows didn't have much energy storage capability. I doubted a dozen would be able to fill more than one container. How long had they been at this? How much raw energy did Feille have in his weasely little elven hands? Staring at the containers, I realized that I had far more raw energy contained within me than they could hold. If I overflowed one, would everything explode? Would it set off a chain reaction with the other storage vessels?

I looked into Stab's lifeless eyes with grim resolve. No matter what happened, I'd find a way to take these fuckers out. I'd promised him we'd get out of here. Vengeance for his death would need to be the next best thing.

~33~

S adly, your friend's offspring didn't make it out of the tube
alive. I saved some samples, just in case, but I think he's a
lost cause."

I opened my eyes to see the angel rubbing his hands in
anticipation. They'd removed Stab's corpse at some point, and
I wondered where they'd dumped his body. Probably down
around Richmond, Virginia, if their past pattern of corpse
disposal was anything to go by.

Pash wheeled the mostly empty glass container toward
my table. I'd been sleeping, dozing fitfully as my mind
wandered. I was beginning to hallucinate, which, while
entertaining, wasn't doing anything to help me think of a
strategy for either escape or destruction.

The sorcerer approached the table and picked up the
glowing tube. This all seemed to be going quite a bit faster
than Stab's procedure had. I wondered if they were just trying
to get it over with, or if they'd drawn the other demon's death
out to torture me.

"Hold on." The angel frowned. "Better get one of the
empty containers instead."

The sorcerer met his eyes defiantly. It was the first time
I'd seen him actually have some backbone around the angel.
"This one's almost empty. None of them fill a full one, and I
don't want to waste the space. I'm the one that has to haul
them through the gate while you sit and watch."

The angel glowed slightly, allowing a hiss to escape his lips. I couldn't help a quick grin, because he suddenly reminded me of a wussy version of Gregory. Poser.

"Watch your mouth. You'll do as I say or I'll kill you and tell that elf to send me a new sorcerer."

The sorcerer paled, but I laughed.

"I don't think Feille has any sorcerers left. He's a complete asshole, and they run off regularly. I used to do retrieval, but even I won't work for him anymore."

Pash started, turning to me. "You're the one? The one who brought the guy home in a bag, in little bits?"

"Yep," I told him proudly. "Elves need to give us clear instructions, or they're going to get a dead guy when they wanted him alive."

"Empty. Get an empty one." The angel cut me off with a wave of his hand. Pash complied, wheeling the semi-full container back with the others and brining an empty one forward.

The sorcerer's hands shook as he held the tube toward my chest. Not wanting to make his job any easier, I snarled, grinning in what I hoped was a maniacal fashion.

"Just do it," the angel commanded.

"She's gonna kill me," Pash whined, looking at the angel with pleading eyes. "Chop me into little bits and stuff me into a bag."

"Of all the stupid, weak-willed, cowardly humans, I get stuck with you!" the angel shouted, snatching the tube from his hands. He reached toward me and jabbed it downward.

I twisted as far as I could. The tube missed its mark, plunging into my right lung. A hiss of air exploded, and I gasped for breath. I wanted to consolidate inside myself and escape the pain of a slowly dying body, but I fought the urge. I needed to remain in control of muscles and nerves until the last possible minute, even if it meant my death.

"Hold still," the angel commanded, compulsion in his voice.

"Fuck you." I twisted again, and he jabbed again, missing and hitting the already-deflated lung.

The angel's knuckles were white on the tube as he tried to aim it at my thrashing chest. Instinctively, he reached out with his other hand and pressed on my shoulder, trying to hold me still. Agony lanced through me as his hand hit right on my gunshot wounds, but I smiled. Reaching out to his spirit self through the contact of our flesh, I grabbed hold and pulled.

He screamed, frantically trying to yank away, but I'd gotten a firm hold. He was stronger than I'd expected, and I was so weak — physically, as well as within my spirit self. Yes, I'd seized hold of that portion of Gregory when he'd tried to bind me, but it had been an instinctual response, and I'd never tried to actually devour him. I'd never tried to devour anyone but a demon. I pulled, slowly gaining ground, even in my current state. Haagenti had poured into me like a spool unwinding, Raim had been a desperate struggle over who would devour who, but this angel's powers were unfamiliar, and his will strong. Slowly, he edged closer to me, tantalizingly within reach.

Pain exploded within me, and I gasped, everything narrowing to a pinpoint of white in an endless black. I struggled to hold on, but the angel began to regain the parts of himself I thought I'd won. Again a bolt of pain shot into me, and my grip slipped, allowing the angel even further advantage. Bolstered by the turn of events, he renewed his struggle to pull away. I was weakening. Pain once again slammed through me and I lost my grasp, the angel snapping back into himself.

As my vision cleared, I saw him, on the floor, panting and staring at me in astonishment. I realized the pain I'd been feeling was because of the sorcerer, who'd been slamming the tube into my thrashing body, eventually hitting his mark. I felt the stream pouring from me, and I was powerless to stop it.

"You nasty, disgusting creature," the angel gasped. "How could there be two of you? How? The one that killed Sallep, and now you?"

I'd almost had him. If that fucking sorcerer hadn't suddenly decided to make a stand. I glared at him, and he smirked back, confident and unafraid now that my energy flowed out of me into his glass globe. I guess I couldn't blame him — the angel was likely to keep him alive as long as he was useful, but I would have killed him right after I'd devoured the angel.

"I'm not about to perpetuate a devouring spirit." The angel sneered, getting to his feet and dusting himself off. "I don't want to try to breed this one. We'll just kill her after you've drained off her energy."

"Just as well," I taunted him. "I've got a whole stack of breeding petitions ahead of you, some of them from very notable demons. I can't imagine your request would have met with my favor."

"Sir, the container isn't big enough; it's going to overflow." The sorcerer's voice radiated with fear. I grinned.

The angel raced over, grabbing the tube that protruded from my chest. I struggled against my restraints, trying to push more raw energy forward as he tried to push it back in. The glass vessel foamed as raw energy spilled over the top. Drops of acid rolled down the sides, sizzling as they hit the floor and burned inch-deep pockmarks into the stone.

"Hold it in, hold it in," the sorcerer screamed. He chanted, his hands on the container blistering with contact.

With a pulse of power, the angel wrenched the tube from my chest, rebounding the energy back into the slippery restraints, but not before I'd managed to grab a substantial chunk. Relief flowed through me. I felt lost without access to my energy. All those times in Aaru when I'd been restrained and naked, I'd been in the throes of a panic attack. It wasn't just the lack of corporeal form, it was the defenseless feeling of being without any demonic skills. The amount I now held was a fraction of my usual amount, but it was still a comfort.

Pash knelt, breathing heavy, his hands horribly burned from the acid. The angel shoved him aside, wheeling the glass container off with the others and placing the glowing tube back on the table.

"Come on," he told the sorcerer. "I'll condescend to heal you this time as I need you to have full use of your hands. We'll return afterward, and you can finish draining her."

"Then you'll kill her?" Pash asked, his voice hopeful as he held his hands out in front of him.

The angel shot me a quick look, his eyes meeting mine for the briefest of seconds. "No. She's the last one left. It will take me some time to make arrangements with another demon for an adequate supply. I might as well use her. Who knows, maybe her offspring will actually live. She certainly seems hard enough to kill. I can see her endowing her progeny with a similar will to survive."

The pair of them left and I grinned. I was starved, weak, and in pain, but I'd managed to grab a good chunk of raw energy and hide it safely away. And I'd seen the look in the angel's eyes when he'd met mine. In spite of his bravado, he was afraid. Very afraid.

~34~

I was glad they weren't gone long because I was badly dehydrated, weak from hunger, with one operational lung. My gunshot wounds, dislocated shoulder, concussion, impaled limbs — they all signaled my impending death. I thought about using the energy I'd hidden to fix my physical body, but I didn't want the angel and the sorcerer to return and find me good as new. Plus, I had a rather dramatic plan, and I wanted to surprise them. I especially wanted to see that look of fear in the angel's eyes.

Pash wheeled another empty container next to me with perfectly healed hands. This time I held still as he jabbed me with the tube and raw energy poured out in a silver stream.

"She filled *another* container," he commented in astonishment. "Two! I've never had a demon even come close to filling one, and she filled two."

The angel frowned as Pash removed the tube and began to wheel the glass jar away. "Are you sure she's empty?"

He was right to worry. When a demon died, the raw energy we held burst forth, usually with violent force. Any residual amount could explode the lab, or more.

"That's all. The tube had completed the siphon, so there's no more left to draw."

No more there. The amount I'd hidden away could have filled another of those containers, perhaps more.

"Hand me the box. The sooner we get this over with, the sooner you can go back to Hel with your bottles."

The angel took the metal box from the sorcerer's hands and, as before, removed the crimson rod. It flashed bright red, reminding me of one of those hazard sticks placed around auto accidents. I felt the cold metal of the amulet on my forehead and heard soft chanting in Elvish. A line of dark red began to extend from the amulet through my body and into my spirit self, burning a channel as it went. It felt oddly familiar, and I realized this was a similar process to what Gregory had done to bind me, only he'd used his mouth on the inside of my arm and extended a part of himself into me. Obviously this angel didn't want to get that personal, but the process gave me an idea, and I held back on my plan of attack.

The red seared into my spirit, and I shifted, blocking its progress with the red-purple of my angel that networked throughout me. Pash abruptly ceased chanting then began again, a tremor in his voice.

"What's wrong?" the angel demanded. He tapped the glowing rod and frowned at my forehead and the amulet. "Why isn't she coming out?"

"Stuck. Something's stuck." The sorcerer said, his voice breathless. Again he began to chant.

The red inched forward, trying to burn through the blockage. I held firm, pushing the angel essence further, driving it into the channel the amulet had created in my spirit self and my physical body. I heard the sorcerer scream, felt the amulet turn to dust against my forehead, saw the pulsing rod shatter into fragments.

Everything slowed. Crimson shards rang out as they hit the floor, sandy dust slid off my forehead onto the table. Out of the corner of one eye, I saw the sorcerer writhing on the floor, clutching his head. The angel stared at his empty hands then turned to meet my eyes.

"What are you?"

"The angel of death." I let the raw energy I'd hidden away burst from my being. There was a split second when I saw the terror in the angel's eyes before everything exploded. The facility, the island — everything within a half-mile radius vanished. Nothing living: no matter, no flesh survived.

Including me.

I'd used it all to ensure I actually killed that fucking angel. I had no energy left to form myself into anything, and I was dying — a being of spirit with no corporeal form. This had been a far too quick and easy death for both the angel and the sorcerer, but I had to take satisfaction with what I had. Dead was dead, and that was better than having these assholes outlive me. Facing my own death was worth seeing that look of fear, that recognition of his own demise, in the angel's face. But even though I was resigned to my own death, I had one last hope, one slim chance to survive this.

Feeling the agony, the painful tearing, I began to come apart at the edges and separate. Without a corporeal form to house myself, my spirit self was slowly unraveling. Soon, I'd be nothing, dissolving into the universe around me. Frantically, I pulled on the red-purple within myself and called Gregory. Could he hear my panic, my desperation? Maybe what happened with the amulet and rod broke our tie. I couldn't feel him like I'd been able to before. I was dying. I was dying and he'd never know.

The pain grew intense as I felt myself ripping apart. I thought of Wyatt, how much I loved him, how much he'd grieve for me. I'd never made it home, never called him to let him know what plane I was on. Did he still have that vodka in the freezer? Was he trying to track me down and find me? He'd feel the sorrow of losing me, but at least he had his sisters. Gregory — he'd be all alone, just as he'd been for so long. Would he mourn me over millions of years, like he did his brother? The thought of him lonely once again, the remembrance of his voice when he said he couldn't lose me, couldn't bring himself to kill me even if it meant saving the world, brought me more pain than the tearing of my spirit being.

My thoughts were fading. Numbness spread inside me, dulling the terrible pain. I'd just begun to feel a sense of peace when, with a jerk and a stab of pain, I returned.

I've got you.

He didn't sound very happy about it. I wasn't sure I was happy about it. Everything had begun to blur out, but now the agony had increased tenfold. Even his gentle embrace, the feel of him carefully touching my wounds was torture.

Oh, Cockroach.

He didn't have to spell it out. I was in bad shape, huge sections of my spirit self missing or damaged. Some of it would knit back together, but nothing would replace what I'd lost. And I'd lost a lot.

More pretty scars? I teased.

They'll be beautiful, he lied. *You're safe now, in Aaru. I'll heal you, and in time you'll recover some lost abilities. You'll be good as new.*

More lies. Crap, he was just as bad at lying as I was. I examined my damage, starting with the considerable cosmetic stuff. The surface of my being had come apart first. It would smooth over, but the scarring would be horrific. I'd be really ugly, but Gregory was the only one who saw me without a physical form, and I got the feeling he didn't really care what I looked like. Other sections were bad, but those abilities would shift to other parts of my being with time. The most disturbing was the damage to the part of me that converted energy into matter. Without that, I'd not be able to form a physical shell to house myself. There was only one place I could exist solely as a spirit being — Aaru.

You can be here with me always, little Cockroach. By my side, as an angel.

Ugh. I loved this angel, but being stuck here for the rest of my life wasn't appealing. I pulled the thin, crisp energy of Aaru into myself and tried to manifest a corporeal form.

Nothing. I tried again, and again, feeling something like a lump in my middle. I wanted to cry, but I had no tears, no eyes.

It will be a different life, but it will be a good one. Beloved Cockroach, everything will be fine. I promise everything will be fine.

I tried again, one last desperate attempt, and felt a spark. It was something, and thanks to the angel, I'd learned that I could exist in just about anything. A chair, a rock, bacteria, even a flame.

I think I can convert energy into matter, I told him. *I just can't seem to pull enough energy from my surroundings to hold a form.*

Give yourself time to recover; a few centuries maybe, and then you can try again.

Fuck that. There's no way I'd recover in Aaru. Already the place was sending me into a near panic attack. Gregory couldn't hold me in his arms forever — although at the moment that seemed a rather appealing prospect. Sooner or later he'd have to go off and do something, and I'd go crazy.

I'd be a cripple, an invalid dependent on him for everything. I'd rather be dead.

Stop it. You'll be fine. As soon as you're recovered, I'll work with you to see if you can create a physical form. Stop this talk about dying. I can't lose you. I won't let you go.

I tried to convert again. Yes, a spark! The energy here was just too thin for me to pull enough together to sustain matter. Aaru wasn't like back home, where the energy flowed thick and heavy all around us, blanketing us in warm plenty.

Home.

Send me home. You need to send me home.

I felt his hurt through our bond. *Home to Wyatt? He wouldn't have time to see you before you dissolved away to nothing. Even if I brought you right to him, he wouldn't be able to see or hear you.*

Not that home. Home to Hel. I need to go back to Hel. The energy there is different, easier to collect and manipulate. I can form there, then I can begin to fix what I can and adapt to live with what I've lost.

Frustration filled his thoughts. *I can't take you there. I can't go to Hel, even for you, my Cockroach. And I fear for you — what if you're wrong? I may not be able to summon you back in time.*

All sorts of improbable scenarios ran through my head. Gregory holding me within his form, then tossing me through the gate at Columbia, releasing me at the last moment. Gregory creating a gate from Aaru straight to Hel and tossing me through it. Gregory. . ..

Banish me.

I felt him shift in confusion. *Banish you?*

You've bound me. If you banish me, I'll return to Hel.

But that will dissolve our bond. I won't know if you're alive or dead. You won't be able to summon me if you need me, and I will no longer be able to summon you.

Yes, and that prospect was more painful than my damaged, shredded being. I felt him, knew if he was near, how he was feeling. Sometimes I read his thoughts, and I knew he could read mine. I didn't want to lose that, but I couldn't stay in Aaru. This was the only way he could send me to Hel.

I felt him sigh, move against me in a caress, careful to avoid the raw sections. *I love you, little Cockroach, and if you die, I will never be the same.*

If I live, you'll never be the same, I teased.

That drew a smile from him — well, what passed for a smile in a being without a mouth.

Niyaz, Az, Jahi, Ereshkigal, Malebranche.

He began to recite my names. It was a short list. I wasn't very old. I curled against him, pushing in slightly so we merged in a line of white. I'd miss this. I'd miss him.

Mal Cogita, Samantha Martin.

One more, I prompted.

Cockroach.

I love you, too, I blurted out. He knew, but I didn't want to leave without saying the words.

I break the bonds between us and release you from service. Banished from my presence, return from whence you came, to be summoned no more.

I was ripped from his embrace, and, with a jolt, felt familiar, thick warmth. Instinctively, I pulled from my surroundings, like taking a deep breath when surfacing from water.

Now. Everything exploded in a flash of light then coalesced back into matter. I lay, exhausted, on a carpet of moss-green grass dotted with yellow flowers. The smell of the forest filled every pore — life, sunshine, growth, and decay. I was alive. I'd done it. I'd somehow managed to manifest a physical form to house myself. It wasn't ideal, and it sure as hell wasn't attractive, but it would do. I just needed to recover, to fine-tune whatever conversion skills remained. I'd grow stronger, repair what I could. Make it to my household and contact Wyatt through my mirror, to let him know I was alive and okay. Then I was going back. Going back to my family. Going back to my angel.

About The Author

Debra Dunbar primarily writes dark fantasy, but has been known to put her pen to paranormal romance, young adult fiction, and urban fantasy on occasion. She lives on a farm in the northeast section of the United States with her husband, three boys, and a Noah's ark of four legged family members. When she can sneak out, she likes to jog and ride her horse, Treasure. Treasure, on the other hand, would prefer Debra stay on the ground and feed him apples.

Connect with Debra Dunbar on Facebook at DebraDunbarAuthor, on Twitter @Debra_Dunbar, or at her website http://debradunbar.com/.

Sign up for New Release Alerts:
http://debradunbar.com/subscribe-to-release-announcements/

Feeling impish? Join Debra's Demons at http://debradunbar.com/subscribe-to-release-announcements/, get cool swag, inside info, and special excerpts. I promise not to get you killed fighting a war against the elves.

Thank you for your purchase of this book. If you enjoyed it, please leave a review on Goodreads, or at the e-retailer site from which you purchased it. Readers and authors both rely on fair and honest reviews.

Books in the Imp Series:

The Imp Series
A DEMON BOUND (Book 1)
SATAN'S SWORD (Book 2)
ELVEN BLOOD (Book 3)
DEVIL'S PAW (Book 4)
IMP FORSAKEN (Book 5)
ANGEL OF CHAOS (Book 6)
IMP (prequel novella)
KINGDOM OF LIES (Book 7) Fall, 2015 release

Books in the Imp World
NO MAN'S LAND
STOLEN SOULS
THREE WISHES

Half-Breed Series
DEMONS OF DESIRE (Book 1)
SINS OF THE FLESH (Book 2) Summer, 2015 release
UNHOLY PLEASURES (Book 3)Spring, 2016 release

23732395R00184

Made in the USA
San Bernardino, CA
30 January 2019